Isobel's Promise

Maggie Christensen

Dedication

To Jim, my own soulmate

Also by Maggie Christensen

Oregon Coast Series
The Sand Dollar
The Dreamcatcher
Madeline House

Champagne for Breakfast

Sydney books
Band of Gold
Broken Threads
The Good Sister (set in Scotland)

Check out the last page of this book to see how to get
a free download of one of my books.

One

It was a typically dreich Scottish day. Isobel Davison stood dry-eyed beside Matt Reid as her aunt's coffin was lowered into the grave.

She'd shed all her tears in the days leading up to this occasion. There were none left. Isobel MacDonald had been an unusual woman, one whom Bel had only fully appreciated in the weeks before her death.

At ninety-six and suffering from emphysema, Isobel's death hadn't been unexpected, but Bel was still in shock. Nothing could have prepared her for the sense of loss. The day was in perfect synch with her mood – grey and miserable. She shivered, and Matt wrapped an arm around her shoulders.

'We can go now,' he said, as the gravediggers began to fill in the grave, the shovels of soil making a loud thumping sound on the coffin, each one seeming louder than the one before.

Bel looked around.

All the others were beginning to walk away. It was a small group. Besides Matt and Bel, only Betty, Isobel's housekeeper, and Mary, Bel's old schoolfriend and a long-time neighbour of her aunt's, had braved the cemetery, even though the church had been full of mourners – Isobel had been a popular woman, and many had come to pay their last respects.

'We should get you home.' Matt began to lead Bel away from the graveside to the car park where his car was waiting.

'Home?' Bel couldn't think of the Kelvin Drive house as home. Although she'd grown up there, she'd left as soon as she was able, only returning for her mother's funeral all those years ago, and now, to witness the final weeks of her aunt's life.

The house belonged to *her* now, but not for long. Soon the renovation would begin, a renovation which would turn it into a home for disabled children and their carers. It had been her aunt's wish, a legacy from a woman who'd had no children of her own.

'Or we could go straight back to my place on the loch,' Matt suggested, referring to his modern house on the banks of Loch Lomond.

Bel's eyes lit up at the thought of that refuge, the place where she'd found love at the ripe old age of sixty-five, but she shook her head. 'No, I need to go back there sometime, so it might as well be now.'

'If you're sure?'

'You'll come with me?'

'Always.' Her companion grinned, and it was as if a shaft of sunlight pierced the greyness of the day.

'You're a good man. Aunt Isobel always said so, and she was right. She was right about so many things.'

But once she was back in the old house, Bel shivered again. The walls seemed to close in on her, telling her she didn't belong. Despite the warmth of the man beside her, Bel experienced an unexpected yearning for the sunshine of her home in far-off Australia.

'What's the matter?' Matt closed the door behind them, shutting out the wind and rain.

'I don't know… Something… Aunt Isobel would say someone walked over my grave.' Bel's eyes filled with tears at the memory of her aunt.

'You're letting the day get to you. You've never been comfortable in this house. We should have…'

'No.' Bel smiled wearily. 'There are things I need to do, sort out, before…' She raised her eyes to meet his, comforted by the love she could see there. 'You do know I have to go back to Sydney?'

'Sometime. But surely not just yet?'

'Soon. I have things to sort out there too; matters I need to take care of before we can be together.'

Matt enfolded her in a tight hug, resting his chin on her head. 'It'll all work out,' he muttered into her hair. 'You see if it doesn't.'

'Mmm.' Bel disentangled herself. Their relationship was so new, so untested. Who knew what trials distance would exert on it once she was back in Australia? She loved him – she did. But this was Scotland. She'd only intended to be here for a few weeks. It wasn't her home. She'd spent most of her life on the other side of the world. Maybe this had just been the interlude she'd first believed it to be when... Her thoughts flew to the passion she'd found in this man's arms, a passion she'd never imagined she'd find again.

'You're not going to bail out on me now Isobel's gone, are you?' Matt asked, raising one eyebrow, his hands falling to his sides.

'No, I just...' Bel rubbed her eyes and dropped into the nearest chair. 'I think I need time to digest all this.' She waved a hand around the room, her eyes settling on the old furniture she'd known since childhood, the chair which had been the favourite of her aunt, the tartan rug folded over its back as if waiting for her. She could almost see Isobel sitting there, a cup of tea in her hand. 'I can't believe she's really gone.'

Matt gazed around the room as if trying to see it through Bel's eyes. He rubbed his chin. 'We shouldn't have come back here. It's too soon. Why don't you pack a wee bag and come home with me?'

Bel was sorely tempted and, for a brief moment, almost gave in. Then she shook her head. 'No. You go on. I need to be alone for a bit. I'll have a bite to eat, then get started on the house. Betty promised to come in tomorrow and, between us, we should have it cleared in a day or two. I'll come then.'

Bel stood up and hugged Matt, relishing the feel of his strong arms around her, then followed him to the door.

She sighed as she turned back into the empty house. She'd never liked the place. And, now Isobel had gone, the whole house echoed, its emptiness seeming to threaten her with all manner of things. It was a house populated with ghosts – the ghosts of her mother, aunts and grandparents. Everywhere she looked, the past seemed to rise up to greet her.

The sooner she could leave, the better.

Two

The crowded airport didn't provide the most favourable setting to say farewell under any circumstances. It was six o'clock on a Tuesday evening and to Bel, it felt as if half the population of Glasgow had decided to come there. Walking through the terminal, she and Matt were buffeted by what felt like hordes of people all pushing them in different directions.

'Let's get out of here. A drink and something to eat?' Matt suggested, taking Bel's arm and leading her into a coffee outlet.

She nodded and dropped her bag at her feet, her eyes following his erect figure elbowing through the throng of people, all hellbent on grabbing something to sustain them before their flights.

Her breath quickened, and a warm glow suffused her as she remembered the past few weeks spent with Matt at his home by Loch Lomond. When she'd arrived in this country, only a few months earlier, the last thing on her mind was a relationship. Then she'd met Matthew Reid, her aunt's solicitor, the enigmatic Scotsman who had dispelled all her prejudices and with whom she'd fallen in love. Not with the wild passion she'd known as a younger woman, but passion, nevertheless. With Matt, she had a sense of having come home, having found something she hadn't even known she was looking for.

Her mouth turned up in a smile even now, remembering... And to think her aunt had planned it all along.

'Will this do?'

Drawn out of her musings, Bel looked up into the deep brown eyes that had captivated her, the silver-streaked hair, the long legs encased in jeans, and the broad shoulders filling out the worn checked jacket which was his usual outfit. Matt placed a tray containing two paper cups of coffee, a couple of packs of sandwiches and two apples on the table.

'Are you sure you wouldn't like something stronger? It's nearly seven and...'

'No. This is fine.' Bel laid a hand on Matt's arm. 'Sit down and stop fussing. I just want to...' Her voice almost broke at the knowledge that in a few hours she'd be on a plane flying to the other side of the world. She'd be leaving this man who had come to mean everything to her.

'It's not too late to change your mind,' he said. 'We could...'

For a moment, Bel was tempted, but she knew she had to catch this plane. It had been five weeks since Aunt Isobel had died. Since then she'd spent four weeks living with Matt, overseeing the renovations to the old house, relaxing... It had been four weeks of heaven.

But now it was time. She had a life back in Sydney – a home, a business and her dear little Toby, the dog who was a twin of Matt's Hamish here in Scotland.

'I *will* be back,' she said, as if to reassure herself as much as her companion. 'Just as soon as I can settle things back there.'

'Mmm.'

Bel took a sip of her coffee and broke open one of the sandwich packs, but she couldn't take a bite because of the lump in her throat. She put the triangle of bread down carefully and looked up to meet Matt's eyes. Now that the time had come – her flight was due to leave in just over two hours' time – she didn't know how she could bear to leave. She saw a similar reluctance in Matt's eyes.

'I should be coming with you,' he said, taking both her hands in his, his thumb rubbing the back of one. 'It's not too late.' He started to rise.

'Don't be silly!' Bel pulled him back down beside her. 'We've been through all this. You have things to do here. And there's...' She visualised Matt's daughter's face if he took off with Bel.

Matt sighed and ran a hand through his hair. 'You're right. Elspeth would never forgive me if I disappeared to the other side of the world.'

'And Fi would never forgive you if you went without her,' Bel replied, referring to Matt's twelve-year-old granddaughter whose ambition it was to travel to Australia.

Matt linked his fingers in Bel's. 'Christmas? You'll be back by then?'

'Promise.' Christmas seemed aeons away, but it was only three months, the same length of time she'd been here, the same length of time she'd known Matt. It felt like forever.

She was about to say more when Matt checked his watch. 'It's time!'

Bel picked up her bag and the pair made their way to passport control and security for international travellers. Bel felt she was at the gate of no return. It was foolish. She was coming back – just as soon as she could arrange everything at home in Sydney.

'Remember – Christmas,' Matt said, his lips turning up in that lopsided grin she found so endearing. 'Don't forget – *Barkis is willing*,' he repeated. They hugged, then she shrugged off his embrace and walked through the archway without a backward glance. She knew that, if she did glance back, take one more look, she might be undone, might never leave.

*

Matt gazed after Bel's tall figure as she walked away from him, head up, shoulders squared. He knew she'd be back. She'd promised. But Christmas seemed such a long way away. What if, once she'd got back to Sydney, she had second thoughts?

For a moment, he toyed with the idea of heading to the ticket counter and buying himself a ticket. Not for today, but for some time soon – maybe next week. He almost did, but turned in the opposite direction instead. They'd discussed this. The decision had been made. He had to trust Bel. And there were the renovations on the Kelvin Drive house to oversee.

Bel's aunt had left the house to Bel with clear instructions for its use. She'd have liked Bel to stay in Scotland to ensure it was done exactly to her requirements – Matt would too, but Bel had been anxious to get back to Sydney, making the sensible point that the sooner she left, the sooner she'd be back.

They'd spent a blissful four weeks together at his retreat by the loch but, as soon as the development permission had been approved, she'd booked her ticket. Now Bel was gone, and Matt felt as if there was a hollow space where his heart had been. He'd never intended to fall in love again after Ailsa had died, thought he was too old for passion. Then Isobel MacDonald had introduced him to her niece from Australia, and emotions he never thought he'd experience again had overwhelmed him.

After avoiding the clutches of groups of women of a certain age in his home town, he'd been undone by this tall, elegant, sixty-five-year old from the other side of the world.

He sighed. Bel was right. He had his family to think about and a job to do. He stood watching from the windows until he saw the Emirates aircraft taxi down the runway, then he left, making his way to the stairs leading down to the car park.

*

Bel leant back in her seat as the aircraft lifted and rose into the sky. She was on her way home. Sydney was where her home was, so why did she feel as if she was *leaving* her home instead of going there? She'd lived in the harbour city since emigrating at the age of twenty-two as soon as she'd finished uni. She'd been glad to leave the claustrophobic atmosphere of the house she'd grow up in, and a disastrous relationship.

She'd taken this same trip back then, full of anticipation, excited to begin a new life as far away as possible. Back then, she'd flown from London, having taken the train there from Glasgow. She could still picture the faces of her mum and Aunt Isobel holding back the tears as they waved her off.

As soon as the seatbelt sign was switched off, Bel relaxed and closed her eyes.

*

At London's Heathrow Airport, Isobel MacDonald, wearing a floral-print suit with a lace-edged collar and high-heeled white sandals, boarded the British Airways flight that would take her to Australia. She had to pinch herself to make sure she was really here, on her way to a new life on the other side of the world; far away from Callum, the art student who'd abandoned her at the first hint she might be carrying his child; far away from the confines of her Presbyterian upbringing and what always seemed to be the crowd of women who filled the family home.

When she'd seen the advertisement to Come and Teach in the Sun, *the picture of the tanned young man wearing a gown and mortarboard – the gown hanging open to reveal a naked chest and a pair of navy blue swimmers – it had sent shivers up her spine. She'd sent in her application to teach in New South Wales, travelled to London to attend an interview at the Australian High Commission, and now she was heading to Sydney.*

She knew it would be a long flight, but was too excited to sleep much, gazing out at the fluffy white clouds as the airplane took her farther and farther away from all she'd known. There was one brief stop in Bahrein, then she was permitted to disembark at Darwin – her first opportunity to set foot on Australian soil. It was two in the morning, but the airport was busy, the bar seeming to be full of men wearing knee-length shorts and long socks drinking beer. And it was hot, a humid heat which sapped any energy she had. Was this what Australia was like? It felt very foreign.

Isobel was glad to arrive in Sydney where she discovered she was one of a group of teachers who'd answered the advertisement. She quickly made friends and, after a couple of weeks in a hostel in the suburb of Marrickville, eating meals in a Chinese restaurant, she and a fellow teacher managed to find a flat to rent on the north shore of the harbour – they were called units here. Her new life was about to begin.

*

The sensation of lights coming on and the rattle of trolleys caused Bel to open her eyes. Since the brief stopover at Dubai thirteen hours ago, she'd slept on and off.

For a moment, she was confused. Then she remembered. She was on the plane to Australia. Looking out the window she saw a familiar red sunrise as the sky changed from gold to red. She stretched her neck and wriggled her toes. It was a long flight.

The cabin was beginning to awaken as the flight attendants wheeled through the breakfast trolleys. Bel picked at her meal. She wasn't hungry. She could never eat much on planes. She'd be home soon, back to the life she'd left behind, back to the same routine. But Bel wasn't the same person who'd flown off to visit her Aunt Isobel. She sipped the airline coffee and grimaced. She couldn't wait to see her Toby again – and to put her house on the market, investigate selling her business and, most importantly, buy her ticket back to Scotland, back to Matt, back to the love she'd never expected to find and to a future she could only imagine.

Three

Bel gazed around the familiar kitchen. She felt disoriented. It was as if the sunshine streaming through the open window was mocking her. She sighed and reached down to where her small Westie, Toby, was trying to nibble her bare toes. She was home, back where she belonged. So why did she feel so unsettled? She opened her computer and, sure enough there was an email from Matt. Her lips turned up in a smile, and she had a familiar warm feeling as she read the amusing anecdotes of his daily life and words of love. She'd only been back three days and missed him so much.

Rising from her desk, Bel gave herself a shake. Usually well organised, since returning to Sydney she'd been unusually lethargic. It had taken her all weekend to recover from jet-lag. But last night she'd made a list. Today she needed to return to work but planned to take time out to book her ticket back to Scotland and to contact the realter about putting her house on the market. Her mood rose at the thought of Christmas with Matt – Christmas by the side of Loch Lomond in the arms of the one person with whom she wanted to be.

But there was a tiny part of her holding back; a hint of reluctance to take this step which would be so final. Bel told herself not to be stupid, that she was having the equivalent of buyer's remorse. She chuckled at the inappropriate comparison, headed to the kitchen, turned on the coffee maker, and dropped a couple of slices of bread into the toaster.

Sitting down to eat breakfast, she picked up the postcard that had been propped against the fruit bowl. It had arrived the previous

Friday. *Who sent postcards these days? Matt must have mailed it before she left for it to arrive so soon.* Bel stroked the surface. The scene of Loch Lomond reminded her of Scotland – the yellow and purple of the gorse and heather prompting memories of moments with Matt. A dozen or more incidents bubbled into the forefront of her mind. Turning the card over, she read the message for what must have been the hundredth time: *You are the light of my life. Can't wait for Christmas! Hamish says Hi. Missing you. Mx*

Bel rubbed her eyes. She gave herself a shake. She couldn't sit here all day. She had to open Isabella, get back into some sort of routine. The boutique that had been her life ever since her marriage had ended all those years ago, suddenly seemed less important.

She dropped the postcard into a drawer, closing it with more determination than necessary, and made her way to the bedroom.

Once showered and dressed, she stood staring at her reflection, arm upraised in the midst of brushing her silver hair. Who was the woman in the mirror? She barely knew. Three months earlier, before her hurried departure to Scotland at the bidding of her terminally ill aunt, she'd known exactly who she was.

She was Bel Davison, sixty-five years old, owner of Isabella, a successful boutique in the upper-class suburb of Mosman in Sydney. She lived alone – by choice – had a few good friends, her loyal dog, Toby, and enjoyed walking along the harbour, dinners in her favourite wine bar, and occasional visits to orchestral concerts, the opera, and the theatre. It was a good life. She was satisfied with it. No highs, few lows. She lived on an even keel.

But the woman who looked back at her today was a stranger. Her eyes had a faraway look, a longing for something other than the everyday routine of her life. Her skin seemed softer and there was a passing smile on her lips that owed nothing to the glorious weather outside.

While in Scotland she'd broken her rule to avoid men, to evade involvement and… Her lips twitched into a wide smile as she remembered the comfort of Matt's warm body and his final words. *'Barkis is willing.'* The line from Dickens' *David Copperfield* when her aunt had been so ill had been the first indication Bel had that Matt saw a future for them together. Those words meant a lot to her.

She had a lot to thank Aunt Isobel for. Bel had become close to the woman whose words and attitude had irritated her during her teenage years. As she'd learned more about the older woman's life, she'd begun to understand her resilience and to respect her. And it had been due to her that Bel had met Matt. She was a bit of a witch, Bel decided.

She exhaled loudly, gave her hair one final pat and turned away from the mirror. She had more to worry about than the enigmatic Scotsman, regardless how much he meant to her.

*

'Can we have a chat?'

After having been gone for three months, Bel had been kept busy all morning with customers calling in to welcome her back, and unpacking a delivery of summer outfits. She glanced up as Jan popped her head into the back room where she was grabbing a quick lunch, a sandwich in one hand, while checking a spreadsheet on the computer with the other.

'Mmm,' she mumbled, then swallowed quickly. 'Right now?'

She put down her sandwich, realising she'd been so busy since her return, that they'd barely had time to talk, apart from Jan's brief handover first thing.

Jan nodded.

'Sure.' Bel smiled. 'Sit down. I'm sorry I haven't taken time to talk with you. Trying to catch up.' She ran her fingers through her hair. 'What's up?'

Jan perched on the only other chair in the tiny room and cleared her throat. 'The zoo...' She paused. 'That course you encouraged me to apply for – the one in Animal Care.'

Bel remembered only too well. A year earlier, when she'd first met Jan, the woman was in dire need of a fresh interest. In addition to working with Bel on a casual basis, she'd begun volunteering at the zoo, finally gaining a position as an Education volunteer. But her real goal was to become an Education Officer and for that she needed an additional qualification. Bel had reinforced Jan's sister's advice to go for it.

'You've completed it? That's wonderful!'

Jan smiled widely. 'Thanks. The thing is… a position has come up… an Education Officer and I've been offered… I don't want to let you down, but…' Jan shifted in her seat. 'I know you're just back. I hate to dump it on you like this.'

This, on top of everything else! But it might not matter. Bel knew she still had to contact the solicitor who'd written to her while she was in Scotland with an offer to buy Isabella. She'd gasped at the amount his client was prepared to pay, and had dismissed the offer out of hand, but now her plans had changed, she intended to contact him. One more item on her to-do list.

'You must accept it,' she said, seeing Jan was nervously waiting for her response. 'I can sort something out here.' But she frowned. She'd need help until she sold. Would she be able to find anyone on a temporary basis?

'I have someone who might be interested.'

Bel's eyes widened. Jan had really thought this through. She'd relied on Jan ever since she'd walked into Isabella and had hoped she'd be able to help her out. But a sale wouldn't go through overnight. She exhaled and leant back in her chair.

'Remember Celia Ramsay?'

'Chloe's mum?' Bel said, remembering only too well the glamourous ex-model, the mother of the young girl who had given birth to Jan's grandson just over a year earlier.

'Yes. We've become friends of sorts having little Simon in common. Well, she's finally decided to stand up to that bully of a husband of hers. Now that both girls have left home, Celia's been spending more and more time with Chloe and little Simon and has decided that, if she can find a job, she might even leave the bastard.'

'So she's looking for work?'

'She helped out a bit when you were gone; when your usual casuals weren't available. She knows her clothes, and the customers loved her. Many of them remembered her face on the covers of *Vogue* and the pages of the *Woman's Weekly*.'

'When does the zoo want you to start?'

Bel saw Jan bite her lip. 'Monday week.'

'And Celia's available?'

'I gave her a call.' Jan reddened. 'There was no sense in my mentioning her if she already had something, so...'

Bel had the distinct feeling that things were moving beyond her control. But she *did* need help, and Jan must take up this opportunity. She sighed, then smiled warmly. 'You'd better ask her to come in and see me.'

*

Lunchtime arrived and, with a quick word to Jan, Bel popped out to visit the realtor along the road. Rod Miller was an old friend, and she knew he'd see her right.

She was feeling buoyant. There was a spring in her step as she strode along. As soon as she'd arrived at the store this morning, she'd logged onto the Qantas site and booked a ticket for Tuesday December fifteenth to arrive in time for Christmas as promised. Then she'd sent a quick email to Matt. It would be almost midnight there, but she hugged herself to the knowledge that he'd receive it as soon as he awoke.

Bel could imagine his delight. On their skype call the night before, he'd wanted to know why she'd delayed booking her flight, and she'd shrugged it off. She really didn't know herself. But now it was done, and she felt relieved, if somewhat anxious.

She was planning to leave everything she knew for a man – a man she'd only met three months earlier. Did she really know what she was doing? Was she caught up in a euphoria of excitement, a bubble that would burst in the cold light of reality? Her steps faltered. Once she put her house on the market, the wheels would start to turn. She'd be caught up in a spiral of viewings, open houses and all the other palaver that went along with selling.

Then there were all her belongings – her furniture, books, all the possessions she'd jealously guarded over the years, carefully carted from place to place until they ended up in the house in Cremorne, the house where she'd expected to spend the rest of her life. Was she mad to think of leaving all that behind her for a man she barely knew?

Her previous experiences with men hadn't led her to place much trust in them. First there was Callum in Scotland who'd vanished almost overnight at the hint of commitment, then Pete, who had seemed to be the answer to all her prayers yet had let her down so terribly. Why should Matt prove to be any different?

But he *was* different. She *knew* he was. There was something about him, a confidence, a sense of belonging that she'd never experienced before. And there was Aunt Isobel who'd done her damnedest to match them up. Then there was… Bel grew hot remembering how Matt made her feel in bed. But that wasn't the basis of their relationship. They'd found they had a lot in common. They liked the same books, enjoyed the same music, thought the same way about things, had the same values.

While these thoughts were milling around in her head, Bel's feet had taken her to her destination. She glanced up at the sign *Miller's Realty*, took a deep breath, and pushed open the door.

'Bel, you're back!' Rod himself came to greet her. 'It was your aunt, wasn't it? Not a happy trip then. How did it feel to be back in the old country?'

Trust Rod to be his effusive self. He must be wondering what she wanted.

'It was… different. It was sad to see Aunt Isobel so sick, of course, but she was a wily old thing and, in the time we had together, I got to know her better, saw a side of her I hadn't known. I'm glad we had some time before she went.' Bel felt a tear come to her eye at the memory of the feisty old woman. How she wished they'd had more time together before she'd passed away.

'I'm sorry for your loss. But we don't usually see you in here. What brings you?'

Bel hesitated, knowing her next words would change her life.

Rod Miller raised his eyebrows and waited.

'I… I'd like to put my house on the market.' It was as if the words fell out of Bel's mouth of their own volition, and she almost wished she could take them back, pretend she'd made a mistake, go back to Isabella and get on with the life she'd been leading before her trip. But she knew that wasn't possible.

She realised Rod Miller was looking at her strangely. Had she voiced her thoughts, or did her expression give them away?

'Best come into my office.' He led her to a room on one side, took a seat behind the desk and indicated she should sit too.

Bel gratefully subsided into the chair. Her legs were beginning to tremble. What had got into her? She was acting like a foolish old woman.

'So!' Rod drew his iPad towards him. She could see him type in her name and address. Maybe it wasn't too late to change her mind. Maybe...

'It's a good place. Should fetch a tidy sum. There's a lot of demand for these Federation homes. And you're in a good location too. Are you in the market for something else, or have you already...?'

Bel swallowed, feeling her throat tighten. 'I'm planning to return to Scotland,' she said.

Four

Bel pushed the shop door open. The die was cast. She'd signed an agreement, and Rod was bringing a photographer around later in the week. There was no going back now, though she still had to contact her solicitor and get him to draw up a contract of sale. She'd do that tomorrow.

Jan turned from a rack of dresses she was rearranging. 'I had a group of women in while you were gone. They must have tried on a dozen outfits between them, then walked out without one sale.' She peered at Bel. 'Is everything all right? You look flushed.'

Bel put her hand to her cheek. She did feel hot, but it was a hot day. Did her indecision show in her face? 'Leave that for now. Come and sit down. We can see the shop from the back room. I have something I need to tell you.'

Once the pair were seated with mugs of herbal tea, Bel cleared her throat. 'This may come as a shock. I should have told you this morning.' She wrapped both hands around her mug. It was one her Aunt Isobel had sent her several years ago, and had a bright yellow *Mr Happy* on the side along with the words *Glasgow's Miles Better*. At the time, she'd been amused by the message referring as it did to the renaissance Glasgow was having. Today it reminded her of the new Glasgow and Matt. She gripped it tightly.

'I'm going to sell up.' Bel glanced at Jan whose expression went from surprise to concern. 'I'm going back to Scotland.' It seemed to Bel that the words fell into a well of silence.

Jan said nothing for a few seconds then, 'Is it anything to do with that man you mentioned – your aunt's solicitor?'

Bel blushed and she felt a now familiar flutter in her stomach. The image of Matt on her computer screen as he'd been the night before appeared in her mind's eye: his dishevelled hair, his deep brown eyes, his warm grin. 'Matt Reid. Yes. He… we… Do you think I'm mad? To make such a big change at my age?'

Jan hesitated before replying, as if unsure what to say. When she did speak, her tone was cautious. 'Are you sure, Bel? It *is* a big step. How long have you known this Matt?'

Bel put down her mug and dragged a hand through her hair. 'Three months. I suppose it's not really very long, but… Hell, maybe I'm making the biggest mistake of my life. But,' she added with more confidence, 'it feels right.'

'Then I wish you well. But what about Isabella?' Jan gazed around the tiny back room, the desk and chairs almost hidden beneath piles of boxes, a rack of clothes stuck behind the door and a filing cabinet, its surface crowded with a dying plant, an electric jug, and a couple of mugs. 'It's your life.'

Bel's eyes moved to encompass the inside of the shop filled with the latest spring and summer collections. She carefully placed her mug on the desk, clasped her hands, and leant back. 'I had a letter… from a Sydney solicitor… while I was overseas. It seems someone wants to buy this whole line of shops, turn them into a block of units or some such thing, so…'

'Oh, you're not going to sell to *them!*' Jan wailed. 'Sorry. I know it's none of my business, but I know that Season, The Junction Boulanger, the Craft Gallery and The Potter's Studio are all against it,' she said, naming four of the neighbouring shops. 'I thought you would be, too. I never imagined… This will set the cat among the pigeons. There was a meeting last week. I went along and promised your support. Heck, I suppose I should have talked with you first, but I just couldn't imagine you'd want to sell.'

'You're partly right. When I opened the email, besides being surprised and flabbergasted at the size of the offer, I had no intention of even considering it. But things changed, and it's beginning to look as if it was meant to be. So, you're saying the others are holding out?'

'Most definitely. Are you really sure about this? What about your lovely home? And Toby?'

'I've put the house on the market. That's where I've been, seeing Rod Miller. And Toby – well, he goes where I go. Matt's Hamish could be Toby's twin brother. I'm sure they'll get on well together. I *was* a bit worried about him, but I needn't have been. I checked it all out this morning. Unlike Australia, Scotland doesn't have any quarantine requirements, so we won't be parted. There's something called a Pet Passport which entails a microchip and vaccination. It all seems very straightforward.'

'Well, you seem to have thought of everything. But I just can't get my head around the idea. When are you planning to leave?'

'I've promised to be over there for Christmas. I've booked...'

But, before Bel could say more, Jan interjected, 'What! That's only three months away!'

Suddenly the anxiety which had lain dormant, just beneath the surface, came to the fore and Bel's chest tightened. Maybe she *had* acted precipitously; maybe Jan was right. Then she thought of Matt, of his strength, his affection, his passion, his humour, his kindness, and, above all, his basic decency and care. 'My mind's made up, Jan. My ticket's booked. It's a white Christmas for me. Though Scotland doesn't always get snow in December.'

'But... Celia...'

'I'll have to find out if she'll be happy with a short-term arrangement. And I guess I need to talk with the other shopkeepers – find out exactly what their position is re this development proposal.'

The rest of the afternoon passed smoothly, though Bel caught Jan glance at her oddly a couple of times.

'I'll call Celia tonight, shall I? Or would you prefer to contact her?' Jan asked, as she was preparing to go home.

'It may be best if you call, then you can sound her out about the timing. If she's looking for something more permanent, there will be no point in my meeting her.' *And I'll have another headache trying to find someone else*, Bel thought.

*

Bel was glad to arrive home. She was exhausted. In the short time she'd been gone, she seemed to have distanced herself mentally from her business, and it was taking all of her energy and concentration to get back into the swing of it. It was a relief to open the door and be greeted by Toby. The little dog had been delighted to see her again, even though Bel was sure he'd been completely spoiled by Jan's son, Andy, who'd taken care of him during her absence.

She poured a glass of wine, sat down at the computer and opened Skype. Soon Matt's smiling face filled the screen and Bel settled back for a long chat. As she'd anticipated, he'd been delighted to get the news that she'd booked her flight, and she was now able to also tell him about putting her house on the market.

'But it may not sell immediately, and there seems to be a hitch in the proposed sale of the shop,' she said, a niggle of the worry she'd been suppressing since the conversation with Jan, popping to the forefront of her mind. Her indecision must have shown on her face, because Matt frowned. She was quick to reassure him. 'I'll still be there for Christmas. I can't wait. It's just that things may take longer to settle here than I'd thought.'

'You'd better be here. I've ordered a white Christmas specially.'

Bel laughed.

'And how is your family? Have you told Elspeth yet?'

Matt frowned again. 'Not yet. I need to wait for the right time. I need to prepare her, to persuade her to be less dependent on me, but it's not easy.'

'Aunt Isobel said you made a rod for your back with her,' Bel said without thinking.

'Easy for you to talk.' There was a harsh note in Matt's voice, one Bel hadn't heard before. She flinched. His relationship with his daughter was really none of her business. She'd overstepped the mark and hastened to try retrieve the situation.

'I know.' She sighed. 'I'd probably think the same as you if I had children. I know you're doing your best and that she was there for you when you most needed her. It must be hard to extricate yourself from her support when you no longer need it so much. I guess helping you has helped Elspeth deal with her grief too.'

'You're right.' Matt appeared to relax. 'And it can't be changed overnight. But I'm working on it. At least Duncan is on side,' Matt said, referring to his son who'd expressed his delight that his father had someone new in his life.

'And what about the young ones?'

'They're all well. Fi tells me she's been doing more research on Australia and has mapped out an itinerary for the trip she plans to make some day. You really made an impression there. That won't please her mother either.' He sighed.

Matt then began to fill Bel in on the latest news on the renovation to her aunt's house – now hers – which was proceeding according to plan, and they ended the call on a positive and loving note.

As Bel logged off, she felt hollow. While speaking with Matt, seeing his face right there in front of her, it was almost as if she could reach out and touch him. Then, suddenly, he was gone, and she was left in an empty house on the opposite side of the world from the one person she longed to be with.

Five

Matt sat looking at the empty screen. Had they almost had an argument? He pulled on his ear. He wasn't good with distance. He wished again that he'd gone to Australia with Bel. He'd have been there to support her and help organise the move. He longed to hold her in his arms again, to feel her soft skin against his, to kiss her lips, to… Shit, he'd need to take a cold shower if he continued thinking like this.

Calling to Hamish, he slid his arms into his well-worn *Barbour* and, the little dog at his heel, he set off walking briskly, heading for his favourite spot high above the loch. But, when he reached it, Matt wondered if he'd made a mistake. This was his private place where he came to enjoy the solitude, and to think, but today it was failing to soothe him.

When Bel had been here, she'd often joined him, and they'd sat there together, hands entwined, both enjoying the sense of peace. This was the first time he'd ventured up here since she left. Now the air seemed to be filled with memories. Matt sat on his usual boulder, gazing down at the blue-grey water of the loch, at Ben Lomond rising up behind it, at his house in the distance. It looked so tiny from up here, and the few fishing boats appeared like small dots on the surface of the loch.

Matt dropped onto the heather and lay back, hands behind his head, trying to enjoy the solitude. He looked up into the pale blue sky, to the few clouds scurrying along, seeing what looked like a golden eagle soaring high above. Letting his hand rest on the springy mix of heather and mountain thyme, he closed his eyes and let his mind wander, while Hamish went running off searching for new smells.

The sound of loud barking roused him. He opened his eyes. But it was only Hamish trying to catch a bird that had landed close by. Checking his watch, Matt stretched out his legs with a groan. He became stiff more easily these days when he sat for a long time. He needed to move, to go back down again. He had an appointment with Isobel's architect in a couple of hours and had to change, then drive into town.

As he descended, he wondered that he still thought of Andrew Forrest as *Isobel's* architect. He was more correctly Bel's, now Isobel was gone. But the old lady had been so vital, her presence seemed to linger.

*

An hour later, Matt was driving into Glasgow in his little sports car. He usually took the sedan into the city, but this morning he had the urge to feel the wind in his hair. Maybe he'd get rid of the other vehicle, though it came in useful when he was ferrying the grandchildren around or when he wanted to appear more professional.

Unable to believe his luck, Matt found a parking spot close to Andrew's office. He hopped out of the car, pushed open the heavy glass door and, eschewing the lift, took the stairs two at a time, arriving at the office door somewhat breathless, his legs aching, but pleased to feel the blood coursing through his veins. There was still life in the old dog.

'Matt!' A slightly dishevelled red-haired man wearing large dark-rimmed glasses came to greet him, hand outstretched. As always, Andrew's business shirt had pulled out of a pair of worn jeans, his tie hanging loosely from an unbuttoned collar. 'No Bel today?'

Matt's ebullience immediately faded as he remembered his previous visits with Bel by his side, and how they'd developed the habit of lunching together afterwards, just as they had on the very first occasion. Back then, they'd been almost strangers, but he'd known even then that she was a special lady, someone he wanted to know better.

'No, not today. Bel's gone back to Sydney to sort out a few things there.'

Andrew looked puzzled. 'But I thought you two were together – up there in Inveruglas.'

'We were. We will be. She'll be back by Christmas,' Matt said confidently. 'Now what was it you needed to see me about?'

The next hour was taken up with discussion of the Kelvin Drive house. When they finished, Andrew began packing away the folders relating to the project. 'Are you staying in town for lunch? Fancy a pie and a pint across the road?'

As the two men walked across to the pub, Andrew said, 'That granddaughter of yours is a clever wee lassie. She'll make a good architect one day. Maybe she'd like to drop by on a regular basis to keep her eye on things – make sure we don't put a step wrong?'

'I'm sure Fi would love that,' Matt laughed. 'But her mother might have a different idea. There's time enough for her to take to the drawing board when she's older.'

The two men skirted a group standing in the doorway and, leaving the brightness of the day behind, entered the dimly lit hotel bar and made their way to a table in the far corner.

'What'll you have? They do a smashing steak pie here, unless you want something fancier.'

'Steak pie sounds just fine. Let me get it. A pint to go with it?'

'Please.'

'A pint of heavy?'

'Make it a lager.'

Matt pushed his way to the bar, his mouth watering at the thought of a good dish of his favourite comfort food. He liked young Forrest. He'd done a good job on Isobel's place, just as he had on Matt's own home a few years earlier. It was good of him to take on the project management too – gave Matt some breathing space. Not that he needed it. With Bel gone, it seemed there were too many hours in the day. He missed her. And she'd only been gone a few days. The thought of the next three months stretched ahead like a seemingly endless tunnel.

Lunch passed quickly, and soon Matt was ready to go home. On a whim, he took a detour to the house – Bel's house, as he must now think of it, even though it was the last place she would want her name associated with. He wasn't sure exactly why she felt such an antipathy to the place. She'd told him a little of her early life there. It appeared to have been happy for the most part. She was loved and cared for – maybe too much so. What he did know was that the house seemed to stifle her. She'd become a different person away from it – more carefree and relaxed. They'd never made love in that house. For her, it had been a house of memories, some good, some bad, but all reminding her of times she wanted to forget.

There was a flurry of raindrops as he parked outside the old sandstone terrace, and Matt pulled up the hood of the car before running up the steps to the front door. The door stood open, and from the entrance, he could hear the workmen's voices, a few thuds, and the echo of a radio playing in the distance.

He walked into the wide hallway to find a painter perched on a ladder, while another man was stripping the carpet from the large front room which had been Isobel's bedroom. For a moment, he pictured the old woman lying there on her deathbed, then his vision cleared and all he saw was a large empty room.

'It's been a braw hoose in its day,' the man said, glancing up as Matt stood transfixed in the doorway.

'And it will be again.'

'They're saying it's going to be a home for crippled children?'

Matt flinched at the words, though he knew he shouldn't be surprised that some people still used the derogative term. He never thought of it in relation to his granddaughter who'd been in a wheelchair since a car accident over five years ago. Although she'd lost the use of her legs, wee Fiona was as bright as a button and could run rings around her older brother when it came to academic pursuits.

'For children with a disability,' he corrected, 'and their carers. It'll be a happy place filled with love and laughter. It was the wish of the previous owner.'

'Oh aye?' The man paused in his work, stood up and stretched, a hand going to his back as if to relieve a pain. 'And you'd be…?' His eyes raked Matt up and down as if wondering what his role was.

'I'm her solicitor. The owner's solicitor.' *Bel's solicitor*, he thought with an inward smile. 'You seem to be making good progress.'

'This is the last lot of carpet up. Jock there will get in here tomorrow, then we'll both be done with the downstairs. It's coming up a treat.'

'It is that. You're doing a grand job.' Matt left and walked through the rest of the downstairs rooms, noting that the kitchen had been gutted ready for the new cabinets and appliances. Isobel would barely recognise the old place. It was all proceeding just as she'd planned it. By the sounds coming from upstairs, the new room partitions were well underway too, and he could see the well for the lift was almost complete. That had been one of Isobel's last instructions, and one with which Fi heartily agreed. The young girl's contribution had been to look at the house from the point of view of someone who'd be living there, and Matt, Bel and Andrew had welcomed her suggestions on height levels, lights and power outlets.

Matt contemplated going upstairs, then decided he'd seen enough for the day. The rain that had been threatening when he arrived, was now teeming down, a solid curtain of water pouring into the gutters. Matt turned up his collar and ran to the vehicle, shaking the raindrops from his hair as he closed the door.

The weather matched his mood as he drove out of the city. He switched on the radio, but it provided little relief as he turned the knobs to get a better reception. Discouraged by the white noise of the interference, he gave up and drove on in a silence only interrupted by the swish of the windscreen wipers.

Back home, he wandered around the house, unable to settle, while Hamish, seemingly unable to understand his master's restlessness, followed at his heel before settling down in his basket, head on his paws. Matt paced aimlessly around the room before finally going to the fridge to pour himself a beer.

There was no sense in being anxious. Bel would be back. The three months would pass quickly, and they'd be together for Christmas – a family Christmas. The image of sitting beside Bel at the dining table along with all of his family, a gaily decorated tree in the corner and snow-covered ground outside fuelled his imagination. He couldn't guarantee the snow, but maybe he could make the rest happen.

He sighed and opened his computer to deal with a particularly knotty legal matter his son had passed on to him. Duncan was worried about something more than he'd let on to his dad, but this problem would keep Matt occupied and take his mind off his own issues for now.

He'd keep busy, and Christmas would be here in no time.

Six

'Are you sure about this?' Louise Connolly waved her glass of Chardonnay in the air as she stood in the middle of Bel's kitchen.

'What? Oh, you saw the sign out front.' Bel continued filling a platter with cheese, biscuits and fruit. 'Let's take this outside.' She slid open the glass door with her free hand and led the way to a sheltered courtyard, where the heady scent of jasmine hung in the air.

'See it? I couldn't miss it.' Lou followed Bel and settled into one of two white cane chairs. 'Rod Miller doesn't do things by halves. So, *are* you sure? I mean, to leave all this? It's a huge step for someone you've just met.'

Bel took a deep breath before replying. Lou was her oldest friend. They'd met at a yoga class when both were experiencing the after effects of divorce, and despite the five years between them – Lou was five years younger – had bonded over their joint distrust of men. The yoga classes had long gone, but their friendship had continued.

Despite their apparent differences, they'd become good friends who enjoyed each other's company and Bel usually valued Lou's opinions, even though they were often stated bluntly. They'd had some good times over the years, and Lou was generally Bel's first port of call in times of difficulty.

But, for some reason, Bel had kept Matt's name out of her emails to her friend while she was in Scotland, so it was only recently Lou had learned both of Bel's new-found relationship and her plans to move to Scotland.

Bel carefully cut a piece of camembert and placed it on a water cracker, then looked up to see the concern on Lou's face. 'No, Lou, I'm not really sure. But how can any of us be sure what the future holds?' She repositioned the cheese before popping it into her mouth. 'I just know fate doesn't give us too many chances at our age.' She paused. 'It was seeing Aunt Isobel so alone. She wrote a sort of diary, you know. It spelled out episodes in her life, her regrets; how awful to die with regrets.'

Bel gazed into space, transported to Glasgow, to the house she'd grown up in, the house where her aunt had died, the house where she'd met Matt. 'It won't be easy – to leave all this. To leave my home, my business, my friends – to leave you, dear friend.' She placed a hand on Lou's arm. 'But what if I don't go? What will my life be like here, knowing that maybe, just maybe, I could have had love again?'

Lou let out a rasping laugh. 'Love? Lust more like. Come on, Bel. This is me you're talking to. So, you had a fun roll in the hay with some hunky Scotsman and now you think you've found the love of your life? At sixty-five? Well, you know what they say – there's no fool like an old fool.' She shook her head.

Bel's muscles began to quiver, her body tensing as if to ward off her friend's harsh words. But she recognised the sentiment. It was one she'd often expressed herself in the past, when a friend or acquaintance had behaved in what she considered to be an outrageous fashion. She took a gulp of wine. She looked at her friend whose grey curls owed nothing to the ministrations of a hairdresser. With Lou what you saw was what you got. Her arty friend was almost the direct opposite to her own elegant appearance. But, despite that, they were a lot alike. They'd both been through the divorce mill and come out the other end, if not unscathed, then scarred in indefinable ways. But, whereas it had left Lou impervious to all approaches from the opposite sex, Bel had remained optimistic and had often tried to help her friend see things in a more positive light.

Lou was jealous.

As if reading her mind, Lou said, 'We'd all like to find that someone, but don't you think it's going a bit far to travel to the other side of the world for him?'

Bel leant back. 'Maybe. But, Lou, it just seems so right. And Aunt Isobel approved. In fact, she encouraged me – us.'

Lou moved forward, her arms folded on the glass-topped table. 'She was an old woman, Bel. Can you base the rest of your life on something she wanted as a way of making up for her own past mistakes?'

Bel shook her head. Lou didn't understand. She could have no idea how Bel felt, how Matt made her feel. She had a new confidence, a fresh outlook on life. And it was all due to Matthew Reid, the enigmatic Scotsman who'd been her aunt's solicitor.

'Well, I'm going,' she said at last. 'My ticket's booked, and I'll be back home for Christmas.' But as the word *home* escaped her lips, she felt a strange tremor. This was home – this harbour city that had welcomed her over forty years ago, when she'd fled from her past determined to make a new life for herself.

*

Sydney had been a magical place to the newly arrived Bel. The constant blue skies made her think of the picture postcards she'd collected as a small child – they didn't seem real. She'd lie by the pool of the apartment block, gazing up into that blue sky, pinching herself that she actually lived here. It was as if every day was a holiday or a dream she'd wake up from to find herself back in the dark, damp house in Kelvin Drive, the house filled with women. Women whose prime purpose in life, it seemed, was to act as gatekeepers to foil Bel's plans and ruin her life.

But she'd escaped from all that.

Here, it was easy to take the bus to the beach, or the ferry to the city. It was like a wonderland with so much to explore. Even teaching was different. Bel had been lucky enough to find a placement close to one of Sydney's beaches and could swim after classes finished for the day. She had no time to feel homesick. Life was one long holiday.

*

Bel sighed. It was a lot to give up, an entire way of life – a life she'd been accustomed to for such a long time. To have to dismantle the life she'd put together with such care and pride. But she'd made her decision and wasn't going to change her mind, not for anyone, not for anything.

'The shop – Isabella?' Lou prompted. 'I spoke with Jan, and she said you were in touch with the lawyer in the city – the one that wants to buy you all out.'

Bel flinched. The small craft shop that sold Lou's art-work was situated at the end of the row. She'd conveniently forgotten it would be in the firing line too.

'I received an email from him – probably the same one we all got. And, yes, I've replied. But that's all at this stage. But I'll have to sell, Lou. If not to his clients, then to someone else.'

'You can't let us all down.' Lou thumped her glass down on the table so firmly Bel thought it was going to shatter.

'Careful!'

'I mean it. We haven't spent all these years building up our businesses for some big-shot from Melbourne to jump in and take it all away.'

'Well, they won't buy Isabella if everyone else is against it.'

'Mmm.' That seemed to satisfy Lou. She helped herself to a piece of cheese and fell silent.

'Now, what's been happening with you? Have you finished that project yet?' When Bel left, Lou had been working on a set of banners depicting the changing seasons on the harbour. They were to be hung in the local library. The two women had spent hours discussing the various scenes, as Bel helped Lou decide on which aspects to concentrate. It was a labour of love for Lou and a matter of pride to Bel that her friend valued her opinion on such an important scheme.

As Bel predicted, Lou was easily distracted into describing her progress which had been hampered by various local events and a bout of sickness, but was now back on track. By the time she rose to go, the two had forgotten their differences.

As Lou was leaving, she dropped the news that shocked Bel. The pair hugged at the gate, and as Bel turned away, Lou said in a halting voice. 'By the way, did you hear Pete's back in town?'

Bel felt her gut shrivel as her friend drove off, seemingly oblivious of the wound she'd just inflicted. Pete! When he left the state all those years ago, she'd never expected him to return, never expected to hear of him again. What had started out as her antipodean romance, a love affair to rival any she'd ever read as a teenager, had ended badly.

But the early days had been good, and she'd been in love. As she gathered up the empty glasses and crumb-filled platter, Bel remembered.

*

Bel hadn't wanted to go to the party. In a careless moment she'd gone over on her ankle a week earlier and now she was using crutches to get around. But she'd been stuck at home all week, and it didn't take too much urging on her flatmate's part to encourage her to overcome her initial objections.

'You can just sit in a corner nursing a glass of wine,' Ann had said. 'It's better than staying here on your own.'

So, Bel had agreed and was perched by the kitchen door with a rather large glass of cheap plonk, when a tall dark-haired rugby type almost tripped over her, a stream of beer from his can dripping over her feet.

'Sorry,' he muttered, then paused to give her a closer look. 'What's a lovely girl like you doing sitting here all alone?'

Bel sighed at the less-than-unique line and nodded towards her crutches which were leaning against the wall. 'Skiing accident,' she said, having decided this sounded much more interesting than the reality that she'd tripped over her own feet after a night out on the town.

'I'm Pete,' the man said, crouching down beside her and trying ineffectually to pat her feet dry with a large white handkerchief. 'Just got back from the snow myself. Bad luck.' He pointed to her foot encased in a large, now damp, bandage. 'Where'd you go?'

Bel had managed to provide a fictional account of her skiing trip which satisfied Pete who, to her amazement and delight, stayed by her side for the remainder of the party, refilling her glass and bringing her titbits from the buffet. She couldn't think what she'd done to attract the attention of this hunk. Since Callum, she'd been wary of forming relationships, preferring to keep guys at arm's length and only go on group dates. But there was something about this guy that made her heart beat wildly and her limbs turn to jelly.

She knew right from the start Pete was going to be someone special, that he wouldn't be satisfied to see her as part of a group. To her surprise, she didn't want that either. For the first time since arriving in Australia, she felt an attraction she was unable to ignore.

Pete became a fixture in her life. He was older, owned his own business and seemed extremely sophisticated to the young Bel. After a few dates, Bel admitted there had been no ski trip, and they'd both laughed at her subterfuge. He'd promised to take her skiing. He'd made lots of promises in those early days, declaring himself to be smitten by her Scottish accent, and clear Scottish skin. And some of them he'd kept.

In Pete's company Bel had come to see Sydney – and Australia – through different eyes. Whereas before meeting him life had been one long holiday, in Pete's company she'd begun to discover the real Australia, and the harbour city had become home. As he proudly squired her around his city, and they visited other parts of the country – the Gold Coast, the Whitsundays, Uluru – she developed a love for this country. With Pete, she swam with the dolphins and took a camel ride along the beach in Broome, fascinated to learn more about this enthralling land. By the time Peter Allen recorded I Still Call Australia Home *some thirty years later, it became her anthem, just as* Scotland the Brave *had been in her formative years.*

*

But to think he was back in town. Bel stopped in the midst of putting the glasses into the dishwasher. She suddenly remembered the couple of odd calls on her answer machine with no message. At the time she'd shrugged them off as a wrong number. But what if it was Pete trying to reach her?

Seven

'So, that woman's gone home now?' Elspeth paused, looking around as if to make sure she and her father were alone.

'*Bel*'s been gone a few weeks as you very well know.' Matt flicked on the coffee machine and turned away from his daughter as it began to gurgle and hiss. He wondered if he should add that she'd be back – for good this time – but decided it was too soon to share that news with Elspeth. Since he'd been widowed five years earlier, she'd taken on her mother's role, jealously guarding him from anyone she viewed as a threat to their close relationship.

'She didn't stay for the renovation to be completed, then? Fiona said…' Her mouth turned down in a moue of disgust.

'No, there was no real need, once the approval came through. I took Fi to Kelvin Drive before Bel left. She'd promised to let her have a look at the house to give her opinion on…'

'I can't imagine how the opinion of a twelve-year-old would influence anything.'

Matt sighed. He dearly loved his daughter, but sometimes he felt like strangling her. He pressed his lips together to prevent telling her exactly what he thought of her insensitive remark. 'She was a great help. It takes someone who's been in a wheelchair herself for years to really understand what the needs of the new residents will be.'

'Yes… well…' she bridled.

Matt could see he'd won that round.

'Coffee's ready,' he said to break the tension. 'Shall we have it outside? It's not very cold today, and there won't be too many more days like this.'

Once they were settled in a sheltered spot with a good view of both the loch and Ben Lomond rising up behind it, Elspeth returned to the subject of Bel and the house on Kelvin Drive. She was like a dog with a bone, he thought, worse than his little West Highland Terrier, Hamish, who knew when his master had had enough.

'I don't know why you have to bother with that place now the old woman's dead. Surely you could have put the renovation in the hands of a good project manager, and Duncan could take care of any legal work. You're supposed to be retired, Dad.' Elspeth smiled in what she no doubt thought was a winning manner.

Matt wasn't to be swayed. 'Your brother has enough to do, and Isobel MacDonald was *my* client. She was a friend too, and I want to see her wishes carried out. Bel is her niece and next of kin,' he added, watching his daughter's face redden at Bel's name.

For an instant the image of Bel's face flitted behind his eyes – her clear blue eyes, mobile mouth, skin darkened by the Australian sun and surrounded by a smooth helmet of silver hair, and her smile. He couldn't get that smile out of his head. Matt felt a pang. He missed her so much. He'd never thought to fall in love again, imagined he was finished with all that. But life had a way of creeping up on you when you least expected it.

Neither of them had wanted or expected the complication of a relationship at their age, but perhaps it was all the sweeter for that.

'And is she – this Bel – is she your friend, too?'

Matt was pulled back to the present by Elspeth's voice. 'Yes, a good friend,' he said. 'A very good friend.'

'Fi said…' Elspeth paused as if she knew her next words might offend her father. 'Fi said she was staying here… with *you. Alone.*'

'And is that such a bad thing? We're both a bit too long in the tooth to need a chaperone.'

Elspeth turned away and bridled.

'Och, come here!' Matt drew his daughter into a warm hug. 'I can have women friends, you know. It doesn't mean I have any less affection for you. You're my daughter. Nothing can change that or interfere with how I feel about you. But your old dad has a life too. I loved your mother. You know I did. We grew up together and, as long as she was alive, neither of us wanted anyone else.' He held Elspeth at arm's length and brushed a stray strand of hair out of her eyes. 'But she's been gone for five years now, honey. I have a lot of years left to me. Is it too much to ask that I find a woman I can be friends with?'

Matt saw a tear begin to slide down Elspeth's face. 'Nooo, but…'

Matt put a finger to her lips.

'You've been a great help all this time. I truly don't know what I'd have done without you and the kids dropping round, without your delivering all those food parcels. Sometimes I almost felt like I was a recipient of meals on wheels.' He laughed. 'But you know it can't go on forever. You have your own life too. I need to learn to fend for myself. Now, go and wash that face and be off with you. By the time you get back to Glasgow it'll be time for you to pick up Fi from school, and Robbie will be getting home, too.'

Elspeth sniffed. 'You always try to make out you don't need me, but…'

'Wheesht.' Matt gave her a small push towards the bathroom, sighing as she closed the door behind her. He'd allowed Elspeth to become too dependent on him. Alasdair had put up with her mollycoddling her father and, as far as Matt knew, his son-in-law had never complained. But Isobel MacDonald had warned him he was letting Elspeth do too much, take her mother's place, organise his life.

Oh, not in as many words. That hadn't been Isobel's way. Just the odd comment here and there to let him know she didn't approve, that she thought he might one day regret giving in to his daughter. Isobel had been a wily old bird. He'd been sad to see her go. He missed her.

But she'd introduced him to Bel, and it had turned out Isobel had known – *loved* – his father. That had been a shock. It took a bit of getting used to, to think that the old woman and his dad… And look at the crafty way she'd thrown him and Bel together. Though they'd have managed it without her interference, he was sure of that. As soon as he set eyes on Bel, he'd known she was someone special.

Elspeth joined him, a forced smile on her face. 'Well, it seems I'm not wanted here, after all.' She looked as if she was going to burst into tears again. 'I must be getting back. As you said, Fi will be waiting for me and… Oh, Dad. I know you're right. Alasdair's often told me, but…'

'I know, I know. You've got into the habit of dropping round here, and I don't want you to stop doing that. I'd really miss you and the young ones.' Matt wondered what more he could say, how he could phrase it so that Elspeth didn't feel any worse. 'Just keep your fussing for Fi and Robbie in the future. They're going to need it, if they're anything like you and Duncan were as teenagers. Let me choose my own friends. And I promise you, you'll be the first to know if anything in my life changes.'

He realised as soon as he said those words that he wasn't being entirely truthful. Things *had* changed, *he* had changed. But Christmas was still months away. There was time enough for him to break the news of the prospect of Bel's return. Maybe he could win Elspeth round by then.

'Well, I'll be away. You have everything you need? I've left a casserole in the fridge and…' Her voice tapered off, perhaps remembering his earlier words.

'That's lovely, honey. You know how much I enjoy your cooking.' A thought occurred to him. 'Maybe you could give me cooking lessons sometime?'

'Maybe.' She smiled – a real smile this time, seemingly amused at the thought of her dad actually learning to cook.

Matt watched his daughter drive away. He shook his head. That one wasn't going to be easy. He called to Hamish. A walk across the muir would clear his mind. It was the wrong time to call Bel. He'd have to wait till late evening and try to catch her before she went to work. There was so much he wanted to say to her, and he was eager to find out how the sales of her house and business were progressing. He'd noticed a slight reluctance on her part to discuss it. It was a big step, he knew. He just hoped she wasn't getting cold feet.

Eight

It was Jan's last day at Isabella, and Bel had arranged a small gathering as a send-off and thank you. Her meeting with Celia had gone well, and the woman had agreed to accept Bel's offer of temporary employment. She'd seemed grateful to find anything at all, though Bel felt slightly guilty knowing she'd be gone by Christmas and Celia would have to find something else.

Once the shop had closed for the day, Bel and Celia set out champagne and glasses and took delivery of a tray of delicious nibbles from the nearby deli. They'd tried to keep it secret, but Bel felt sure Jan had detected the supressed sense of excitement that had permeated the atmosphere all day.

'You shouldn't have,' Jan said in a breathless voice, as the others raised their glasses in a toast. She looked around the small group which included her sister Anna, several local shopkeepers, and a few of their regular customers who Bel and Jan had come to regard as friends.

'We all wanted to wish you well,' Bel said, presenting Jan with a large bouquet of native blooms. 'I'm sure we haven't seen the last of you. Don't forget us once you become entrenched in your new role.'

'I won't.' Jan blinked away incipient tears. 'You've been so good to me, Bel. I don't know what I'd have done this last year without your support and guidance. 'And you too, Anna.' She turned to her sister with a smile. 'And dear Heather.' Jan grasped the hand of one of Bel's oldest customers. Heather had been Jan's sister's boss for many years and had helped Jan through a difficult patch.

'Get away with you. You have an inner strength that would have seen you through,' Heather said, referring to the untimely death of Jan's son, and its ensuing consequences the previous year.

'Well, thanks anyway,' she said, burying her face in the flowers. 'These are beautiful.'

Bel refilled the glasses, and the conversation flowed as Jan accepted congratulations and answered questions about her position with the zoo. After a time, the women began to drift away. Heather claimed a concert at the Opera House, Lou muttered something about an urgent meeting, Celia said she had to get back home before she was missed, and Anna and Jan were to meet their husbands for dinner in nearby Neutral Bay.

Left alone, Bel dropped into a chair and contemplated how much she was going to miss this place and those women. She sighed. The solicitors hadn't replied to her request for more information about their offer on the shop. And her neighbours were urging her not to sell. But what option did she have? She couldn't manage Isabella from Scotland. It had worked for a few months, but it wouldn't be possible on a permanent basis. And Jan was no longer here to manage it for her.

It was all very well for the others to insist she remain as owner, but she had her own life to live, and that life wasn't going to be here, regardless of how comfortable it was. That was the problem, Bel realised. Life here *was* comfortable. It was a way of life she'd made for herself and it suited her. Scotland was an unknown quantity. But Matt was there. He was the one thing she *was* sure of.

As she mulled over the evening, it occurred to Bel that Celia had been very quiet. In fact, she'd become quieter and quieter as the evening progressed. Bel made a mental note to keep an eye on her new employee. She had the distinct impression all was not well there, and that Celia might be in need of more support than simply a job.

Bel sighed, picked up her bag, and was taking one last look round prior to turning off the lights, when a dark shadow at the door caught her eye. What the…? The shape was indistinguishable in the darkness due to the shop lights. There was a sharp knock on the glass. Moving closer, Bel peered out into the night. It was the figure of a man – tall, thin and slightly hunched.

*

Celia Ramsay hurried along the road. She knew she should have left the gathering earlier, but it had been so refreshing to spend an evening without having to look over her shoulder, without worrying she might say or do the wrong thing. She enjoyed the company of the women. They were a good bunch. And to think she'd never have met them if Chloe hadn't become pregnant, if Simon hadn't died, if... She thought of the old saying, the one her grandmother had often repeated to her as a child – *If ifs and ands were pots and pans there'd be no work for tinkers' hands.*

All too soon, it seemed, she reached home, and her heart sank to see Bill's car in the driveway. His dinner meeting must have finished early. He'd not be happy to find the house empty. Who was she kidding? He'd be bloody furious!

Biting the inside of her cheek, a shiver of apprehension running up her spine, she pushed open the door.

'You decided to come home, then?' Her husband's voice boomed from the living room.

Celia could tell he'd been drinking – a lot. She carefully placed her bag down and took a deep breath before replying, 'Did you have a good evening?' She'd learned over the years that a conciliatory attitude often worked best when he was in this mood, when he was in any mood, really.

They'd been married for over twenty years, and for most of those years she'd had to suffer Bill's mood swings – along with his unfaithfulness, she reminded herself. Although there hadn't been so much of that in recent years. Probably not for lack of trying on his part. But he'd become more belligerent as he grew older, and his excessive drinking was taking a toll on the good looks of his younger years. The former nationally renowned rugby player, the darling of the media and the girls who were the team groupies, was fast becoming known as the beer-swilling bully he'd always been under the surface.

Celia was aware he'd been known as Bruiser Ramsay in his heyday, but had brushed off the nickname as the jealous opinion of his opponents. Now she knew better. Through his one-eyed thinking and bully tactics, she'd almost lost their two daughters.

To begin with, it had been easier to agree with him, to take his part when their older daughter, Hannah, told them she was in love, and her partner was Ingrid, the friend she'd been sharing a house with as a student. But it had been harder to side with him when their younger daughter, Chloe, became pregnant at seventeen. She'd refused to have an abortion, and he'd refused to have her in the house.

For Celia, that had been the beginning of her disillusionment and, when little Simon was born, she'd defied Bill's edict to have nothing to do with *that slut and her bastard* and visited the pair in hospital. That had led to a more gradual acceptance of her older daughter's relationship and, more slowly, to a friendship with Hannah's partner. Now she visited them all on a regular basis, albeit surreptitiously most of the time. But she was becoming tired of the subterfuge, tired of hiding her true feelings, tired of living with a bully for whom she'd ceased to have any feelings or respect.

'Don't try to wriggle out of it,' he said, his voice rising. 'Where have you been? Sneaking off to God knows where as soon as my back is turned. Did you think I wouldn't know? That I wouldn't discover your deceitful behaviour?' His voice slurred on the word deceitful, and he drained the glass of scotch he was holding.

Seeing he was unsteady on his feet, Celia moved toward her husband and gently took him by the arm. He had no doubt drunk more than the recommended amount of wine during the dinner, had driven home in an inebriated state, and was now topping up from his private supply.

'It was Jan's farewell party at the shop. Remember I told you it was tonight?'

But Bill was in no mood to listen. 'I don't know why you have to bother with that place. It's not as if you need the money. You should be here at home, where you've always been. Your place is here, not in some tomfoolery clothes shop catering to the whims of fancy women,' he blustered.

Celia stood looking at him for a moment, wondering why she was still here, why she hadn't left him years ago. She'd been afraid; afraid of being alone; afraid of what people would say; afraid of what Bill might do. But no longer. Now she saw him for what he was – a sad middle-aged bully, running to fat, his face blotched as a result of too much alcohol, who'd do anything to get his own way.

'I'm going to take a bath, then I think I'll have an early night.' She picked up her bag and mounted the stairs without a backward glance.

Nine

Carefully, Bel opened the door a crack and peered at the figure standing there. Emaciated, and wearing an expensive leather jacket, a familiar and long-forgotten face gazed back at her. *It wasn't... it couldn't be...*

'Pete?' she gasped, shrinking back into the shop, a tingling in her chest signifying the need to sit down before she collapsed. Surely she wasn't having a heart attack? She put a hand to her chest.

'Surprised to see me?' the familiar voice asked. 'You didn't answer my calls. They said I'd find you here.'

The idea that the strange calls had been from him and the question of who *they* were jostled for supremacy as Bel tried to come to terms with the fact that her ex-husband was standing in the doorway of her shop. She stood in silence, her tongue stuck to the roof of her mouth as she tried to work out what to say.

'Pete,' she repeated, then finding a strength she didn't know she possessed, added, 'What are you doing here? The last I heard you were in Melbourne. That's where you ran off to, wasn't it – when the business went belly up?' *When you had to escape your creditors and left me in the lurch.*

'Can I come in?' Pete's voice was hoarse. 'Please, Bella.'

Pete had been the only one to call her Bella. When Bel arrived in Sydney as Isobel Davison, she'd been shocked to discover most Aussie's immediately sought to abbreviate her name and Izzy was the most popular choice.

She didn't feel like an Izzy, didn't want to become Izzy – her pet name for her Aunt Isobel as a young child. But Bel had soon realised her friends wouldn't be satisfied to call her Isobel, so had determined to become Bel. It suited her. It fitted the person she'd become in her new life in this new country. When she'd met Pete, he'd told her she was beautiful, *bella* in Italian, and the name Bella had stuck, had been his special name for her. Perhaps it had even subconsciously influenced her to name her boutique Isabella.

Bel gave a frightened glance behind her. 'No,' she said. 'Not here.' But she realised he wasn't going away. She'd need to talk to him somewhere. And she didn't want him in her home either. Both of these places belonged to her, to the life she'd made for herself after he'd left, the life she was about to leave.

'I'll just lock up, then…' She thought quickly. The wine bar on the corner would be open. There would be people there. It would be safe. Bel wasn't sure why she felt the need to have others around her. This was Pete, the man she'd been married to in her twenties. But she hadn't seen him for thirty-five years. *What did he want of her? Why had he turned up in her life now? Just as she was making a fresh start.*

It wasn't till they were seated in the wine bar that Bel was able to get a good look at her companion. The years hadn't been kind to him. The once handsome face, now thin to the point of emaciation, was gaunt. The skin was tinged with grey and a battery of lines extended from his mouth and eyes, eyes which had once been bright and eager and were now dull and rheumy. His formerly luxuriant head of hair had thinned and, she noted, he'd taken to combing a few of the remaining strands across to hide what was no doubt a bald patch. The distinct odour of alcohol emanated from him. Despite all of this, Pete was dressed as immaculately as she remembered in a brown leather jacket and a pair of smart beige pants. But the jacket hung off him as if it had been made for a much larger man, and the pants sagged around his ankles.

The Scots expression *shilpit,* she'd heard her grandmother use as a child, emerged from the recesses of her mind. He looked so pale and feeble – sickly, even. *What had happened to the tall handsome man she'd fallen in love with all those years ago?*

'Coffee, I think,' Bel said. 'I'll get them.' She rose and headed for the bar, glad to have a respite and a few moments to decide what to say to this ghost from her past. Pete Sadler was the last person she wanted to see right now. She had no idea why he was here, what he wanted of her. But she knew it couldn't be good. The Pete Sadler she'd come to know in the years they were married was a manipulating bastard. He'd run off and left her to face the music when his business went south, disappeared without a word, and she'd been left to pick up the pieces – and herself.

*

'I'm home!'

Bel was glad it was Friday. She'd had a hectic week at school. The combination of a school inspection, a run-in with an irate parent, and a reprimand from the principal on her handling of a playground dispute made her wonder how much longer she could continue teaching. The joy she'd once felt in helping young people learn wasn't there anymore; it had been buried under a mountain of bureaucracy.

Maybe she could help out at the car yard? Pete never talked much about it, preferring to keep his work separate from their home life. Or maybe it was time to think of starting a family? When they'd first married, they'd both been content to wait, enjoy each other before bringing a new life into the world. And recently, if she was honest, things hadn't been so good. It seemed ages since she and Pete had spent any quality time together. Weren't children supposed to bring a couple together?

Though that was a poor reason to have a child. But the thought of a baby, a child to call her own, different to the roomful she dealt with every day, was a wonderful idea. It would be a daughter, of course, and Bel could almost feel the soft skin against her cheek, smell the fragrant aroma of a small child. Maybe Pete would spend more time at home if they had a baby of their own. They'd be a real family.

With these thoughts in the forefront of her mind, Bell dropped her bag in the hall and went through to the kitchen. It was empty. She then popped her head into the study where she found Pete emptying the filing cabinet, throwing some papers into the wastepaper basket and stuffing others into a briefcase.

'What on earth are you doing?' she asked, as he continued to rifle through documents seemingly unaware of her presence.

'*Oh!*' *Pete turned around, his usually immaculate hair dishevelled. 'No dinner for me tonight. I have to go out again.*'

So much for a cosy evening at home discussing the future, *Bel thought, dragging her tired body back to the kitchen, fixing herself an omelette and pouring a generous glass of wine. She should have known better than to expect Pete would make time for her. The yard always came first, that and his somewhat dubious mates or business colleagues. She was never sure of the identity of the various shady characters he seemed to spend time with.*

Bel was swallowing the last drops of wine when she heard the door of the apartment bang closed. He'd gone without a word!

That was the last time she'd seen Pete. His side of the bed remained empty that night, and the following two nights. Bel wondered if he was all right, who she should call – the police, hospitals, his friends? It was only then, she realised, she didn't know any of his friends. That was another part of his life her husband had kept secret from her. She spent the weekend alternatively worrying – afraid of a phone call or knock on the door telling her he'd been in an accident – and cursing him as a selfish bastard.

By Monday morning, she'd convinced herself he'd gone on a bender, crashed at a mate's place to sleep it off, would have gone straight to the yard. He'd no doubt return home in the evening, full of apologies and, maybe, with a bunch of flowers begging forgiveness. Well, she'd not be so forgiving this time. It had happened too often over the years, and she was tired of being treated like a doormat. Something had to change.

Bel turned on the television while eating breakfast. It was out of character, but she wanted to check if there was any news of the baby supposedly taken by a dingo at Ayers Rock. She couldn't imagine the anguish the parents must be experiencing. She was listening with half an ear, only glancing at the screen from time to time, when a news item caught her eye.

Surely that was Pete's car yard on the screen? But where were the cars? *Bel turned up the sound to hear the reporter speculate about the disappearance of car dealer Pete Sadler and his stock of cars over the weekend. Shocked, Bel dropped her cup, the coffee spilling over the beige carpet. It would leave a stain, she noted instinctively as she tried to take in the news report.*

The announcer was saying Pete had disappeared, along with thousands of dollars' worth of cars. That couldn't be right. Pete was... But where was

Pete? The last time she'd seen him was Friday evening. By now he could be anywhere. And that was his car yard on the screen. How could a whole car lot disappear almost overnight? Where...?

The doorbell pealed, followed by a loud knocking. Startled, Bel jumped up, automatically smoothing down her skirt and patting her hair before answering the door.

'Mrs Sadler?'

The two men who stood there could have been straight out of her favourite TV drama. Bel sighed as they showed their badges and introduced themselves. It was all about to begin. And her life was going to change forever.

Pete was finally run to earth on the Gold Coast, recognised by a former customer who was up there on holiday and had shopped him to the police. Australia might be a big country, but it was a difficult one to hide in. There followed a time in prison for him and a divorce for Bel. She'd heard he'd gone to Melbourne when he was released but, by that time, she'd made a new life for herself. Bel had resigned from teaching and taken the money from her paid-out long service leave plus a small loan to set up her boutique. She had relegated Pete Sadler to the past and got on with her life, never expecting – never wanting – to see him again.

*

'One cappuccino and one latte. That'll be eight dollars.'

The voice of the barman broke through Bel's thoughts forcing her back to the present. 'Thanks.' She forked out the change and carried the drinks back to the table where Pete was sitting. He didn't appear to have moved while she'd been gone. Bel frowned. Pete had always been so full of energy, the life and soul of any crowd. His unbounded confidence had been one of the things that had attracted her to him. This man was a shell of his former self.

She knew he'd been to prison, but that had been years ago – thirty-five to be exact. His confinement couldn't have any bearing on his present state, could it?

'So?' Bel picked up her cup, grasping it with both hands and propping her elbows on the table. She fixed her ex-husband with the stare she used to use on recalcitrant school children. She hadn't used that particular stare for years but, after teaching a class of eight-year-olds for so long, it was easy to recapture.

Refusing to meet her eyes, Pete stared into his cup. 'It's a long story, Bella.'

'Don't call me that!' The words shot out like bullets. 'My name's Bel,' she said in a slightly gentler tone. 'Bella was... back then.'

He looked up, seemingly surprised at Bel's outburst. 'You'll always be Bella to me. My Bella.' His lips turned up in what was probably supposed to be a smile, but ended up as more of a grimace.

Bel shifted uncomfortably in her seat. She took a sip of coffee and put her cup down on the table, letting her hands drop to her lap. She glanced down at the garnet ring on the third finger of her right hand. It had belonged to her aunt, given to her by Matt's father so many years ago. Seeing it on her own finger brought home to Bel yet again how much she missed her aunt, missed Scotland, missed Matt. She rubbed the garnet with her thumb, unconsciously mirroring Isobel's habitual gesture.

The now familiar feel of the stone comforted her, and with the strange sensation her aunt was somehow with her, Bel regained her composure. 'Spit it out! What are you doing back in Sydney? Why have you been trying to contact me? Why the hell were you lurking outside my shop like... like...' She was lost for words.

'I've always thought of you as Bella – my beautiful Bella.' Pete coughed, a hacking cough, took a gulp from his cup, and cleared his throat. 'I've always regretted things ended the way they did. They'd been going bad at the yard for a while, but I thought I could make it through. Then one of the guys suggested I join them at a poker game. I'd always been good with the cards.'

A faint grin lit up Pete's face, and Bel caught a glimpse of the man she'd known in her twenties. He'd been so handsome back then, and she'd fallen for his undoubted charm and zest for life. Where had all of that gone?

'At first I won. Maybe they let me win.' He sighed and clasped his hands on the table. Bel saw they were trembling. 'But my luck didn't last. They fleeced me. I lost big, until the only thing I had left to wager was the yard.' Pete looked up. 'I couldn't let that go without... so I had to leave.'

'But…'

'Right. I didn't own the cars. So…' Pete sighed again. 'I then had the police after me, as well as the guys I thought were my friends. I knew they were into a few shady deals. I'd borrowed from them in the past, but this time they wanted their pound of flesh. And I didn't have it. Prison was probably a better option than being held for ransom by those guys. You'd have been in their sights too. At least by leaving as I did, I hoped they'd spare you. They did, didn't they?'

Bel's eyes widened as she experienced a sense of bewilderment. Was Pete trying to say he'd left to protect her? Protect her from what? And it didn't explain what he was doing here now. She opened her mouth, only to be silenced by Pete raising his hand.

'I know that's not what you asked. It was something I wanted you to know. Something I've wanted to say to you ever since.'

Bel remained silent, her mind in a whirl. If he'd been able to tell her back then, would it have made a difference? Would she have been able to forgive him? Would it have improved their relationship if she'd been able to understand what was worrying him? Probably not, she decided. There had been more wrong with their marriage than lack of communication, more than she could enumerate on two hands. But his explanation did go some way to clarifying the situation she'd found herself in that dreadful Monday morning.

It was a time she'd never forget; a time she didn't want to forget; but a time that had given her the impetus to become the independent person she was today.

'So why now?' Bel's foot began to tap impatiently under the table. It was all very well for Pete to express regret for what happened thirty-five years ago, but it didn't explain why he'd sought her out now.

'I'm coming to that.' Pete sounded weary, as if talking was using up all his energy. 'I don't have much longer. I'm sick, Bella.'

This time, Bel didn't correct him.

'While I was in prison I had to do without the drink.' He rubbed a hand across the top of his head. 'It was bad. I hadn't thought I was an alcoholic. Thought I could take it or leave it, but in there… I was lucky I guess. I got to speak to a guy – one of those counsellor chaps. He got me hooked up with this AA group when I was released. I learnt about the importance of making amends. I knew I had to find you, but kept putting it off.

'When this hit, I knew I had to look you up, to tell you. I didn't want to die without your knowing, without seeing you one more time.' He paused and dropped his eyes. 'I'm drinking again. You can probably tell. There didn't seem much point in staying sober now. It's cancer.'

Bel was speechless. Her eyes began to fill with tears. She had no idea why. But she had once loved this man and to think of him suffering brought home to her how fragile life was. She'd just buried her aunt and now here she was faced with a dying man. A man she had once loved to distraction.

Ten

Bel awoke to the sound of rain pounding on the iron roof. She slowly opened her eyes. For a moment she lay still, remembering the previous evening. Pete Sadler! Could she believe him? He'd lied to her so often in the past, it was difficult to know if he could even distinguish truth from fantasy. But he had sounded genuine, and she'd had a flash of something resembling compassion before common sense prevailed. She'd left him gazing at a second cup of coffee with the distinct impression he'd be ordering something stronger as soon as she'd gone.

Pulling on a towelling robe, Bel went into the kitchen, turned on the coffee machine and dropped a couple of slices of her favourite *Vogel* bread into the toaster before heading to the study and logging onto her laptop. As she'd anticipated there was the usual email from Matt. Her lips curled into a smile as she read his words and pictured him sitting in his home with his little dog, Hamish, at his feet. She frowned when she saw that he still hadn't broken the news to Elspeth that Bel was returning.

Although initially antagonistic towards Bel, Matt's daughter had seemed to warm to her when they discussed the plans to renovate the Kelvin Drive house. But maybe it had been Bel's stated intention to return to Australia that had caused the change in her attitude, Bel surmised, reading between the lines. She shrugged. No doubt Matt knew his daughter best, but it was worrying that he was keeping their relationship secret from her. It made Bel wonder what would happen when she returned to live with Matt as they'd planned. She was giving up a lot to go back to Scotland; she didn't want to be the cause of a rift in Matt's family. He was so close to his children and grandchildren and loved them dearly. Was she making a mistake in thinking she could find a place in his life?

But Bel had more to worry about than Matt and his daughter. She wrote a brief reply and logged off. Last night, in a weak moment, she'd made arrangements to meet Pete again. He'd explained he was currently living in a hotel in North Sydney, and that his intention was to return to Melbourne where a place in a palliative care home would come available for him in due course.

When questioned further, Pete had revealed he'd never formed another permanent relationship, never remarried. There was no one to care for him.

'You were my one and only love, Bella and I screwed that up right royally,' he'd said.

And so she'd agreed to meet him for lunch on Sunday.

*

It was still raining when Bel arrived at Isabella. She was standing at the door shaking the raindrops from her umbrella when Celia arrived, immaculate in a trendy pale blue raincoat.

As she grasped her umbrella in one hand and turned the key in the door with the other, Bel noticed dark circles under Celia's eyes which she'd attempted, unsuccessfully, to disguise with makeup. She waited till they were both settled, and Celia had brewed them tea before speaking.

'Are you all right, Celia? You look...'

'Oh, I'm fine. I just didn't get much sleep.'

Bel felt there was more to Celia's shattered appearance than simply a lack of sleep, but decided to leave it for now.

Despite the rain, there was a steady procession of customers, and the day passed quickly. Bel was preparing to cash up when Celia popped her head through the office door.

'I'm off now. I...' Her eyes filled, and Bel could see that tears weren't far away. 'I'm sorry, I don't...'

Bel rose, took Celia by the shoulders and guided her into a chair.

'Sit down here. Now, tell me what's the matter. You haven't been with it all day. It's more than lack of sleep, isn't it?'

Bel pushed a bundle of papers aside and perched on the edge of the desk.

'Last night, when I got home… Bill… Oh, you don't want to hear all my woes.' With one hand, Celia dashed away the tears which were now streaming down her cheeks, ruining the immaculate makeup and leaving streaks of mascara on her otherwise perfect complexion.

Bel focused her attention on Celia, wondering how to deal with the situation. The tearful woman sitting opposite was her employee, and something was clearly upsetting her. Usually composed, it was completely out of character for the woman to break down like this. Although Bel had only known Celia for a few weeks, in that time she'd proved herself to be an efficient, competent worker, one who Bel would have said had her life together. Although… Bel tried to recall what Jan had said about her – something about her husband? Had she said he was a bully, or was Bel imagining it?

'I'm here if you want to talk.' Bel thought of her own experiences with Pete, her own marriage, the excuses he'd come up with last night, and her lips tightened. Men! Maybe Lou was right, and they were better off without the lot of them, Matt included.

Celia scrubbed her eyes with a tissue, leaving dark rings around them, and scrunched the sodden bundle in her hand. Haltingly, she began to speak.

*

'So that's my story,' Celia concluded. 'Not pretty, but not so unusual either, I suspect. There are a lot of bullies out there, men who can't keep it in their pants too. Though Bill seems to be finding it harder to meet willing victims these days. Maybe that explains why he's become even more difficult to live with.' She dropped her eyes and picked at the skin around her thumb.

Bel gazed at Celia. 'If there's anything…'

'No, thanks. It helps to say it out loud. Helps me come to a decision.

I've been thinking about leaving Bill. I told Jan that when I asked about the job. And I'm grateful to you for giving me this opportunity. I know it's only short-term, but it's helped me, made me come to appreciate that I *can* make another life for myself, that I don't need to be dependent on a man – on Bill – to take care of me, to provide for me. I can stand on my own two feet.'

'So what'll you do now?'

'Right now, I need to go home and face him.' Celia's face crumbled, then she appeared to find some inner strength. 'Then I'll go to my daughters. Hannah and Chloe will understand – and Ingrid. They don't have a lot of room, but I'm sure I can find somewhere to bunk down till everything's sorted.'

Bel blenched at the thought of this elegant woman who used to grace the covers of Sydney's glossy magazines *bunking down* somewhere in her children's home. Without thinking, she said, 'I have a couple of spare rooms at my place. You'd be welcome to stay there for a bit.' As soon as the words were out, Bel wished she could take them back. What was she thinking? She hadn't been. She'd spoken from the heart.

The memory of her own heartbreak had come closer with Pete's reappearance in her life. She knew what it was like to have nowhere to go, to feel isolated. When Pete left her, *Bel* had been forced to stand on her own two feet, to restructure her life. It hadn't been easy, but she'd managed it. That was when she'd met Lou. She knew how vital the support of a friend could be at such times.

Celia's face lightened. 'Do you mean it? I couldn't… But thanks. Thanks so much. I'll go to Hannah's tonight, and see…' Her voice tailed off.

'Well, the offer's open. You can take it up any time.' *More fool me. I'm supposed to be downsizing and selling up, not taking in a lodger. But it won't be for long, and Celia needs help.*

Bel slid down from the desk. 'Here are my home and mobile numbers.' She jotted them down on a scrap of paper. 'Feel free to ring me anytime.'

'Thanks.' Celia carefully stowed the piece of paper in her bag, flashed Bel a watery smile, and left.

Bel watched Celia leave and returned to her task, but the other woman's plight remained with her. Heaving a sigh at the difficulties many women had to endure and the different ways in which they managed to continue to live with them, she finally checked her watch. It was almost six o'clock. Bel now regretted she'd arranged to meet Lou that evening. They'd been subscribing to the Sydney Theatre Company for as long as she could remember, and Bel usually looked forward to the productions with a sense of anticipation. But this evening she'd have preferred to stay home.

While she'd been in Scotland, she'd missed several plays, and the remainder of the season had been something she'd looked forward to on her return. Bel loved the ambiance at both the Wharf Theatre and the Drama Theatre at the Sydney Opera House. Tonight's play was being performed at the latter and, normally, Bel would already be home dressing for the occasion. But tonight, the last thing she felt like doing was sitting in the theatre watching a romantic drama. She'd studied Shaw's *Arms and the Man* at school, and the teenage Bel had thrilled to the classic love triangle; the tale of the girl who wanted more out of life, who wanted to leave the town she'd grown up in, had resonated with the young Bel.

Wearily, she bundled her papers together, thrust the day's takings into the safe and logged off the computer. She couldn't let Lou down at this late stage. There was nothing for it. She'd have to go.

An hour and a half later Bel, wearing a freshly ironed tunic and long pants in her favourite shades of lilac and purple, alighted from the ferry at Circular Quay and made her way towards the Opera House along the harbour promenade. As she hurried along, Bel took time to enjoy the familiar sight of the green and yellow ferries ploughing across the harbour. Tonight, they were joined by a flotilla of small yachts making their way upstream toward the bridge, small white dots in the darkness.

Bel stopped for a moment, her eyes moving slowly across the stretch of water, the city lights reflected in its glassy surface. Then she looked up at the soaring white shell-like sails of the Opera House mimicking the sails down below and glistening in the moonlight. She was going to miss this. She remembered telling Matt the Clyde Waterfront was almost like Sydney Harbour. She'd been wrong. There was nothing quite like this place.

Giving herself a shake, she moved on. There was no sense in

becoming melancholic. She'd made up her mind, hadn't she? Pete's arrival on the scene was another reason to keep to her plan. But there was something, a niggle of something she couldn't put her finger on. Telling herself not to be stupid, she kept on walking, smiling with relief and waving when she saw Lou waiting for her on the forecourt.

*

Despite her initial reluctance, Bel enjoyed the play and was glad she'd made the effort. As the performance progressed, she began to relax and, during the interval, she and Lou sat in *Eat, Drink* adjacent to the theatre and enjoyed the special snack, designed to accompany the play – a glass of *Madam Coco Brut Blanc des Blanc*s accompanied by a decadent Chocolate Cream Soldier dessert. It was a trio of chocolate mousse, cinnamon cream, and hazelnut caramel which melted in the mouth.

'Glad you came?' Lou asked, as she swept her spoon around the goblet to trap the last remnants of the delicious sweet, her words almost drowned out by the loud chatter of other patrons.

Bel was stunned. *How did her friend know how close she'd come to cancelling?*

'Mmm.' Her mouth was too full of chocolate mousse to form a coherent reply.

'I know you too well. Your face… It had that look you get when you're wishing you were somewhere else. Did something happen today?'

Bel swallowed. 'You don't want to know.' Then, seeing Lou's concerned expression, added, 'Later. I *am* enjoying the performance. Don't let's spoil it.'

Bel could tell Lou wasn't going to let it go at that but, just then, the bell rang to signal the end of the intermission, and they rose to return to the theatre and resume their seats.

When the play finished Bel and Lou joined the throng of people moving through the doors and out into the fresh night air. It was a clear balmy evening heralding a hot summer ahead.

'Shall we have a drink somewhere?' Lou peered around. 'Everywhere's probably busy at this time on a Saturday night. It's after ten.'

Although eager to get home, but dreading her lunch next day, Bel allowed herself to be cajoled into walking along to the Opera Bar. Once there, it seemed half the audience from the theatre had combined with that from the Concert Hall and the ballet to produce a milling crowd of well-dressed and expensively perfumed Sydney theatregoers.

Pushing their way through the melee, the pair managed to find an unoccupied spot, where Bel thankfully subsided onto a seat. Most people were standing around under the large sails and enjoying the view of the harbour.

'I'll fetch drinks,' Lou said, turning to make her way back through the crush. Bel leant back, enjoying the bustle, while still feeling apart from it. She relished the delay of the inquisition she knew would ensue when her friend returned.

It wasn't long before Lou reappeared balancing a platter of potato churros and crispy basil prawns along with two glasses of sparkling wine. 'I thought we could do with a bite to eat, too,' she said, reaching out to allow Bel to take a glass before placing the food on a nearby table.

'Now, what's up?'

Bel took a sip of the cool sparkling drink before replying, enjoying the fizzy sensation on her tongue.

'It's Pete,' she said, when she knew she couldn't put off replying any longer. 'He came to see me last night – to Isabella.'

'He what? You didn't let him in, I hope.'

Did Lou think she was a complete fool?

'No. We went for coffee.'

By the time Bel had finished recounting Pete's explanation and her subsequent conflicting emotions, the crowd was beginning to thin.

'So, you're seeing him again tomorrow. Is that wise?'

Bel exhaled loudly. 'Probably not, but I feel a sense of… Hell I don't really know. If you'd seen him, Lou, heard him speak. He's a sad ghost of the man I knew all that time ago, of the man I was married to.'

'Well, as long as you didn't offer to give him house room.'

Bel reddened.

'You didn't, did you?'

'Not him,' Bel replied quickly, though the thought had crossed her mind, albeit briefly. 'But I did offer a room to Celia.' She bit the inside of her cheek, predicting Lou's reaction.

'Celia? As in Celia Ramsay, Bruiser Ramsay's wife? Are you out of your mind?'

'Keep your hair on, Lou. I only said if she was stuck, if she finds it too cramped at her daughter's place. She's planning to leave him and she *is* my employee. I have some sort of obligation to help if I can.'

Lou pushed her empty glass to the centre of the table and, licking her forefinger, mopped up some crumbs. 'What happened to you in Scotland? You've gone soft in your old age. Letting your guard down to feel sympathy for the bastard who left you high and dry and now turning your home into a women's refuge. The old Bel would never have done either of those things. And what's going to happen to this Celia when you toddle off back to your Scotsman? Is she going to lose her job and her home in one fell swoop? You haven't thought this through.'

Bel bit her lip. She should have known better than to have told Lou about Celia. 'It might never happen,' she said. But she wondered if her friend had hit on the truth. Had she really changed in her months away?

Had her experiences with Aunt Isobel and her meeting Matt softened her, made her more vulnerable, more sympathetic to the woes of others? If so, was it a bad thing? She'd kept herself buttoned up for years, forced to forge a life for herself, to be independent. Had that made her hard? Had she become so tough, so rigid that she'd been uncaring? Surely not?

'Well, it's done now. And it may never come to that.'

'It's your life. But if it all goes pear-shaped, don't come to me for tea and sympathy. We should probably leave now.'

When Bel looked around, she saw that the space around them had emptied and the wait staff were moving about clearing the debris.

As they rose to leave, Lou squeezed Bel's arm supportively. Although they often saw things from a completely different perspective, when the chips were down, Bel knew she could rely on her friend and that Lou *would* be there to pick up the pieces if things did go pear-shaped.

'Thanks,' she said, as they made their way to the ferry terminal where they hugged and parted with promises to get together again soon.

Eleven

Celia took a deep breath before turning her key in the lock. The five-bedroomed white house was set on the edge of the harbour and designed to impress. When they'd bought it in the early days of their marriage, at the height of Bill's rugby fame and when she was still the darling of the fashion magazines, both Celia and Bill had fallen in love with it. The tri-level architect-designed home graced a number of glossy magazines before Celia retired from modelling to start a family, and Bill's football career came to an end.

When the girls were growing up they loved swimming in the partially enclosed ocean pool, the setting for many wild parties in the days of the Ramsays' early married life.

But now, with her daughters both gone, Celia felt that she and Bill rattled around in the large house. They had no need of the three fireplaces, the two studies and the four empty bedrooms. Unlike other families, there was no likelihood of grandchildren coming to stay – or even visit.

Celia trembled as she walked into the wide hallway from which the curved stairwell stretched up to the bedroom level. But the house was silent. Bill wasn't home. She walked to the kitchen, her footsteps echoing on the Italian tiled floor, picked up a glass and, opening the fridge, filled it to the brim from a half-full bottle of Chardonnay.

Still carrying her bag, Celia stepped into the sunroom, her favourite part of the house. It curved out onto the veranda and over the harbour. In daylight, it offered a premier view of Mosman Bay filled with yachts.

Bill's forty-footer was moored at their private jetty ready to take part in Thursday's twilight sailing. Gulping the wine down, she sent a text to Hannah.

I'll be over in an hour. Can you put me up for the night? Love, Mum.

That done, Celia went upstairs to pack a small overnight bag. She'd fetch her other clothes later when she'd decided what to do. The important thing to do now was to get out before Bill returned home. She dreaded his reaction, especially if he'd been drinking. He'd never actually hit her, but she'd never openly defied him before now. And he'd been pretty belligerent the previous night.

Celia shivered as she removed her toiletries from the bathroom. Bill might not notice the absence of a few items of clothing, but the empty spaces on the bathroom shelf would announce her absence.

Slipping downstairs, Celia had almost reached the front door when it opened. She stopped in her tracks, a knot forming in her gut. *This is what she'd been afraid of.*

'Going somewhere?' Bill's wide shoulders barred her exit. She could smell the expensive whisky on his breath.

'Over to see the girls.' Celia gripped the overnight bag tightly and held her breath. Would Bill accept her excuse? 'I'm taking over a few things for little Simon.'

'Don't know why you bother with that bastard. That slut made her own bed. And the other two are a pair of freaks. What about dinner?'

Celia pressed her lips together, to prevent an outburst of anger. *Simon was* his *grandson, Hannah and Chloe were* his *daughters.*

'There's some of last night's roast in the fridge.' She tried to sound calm, while inwardly shaking. *What if he asked to look in her bag? What if he demanded she cook dinner first, went upstairs and noticed…?*

'Don't stay too long,' Bill said, pushing his way past her and into the kitchen. Celia heard the fridge door open and close, then the pop of a beer can opening. She opened the front door and walked out.

Once in the car, Celia breathed more easily, but her hands were trembling so much she had to wait a few seconds before turning the key in the ignition. As her little red mini made its familiar journey along Military Road to what she regarded as a safe haven, her self-confidence gradually returned.

'Hi, Mum. What's up?' Chloe, with young Simon hanging onto her leg, her Siamese cat, Bindi, padding behind her, greeted Celia at the door. 'Can you look after this one for a bit while I see to dinner?'

Celia picked up her grandson and carried him into the large open living space where Hannah and Ingrid were engaged in what appeared to be a serious conversation. Deciding not to interrupt, she settled Simon on the floor with some soft toys.

'Mum! Have you really done it?' Hannah broke off her conversation to give Celia a hug. 'You have, haven't you? You've left him. Good for you. It's about time.'

'I don't know.' Celia dropped into a chair. 'He thinks I'm only here for the evening. I don't know what he'll do when I don't go back. Maybe I shouldn't have come here. I…' She looked around wildly.

'Where else would you go? It'll be a bit tight, but there's the sofa in the sunroom. One of us can bunk down there.'

Celia could see her daughter mentally working out the logistics of housing another person.

'It's only for a couple of nights. Bel – my new boss – has offered me a room. I don't know her very well, and her house is on the market. But it's somewhere till I work out what I want to do.'

'Is this all you brought with you?' Ingrid pointed to Celia's bag. 'Surely you'll need more?'

'I packed what I could fit. Maybe…' Celia hadn't thought beyond getting out of the house and spending the night with her girls. She'd talk with Bel on Monday and find out if she was serious about the offer of a room.

Chloe had cooked dinner, and when Celia sat down at the table, the delicious aroma of an Italian chicken casserole rose to greet her. She looked around the table at the smiling faces of the three girls, at her grandson sitting in his high chair beaming his toothy grin at her while pounding on the tray with his spoon. Although exhausted after a day at work, followed by the stress of leaving home, she felt as if a load had been lifted; lightness began to fill her. It was like being re-born, as if she'd finally managed to shake off the shackles of the marriage she'd been locked inside for so many years. This was her family. She was welcome here. She was safe.

'What did you tell Dad?' Hannah's eyes met hers across the table. 'Does he know you've gone?'

'I said I was dropping over a few things for Simon.' She smiled at the little boy who was now chewing on a crust and trying to turn his drinking cup upside down.

'And I bet he was ropeable about that,' Hannah said. 'So he'll be expecting you back?'

'I guess so.' Celia shifted uncomfortably in her chair. She hadn't thought that far ahead, hadn't considered what Bill might do when she didn't return. 'Do you think...?' Should she call him? What if he imagined she'd been in an accident? Called the hospitals, the police? For a brief moment she imagined him reporting her missing, being accused of her murder. Hadn't there been a case in Brisbane? It would serve him right. But she wasn't missing. It was more likely he'd turn up here – at the door – blustering and demanding to see her.

'Maybe you should call him,' Ingrid said. 'Let him know you're here and safe. Tell him you won't be back tonight.'

'You don't know Dad,' Chloe said. 'He'll be over here beating down the door. He thinks this house is a place of evil. My God, it's home to two lesbians an unmarried mother and her bastard. What can you expect?'

'Chloe!' Celia winced at her daughter's words, but it was exactly how Bill thought and, if he believed she was here, he might well come beating down the door. It was one thing for him to disown his daughters and throw them out of his house, but quite another for his wife to walk out on him. 'I'll call him after dinner,' she said quietly, inwardly quaking at the thought.

*

Celia awakened to the muffled cries of a small child, the sound of cheerful voices and a radio playing in the background. For a moment she wondered where she was, then remembered. She was with her daughters, and the sounds she could hear were Simon's cries and the usual morning chaos that occurred in most family homes. Stretching out, her feet met the end of the sofa she'd insisted on sleeping on. The few aches in her back and crick in her neck reminded her she wasn't as young as she used to be and had her wishing she'd accepted Hannah's offer of a *real* bed.

'Are you awake?' Chloe, with young Simon clinging to her hand, peered through the door, a mug in her hand. 'I thought you might like a coffee. It's a bit hectic here on weekends, so you might want to stay put till Hannah and Ingrid have gone. They go to the markets on Sunday mornings. Then it'll just be Si and me. No word from Dad?'

Celia sat up, pushed a strand of hair out of her eyes and blinked before accepting the mug of coffee. 'Thanks. No. I turned my phone off after I called him. Let me see.' She picked up her phone from the floor where she'd placed it before dropping off to sleep and turned it on to see a barrage of missed calls and text messages.

'He's been trying to get hold of me. The last was around two. He was probably completely drunk by then.' She turned it off again. 'I can't talk to him. Not yet.'

'Maybe you should change your number.'

Celia took a sip of the warm coffee before replying. The caffeine gave her a buzz as it hit her stomach. 'Oh, that's good. But, if your dad can't reach me, he may come round here looking for me. I said I was staying with a friend for a bit, till I worked things out.' She bit her lip. 'I'm not sure he believed me. It's lovely to be here with you, to spend time with this little chap. But I can't stay for long. There's no room here. I can ask Bel…'

'Don't be in too much of a rush. The sofa's yours for as long as you want, though I guess it's not very comfortable, not what you're used to.'

'It's wonderful. And it's good of you to take me in.'

'You're our mum,' Chloe said, as if that explained everything.

But Celia knew quite well that it could have been a very different story. It had taken the birth of her grandson to drive her to reunite with both Chloe and Hannah. To think how easily she could have missed out on the joy of that little one, could have remained estranged from her two girls, could have missed out on making friends with her daughter's partner.

'I was foolish. I accepted your dad's views for far too long, let myself be blinkered by his narrow-minded prejudice.'

'But not anymore, Mum.' Chloe gave Celia a hug. 'We're all together now, and…' She stopped, pursing her lips. 'No, it's not for me to tell you. It's not my surprise.'

Celia looked at Chloe, then shrugged. She was past being surprised by her offspring. They'd already sprung enough on her. First there had been Hannah and Ingrid, then the pair had hotfooted off to London only to return as Chloe was about to give birth at the tender age of eighteen, the baby's father having died in a surfing accident. Now all four were living here as happy as pigs in muck. Where had that expression come from?

Celia shook her head. She was surprising herself this morning.

Chloe disappeared, leaving Celia to contemplate what to do next. As she slowly drank the coffee, it occurred to her that she'd left her family home somewhat precipitously. She could have planned it better, prepared herself for the move, managed to bring more with her than the few outfits she'd crammed into her overnight bag.

But she'd done it. She'd left Bill – and her marriage. She'd finally had enough, taken her courage in both hands, and was now drinking coffee in the sunroom of her daughters' house with barely more than a change of clothes to her name.

'Morning, Mum. We're off to market. Anything special you fancy?' Hannah's dark head popped round the doorway. Her daughter seemed full of suppressed excitement this morning. No doubt something to do with the *surprise* Chloe had referred to.

Celia shook her head, and Hannah's head disappeared. There was the sound of excited voices, then the front door closed, and the house seemed to settle into itself. Celia reflected that this house was a home in a way the big house on the harbour had never been. It was cosy, lived in, not a showpiece. It was a happy place.

The kitchen was empty by the time Celia had showered and dressed. Chloe had left a note to say she'd taken Simon to the park and that Celia should help herself to breakfast and make herself at home. They'd all be back for lunch and they could talk then. Feeling slightly disappointed she wasn't going to enjoy the promised time with Chloe and Simon, Celia wandered around the room before fossicking in the pantry and the fridge. Having eaten very little for dinner, she discovered she was hungry and decided to scramble a couple of eggs to have on a slice of wholemeal toast and to accompany it with a cup of some lemongrass tea she'd found in the pantry.

Breakfast over, Celia made a second cup of tea and took it out into the garden. Chloe's cat, Bindi, followed her, jumped into her lap and curled up. Celia's hand automatically began to stroke the little creature, finding the repetitive movement comforting.

She'd been here many times now, but her mind went back to the very first time. It had been a barbecue, and Chloe had been very pregnant. She hadn't wanted to come, but Chloe had insisted. Celia was ashamed now, of how rude she'd been to Ingrid. Bill's prejudices had tainted her back then forcing... No, she thought, no one had forced her to do or think anything. It had been her choice.

It had been a Sunday then, too. And she'd met Simon's family. Simon – little Si's Dad. She'd known Simon, of course. Both she and Bill had approved of the tall blonde surfer who'd appeared in their daughter's life in her last year at school. He was well-mannered and seemed more sensible than many of her peers. It had been a shock when he'd died, an even greater one when Chloe revealed her pregnancy.

Celia looked across the garden. It was under that very tree she'd met Simon's great-grandparents. She could pinpoint that as the time she began to thaw towards her daughter's pregnancy. It was only later, after her grandson's birth, she started to visit on a regular basis and discovered the deep love between Hannah and Ingrid.

Her eyes grew moist. She now understood that her older daughter had a better relationship with her partner than she'd ever had with Bill. It was based on mutual trust and respect. Bill had never respected her as a woman, as a person in her own right. She'd always been a possession, albeit one he was proud of.

Finishing her tea, Celia let Bindi drop from her lap and made her way back into the house. She felt at a loose end. It was strange to be here on her own. She wandered through the house admiring what the girls had done. It was a typical Sydney Federation home. The white plantation shutters shaded the kitchen which looked out onto the garden. Further in was the large open living/dining area which must originally have been divided into two rooms. This area was comfortably furnished with matching sofas in soft blues and bright yellows, a nod to the nearby beaches. Celia smiled with approval. She recognised Hannah and Chloe's influence at work. Her girls had inherited her flair for design. The large scrubbed wood table where they'd had dinner was the perfect foil to the soft furnishings.

Celia dropped onto one of the sofas, leant back, and closed her eyes.

She must have dozed off. There was the sound of a door banging, the clatter of footsteps and voices coming closer. She pushed herself upright.

'We're back!' Hannah and Ingrid said in unison as they trundled through the room carrying several boxes which looked as if they contained their week's supply of fruit and vegetables. 'Chloe's on her way. We passed her and Si at the corner.' She peered at her mother. 'You're looking better than you did last night. Not so haggard, more relaxed.'

'Thank you very much!' Had she looked haggard last night? Probably. She'd been feeling that way for weeks, but had hoped no one had noticed through her make-up. Her days as a model had taught her a lot of make-up tricks which she'd put to good use over the years. Maybe they weren't working anymore.

'Don't worry,' Ingrid said, clearly seeing her consternation. 'You still look too young to have two grown-up daughters.'

Celia was reassured. She didn't consider herself vain, but she'd always taken pride in her appearance. That was one of the things Bill… She stopped herself. She wasn't going to think about Bill. Not yet.

It wasn't till they were all seated, eating lunch, that Celia remembered Chloe's hint of a surprise. 'Did one of you have something to tell me?' Her eyes flitted from Hannah to Ingrid and back again.

The pair grinned, and Celia saw Ingrid take Hannah's hand.

'How do you feel about becoming a grandmother again?' Hannah asked.

'You're not…?' Celia knew the two had discussed having a child, joked that they'd practice on Simon before having one of their own. But no more had been said, and Celia hadn't taken it seriously.

Hannah laughed. 'Not yet, but soon.' Celia saw her hand tighten in Ingrid's. 'We've found a sperm donor.'

'Oh.' Celia could think of nothing else to say. She knew lesbian couples often had children, but had never delved into the details of how they organised it. And now, she was to be grandmother to a child whose father she didn't know, might never meet. It was a lot to take in.

'Don't sound so shocked, Mum,' Hannah said, releasing her partner's hand. 'Don't you want to know who it is?'

'Who it is?' Celia repeated weakly.

Clearly taking this for an indication of interest, Hannah continued. 'We have to work out whether Ingrid or I will actually carry the baby, but Bob Frazer has agreed to donate his sperm.'

'Bob…?'

'You know. Jan's brother. He and his partner like the idea of having a child too, one we can all share. Our child will be related to young Si. It'll keep it in the family.'

All Celia could think of was how Bill would react to having a grandchild both of whose parents were gay.

Eleven

Bel wondered if she was doing the right thing as she parked on Macquarie Street and made her way to the entrance of Sydney's Botanic Gardens. She hadn't been here for years, surprised when Pete suggested it as a meeting place.

It had been one of their favourite spots when they'd first met. Pete had brought her here on more than one occasion when he'd delighted in introducing her to all manner of Australian native plants, most of which she'd never heard of before. She smiled as she walked past the conservatorium, remembering student concerts they'd attended together, and skirted the herb and oriental gardens on her way to the café where they'd arranged to meet.

It had been clever of Pete, she reflected, to choose a spot which held so many pleasant memories – memories of a time when they'd been besotted with each other, when they'd imagined they'd be together forever, when they'd given no thought to what the future might bring.

But that wasn't why she was here. Bel had no desire to relive the past. If it had been Pete's intention to soften her up that way, then he'd failed. But soften her up for what, she speculated? He'd made his so-called amends the other night, explained he was sick – terminally so – and pleaded with her to meet him again. Today. For lunch.

Bel still wasn't sure why she'd agreed. Surely she hadn't fallen for that hang-dog, little-boy-lost expression he'd used so often in the past to sway her to his way of thinking? No. His ability to influence her opinion – and her thinking – was a thing of the past.

Yet, here she was, at twelve o'clock on a Sunday, when she had so many other demands on her time – and a lover in Scotland – taking a trip down memory lane to fulfil some weird request or – as she was beginning to think – fantasy, of Pete's overactive imagination. Lou was right. She must be mad!

Bel rounded a corner and she was at the café. She stopped for a moment, struck again by memories, and saw Pete. He was standing by the duck pond with his back towards her and just for a moment, with the sun shining on him, she caught a glimpse of the man she used to know, the man she'd fallen in love with.

Bel's skin tingled. Her hand flew to her chest.

It was only a momentary glimpse and was over almost as soon as it occurred. Pete turned, smiled, walked towards her and became once more the sick, skeletal, middle-aged man who'd accosted her outside her boutique two nights earlier.

But for that brief moment, she'd been taken back in time, back to the proposal of marriage by the younger version of Pete right here by this very duck pond all those years ago.

Bel felt a flare of adrenaline and stiffened her resolve not to be influenced into anything untoward. He was definitely up to something.

'Bella!'

Bel evaded Pete's outstretched hand, stuffing hers in her pockets.

'Pete.'

They stood facing at each other – a bit like two combatants who couldn't make up their minds whether to fight or flee.

She was the first to break the impasse. 'Shall we have something to eat?' she asked, gesturing to the outdoor café. It hadn't been there all those years ago. The old one had long since burned down and been rebuilt. There were no memories to intrude on whatever Pete had to say.

They studied the menu in silence, then ordered. Bel didn't feel hungry so ordered the plate of antipasto, while Pete chose a bacon and egg roll. Both opted for sparkling mineral water.

Bel waited for Pete to speak, but it seemed that, now she was here, he was in no hurry to begin. She fiddled with the cutlery, repositioned the salt and pepper. But it wasn't till their meals arrived, and she was loading a piece of smoked fish onto her fork and preparing to take a bite that Pete began.

'Thanks for coming, Bel.' He seemed to hesitate, maybe remembering she preferred Bel to Bella and regretting his earlier greeting. 'I know you probably don't want anything to do with me.'

He was right. What was *she doing here?*

'It seems you've made a good life for yourself. You've made a better fist of it than I have. No thanks to me. But I'm happy for you. Happy to see you looking so well, so…' He gestured with his hands to indicate her elegant appearance. 'Who'd have thought it, eh? A schoolteacher, back then, now a business owner.'

Bel was perplexed. She hadn't come here to hear him praise her achievements. *Why* had *she come?* She still wasn't sure. It seemed easier at the time.

'My Bella,' he said.

'Not Bella, and not yours. I've met someone. In Scotland. I'm going back there to live.'

'Scotland? But you said you hated it there. You hated the weather. You hated your family. You can't be.'

Bel popped a bite-sized piece of bread into her mouth and chewed it carefully before replying. 'Yes, I guess I did. And I meant it at the time. But that was years ago, Pete, another lifetime. Things have changed. My aunt died. I was there. It was…. different. And…' Bel could feel herself blush, 'I fell in love.'

It was Pete's turn to redden. He clearly wasn't prepared for this. Why had she told him? It was really none of his business. But Bel knew that, subconsciously, she'd wanted to annoy him, to overturn his smooth assumption they were still… what? Friends? More than friends? They were divorced for God's sake, had been since forever. But Pete was acting as if they were old friends meeting up after a long absence.

That was it, she realised. That was what irked her, what forced her to tell him her plans. And now she regretted the impulse.

'Scotland?' he repeated as if he couldn't believe his ears. Then he was silent again and began to eat, taking small bites of his food and washing each down with large gulps of water. He seemed to be considering how to proceed.

He pushed his plate away. 'I'm not eating much these days,' he said. 'Everything seems to taste the same.'

'Cancer, you said?'

'Mmm. Tried the chemo, but it came back and there's not much they can do now.' He gazed at Bel, a plaintive look in his eyes. 'I just have to make the most of what time I have left. That's why... I had to see you one more time. To see if...'

Bel was at a loss for words. What did you say to someone who was terminally ill? She thought of Aunt Isobel. The old lady had been ready to die, accepting of the inevitable. She'd had a long life and, although she had regrets, she'd made peace with herself and her Maker.

But Pete wasn't that old – he must only be around seventy. He should have many fruitful years ahead of him. Did he have regrets? Other than those he'd already expressed to her? What had the years been like for him since he came out of prison?

'What happened with you, Pete? After...? When you went to Melbourne?' Bel asked in a quiet voice, laying down her fork.

Pete exhaled and propped both elbows on the table.

'It's a long story. I came out a changed man. It wasn't only the drinking. I'd learned to live with myself, to accept less, being less, having less. And the strange thing was that everything I touched turned to gold, in a manner of speaking. I had a bit put by...' He threw an apologetic glance at Bel. 'It was in a hidden account – my running away cache.' He gave a sly grin.

'Well,' he exhaled loudly, then coughed, a racking cough, 'it was enough to set me up, to allow me to buy into the Melbourne property market. I started with a run-down house in the outer suburbs, renovated, sold, bought again. I discovered I was good at this. It was something I enjoyed. Houses are better than cars – they improve in value. But it was a lonely life. Over the years there have been ups and downs but, on the whole, I've done reasonably well. But all the money in the world won't help me now. It'll go to you when I die. There's no one else. And you deserve it for the way I treated you.'

Bel stared at him incredulously. A shiver ran up her spine. This was Pete – discussing his death as cold bloodedly as Aunt Isobel had, but... it wasn't the same. Despite his pragmatic words, Pete didn't seem to have the same acceptance of his fate as her aunt. There was a hint of bitterness. That didn't surprise her. Pete had always liked to be top dog and here he was, with death snapping at his heels just as he'd made a success of his new life.

'I don't want your money.' It was all she could think to say.

'I didn't ask you. It's yours.'

'You could leave it to some charity. Surely there's…?'

'No, Bel. I've made up my mind. It's all legal.'

Bel flinched. She didn't want any of this. She had her life in order, her plans in place. She didn't want to be beholden to Pete of all people. This was a conversation stopper. What could she say now?

But Pete seemed to have no such qualms. It appeared that, having the reference to his death and will out of the way, he'd shed a burden, and was ready to talk of other matters.

'Tell me about this shop of yours,' he said. 'Looks pretty classy.'

For the next half hour or so, Bel told him how she'd come to set up Isabella, leaving out any reference to the pit of despair she'd fallen into after his desertion, and the difficulties she'd had coming to terms with making a new life for herself.

When they finally rose to go, Bel suffered his peck on the cheek secure in the knowledge, he was about to return to Melbourne.

She'd never need to see Pete Sadler again.

Twelve

It had been raining steadily all day when Matt heard a car draw up outside, a door slam, and the sound of hurried footsteps. He saved the email he was writing to Bel and, Hamish trotting at his heels, went to open the door.

'Hi, Dad. Fine day for the ducks.' Duncan shook the raindrops from his jacket and hung it on the hallstand. 'Can I beg lunch? I've been with auld Alex Strachan all morning, trying to sort out his last will and testament and I could eat a horse.'

'No horses here,' Matt chuckled, 'but I could manage a sandwich and maybe a beer to wash it down?'

'Now you're talking.'

Matt carefully exited the computer, before going to the kitchen to take a couple of cans from the fridge and set out some sandwich makings.

'How's your lady friend?' Duncan gestured towards the laptop. 'Still planning to be back for Christmas? You really need to tell Elspeth, Dad. Break it to her gently.'

'Hmm.' Matt began to spread slices of bread with butter and top them with lettuce leaves, tomato, and thick slices of corned beef. He carried them over to the table without speaking. He knew he should broach the subject with Elspeth. It was just so damned hard. His feeble attempt to loosen her dependence on him hadn't worked. She was still dropping off food and turning up unexpectedly so frequently he was beginning to wonder if all was well with her and Alasdair.

'Has she been here recently – Elspeth?' Duncan asked, as if reading his thoughts.

'She drops in on a regular basis.' Matt dragged a hand through his hair, making it stand on end. 'I've tried to talk to her about it, but it doesn't seem to have worked. Is everything okay with her and Alasdair? You'd tell me if you knew anything, wouldn't you?'

'Elspeth doesn't talk much to me anymore.' Duncan drew out a chair and took a mouthful of beer. 'I occasionally see Alasdair at the golf club, but he's always caught up in some deal or other. Doesn't have time for a small-time solicitor.'

'Hey. Less of the small-time. My uncle and I built up that practice, and it's as good as any around Glasgow.'

Duncan held up his hands defensively. 'I know, I know. It's just that it sometimes seems my brother-in-law is too busy to make conversation. If he's like that at home, too, maybe Elspeth isn't finding it easy.'

Matt exhaled loudly. 'I guess I need to get her to open up, tell me if there's a problem. Though what I can do about it, God knows. We never know what goes on in someone else's marriage, and your sister has always been a law unto herself.' He took a bite from his sandwich, chewed it carefully, then asked, 'Everything's fine with your lot, I presume?'

'No problems there. Kirsty's good, and Jamie's still a wee devil. He's in the school team now. You must come along one Saturday and see him play. He's a terror when he gets the ball.'

This led to a discussion of how well their teams were doing in the league tables and their usual debate over the superior qualities of St Mirren and Queens Park. It was a well-worn argument, but one which never failed to entertain the pair.

Finally, Duncan rose to leave, brushing the crumbs from his shirtfront. 'So, I'll tell Jamie you'll be there on Saturday, then.'

Matt grinned. Duncan was so like him. It wasn't a question. He'd no doubt already told the boy his grandfather would be at the game.

'Sure. Maybe we can all catch up afterwards.'

Duncan frowned. 'By *all*, I suppose you mean Elspeth's lot too? Might be a tad difficult to arrange.'

'Oh, I'm sure you or Kirsty can work something out.' Matt busied himself collecting the empty plates and cans as he spoke to hide a smile. It was time the whole family got together. The last time had been… He could barely remember. Certainly before the advent of Bel in his life.

'Hmm. We'll see. You're a hard taskmaster. Well, I'll be off, or Mandy will be sending out a search party,' Duncan said, referring to the office receptionist who'd been there since Matt's day and always said she couldn't leave because she knew where all the bodies were buried. He shrugged into his jacket and gave Matt a hug. 'So, Saturday. The game starts at eleven on the school oval. I guess you'd like us to get together for lunch?'

'Sounds good. I look forward to seeing you all then. And tell wee Jamie I expect to see him score.'

'He'll do his best. Take care, Dad. And remember what I said about Elspeth. You need to tell her.'

Matt shook his head as he closed the door behind Duncan, hearing the sound of the company BMW going off into the distance.

'Family!' he said to Hamish, who had been lying beneath the table hoping for some stray food. 'Can't live with them, can't live without them. As Mum used to say, "You can choose your friends, but you can't choose your family". If Ailsa were here, she'd know how to handle Elspeth.' Then he realised the foolishness of the thought. If his wife was still alive, there would be no Bel, no need to tell Elspeth anything, and no need to ask Duncan and Kirsty to set up a family get-together.

Matt rubbed his chin. When had everything become so difficult? Before Ailsa's death, the family had all gathered for lunch in the old Anniesland family house every Sunday. It was something that had slipped through the cracks since she'd been gone, and Matt had moved house.

At first, they'd all been too grief-stricken to continue, to have to look at the empty place at the end of the table. He'd taken to eating in front of the television to avoid that very emptiness. Then Elspeth had managed to persuade him to sell up, and he'd built this modern edifice of wood and glass.

It had been a good decision for him, given him a fresh start, and the planning that had gone into its construction had helped with his grief too. But now he wondered if, by moving out here, he'd distanced himself from the children and grandchildren in more ways than one.

No. Elspeth still visited often – too often, that was the problem. And he and Duncan still had a few clients they could discuss. But it was a lonely life. That was why… His eyes settled on the laptop with the abandoned email. Bel! She was his future. He just had to work out how to make Elspeth understand that her dad had a right to a life of his own.

Matt finished the email and pressed *send*, then he shrugged on his weatherproof jacket, and instructed Hamish to stay. He felt like company. Since Bel had left, the solitude he'd once enjoyed had morphed into loneliness. He'd only known her a short time, but in that time she'd found a special place in his heart and in his life. Her presence had been a balm to his soul, providing a sense of love and comfort he'd never thought to find again.

Why couldn't his daughter see that? Be glad for him? Duncan could. Maybe sons were different, could see his point of view, his desire for companionship in his old age. Who was he kidding? What he had with Bel was a damned sight more than companionship. It was passion, a different sort of passion from that he'd experienced as a young man, as a married man. He couldn't explain it. It was as if he'd been given a special gift at this late stage in life, at a time when he'd fully expected to slip gently into his later years – father, grandfather, friend, retiree, pensioner even.

Matt hopped into his vintage sports car and headed for the city. Driving along, he pictured Bel sitting there beside him, the wind blowing through her silver hair, her infectious laugh, her… He turned the radio on to drown out the memories. Bel wasn't here. She'd be back, but not for a couple of months yet. Until then, he needed to get on with his life instead of behaving like a lovesick fool. There's no fool like an old fool, he told himself as an old Beatles melody began to swell from the radio. The song matched his mood. Even though, unlike the words of the song, Bel hadn't just gone that morning and wouldn't be back again that night, she *would* be back. Feeling more cheerful, he sang along to the familiar words.

Thirteen

Bel finished serving her last customer and breathed a sigh of relief. It had been a busy Saturday and she'd be glad to get off her feet. She was getting too old to be on them all day.

'Can I have a word?' Celia spoke tentatively, her fashionable blonde bob swinging across her cheek. She'd been a good choice. Jan had known what she was doing when she recommended her replacement. Not only did Celia Ramsay relate well to customers, her modelling background meant she showcased the merchandise without even trying. She'd kept her figure and the expensive garments hung on her slim frame as if they'd been specially designed for her.

'Sure. Come through the back. I'll put on the electric jug. I think we could both do with a cup of something after the day we've had.' Bel led the way and, taking a seat, kicked off her shoes before brewing some peppermint tea and emptying the remains of a packet of rice biscuits onto a plate.

'Now,' she said, 'what's up? You've not been looking too good the past couple of days. Have you…?' Bel remembered Celia sharing her plight and her own rash offer. No more had been said and, though Bel had wondered if Celia's home situation had improved any, she'd been too courteous to ask, figuring the other woman would tell her in her own good time.

Celia gazed down at her fingers twisting in her lap, a rueful expression on her face. 'I've left Bill.'

'So, you did it?' Bel wasn't surprised. From what she knew of

Celia's husband, he couldn't have been easy to live with. And now her daughters were no longer living at home… But where was she living?

The question must have shown in her face.

'I'm at Hannah's. But I can't stay there. It's pretty cramped and, although they're very kind and welcoming, the girls all have busy lives. I feel like an intruder. I know it's silly. They're my own daughters. At least, Hannah and Chloe are. And Ingrid's been very good, too, but…'

Bel knew what was coming and, although regretting the sudden impulse, she *had* offered Celia a room.

Celia raised her eyes to meet Bel's. 'Did you mean it? When you said I could stay with you for a bit. It wouldn't be for long,' she added hurriedly, the words tripping over each other. 'Just till I get things sorted out with Bill; till I decide what to do.'

'Of course.' Bel's heart sank. She wasn't sure how she would cope with sharing her home with another woman, one whom she barely knew. But there was no way she would withdraw her offer of accommodation. 'Why don't you come home with me now and take a look? The rooms are quite small, and the house is pretty old. It won't be what you're used to.'

Hell, did that sound ungracious?

But if it did, Celia didn't seem to notice. Her face cleared, and a grateful smile etched across her lips. 'Really? Oh, thanks. I'd appreciate that.'

The two left together, Celia following Bel's car, and parking at the roadside while Bel drove directly into the garage.

'Watch out for Toby,' Bel said, leading the way inside as a small dog hurtled towards them. Then she paused. 'Oh, I forgot to mention I had a dog. You don't mind them, do you? He's an old fellow and usually pretty calm. But he doesn't enjoy being cooped up all day. It was raining when I left this morning, so…' Stop babbling, Bel told herself.

'No, though I'm more accustomed to cats.' Celia bent down to fondle the little dog, who immediately began to rub himself against her legs. 'He's cute. Toby, did you say?'

Bel dropped her bag in the hallway, reflecting she'd have to develop some tidier habits if Celia moved in. Though that probably wasn't a bad thing. She should be clearing the house out anyway, now it was up for sale. She sighed. There was so much to do.

'The kitchen's through here.' Bel led Celia through to the back of the house and into the light-filled kitchen, the dying sun streaming in through the glass to form puddles of light on the marble surface.

'This is lovely. It's so light, even at this time of day.' Celia spun round, taking in the entire room. Her eyes settled on the large fridge and the nearby pantry. 'Do you…? Have you considered…? What about sharing meals, food and things?'

'I haven't shared a house since my divorce. And that was more years ago than I care to remember.' The spectre of her ex-husband as he'd appeared the previous week flashed past Bel's eyes. 'And I haven't shared with another woman since before I was married. But I guess the same rules apply. We can keep our food separate or eat together if the mood takes us. I tend to keep unsociable hours. And maybe we can eat out together from time to time too.'

'That sounds good.'

'I'll show you around the rest of the house before you decide.'

It seemed that, by the time they returned to the kitchen, Celia had made up her mind. 'How much…?' she asked.

'I've no idea.' Bel smiled at Celia's confused expression. 'How about we start off by sharing the utilities? I don't need rent. Remember it'll only be till Christmas.'

'Oh, I should have things worked out by then. I know your plans, and I saw the *For Sale* sign outside. Have you had much interest?'

'Not yet.' Bel frowned. She must check with Rod Miller. He'd mentioned something about an open house, but they hadn't set a date. She'd really need to make some changes before that happened.

'When did you want to move in?'

'Would next weekend be too soon?'

Bel swallowed. 'No, that'd be fine,' she said, mentally figuring out what she needed to do before then.

*

After seeing Celia out, Bel poured herself a glass of wine and took it into the courtyard where she sat contemplating her pot plants in the dying rays of the sun. She wished she could wave a magic wand and all of this would disappear – that she could close her eyes and when she opened them again, she'd be there, in Scotland, with Matt in that beautiful house. If she closed her eyes now, she could visualise him and his little dog, the floor-length glass windows looking onto the loch and the heather-covered hillside, the…

Bel's eyes snapped open. Where had all that come from? She wasn't given to being fanciful. Her stomach felt empty. She'd skipped lunch, and the tea and biscuits with Celia had barely taken the edge off her appetite. 'This won't do,' she said to Toby, rising and taking her glass into the kitchen. But once there, she was undecided as to what to prepare for dinner. She opened the fridge, but nothing appealed.

Her phone rang.

Seeing Lou's face on the screen, Bel was relieved. Even more so when her friend suggested meeting for dinner at their favorite spot, The Oaks in Neutral Bay. Getting out of the house was exactly what she needed. She loved her home and the thought of the task ahead of her seemed almost insurmountable. She'd get it done. She knew she would. But not now, not this evening.

Bel was first to arrive and settled herself at a table under the large oak tree from which the hotel took its name. She leant back, enjoying the familiar atmosphere, letting the babble of voices flow over her. It being Saturday evening, the courtyard was quickly filling up with groups of young people all intent on making the most of their weekend. Bel smiled as a trio of chattering girls in their twenties walked past, oblivious to everything but themselves and the mobile phones they carried as if they were an extension of their hands. *Had she ever been that young and carefree?*

This place was something else she'd miss. Bel's mind went back to another hotel, one on the side of Loch Lomond where she'd experienced the first indication there might be more to her friendship with Matt than merely one of a client and her solicitor. That moment she'd felt the first stirrings of lust. At first she'd dismissed it as foolish – to feel such intense attraction at her age. But later, when it appeared her feelings were reciprocated, when lust had turned to love, she'd accepted there was no age limit to either love or lust.

Bel was remembering how Matt had made her feel, how with him she'd experienced heights of passion she never had before, when a cheerful voice interrupted her musings.

'Sorry. I got held up. Have you been waiting long? Have you ordered?' Lou bent down to touch cheeks with Bel. They'd never been much for hugging, not like some women she knew.

'No to both. I was just sitting here reminiscing,' she lied.

'Goodness, yes. Our old stamping ground, back when we thought there might be someone out there, that we might meet the one who...' Lou's voice faltered, no doubt remembering that Bel believed she *had* found that elusive someone. 'Well. We didn't, did we?'

'Not then.' Bel smiled faintly, as she too remembered all those evenings spent here under this very tree, surreptitiously glancing around in the hope of spying some eligible male who might, just might, choose to join them, or at least send over a drink.

Lou ignored the implicit message in Bel's response. 'What'll you have?'

Bel checked a menu before replying, 'The grilled barramundi for me, with salad. Hold the fries. And I think I'd better stick with white wine, I had a glass earlier after Celia left.'

Bel saw her friend's eyebrows rise at this piece of information and knew she was in for a grilling later. But all Lou said was, 'I'm happy to stick with white. And I think I'll have the prawns with angel hair pasta. Shall I order a bottle?'

'Not unless you want to drink most of it yourself. I think one glass will be enough for me.'

Once they'd placed their orders, the two women sat back, and Bel prepared herself for the interrogation she was sure Lou was planning. She didn't have to wait long.

'So, Celia?' Lou's eyebrows rose again.

'Yes.' Bel fiddled with her cutlery before replying. 'She came back with me after work to have a look at the room.'

'And?'

'She's going to move in next weekend.'

Their conversation was briefly interrupted by the arrival of their drinks, then Lou fixed Bel with her eyes. 'I'm presuming she's left him then. Doesn't she have family to go to? Didn't you say there were two daughters? Where do they live? It's really beyond any expectation for her to land on you. As if you haven't enough on your plate without...' Louise raised both hands in the air as if to imply the magnitude of Bel's current situation.

Bel allowed Lou to rant on, almost laughing at her friend's indignation on her behalf. Although younger, Lou had often taken on a protective role in their relationship. Sometimes it had saved Bel from making a disastrous error of judgement. But this wasn't one of those occasions.

'Keep your hair on. I *did* offer, remember? And, yes, she does have two daughters. They live in Cremorne too. That's where she is now.' Seeing Lou's mouth open again to speak, Bel held up her hand to stem another outburst. 'They're a bit cramped there, I understand. There's a grandchild too. Anyway, it's done now. And I'm sure we'll rub along okay till she sorts herself out and finds something more permanent – or goes back home. This looks like dinner,' she added, seeing a waiter heading towards them carrying two plates.

The pair were silent as they tucked into their meals. But Bel could feel her friend itching to return to the topic of her impending house guest. However, it wasn't to Celia that Lou returned over coffee.

Taking a sip of her latte, Lou peered over the edge of the cup. 'Heard from Pete again?'

'No, thank God. I don't expect to. You don't think…?'

'He's still in town. I heard on the grapevine. You saw him again that Sunday, didn't you? He didn't say anything about staying in Sydney?'

'No!' Bel wracked her brain, trying to remember the conversation. When they'd met for lunch in the Botanic Gardens, it had been awkward, to put it mildly. She hadn't wanted to be there, regretted the arrangement, while, after an initial awkwardness, Pete had seemed more relaxed. He'd appeared to assume that, now he'd explained his reasons for leaving, they could be friends again, wanted her to be grateful he'd named her his beneficiary. Fat chance! She might feel sorry for him, as she would for anyone in his situation, but friendship was too big an ask.

'No, I'm sure he said he was going back to Melbourne. He's made his life there. He was just here, he just looked me up to…'

'Atone. I know. You said. It seems a long way to come to make amends for something that happened so long ago.'

'He's sick, Lou. He looked like death warmed up, what we in Scotland would call *shilpit*.' She decided to say nothing to Lou about Pete's plans to leave her money. She didn't understand that herself and

82

certainly didn't want anything from him at this stage, legally earned or otherwise.

'Listen to you!' Lou laughed, but it was an embarrassed laugh. '*We in Scotland*. I never thought I'd hear you say anything like that. That trip really did something to you, didn't it? The trip down memory lane seems to have rekindled some nationalistic feelings I'd imagined were long dead.'

Bel shifted awkwardly in her seat. 'It wasn't so much a trip down memory lane as... Hell, Lou, I don't know what it was. If you'd told me six months ago that I'd be planning to uproot myself to return to Scotland, I'd have laughed at you. As you well know, I went back there under sufferance, to satisfy the whim of an old woman, the only living relative from my mother's family. God knows, I never wanted to set foot in that house again. But once there... it was different. Aunt Isobel was different – more approachable than I remembered. Glasgow was different. And I met Matt.'

'Oh, yes. Matt. And how *is* your handsome Scotsman?' There was a sarcastic tone to Lou's voice that grated on Bel. They were good friends, had shared their ups and downs over the years, been able to rely on each other when times were rough.

But now, for the first time, Bel wished she hadn't confided in her friend. Matt was too precious, their relationship too tentative, for it to be bandied around by Lou as a conversational football.

'We're in touch,' she said acerbically, matching her friend's tone. The evening had been spoiled, and Bel was anxious to return home. There should be an email from Matt waiting for her, maybe even a call booked on skype. Forgetting how pleased she'd been to get Lou's invitation to dinner, Bel was now keen for their time together to be at an end. First the snide comments about Celia, then the veiled reference to Pete, and finally the snarky remark about Matt. She'd had enough.

'I'm ready for home. It's getting late – and noisy.' Bel could hear a raucous argument at a nearby table, and across the courtyard a group of women were singing a drunken rendition of Happy Birthday to one of their companions, while a blast of loud rap music emanated from the door of the bar. It was only young people having fun, letting down their hair on a night out. As she rose to go, Bel decided she was too old for this type of evening. The tranquility of the hotel back in

Scotland returned to taunt her. Lou had been right about one thing. The trip to Scotland had changed her. Maybe she didn't really belong here anymore.

Fourteen

The whistle blew for full time and Matt cheered along with Duncan and stamped his feet to get the circulation moving again. The weather had turned cold in the past few days – what old Isobel had called *the turn of the year*. Funny how his mind kept returning to the old woman. She'd made more of an impression on him than he'd realised at the time. Though, even *she* had surprised him in the end. *After being her solicitor and friend for all those years, to discover she'd known Dad...* He wondered if she'd ever have told him if Bel hadn't discovered the connection.

'Did you see me, Gramps?' His grandson's face, ruddy with exertion and the cold breeze gazed up into his. 'I scored. Twice.'

'I did that, Jamie. You helped your team win.' Before he could say any more, the little boy was off again, like a whirlwind, joining his teammates by the sideline to be congratulated by their coach.

'Glad you came, Dad?'

Matt turned towards his son, unsure whether it had been a statement or a question. He decided on the latter. 'I am. Thanks for getting me along. I should have come before now. It was a grand game. They don't stay that age for long.'

'Or that eager. Elspeth's Robbie is already showing signs of turning into the stereotypical teenager. Pretending to be blasé and full of his own importance. Thinks he can outrun and outplay most of his contemporaries. Poor wee Jamie doesn't stand a chance.'

'Oh, I think his sister can cut him down to size. Fi's pretty sharp with her brother. Doesn't let him get away with his cocky attitude. And she can run rings around him when it comes to more academic stuff. But Robbie may have reason to be a bit arrogant at times. He takes after *my* dad, your grandfather. The old boy taught Phys Ed and could outperform me until the sciatica got him. Young Robbie'll be playing for St Mirren before we know it.'

'Don't let him hear you say that. He's all for Rangers at the moment. And he sees himself as the Scottish answer to Ronaldo.'

'Och aye.'

Both men shook their heads at this defection from the family's favourite football teams.

'Young Jamie here knows better,' Duncan said. 'A dyed-in-the wool Queens Park supporter.'

'Hmm.' Matt was keen to change the subject. He enjoyed taunting his son about football teams, but his own interests really lay elsewhere. He'd never been the sportsman his father had hoped for. 'You managed to organise lunch?'

'Sure did. Or rather, Kirsty did. That's more her department. We're meeting up with Elspeth and her two at Gennaro's. Kirsty thought the kids would enjoy fish and chips. I'm not sure if Alasdair will make it. He seems to keep pretty busy these days. Not too much time for family.'

*

By the time they'd all gathered in the café, an icy wind had blown up. Matt rubbed his hands together, then took his place at the head of the table. Fiona pushed her wheelchair in next to him, and young Jamie claimed his other side, while Robbie chose a seat at the other end.

'Don't you youngsters want to sit together?' Kirsty asked, in a fruitless attempt to provide the adults with some breathing space. But she was howled down by Fi and Jamie, while Robbie managed to look supercilious. Kirsty sighed.

'Fish and chips for everyone?' Elspeth took charge. She was good at doing that, Matt thought. She needed something to occupy her, to use her undoubted skills. Maybe she needed a job. He might suggest that, if he could find an appropriate time, one when she wouldn't think he was trying to distract her from *his* life.

Once the meals arrived, accompanied by coffee for the adults and smoothies for the children, Matt relaxed until, forking up a piece of battered fish, Kirsty spoke.

'I was sorry I didn't meet your friend – Bel isn't it?' she said. 'Duncan said she's gone back home.'

'She left a few weeks ago.' Matt stole a glance at Elspeth to see if she was listening, but she appeared to be fussing over Fi. Damn Elspeth. She always seemed to need someone to fuss over these days, and he knew Fi didn't enjoy it any more than he did.

'I guess I'll meet her at Christmas then.'

Out of the corner of his eye, Matt saw Elspeth's lips tighten. She bridled, just like her mother used to when she was displeased.

'Christmas? What about Christmas?' Elspeth asked. 'You did it last year, Kirsty, so it'll be Dad's turn this year. What?' Elspeth asked as there was a stunned silence, even Jamie stopped his continual chatter. Her eyes flickered across the group as if anticipating some disaster.

'That's when Dad's friend is coming back to Scotland. For good this time, isn't it?' Kirsty didn't know what a wave of white anger she'd released in her sister-in-law.

'Is this true, Dad?' Elspeth's voice was so loud Matt glanced around to see if other diners had heard. But it was a busy Saturday lunchtime, and all the other diners were minding their own business, caught up in their own dramas.

Matt cleared his throat, trying to avoid meeting his son's eyes. Duncan had been right. He should have told Elspeth before now. He'd known that all along. He'd hoped he could win her round first, prepare her gradually. But now it was out in the open, and he had to say something.

'Dad?' Elspeth spoke again, her voice brittle with suppressed rage.

Matt took a deep breath. 'Yes, Elspeth. I've been meaning to tell you.' He ran a hand over the top of his head. The fat was really in the fire now. He could see his daughter's eyes harden, her body tense and her nostrils flare. The younger Elspeth would have thrown herself on the floor in a temper tantrum; the adult was more contained, but just as disturbing.

Matt found himself thinking yet again that Ailsa would have known how to handle her. She'd always been able to pacify their fiery daughter. But Ailsa wasn't here.

'What's wrong, Mum?' Fiona pulled on Elspeth's arm, clearly recognising her mother's fury.

Elspeth turned on her, her lips curling. 'I suppose you knew this too, Fi? Everyone knew but me. How could you, Dad? How can you bring that woman here? Into our family? To take Mum's place? We're going home. Fi! Robbie!' She rose, pushing her chair back with such force that it overturned.

'But, Mum... I haven't finished my...' Robbie's complaint was silenced as Elspeth took hold of Fiona's wheelchair and, grabbing her son's hand, pulled them both towards the door.

'Bye.' Fiona glanced back, eyes wide, as she was propelled out of the restaurant.

'Did I say the wrong thing?' Kirsty turned her shocked gaze to Matt. 'I didn't know...'

'No, Kirsty.' Matt sighed. 'You were quite right. Bel will be here for Christmas. It's all my fault. I've been putting off breaking the news to Elspeth. For some reason, she's been difficult about Bel. She doesn't even know her. She's only met her twice, but...' He drew a hand over his hair. 'Maybe I should go after her.' He began to rise, but Duncan put a restraining hand on his shoulder.

'No, Dad. Let her go. You know what Elspeth's like. She'll rage and fume for a bit. Probably take it out on the poor kids. Then she'll see sense and regret her outburst. She'll come to her senses and be on the phone with an apology. You'll see.'

Matt sank back into his chair, but he wasn't so sure. He knew his daughter well, too. He knew how she could hold a grudge, remain incommunicado for weeks at a time. Not recently, not since Ailsa had died. But, as a teenager, Elspeth had been the more difficult of his two children. He sighed again, wondering what he could do to repair the breach which he had exacerbated by postponing the inevitable.

Fifteen

Bel shut down her computer with a rueful smile and drained her glass. Matt had finally told Elspeth about their plans. Well, not exactly. According to what he said, Kirsty had let the cat out of the bag at a family lunch, and Elspeth had stormed off.

She shook her head, went to the fridge and poured another glass of wine. Matt's daughter didn't like her. Probably wouldn't like anyone she viewed as taking her mother's place. Bel carried her wine out into the courtyard, hoping the balmy evening air would go some way to calming the annoyance she felt. She looked up as a flock of black cockatoos flew past, their loud cackling disturbing the silence, the flash from under their wings creating a scarlet splash in the night sky. She loved the raucous noise of the birds here, so unlike the cheerful twittering of those in Scotland.

What was she to do? Could she be responsible for a falling out between Matt and his daughter? Was what they had together worth such a price? Matt seemed to think so. He'd been surprised, but not shocked by Elspeth's reaction. And he knew her well.

But Bel wasn't so sure. She remembered the woman's tight lips, her shocked expression when she'd found Bel in her father's house. What if she refused to meet Bel? There were the grandchildren to consider. Matt was very attached to Fiona and Robbie, and they to him. If their mother kept up this cone of silence, as Matt put it, they'd be bound to suffer. *How could she and Matt build a future on his daughter's anguish?*

Well, there was nothing she could do from here. Matt would have to handle his daughter. And he remained adamant that Bel was to keep to their plans, that she should arrive for Christmas. Though the idea of a family Christmas to welcome her into the fold seemed to be unlikely right now.

But at this end, things were moving forward. The first open house had been held yesterday while Bel had been at work. She'd tried to leave the house looking as welcoming as she could, filling usually empty vases with flowers and leaving bread cooking in the electric bread maker. She'd read somewhere that the smell of baking helped provide prospective buyers with a sense of comfort, helping them to want to live there. Who knew? But she'd done her best. Now it was up to Rod Miller and his minions to work their magic.

'Is everything okay?'

Bel turned her head.

Celia stepped through the French doors, mobile phone in hand. 'I wanted to show you the latest photos of my grandson. Is this a good time?'

'Yes and yes. I'd love to see them.' Bel had forgotten Celia had been spending the evening with her children and little Simon. She'd moved in the previous Saturday and the two women were managing to get along well together.

As she pored over the small screen, flicking between photos of the little boy and a few of the older girls, Bel reflected again how important his grandchildren were to Matt. Elspeth's behaviour was putting her in a difficult position. She was preparing to leave Sydney for Scotland, to leave her familiar surroundings for the unknown. Well, not completely unknown. She'd grown up there after all. But the Scotland she planned to return to was a very different one from the one she'd left with such high hopes all those years ago.

And the woman who was returning was a very different woman too, she thought. She'd left there a disillusioned young twenty-two-year-old and here she was in her mid-sixties. A lot of water had flowed under the bridge during those years. The Bel Davison of today was a far cry from the Isobel Davison who'd fled to Sydney to mend a broken heart. Matt had referred to her as the older and wiser woman. She laughed inwardly. Older, certainly, but wiser?

'He looks lovely,' she said. 'Can you say that about a little boy?'

'He is, isn't he?' Celia beamed proudly. 'It's just such a shame that…' She buttoned her lip as if afraid to mention her husband's name.

'You haven't spoken to Bill since you left?'

Celia shook her head. 'He's left a few abusive messages on my phone. Several texts. Chloe got a few of those too. He doesn't have a number for Hannah. Thank goodness he hasn't fronted up at their door. I was afraid that would be the first place he'd look for me.'

'Do you expect him to come looking for you?' Bel felt a slight quiver. She didn't want a scene at the shop, and Bill Ramsay *did* know where Celia was working.

'Probably not.' Celia exhaled loudly. 'He's a coward as well as a bully. Sending threatening messages is one thing, but he wouldn't want anyone to see or hear him being aggressive. It wouldn't do his reputation any good – such as it is. I'll drop by Thursday evening to pick up some things. He'll be out sailing, so I can slip in and out again without seeing him.'

'Would you like me to come with you?' Bel didn't like the thought of her house guest sneaking into her former home, risking the discovery and wrath of an abandoned husband.

'Would you? I'd love it. I'd feel more confident, less exposed somehow.' Celia gave a nervous laugh. 'Sounds silly, doesn't it. It's my home. Bill's my husband. I have every right to be there. But…'

'Say no more.' Bel leant over to hug Celia, reflecting as she did so that the woman had the build of a sparrow. There was nothing of her. Had she always been this slender or was all this worry making her ill? Then she remembered Celia's modelling background. Of course, the woman had always been stick-thin, a clothes horse. But maybe, now she was in her forties, she should take more care of herself. Bel silently vowed to ensure Celia ate properly, at least while she was living here, see she put a bit of flesh on her bones and got rid of that haunted look.

As she prepared for bed, Bel caught a glimpse of her naked body in the mirrored wardrobe. Not too bad, at least Matt didn't think so. At his modern home on the side of the loch, this old body of hers hadn't let her down. She sighed as she slipped her white lawn nightdress over her head. Now she had Celia to worry about too. At least that should take her mind off her own worries. She needed to allow Matt to work out his own problems.

Bel lay on her back but didn't find it easy to fall asleep. Thoughts whirled around in her mind. *Celia. Would Bill really be out sailing when they arrived on Thursday, or would he be waiting for them, expecting Celia to return? And how would he react to Bel's presence? Would Matt manage to pacify his daughter? Would Elspeth ever accept Bel in her father's life? Could Bel live with Matt if it meant he was estranged from his daughter and grandchildren? Would her house sell easily? And then there was the shop, the pressures from the other business-owners not to sell up.*

She wished she could see into the future. Maybe she needed to visit someone like the old fortune-teller her aunt wrote about – the one who predicted her meeting the love of her life. But Bel didn't believe in such things, had often rubbished those who frequented the clairvoyants of this world, called them stupid, accused them of clutching at straws, hiding from the real world. Bel was a pragmatist. What would be would be, and it was up to her and Matt to work it out.

Eventually she fell into a disturbed sleep to dream of being chased by a crowd of very angry children throwing rocks. When she awoke with relief and a start, it was to see the sunlight streaming through the window and to the welcome aroma of coffee seeping through the doorway.

*

'I think that's it.' Celia hefted the final bag into the boot and closed it.

It was Thursday evening and the end of a busy day at the shop. Bel watched her standing in the driveway gazing up at the house. It was a mansion compared to Bel's own small Federation cottage, but it didn't have the cosy ambiance Bel was used to. Luckily, Celia had been right about Bill. There was no sign of him in the house, and the yacht, which Celia said was usually moored at the foot of the long garden, was absent.

'We should go.' Bel was wary, afraid Bruiser might return at any moment, but Celia seemed strangely hesitant to leave. Understanding her reluctance – it *was* her home – Bel took Celia's arm. 'Come on. You've got what you came for. You don't want to run into Bill.'

'It's Mrs Ramsay, isn't it?'

The pair turned round with a start to see a young woman carrying a bundle of leaflets and accompanied by two small children. She waved the bundle in the air. I'm delivering these fliers about our local school fete in two weeks' time. And we were hoping you...' She faltered, obviously seeing their surprised looks, then continued, 'You and your husband have always supported our efforts in the past, Mrs Ramsay, and we were hoping you'd be generous enough to contribute this year. Maybe an item for the silent auction?'

Celia composed herself first. 'Thanks.' She accepted a flier. 'I'll see my husband gets this.'

The woman turned to Bel. 'And do you live in the neighbourhood too?' She held out a flier in Bel's direction. Bemused, Bel nodded and accepted the leaflet. The woman left, the children skipping behind her.

Bel and Celia looked at each other and burst out laughing. The woman's arrival had interrupted what had been a tense moment. Celia was now ready to leave.

'It's not easy,' she said as they drove back. 'It's been my home for over twenty years. It's hard to leave.' Her voice broke, then she seemed to find an inner strength. 'But I won't give that man the satisfaction of seeing me weaken. I can start again. I can!'

Bel saw Celia's hands tighten on the steering wheel. Her companion was stronger than Bel had given her credit for. She may have been under the thumb of a bullying husband for all the years of her marriage, but she'd been a top model. Bel had heard it was a tough life. Celia had been tough once and had that strength of purpose to fall back on. She'd be all right.

Sixteen

'I'm going out for a walk,' Bel called into the room where Celia was trying to find space for her collection of designer clothes and the various knickknacks she'd rescued from the Mosman house a few days earlier. Celia was easy to get along with, the woman was barely there, but sometimes Bel just needed to spend time alone. She needed a breath of fresh air and time to consider all that had happened recently.

Attaching the lead to Toby's collar, she walked out through the gate and headed down the street with no clear idea of where she was going. She strolled along, her mind filled with thoughts of Matt, Pete and her impending departure, soon finding herself on Military Road. When she reached Isabella, she stood gazing at the window. A blue sundress was displayed in one corner, a matching cartwheel hat lying beside it. Bel had always believed that when it came to windows less was more, and the discerning ladies of Mosman agreed with her, if the shop's popularity was anything to go by.

Bel tried to look at it with the eye of a stranger, wondering how attractive the shop would be to a prospective buyer. She had to find one somewhere if the purchase from the developer didn't go ahead. She'd been so busy preparing her house for sale that the business with the shop had been pushed to the back of her mind.

'Hello there! It's a lovely display, as ever.'

Bel turned to see a familiar face. The last time she'd spoken to Heather had been at Jan's farewell. The woman who Bel had first met as a customer had become a good friend over the years.

'Is everything okay? You look worried.' Heather's eyes met Bel's and the other woman's expression almost brought Bel to tears.

She blinked. 'Oh Heather. It's you. No, everything's fine.'

'You don't look to me as if everything's fine. It's not for me to say, but you look like someone who doesn't know where to turn. My ear is always open, and I can keep a confidence. How about you come home with me for a nice cup of tea, and we can find some water for the little fellow too,' she added, glancing down at Toby.

'Oh, I don't...' Bel began. Then Heather's arm was in hers and before she could protest further, she was being led away.

Heather didn't speak much on the way, apart from commenting on the weather and the state of the road, making remarks on the efficacy of the local council and its maintenance program.

'Now you sit down here,' Heather instructed Bel, once they were ensconced in her harbourside home, 'and I'll make some tea and see to this young fellow. What's he called?'

'Toby,' said Bel weakly as the little dog happily trotted out of the room after Heather.

Bel relaxed against the back of the sofa wondering what on earth she was doing here. Although she regarded Heather as a friend, this was the first time she'd been in the woman's home. They didn't have that sort of relationship. Their friendship had been confined to Heather's visits to Isabella and the occasional coffee in a nearby café. They'd never shared confidences.

Bel knew Heather had been the headmistress in the school Jan's sister had taught in for years. A few years older than Bel, she'd been a mentor to Anna. Jan had been housesitting in this house when she'd taken the job with Bel while Heather had been overseas recovering from a bad bout of her emphysema, the same illness that had taken Bel's Aunt Isobel – a result of a lifetime of smoking. But Bel knew nothing at all about Heather's private life.

She looked around the room. It was a comfortable space filled with mementoes from overseas trips. What looked like Indonesian carvings vied for space on the bookshelves with photographs which from the distance, appeared to have been taken in New York. And there was one which Bel recognised as the Trossachs, not far from Matt's home at Inveruglas.

'Here we are.' Heather returned with a tray on which were set two dainty china cups and saucers and a plate of *TimTams*. 'Peppermint,' she said, as the tea's tangy aroma hit Bel's nostrils. 'I find it helps when…' She waved a hand in the air as if to explain.

'Thanks.' Bel lifted the cup to her lips and took a sip. It was refreshing and soothing. She savoured the sharp flavour on her tongue.

'Now, what's bothering you? And don't try to put me off by saying it's nothing. I know that's not true. I've seen enough in my years as headmistress to know when someone's worried to death.'

Bel flinched to have been so transparent. But Heather was right, Bel *was* worried, though maybe *worried to death* was an exaggeration. Still, it might help to talk to someone who didn't know her well, someone who was completely unfamiliar with her situation. Despite knowing very little about Heather, Bel knew this woman would listen without judgement, would understand her predicament.

Cradling her cup in both hands Bel began to speak.

'Everything seems to be getting on top of me. I'm not usually like this. But, since I returned from Scotland,' Bel shook her head. 'I feel my life hasn't been my own.'

'You met someone over there, I heard. And plan to return?'

'Yes.' Bel smiled, remembering the strength she'd found in Matt. If he were here now, if she'd agreed to his pleas to return to Sydney with her, would she still be in the same mess? 'But it's not that simple.' Bel paused, took another sip of peppermint tea, then the words poured out of her.

Heather was a good listener. She sat silently as Bel articulated all the things she was worried about: Pete's reappearance in her life, and the possibility he was still in Sydney; Matt's difficulties with his daughter; the challenges in selling Isabella; Celia's arrival in her life with her own marital woes. To her surprise she also revealed her doubts, unspoken even to herself, that she might find it too difficult to adjust to a new way of life at her age.

'Is that all?' Heather asked, when Bel finally paused for breath.

Bel's eyes widened. *All? Surely Heather wasn't going to make mild of the issues that were keeping Bel awake at night, making her wonder if she was going mad? Why had she come here? What had she expected of Heather? Did the woman think a cup of peppermint tea could put paid to all her doubts and fears, make everything right?*

'I'm sorry. That didn't come out right. But I do know what you're up against. I've seen it so often during my long life – and I'm quite a few years older than you, my dear. I haven't had an easy life either, but there's no need to hash over that. No, what I meant to say is that it's only natural in your position to have what I like to call the fuds – to be beset with fear, uncertainty and doubt. That's what's at the heart of this, isn't it?'

Bel thought for a moment. Heather's words made sense. 'But…'

Heather held up a hand. 'I know what you're going to say, but think about it. Most of what you're worried about is out of your control.' She paused to let her words sink in. 'Isn't that right?' she asked when Bel didn't respond. Then she enumerated Bel's worries, one after the other, counting them off on her fingers.

'Ye…es,' Bel said at last, 'but how do I deal with them all. I feel that, since I came back here, everything has landed in my lap. I haven't asked for any of it. Oh dear.' She wiped a hand over her brow. 'I sound exactly like the sort of person I despise – the sort who thinks things are never her fault, that the world is out to get her. I'm not really like that, not usually, anyway.'

'Of course you're not. I've seen how capably you manage Isabella, and Jan speaks well of you, and how you helped her cope when her life went topsy-turvy. What happened in Scotland besides meeting this Matt you referred to?'

'My aunt died. And…' Bel thought again, remembering what she'd learned about her mother and her aunt in the past few months. 'She wrote a… sort of memoir, and…'

Heather looked at her expectantly.

'I discovered things. Things I hadn't known about my parents, my mother in particular. I never really knew my father. And about Aunt Isobel. It made me feel… guilty.'

'Guilty?'

'I was pretty unkind to them when I was younger. Thought only of myself. Couldn't wait to get away. I thought I hated them. But reading what Aunt Isobel wrote, I began to see everything in a different light.'

'*O wad some Pow'r the giftie gie us To see ourselves as ithers see us,*' quoted Heather.

'You know Burns?' Bel asked, surprised.

'I spent some time in Scotland in my younger days, in Ayrshire. But, really, Bel, you didn't behave differently from any other teenager. It's natural to rebel against your parents at that age. And your guilt feelings are perfectly natural too. I can understand your feeling it was too late to repair your relationship with your mother, but your aunt?' Heather coughed, a throaty cough which reminded Bel of her aunt.

'I liked her. We did get on. I enjoyed her company and think I gave her some comfort in her last days. She was a wily old dear.' Bel laughed, feeling some release from the tension she'd been experiencing. Then she remembered something. 'And Mum. She came out here to visit me. Aunt Isobel said she'd been happy to see my life here, what I'd achieved. So, maybe…'

'It sounds as if she was proud of you.'

Bel realised Heather was right. She'd been worrying unnecessarily about that. So maybe about all the other things too? But Matt? And Scotland? That was the real worry.

As if sensing her indecision, Heather leant forward, her hands clasped. 'Now the million-dollar question. What do *you* want to do? What do *you* want the rest of your life to be like? That's the crux of the matter. When you get to our age – pardon my classing you with me. I know you're quite a few years younger. But when you reach sixty, you're really past worrying about what other people think. It doesn't matter whether they're this daughter of your Matt's over there in Scotland, the other shopkeepers who don't want to sell to the developer, or your best friend who thinks she knows what's best for you.'

'Lou?' *How did Heather know about Lou's disapproval of Bel's plans?*

'Is that her name? Your hippy friend, the artistic one. I saw how she looked at Jan's farewell when you mentioned returning to Scotland. If looks could kill…'

'She told me it's a foolish idea to make such a marked change at this time of my life.'

'But my bet is she'd be off like a shot if the same thing happened to her. Again, her behaviour is only natural. Yes, she's concerned for you as any good friend would be. She doesn't want to see you hurt. But maybe there's just a hint of jealousy there too?'

This was so close to Bel's own conclusion, she couldn't help smiling.

'You haven't answered my questions,' Heather gently reminded Bel.

'No.' Bel had allowed herself to be sidetracked, rather than answer Heather. She thought carefully about what Heather had asked her. *What* did *she want? How* did *she want her life to be? And where* did *she want to live?*

'All else being equal, there's no question I want to be with Matt.' Bel paused. 'But – and it's a big but – would it be fair to him if it cuts him off from those he loves? And what about…?'

'You're doing it again.'

'What?'

'Thinking about how your actions will affect others. I think it's time you thought about yourself, Bel.'

'I do. I have. I've spent the past sixty years thinking about myself. I've made a life for myself, an independent life.'

'Ha.'

Bel raised her eyebrows. *What did Heather mean by* Ha?

'Are you afraid of losing it – this independent life you've built up and carefully nurtured and protected?'

Bel was stunned. But she respected Heather, so considered her words carefully. Was she right? Was she manufacturing all these obstacles to hide a truth she didn't want to acknowledge? She swallowed and gave a nervous laugh. 'I hope not.'

'Well, think about it. You're the only one who can determine what's really holding you back. And when you work that out, the way forward will be clear. Until then…' Heather began to stack the empty cups on the tray.

'I'd better be off.' Feeling as if she'd been battered by a large stick, Bel rose to go. 'Thanks for listening, Heather. And for your advice. I will give it some thought. I never… Well, it's given me a new perspective.'

Bel walked home slowly, Toby padding at her heels. She had a lot to think about. Part of her wanted to curse Heather for being so blunt, for forcing her to consider matters she'd been unaware of – or had refused to acknowledge. Another part was grateful to her friend for revealing a side of herself she'd managed to ignore, a fear she'd pretended didn't exist, one she now had to deal with.

Seventeen

'Pumpkin,' Matt said, using his daughter's childhood nickname, 'it's Dad. I need to talk with you. Please call me back. We can't leave things like this. I love you. Nothing can change that. I miss you and the kids.'

Matt ended the message and closed his phone with a sigh. It had been over a week since that disastrous lunch, and there had been no word from Elspeth. In addition, she'd been refusing to take his calls. He'd left messages, sent texts, talked to Fi – all to no avail. As far as Elspeth was concerned, he was now the enemy.

At least he was in communication with his granddaughter. Wee Fiona loved him and had taken to texting him every morning before she went to school. From her, he'd learnt Elspeth was being difficult with everyone around her. According to Fi, they were all trying to stay out of her way. Fi was trying her best to please her mum, Robbie was spending a lot of time in his room, and Alasdair was working late and leaving early, rarely at home. It wasn't good.

'Well, Hamish. if the mountain won't come to Muhammad, then Muhammad must go to the mountain,' Matt said to his little dog, as he poured a second cup of coffee.

Winter was drawing in. From the kitchen bench, he could see a fierce wind blowing the branches of the rowan tree by the fence, and an early morning frost glistening on the hillside. A light mist rose from the loch giving it a wraith-like appearance. Matt reminded himself to put out some food for the native birds and to ensure there was water in the birdbath before he left, then settled at his laptop to check the latest email from Bel.

Reading Bel's account of her uncertainty regarding the sale of her shop and of Celia's arrival, Matt detected an unspoken concern. He had the strangest feeling there was something else bothering Bel, something she hadn't told him. He felt uneasy, as if the solution was just out of his reach. He thought about questioning her, asking her to be straight with him, but instead replied amiably, telling her everything would work out just fine, then shut down the computer in disgust with his own paranoia, telling himself it was all in his imagination

It was time he skyped Bel again. He longed to see her face. He was sure that would allay his concern. He checked his watch, but it was useless. She wouldn't be sitting at her computer waiting for his call. He needed to arrange a time, even set a regular time, though they'd tried that and found it too difficult to coordinate. Maybe that was the problem. He sighed. This distance thing was the pits. He wanted her here. Now. Not in two months' time. But he knew he had to be patient. Bel had her whole life to rearrange. It wasn't something that could be done overnight.

In the meantime, he had to sort matters out with Elspeth. He couldn't allow this state of affairs to continue, and it was up to him to try to make amends with his daughter who clearly saw herself as the injured party.

*

When Matt drove into Elspeth's driveway, he still hadn't decided how to approach her. Like her mother, she could be very loving, but was also capable of holding a grudge. He rang the doorbell before he had time to consider whether or not he was making a mistake by arriving unannounced. Under normal circumstances, it wouldn't be a problem. But things were far from normal right now. Since she'd heard about Bel's imminent return, Elspeth had cut off all communication with both him and Duncan. She'd even refused to permit Fi and Robbie to attend young Jamie's birthday party. Yes, this had to stop.

The door opened.

'Dad!'

For a moment Matt thought she was going to close it in his face.

Instead, she turned and walked back through the house, her heels ringing on the tiled surface. Matt closed the door behind him and followed her into the bright kitchen. The early morning mist had cleared to reveal a clear day, the weak sunshine trying its best to brighten the sky.

'We'll have rain again before the day's out,' Elspeth said, much as she would to a stranger.

'Elspeth,' he began. 'We need to talk.'

'I think you've already said enough.'

Matt sighed inwardly and clenched his jaw. This wasn't going to be easy.

'I suppose you'd like some coffee?'

'That would be lovely, Pu...' No, Matt decided, now was not the time for her pet name. 'Thanks.' He drew out a chair and sat down, watching Elspeth fill the kettle and take two mugs out of the cupboard so violently it seemed she'd prefer to throw them at him.

'So, what have you got to say for yourself?' she said, once they were both seated with mugs of steaming coffee. 'If you've come here to beg my forgiveness, to ask me to accept this... this *woman* in my mother's place, you can think again. I'll never...' Elspeth turned her face away, but not before he saw the tears glisten in her eyes.

'My poor baby. I'd never ask that of you.' Matt reached across the table to cover Elspeth's hands which were clasped so tightly the knuckles were white with tension. Instead of a forty-year-old woman, Matt saw the child Elspeth had been, the little girl, jealous for her father's entire love, resentful of her little brother, demanding her mother's attention. That little girl wasn't far beneath the surface of the grown woman sitting opposite him.

When had Elspeth become so insecure? What happened to the independent girl who'd sailed through uni, who'd married the up-and-coming businessman in her early twenties, graced the dinner table at many charity events in the city? What had he missed? When had she changed? Was it when Ailsa died? Since then? Had he been so bound up in his own grief he'd failed his daughter?

'How's Alasdair?'

Elspeth raised her head at this seeming non-sequitur. 'Why do you ask?'

'Something's bothering you. And I think it's more than my friendship with Bel.'

'Friendship? Is that what you call it?' She almost sneered.

Matt could feel the tension in his neck and shoulders. He tried to remain calm. 'Alasdair?' he repeated. 'Work keeping him busy?'

'What do you care? You're so wrapped up in your fancy woman, you don't care for… you can't see…' Elspeth's tears began to flow in earnest, and she tore her hands from his to scrub her eyes, leaving them red and angry.

'Pumpkin,' the childhood name slipped out unnoticed, 'you know that's not true. Mum and I have always been there for you, and now she's not with us.' Matt swallowed hard. 'I don't know what you want of me,' he said, helplessly.

'Oh, Dad. I don't know what to do. I'm at my wits' end. Alasdair's never home. He says it's work, but I don't know. And Robbie's at that difficult stage where he needs a firm hand. He disappears to his room and only seems to emerge for meals, if then.' She paused.

'And Fi?'

'Fi's wonderful. She has so much she could complain about, but doesn't. She's my little ray of sunshine.' Elspeth smiled through her tears. 'When I look at her, at how she…' The tears began to flow again.

'It wasn't your fault, sweetheart.' Matt grasped her hands again.

'But if I'd gone with Fi, if it had been me driving, not Mum, maybe…'

Matt sighed at this evidence of what he'd always suspected. His daughter held herself responsible for the accident that had taken her mother's life and left her daughter disabled. 'You couldn't have known,' he said wearily.

'I should have. If anyone had to die, it should have been me.'

'No! Fi needs you, Robbie needs you. Alasdair needs you. We all do.'

'If Alasdair needs me, he makes a poor show of it.' Elspeth sniffed.

So that's where the real problem lay. He'd been right, but wasn't sure what he could do to fix it. Was it unfair of him to be so happy with Bel when his daughter's marriage might be on the rocks?

'I miss Mum so much.'

'I do, too.'

'You?'

'But life goes on. I've been given a second chance at happiness. Would you deny me that?'

'Happiness? What's that? It's a long time since I've been happy.'

While feeling sad at this revelation, Matt was pleased Elspeth was talking to him again, sharing her feelings. He racked his brains for something he could say to reassure her, to bring back the upbeat, confident girl he remembered.

Elspeth continued speaking. 'While I was dropping round, bringing you the odd casserole, I felt needed. It helped me. Made me imagine that maybe I wasn't altogether a waste of space, that…'

'You were never that!' Matt couldn't believe his ears. What had happened to make Elspeth feel this way? It couldn't all stem from her guilt about the accident.

'Then you said…' She looked away again.

Matt remembered how he'd tried to discourage Elspeth from being so dependent on him. His hands tightened on hers, willing her to face him. She turned slowly towards him and he noticed the fine tracery of lines near her eyes, the creases beginning to form at the side of her lips. A wave of warmth and love for her threatened to overwhelm him. He felt just as he had when, as a child, Elspeth had injured herself or been the subject of a schoolyard fight. *What could he do to make things better?*

'Did it bother you that much? Would you… would it…' His heart filled with dread at the words he was about to speak. 'Would it make you feel better if Bel didn't come back?'

Elspeth drew herself up and, extricating her hands from his grasp, folded her arms on the table.

'You must do what you see fit. Don't worry about me. But then, you haven't. Not lately, have you? I think you'd better go.'

The moment was lost.

Matt sighed and rose. 'I'm always there if you need me. I always will be. I hope you know that. Think on it, and when you're ready to talk…'

Before leaving, Matt turned to Elspeth who was still sitting as if turned to stone. 'But do one thing for me, Elspeth. Don't take your anger with me out on Duncan. He's your brother. He's done nothing to hurt you. You're only hurting yourself and the kids by keeping up some sort of vendetta against him. You need family and if you don't want to include me so be it, but let Duncan in.'

With those words, Matt left, the door closing behind him with a finality that seemed to signal the end of something that was precious to him.

The visit had been a complete waste of time.

Eighteen

Lou had been right.

Bel's heart sank when she saw Pete's face peering through the shop door again. For a moment she felt herself wilt, then, glancing behind her to make sure Celia was busy with a customer, she straightened her shoulders and marched to the door.

'What do you want now?' she demanded, slipping outside and closing the door firmly behind her. If anything, Pete looked even sicker than he had last time she saw him. 'You told me you were going back to Melbourne.'

'You made a promise when we married'

Bel couldn't believe her ears. She and Pete had been divorced for over thirty years – a lifetime. She bit back the blunt remark that came to her lips. It wouldn't help to speak her mind. She hadn't felt anything for this man, hadn't even thought of him for years. Now he'd reappeared in her life, a shadow of his former self. She felt compassion for his plight, as she would for anyone in his situation. But for him to try to capitalise on the promise Bel made at their wedding, expect her to... do what? Words failed her.

'We need to talk again, Bella.'

'I told you not to call me that! And I can't talk now,' she hissed, before throwing a glance back through the shop door to ensure Celia was still otherwise engaged. She didn't want anyone to witness this confrontation.

'Bel then, if that's what you want.'

'What I want is for you to leave. You left me once of your own accord. I managed to survive, and I've made a life for myself. The last thing I want or need is for you to turn up again like a bad penny, trying to… What *are* you trying to do?'

'Don't be like that. You never used to…'

'I never used to be my own boss, either. But I've had to be for the past thirty years or more. What do you think you can achieve by turning up here to make amends as you call it? Does it make you feel better? Because it doesn't do anything for me. I've long forgotten you and your dirty dealings, put it all behind me and got on with my life. We met. We talked. Why are you still here?'

'Is everything all right, Bel?'

At the gentle voice, Bel looked up to see Heather standing behind Pete.

'Yes thanks, Heather. This gentleman was about to leave. I need to go,' she said to Pete and opened the shop door again.

Heather followed her in, and the two women watched as Pete shambled off.

'Was that…?' Heather whispered.

'Not now,' Bel whispered back then nodded and, in a normal tone, asked, 'What are you looking for today, Heather?'

Heather tried on and discarded several outfits before deciding on an aquamarine caftan which looked very elegant on her large frame. As Bel handed her the bag, emblazoned with the Isabella logo, Heather asked, 'Can you spare time for a coffee?'

Bel hesitated, but Celia, who had obviously overheard, said, 'Go on, Bel. You need a break. I'll be fine.'

Checking that the only other customer was browsing languidly through the rail of sundresses, Bel nodded her agreement and, grabbing her bag from the back room, walked out with Heather.

Once they were seated in the nearby café with coffee – a latte for Heather, cappuccino for Bel – Heather leant forward. 'That was him? Your ex?'

'Pete? Yes, it was. He's still here.' Bel spooned up the chocolate from the top of her coffee and licked the spoon. 'I wish I knew what to do.'

'What does he want?'

'He says he wants to talk to me. But he's already done that. We've met twice. He's made his amends as he calls it, explained why he left me. I can't imagine what else he wants. He said…' She swallowed, remembering. 'He said something about a promise. He seemed to be harking back to our marriage vows. But we've been divorced for more years than we were married, a lot more.'

Heather looked thoughtful. 'I don't quite know how to put this, but is he… in his right mind? Sometimes alcohol – you did say he was an alcoholic. Sometimes it can affect the brain. Maybe…'

'I don't know, Heather. All I know is, he's still here in Sydney and he seems to have this bee in his bonnet that he needs to speak to me, needs something from me. As if I didn't have enough to do.' She ran a hand through her hair, ruining the smooth silver helmet. 'At least the house looks as if it's going to sell. Rod Miller rang to say a couple who'd been at the open house were definitely interested.' She checked her watch. 'They're having a building inspection done as we speak.'

'Well, that's good news. Before you know it, you'll be off to Scotland, and this will all be a memory.'

'Nightmare, more likely. But you're right. I'm probably worrying about nothing. It just spooks me when he turns up like that, unannounced.' She grimaced. 'At least it was in broad daylight today. Last time…' She shuddered. 'I thought he was a burglar, skulking there in the darkness.'

The pair chatted a little longer without coming to any conclusion as to what Pete might want or how Bel could handle him.

'Let me know if there's anything I can do,' Heather said as they parted.

*

'Here she is, now.' Celia held out the shop phone to Bel as she walked in, and mouthed, 'Rod Miller.'

'Rod, what's up?' Bel walked through the shop as she spoke, dropped her bag on the desk and settled into her office chair.

'Bad news.'

Bel's heart sank. 'The buyers have pulled out?'

'Worse. The inspection revealed termite damage. It can be pretty costly. I'm afraid…'

Bel didn't need to hear any more. She knew exactly what he meant. No one was going to buy anything with termite damage in Sydney. The little creatures would enter a building, eat the entire wooden frame then leave, triggering the whole building to collapse. What was she to do?

'I can give you the names of some guys who...'

'Thanks, Rod. Email them to me. I guess...' She exhaled loudly.

'We'll need to take it off the market.' He coughed.

'Leave it with me.' Bel needed to think this through. She had no idea of the cost or the time involved, or even if repair was possible. It was an old house and surrounded by trees. She guessed the varmints had moved in from them. But how long ago and how much damage they'd managed to inflict was anyone's guess. The first thing she needed to do was get her own pest inspection, find out how extensive the damage was, and go from there.

'Bad news?' Celia asked, when Bel emerged from the office.

'Termites.'

'Where? Oh, the house. That can be costly.'

'Don't tell me! But I'll need to deal with it before any sale can go through. If it can be dealt with, that is.' Her lips tightened. *One more thing to worry about. It had been one thing after another since she came home. Was the universe trying to tell her something?*

*

Bel could barely wait till she was home to start researching. She'd heard of the damage termites could do to a house – who hadn't? But she'd never thought to be faced with this problem herself.

Fortunately, Celia had gone to see her girls straight from work, so Bel had the house to herself. She poured a glass of wine, grabbed some bread and cheese and settled at the computer. First, she opened the email from Rod to find he'd thoughtfully provided three possible pest companies, then she set about searching websites relating to termite infestation.

After an hour, Bel went to pour another glass of wine. Now she knew what to look for, she went around the house examining window frames, then outside to the back door where the three concrete steps joined the wooden door frame. The evidence was there – signs of little wings and sawdust. How could she have been so blind? The websites suggested probing the wood with a screwdriver or knife, but Bel shrank from doing that, unsure what she might uncover or release. No, she'd leave that to the experts.

Reading on, she shivered at the thought that these little flying insects were feasting on her home, might have been for some time, all without her knowledge. She vaguely recalled knocking down a mud tube from the back wall some time back. It had been empty, and she'd assumed it was the remnants of a wasp nest. Maybe it had been termites. She gazed up at the tall gum trees surrounding her property. She'd always loved them, felt they were standing guard over her. *Were they providing a home for the little beasts?* Her skin crawled at the thought.

Bel read the advice carefully. It appeared there were several ways to eradicate the problem. She was glad Rod had recommended three companies. She'd call first thing tomorrow to arrange inspections, get their reports and quotes, then decide what to do.

*

Bel managed to contact all three companies before leaving for work next morning and arranged with Rod to provide them with access. Thank goodness she'd known him for years, and he was willing to provide service over and above what might be expected from an estate agent. With a bit of luck, she'd have the reports by the end of the day. Then she could decide how to proceed. She'd read about the various types of treatment and was aware that the cheapest might not be the best. Sighing, she closed the door behind her and left for work. Celia had already gone, leaving Bel to make her calls in private.

When she arrived at the shop, it was to find Jan and Celia chatting while the latter changed the window display. Bel had discovered her new employee had a talent for design, so had gladly handed the window over to her. The result was a completely new look and one which had attracted a number of new customers.

Admiring the simulated beach scene Celia was setting up, Bel smiled at the two women.

'Not working today, Jan?'

'No. I have a day off, so thought I'd pop in to see what you two were up to. Looks as if you've been busy,' she said, gesturing towards the new season's dresses which were waiting to be priced.

'Not too busy to take a minute for you. It's still early. As you know, things rarely begin to heat up before ten. I think we can brew a cuppa in the back, don't you, Celia? The window and this lot can wait.' She nodded towards the pile of garments sitting on the counter.

The three trooped into the back room and were soon drinking the herbal tea Bel always kept a supply of. There was also a plate of Anzac biscuits Celia had managed to find in the cupboard.

'Tell us about the new job,' Bel said, when they were settled. 'Is it living up to your expectations? I haven't seen you since you left, though I understand Celia has bumped into you a couple of times when you were visiting Chloe and your grandson.'

The three women chatted about this and that for a time, sharing their news and hearing all about Jan's new job, before Jan rose to leave. 'I'd better go. You two have a shop to run, and I have a host of things to get done today plus lunch with my sister. That reminds me. Anna is organising a barbecue on Sunday week. She'd like both of you to come. It'll be very casual. No need to dress up. She said she's planning a few fun things for the boys, but basically it's to be an adult get-together. You'll come, won't you? I think she plans to invite Heather too, so you won't feel like a stranger, Bel.'

'Thanks. I'd love to.' Bel was surprised to be included. She'd only met Anna, Jan's sister, a couple of times, and had been impressed by her. Jan had told her a little about her sister's history. She'd had a rough time too, and managed to come out the other end, if not unscathed, then certainly with a new fortitude – and a new husband, Bel remembered with a pang.

Matt! He was never far from her thoughts. She hadn't shared this latest hiccup with him yet. Nor had she mentioned Pete's appearance on the scene.

Bel had tried to push her ex-husband's ongoing presence in Sydney to the back of her mind, but it sat there like a festering wound. *What did he want? What could she offer him?* She'd loved him once. Correction. She'd loved the man he'd been once – a long time ago.

Had he really changed? Time changed everyone. It had changed Bel. Maybe Pete had come to his senses. Maybe it was time to forgive and forget. Maybe she should tell Matt about his reappearance in her life.

But Matt had his own challenges at the moment. They'd skyped late last night, after she'd finished researching those blasted insects, and he'd seemed exhausted. There were dark circles under his eyes that hadn't been there before, and she was sure there were more lines around his mouth, though it still turned up in the way she loved at the sight of her.

It was Elspeth who was causing the problem. Maybe if Matt had been open with her in the first place, had told her all about Bel… But maybe not. Now, it seemed Elspeth had decided to boycott her father completely. It made Bel wonder if she should change her plan to join him, or at least delay her trip. She was the cause of the problem, after all. If Matt and she had never met, or if they'd remained only friends; if their relationship hadn't progressed; if they hadn't fallen in love. Then none of this would have happened. Elspeth would have been happy. Matt would still be in contact with his grandchildren. And Bel could continue with her life here as before.

But it *had* happened. Without either of them wanting – or needing – a relationship, they'd met, fallen in love, and made the decision to spend the rest of their lives together. And, she had to keep reminding herself, Matt was adamant that nothing, not his daughter nor anyone else, was going to stand in the way of their happiness – what he called their September song. But could they be happy, Bel wondered, if that happiness was built on someone else's misery?

Nineteen

Matt was chopping wood. The unaccustomed activity was hard work and was raising a sweat, but it took his mind off the stuff he didn't want to think about. It wasn't as if Elspeth had given him an ultimatum – Bel or her and his grandchildren. But it certainly felt like it.

And it didn't help when Bel clearly didn't want to be the cause of this family dispute. She hadn't said as much, but he could tell it was on her mind. It had to be. And she must have noticed his changed appearance. A glance in the mirror – something he tried not to do too often – showed him the ravages the situation had wrought. He seemed to have aged, no longer the youthful sixty-seven-year-old Bel had fallen in love with.

His phone rang. He fished it out of his pocket.

'Matt Reid,' he answered without checking the caller.

'Dad.'

'Son.' Matt laid down the axe and leant against the side of the shed. 'What's up?' It wasn't like Duncan to call him during a work day.

'I need to discuss something with you. Can I drop over?'

'You know you don't have to ask. I'll be here. Would you like me to fix lunch?'

'That would be great, but don't go to any trouble. I can be there at twelve-thirty and I need to be back in the office by three.'

'That'll work. It'll be the usual dad-type sandwich, and I can probably stretch to a beer.'

'Not for me, Dad. I have appointments this afternoon. See you.'

Matt looked at his phone in surprise. It was unlike Duncan to be so brief. And to come all the way out here to discuss something? Must be important. But what couldn't wait till later, or be discussed on the phone?

*

Hamish heard the car before Matt did, rushing to the door and barking furiously.

'Been busy, Dad?' Duncan pointed to the pile of wood now neatly stacked alongside the shed.

'A good morning's work. Come away in. I've put together what you might call a ploughman's lunch – some bread and cheese – and I found a couple of Forfar bridies in the fridge. I thought I'd heat them up.'

'Thanks. Just the ticket. We're having a cold snap this week.' He rubbed his hands together, before clapping his father on the shoulder.

Nothing much was said while Matt prepared the lunch, Duncan spending the time amusing Hamish by teasing the dog with a rubber bone. It was only when the pair were seated at the table that Matt questioned his son.

'So, what's so important it brings you all the way out here in the middle of a work day? Can't manage without me in the office?'

'No, Dad. It's not about work. It's family business.'

'Elspeth?'

'Aye.'

Matt waited but Duncan seemed in no hurry to reveal the reason for this hurried trip.

'Kirsty met her in town the other day,' he said between bites. 'Gosh, this is good. Don't know when I last tasted a bridie.' He chewed enthusiastically on the pastry filled with mince, onions, and suet. 'It's a rare treat.'

'Kirsty met with Elspeth,' Matt reminded him.

'Aye. The pair met up for lunch in one of these fancy tearooms. Kirsty was loath to repeat it to me, but she thought it might explain a few things.'

Matt was becoming impatient. Was Duncan ever going to get to the point?

'It's...' He reddened. 'Women's stuff, you know.'

'No, I don't know.' A thought occurred to Matt. 'She's not pregnant, is she? Elspeth?' His daughter would be forty-one this year, and Robbie and Fiona were in high school. She'd seemed past all that, but women appeared to be having babies later and later these days, so it wasn't completely out of the question.

'It seems she told Kirsty she'd been having problems – women's problems – a bit earlier than...' Duncan seemed to be having trouble getting the words out, but Matt knew what he was trying to say.

'Menopause – is that what it is?'

Duncan nodded. 'Kirsty thought it was awfully early – too young, she said.'

'Why didn't you say so? Her mother went through it at about her age.' *That would explain her moods*, he thought, *her irritability, maybe even her taking against Bel like she had.* 'It's probably genetic. So why the cloak and dagger stuff? Why couldn't you tell me over the phone?'

Duncan cleared his throat. 'Kirsty agreed to go to the doctor with her. Tomorrow. She thought, we thought, maybe...'

Matt waited patiently. He knew there was no rushing Duncan when he was like this. *What was he going to ask Matt to do?*

'There's Alasdair, you see.'

Matt didn't see.

'Evidently Elspeth confided that things hadn't been so good between them. She hadn't wanted to... you know?'

Matt thought he did and wondered how he'd managed to raise a son who was embarrassed to talk about sex to his dad.

'So,' Duncan continued, clearly feeling more comfortable now he'd got that part out of the way. 'Alasdair's been working late, Elspeth thinks it's to avoid her. We wondered – Kirsty and I – if you'd have a word to him. Man-to-man like.'

Matt was amused. 'And what am I to say to my son-in-law, man-to-man like?'

'We thought...'

Matt smiled. He detected the hand of his wily daughter-in-law in this plan.

'If you could maybe speak to Alasdair. Find out how the land lies. Explain...'

'And?'

'We – that is, Kirsty – thought it would be good for the two of them to get away for a bit, on their own, without the children.'

Matt remained silent, allowing his son to battle away in his own time, while wondering what was coming, what part he was to play in this masterplan.

'There's the October school holiday break coming up. As you know we've booked to go over to New York for the week. Young Jamie is raring to go.' He smiled, no doubt recalling his son's excitement. Matt remembered the little boy telling him about the trip and how they planned to visit the Empire State Building, Central Park and the Sea, Air and Space Museum among other things.

'And I'm going to see a real baseball game,' Jamie had enthused.

'Well, we thought,' Duncan repeated, 'you could take Fi and Robbie for the week to let Alasdair and Elspeth have a real break.'

Matt was tempted to ask if Kirsty had already booked the couple into a romantic getaway at Windlestraw in the borders, somewhere he'd thought of whisking Bel away to after the festive period. But he took pity on his son and remained silent.

*

Next day Matt discarded his customary jeans, sweater and sports jacket in favour of a business suit, leaving Hamish in charge of the house, and driving into town for lunch with his son-in-law. Alasdair was Regional Director for a large insurance company, dressed impeccably and expected others to do likewise.

As he drove along the A82 through Dumbarton and towards Glasgow, Matt tried to work out what he was going to say to Alasdair. The phone call yesterday had been awkward. First of all, there had been the difficulty in getting to speak to Alasdair – his secretary had been well-briefed to screen his calls. Then there had been the question as to what to say. Matt had cursed Duncan for putting him in this position. But he supposed someone had to talk to the fellow, and better Matt than either Duncan or Kirsty. He chuckled at the image of his fiery daughter-in-law fronting up at Alasdair's city office demanding to see him. No, Matt sighed, he was the one to do it. He just wished he wasn't.

Fortunately, Matt managed to find a parking spot in Mitchell Street. Alasdair had suggested eating at the Rogano which was close to his office in the centre of the city. It was a bit rich for Matt's taste, but he agreed with his son-in-law's suggestion, and now he was walking towards the restaurant with still no idea of how to broach this delicate subject.

As he entered, he saw Alasdair sitting at a corner table and made his way towards him. It was a cold day, but the brisk walk to the restaurant had warmed Matt, so he was surprised at the blast of warm air which met him as he opened the door.

'Good to see you, Dad.' Alasdair rose to shake Matt's hand and, for some reason, Matt felt at a disadvantage. *Why was he here? Why couldn't Elspeth and Alasdair be left alone to find their own way?* He'd certainly have been annoyed if Ailsa's father had tried to interfere in *his* marriage. And wasn't that what he was doing – interfering?

'Good to see you too, son.' Matt clapped him on the shoulder, remembering how much he admired and respected Alasdair. Elspeth had a good man here, and it was up to Matt to see it stayed that way. If things hadn't gone too far downhill already.

'Shall we order?' Alasdair asked, when they were both seated. 'I usually have the soup and grilled bream. Would you…?'

'That sounds fine.' Matt wasn't surprised to learn his companion often dined here. Established in 1935, the Rogano was Glasgow's oldest surviving restaurant, beloved by powerbrokers and the fashionista alike. 'And maybe a Corona?' he added, glancing at the drinks menu.

When the waiter had taken their orders, Alasdair spoke. 'Now what's this all about, Dad? You said something about Elspeth. I know she's gone to see the doctor today. I think Kirsty's going with her. Is there something wrong? Something she hasn't told me?' He sat back and rubbed his chin. 'I know I haven't been home much recently. There's been so much on, and we've been… Och, you don't want to hear all that.'

'Have you noticed anything different about her?'

'Lately? Can't say I have. She may have been losing her temper with the kids more, but they're getting to that stage, aren't they?'

He grimaced. 'We adults don't know anything. Well, Robbie's there, anyway. Fi's a delight as always. Don't know how she does it.'

'Anything else?' Matt decided to probe.

Alasdair looked embarrassed. 'There hasn't been much time for... She hasn't had much time for me.'

Matt understood. Their sex life wasn't something Alasdair wanted to discuss with his father-in-law.

'It's a passing thing, I'm sure. Once this merger's over, I'll have more time.'

So it was work, not another woman. Matt felt relieved, but it didn't make his task any easier.

Their beers arrived, interrupting the difficult moment.

'It seems she's spoken to Kirsty.'

'Yes?' Alasdair's eyebrows went up. 'Women's talk. I know she seems to be avoiding you at the moment. I think she's making too much of it. It's your life, and if you want to take up with...'

'It's not about me. Well, maybe indirectly.'

Alasdair looked puzzled.

Matt took a deep breath, and a slug from his glass. 'It seems she told Kirsty she's having symptoms which suggest...'

Alasdair wrinkled his brow. Matt could see he was thinking the worst.

'Oh, nothing serious. Well, not terminal anyway. Seems like menopause.'

Alasdair rubbed his face. 'Isn't she a bit young for that?'

'Her mother experienced it at that age. I should have thought – the irritability, the mood swings, her inability to accept Bel.'

'Oh.' Alasdair paused, seeming to be digesting this. 'And what am I to do?'

'Well, *Kirsty*...' Matt emphasised his daughter-in-law's name, aware the other knew exactly how Kirsty operated. While her heart was in the right place, she often rushed in *where angels feared to tread* as the saying went. This was a prime example of that.

'What does Kirsty want now?' Alasdair asked wearily. 'Isn't accompanying Elspeth to the doctor enough?'

Matt gave a rueful smile. 'Not quite. She thinks it would do her good – do you both good – for you to get away for a bit. As a couple. Without the kids.' He paused to let it sink in.

Before Alasdair could reply, a waiter brought their soup course, and no more was said while they enjoyed the cock-a-leekie soup.

When their plates had been removed, Alasdair continued with the conversation. 'Without the kids? What does she think we're going to do with them? They have school, and Fi… Is she proposing to have them at their place? And when is this supposed to happen?'

'During the October school holidays. Duncan and Kirsty are taking Jamie to New York, so they've suggested Fi and Robbie come to me.'

Alasdair's eyes bulged. Matt had often heard that expression, but never quite understood what it meant. Now he did. It was as if his son-in-law's eyes widened till they became so large they looked as if they might pop out of his head. He saw his Adam's apple bob.

'To you?' he asked after a long pause.

'What's wrong with that?' Matt surprised himself with this response. Despite being initially stunned at Duncan's suggestion, he'd come around to the idea. Now he was enjoying Alasdair's reaction. 'I brought up two of my own and they haven't done too badly.'

'I'll talk to Elspeth.'

That was all Alasdair had to say. The meals were served and eaten, the two men shook hands and parted, and Matt returned to his car wondering if he'd helped or managed to completely screw things up.

Twenty

The news wasn't good. Bel now had the reports from the three pest inspection companies, and all indicated she had a major problem. It appeared that the insects had been nesting in her beautiful trees which would need to be treated along with the house. The good news was that the house wasn't in imminent danger of collapsing. The problem could be fixed. But she had to decide which treatment would prove most effective.

Although it was tempting to go for the quick and cheapest fix, and leave it to the next owner, Bel couldn't do that. She wanted to ensure she sold the house in as good a condition as she would like to find it herself. To do that, it looked as if she was going to be up for at least $5000. She blew through her lips. The expense would make quite a dent in her savings. She put the quotes aside, deciding to consult Rod Miller the next day. He was familiar with the pest control companies. He'd be able to advise her.

Meantime, she had a call from Matt to look forward to. What with one thing and another, they hadn't been able to skype as frequently as they'd anticipated. The time difference had often defeated them. They emailed most days, but it wasn't the same as speaking, seeing his familiar face, although sometimes it made it easier to keep things to herself – things like Pete, and the challenges with the shop. Thinking of the shop reminded her. There had been no reply from the developer's solicitor. She'd have to follow that up. There was so much to do, to take care of, before she could leave, and now the house was off the market till the pest stuff was fixed.

Meantime, there was Matt's call. Bel just had time to freshen up and pour a glass of wine, before settling down at the computer for a long chat.

*

Bel closed off the skype call with a thoughtful look. Her sympathies were with Matt. But at least they seemed to be getting to the bottom of Elspeth's problems. She felt for the woman. She was young to be suffering from menopause. Bel herself had been closer to fifty when she'd gone through it. She could well remember the agony of the hot flushes, the discomfort of the night sweats and what seemed to be the constant prickliness.

Matt had been equivocal about Alasdair's reaction. She hoped he'd see sense and go along with what seemed to Bel to be an eminently sensible suggestion that the two of them go off for a romantic getaway. She hadn't met Matt's daughter-in-law, Kirsty, but liked the sound of her. Maybe they could become friends? Duncan had been welcoming when they'd met. They had a little boy too, another grandchild.

It suddenly occurred to Bel that, if she and Matt married, she'd inherit three grandchildren. What would they call her? She couldn't imagine transforming into an instant grandmother. She'd prefer to remain Bel to all of them. That was her name, the one she'd chosen.

Married! What was she thinking? She and Matt had never discussed marriage. But she knew he'd considered it. As had she. She wasn't changing her life, moving to the other side of the world for a flash in the pan. No. At her age, and of her generation, marriage was definitely on the cards. She quivered a little at the thought. It was a big step at any age and seemed even greater at her time of life. But why not?

As she closed her eyes that night, Bel imagined herself cocooned in Matt's arms in a little love nest somewhere in the Scottish borders. His reference to the romantic getaway he had in mind for Elspeth and Alasdair had sparked her imagination. Matt was so unlike Pete. He'd never let her down. She was sure of that.

*

'Will you be okay if I pop out for a bit?'

It had been a busy morning, but the shop was empty now, and Bel thought it might be a good time to check with Rod Miller about the pest control companies.

'Sure thing.' Celia was pricing a delivery of new dresses. She glanced up and Bel noticed she had a glow about her that hadn't been there earlier.

'You seem happier. Has something…?'

'No. It's just that I'm beginning to feel happy again. Bill has kept his distance, although I know I have to face him sometime. And I feel safe living with you, seeing the girls regularly. It's as if I've been given a second chance.'

'Right.' Bel didn't know how to respond. She was glad Celia seemed to be recovering. She'd never let her anguish show at work, managing to keep a smiling face in front of customers and always appearing her elegant and immaculate self. But, when she'd first moved in, Bel had heard the muffled sobs at night and seen the bleary eyes in the mornings. 'I'm glad it's working for you,' she said awkwardly. 'I'm off now. I shouldn't be long.'

Bel was in luck. Rod was alone in his office at the back of the shop. He rose to greet her with a smile.

'I thought I might see you today. You got the reports done?'

'That's why I'm here. It seems the problem's pretty extensive. I need your advice. They recommend different approaches – baits, barrier treatments… I don't know where to start.'

'Let me see.' Rod took the reports and studied them carefully, while Bel waited, tapping her fingers on the desk.

'Right,' he said after a few minutes. 'It's bad, but I've seen worse. I'd recommend the barrier treatment and, of course, getting rid of the nest in the tree. The new owner will need to have annual inspections done as they can return.'

'I know. I've been remiss. It didn't occur to me.'

'Happens a lot in Sydney with those old places – and the surrounding trees. The creatures love them.'

'If I ever find a buyer,' Bel said disconsolately.

'You will. It's a lovely house in a good location. In fact…' He tapped his teeth with a pen. 'I wouldn't be surprised if the original buyers renew their offer – if they haven't found anything else by the time you've had the work done.'

'Really?' A wave of relief flooded Bel. It was going to cost her, but maybe all was not lost.

There was a spring in Bel's step as she walked back to the shop, only to find Celia looking glum.

'What's up?'

'Bill called.'

'I thought you were going to change your number.'

'I was. I am. But there's been so much happening I hadn't got around to it. He hadn't called, so I let it go and now…' She bit her lip, her eyes moistening. 'He wants me back.'

'But you won't go?'

'Nooo. No,' Celia said more decisively. 'But…'

'Come through here.' Bel glanced around the empty shop. She didn't want Celia to break down in full view of any prospective customers. This wasn't like the apparently strong-minded woman who'd fearlessly walked out on Bruiser Ramsay. She led the way to the office, leaving the door open to provide a clear view of the shop.

Bel pointed to a chair, fetched Celia a glass of water and perched on the desk. 'What did the bastard say? Did he threaten you?'

'Not in as many words, but…'

Bel cursed under her breath. Bill Ramsay knew where Celia worked. By now he'd probably worked out where she was staying too. Was she safe from him? Her lips tightened, but before she had a chance to speak, Celia continued.

'He's never been violent, not…' She shivered, then seemed to pull herself together. She took a gulp of water. 'It's all about money with him,' she said bitterly. 'Money and possessions. He thinks he owns me,' she sniffed. 'Always has. In the early years, I quite enjoyed it. It was like I was his Barbie doll, on display. But it soon became tiresome. I thought he'd grow out of it – *we'd* grow out of it. Now it's as if what he's lost is not me – not a real flesh and blood human being. I'm no more to him than one of his precious antiques.'

Bel thought quickly. Celia was a wreck. There was no getting around that. And she wasn't going to be much good here today. But what if her husband took it into his head to fetch her back? Came here or to Bel's home? Where should she go? 'Are the girls home today?'

Celia raised her head from a study of her feet. 'Chloe should be there with Simon.'

'Why don't you go round there? I can hold the fort here by myself. It probably won't be busy today. You look as if you need some family time, and my guess is the company of a fourteen-month-old will do the trick. Get rid of that phone. Have Chloe set you up with a new sim card. I'll see you later. And if Bill dares to show his face here, I'll give him short shrift.'

'Thanks, Bel.' Celia gathered her belongings and was gone in the blink of an eye, leaving Bel shaking her head in disbelief. One more thing to worry about. It seemed that, no sooner was one problem solved than another reared its head. Maybe Lou was right, and she'd become too soft in her old age. Maybe Scotland had changed her, and not for the better.

Well, she had things to do. She opened her iPad to revisit her to-do list for the day. She could check off pest control. Rod would take care of that. But the business with the shop was still outstanding. Bel sighed. She seemed more able to take care of other people's problems than her own these days. She picked up the phone.

Ten minutes later, she finished the call. It was as she'd thought. Only one of the other shopkeepers was prepared to sell. She was out on a limb. There was no way the developer would risk purchasing anything less than the entire row. That meant she'd have to find a buyer for Isabella by herself. For a moment, she wanted to put her head down on the desk and burst into tears, but the shop door opened, and a flurry of customers flooded in. Bel went through to the shop and put on her most welcoming smile.

It was after one by the time they'd all left carrying their purchases as evidence of a successful shopping spree. Bel loved to see satisfied customers walking out with outfits which made them look and feel good. That's what Isabella was all about. It was why she'd started the boutique and what had kept her going through the years.

She was hanging up the discarded garments when she heard the door open again.

'Lunch?' Lou was standing there with a brown paper bag which Bel recognised as being from the local deli. 'I saw Celia leave earlier and thought you mightn't have time to grab a bite to eat. Pastrami on rye with dill suit you?'

'You're a godsend.' Bel suddenly realised she *was* hungry. It had been a long time since breakfast, and she'd packed a lot into the morning.

'What's up with Celia?' Lou asked as they sat eating lunch. 'I saw her rush along the road like a bat out of hell. Someone after her?'

Bel said nothing.

'Husband,' Lou said, biting into her sandwich. 'Always is. Men!'

Bel didn't want to get into this. She'd had this conversation with Lou before, many times. Sometimes she wondered if her friend was her own worst enemy, if she was without a man in her life simply because she could never find it in herself to trust any of them. Bel remembered how, early in their friendship, when they'd occasionally gone to wine bars together, her friend's brash attitude had served to scare away possible suitors.

'Mmm. Not all of them.'

'Well, you'd be prejudiced, of course.' There was that bitter tone again.

'That's enough, Lou. I know you mean well, but we all have our own lives to live – and our own mistakes to make. I know you've saved me from a few in the past and I'm grateful, but this time I'm sticking to my guns.' Bel tossed her empty sandwich wrapper in the bin and stood up. 'Thanks a lot for the lunch. I'd most likely have done without if you hadn't dropped by. But I need to get on now. I have a shop to run even if you haven't. Shall I see you on Saturday?'

'If you still want me to come to dinner.'

'Of course I do. You can meet Celia properly then. Maybe she'll even tell you her story, if you behave yourself.'

'That'll be the day,' Lou laughed. 'I'll bring along the mockups for the library hangings – get your opinions on them. See you then.'

She left as two new customers entered, and Bel barely had time to freshen her lipstick before walking out to greet them.

The afternoon passed so quickly Bel didn't have a moment to think about Celia's Bill or Lou's dire view of men, before it was time to close up for the night. As she locked up, she glanced around warily, fearful of seeing Bill Ramsay, or, worse still, Pete Sadler, lurking outside. But the street was clear, the only figures those of a few late shoppers hurrying to their cars and a couple of local schoolchildren giggling over something on their mobile phones.

Bel breathed a sigh of relief. All was well, but she had the distinct feeling it wouldn't remain that way.

Twenty-one

Bel drew up outside the address Jan had given her and parked behind a car she recognised as belonging to Heather. She must be at the right place, but she couldn't see the house. What she *could* see was a set of worn stone steps leading downwards through a tangle of bushes. She checked the number again. Yes, this was it.

As she carefully made her way down the steps, carrying a bottle of wine in one hand and balancing a plate of brownies in the other, her bag slung over one shoulder, Bel was glad she'd worn her flat sandals. The steps were cracked in places, deadly to someone who might be taking less care. As she neared the foot, she could hear voices and, turning a corner, saw Jan standing in the doorway with a tall dark-haired man. It must be Graham. She'd never met Jan's husband though she'd heard a lot about him.

Before she reached the door, a familiar figure rushed out to greet her.

'How's Toby? Did you bring him?'

'Not today, Andy.' Jan's son loved Bel's little dog and had minded him while she was in Scotland.

'Bel! You found us. Good to see you.' At the sound of Andy's voice, Jan had turned and now reached out to relieve Bel of her burden. 'You shouldn't have. Oh, Marcus will approve of this one,' she said, looking at the label on the wine Bel had brought. 'My brother-in-law can be a bit of a wine buff. Come on in and meet the others.'

Bel allowed herself to be led into the house, through the kitchen and out into a large garden where groups of people were milling around chatting, while a game of cricket seemed to be going on at the far end.

'This is Bel,' Jan announced, breaking into one group. 'Anna, you know, and Heather.' The two women smiled at Bel. 'You met my Graham at the door with Andy. This is our mum.' She brought forward an older woman in whom Bel could see a resemblance to both Jan and her sister. 'Dad and Marcus are over there playing cricket with young Jon, Marcus' son, and it looks as if Andy is about to join them,' she added, as her son raced across to join the cricketers. 'Celia's not here yet. She's picking up Chloe and Simon. The others,' she pointed to another group which was gathered under a large poinciana tree, 'are mostly from uni, or friends of Marcus.'

Bel accepted a glass of white wine and was soon enveloped in the group. Jan's husband drifted off to the barbecue where he was joined shortly by Marcus. It was a typical Australian barbecue, Bel thought – the men cooking steaks and sausages while the women chatted about families. She always felt a little left out at these gatherings. She had no children to discuss, no family anecdotes to share. She listened politely, wondering why she was here, till Heather drew her aside.

'You're like me. It's sometimes difficult to relate to all this talk of husbands and children. Over the years, I've come to accept being the odd one out, and, listening to some of the stories, glad I've never been a parent. Have you heard any more from your ex?'

'No. Thank goodness. I've been more concerned about termites.'

'Termites? You have an infestation? Oh, my dear!'

By the time Bel told Heather her sorry tale and received a blow-by-blow account of Heather's own very similar experience, she was reassured it wasn't the disaster she'd first imagined. Maybe Rod was right, and they would still find a buyer.

'Here's Celia with her daughter and the little boy.'

Bel glanced around to see her employee and house guest arrive with a pretty blonde girl and a small child who was immediately picked up by Jan's mother. Of course, he was her great-grandson.

Suddenly the men called to say the meat was cooked, and a large array of salad platters appeared as if by magic. Tables were arranged and soon everyone was seated with plates full of salads and meat, while Anna's husband, Marcus, moved among them, chatting and topping up glasses.

*

'Hello, Bel. This is my daughter, Chloe.' They'd finished eating when Celia drew the pretty blonde girl forward.

'We've met, Mum,' she protested. 'Remember I told you? When I was living with Jan, I popped into the shop from time to time. I was working just across the road.'

Celia felt her ears turn red with embarrassment. Of course, she should have known. But she'd tried to forget that dreadful time when it was as if Chloe wasn't her daughter. Thrown out of the house by her bullying father, Chloe had sought shelter with the only adult she knew would take her in – her boyfriend's mother, Jan.

And now they were all here, friends together. Celia, Chloe, Jan and Graham, Heather and Bel. It was almost as if it had never happened. But it had, as evidenced by the only one absent – the little boy's other grandfather, Chloe's father, who still refused to acknowledge his existence.

'You have a lovely little boy,' Bel said. 'You must be very proud of your daughter,' Bel addressed the latter remark to Celia.

'I am.' She threw an arm around Chloe's shoulder. 'I was such a fool for so long, I almost…'

'Everything's fine now, Mum.' Chloe shrugged off her arm, and Celia worried she'd been too demonstrative in public. But the strange thing was that she felt she was among family. Jan's family had been so welcoming to her and her daughters – both of them. Even though Hannah and Ingrid weren't here today. Bill could learn a thing or two from this family, she thought, as she accepted a top-up to her glass from Marcus.

Bel moved off, and Celia found herself cornered by Jan.

'I'm glad you came today. Mum and Dad – and Anna, too – consider you part of the family now. And they're besotted by our grandson.' She gestured to where her parents were sitting on the grass with the small child, never seeming to tire of rolling a ball towards him. 'They love it, even though they'll most likely find it difficult to get up again. This was *their* house, you know – the old family home. They were delighted when Marcus bought it, felt it was staying in the family. That was before he and Anna married, of course, but it was on the cards.' She laughed. 'He didn't let the grass grow under his feet, though for a time… But that's not my story to tell.'

Celia wondered what their story was, but was too polite to ask. She knew Jan, herself, had had problems after her son's death. But, seeing her here today with her husband, relaxed and happy, it appeared they were all in the past. And they still had Andy, who was a tender and loving uncle to young Simon, promising to teach him cricket as soon as he could hold a bat, and offering to babysit any time.

'I wanted to talk to you,' Jan said in a low voice, drawing Celia over to the unoccupied bench under the poinciana tree. 'How are you getting on living with Bel?'

'Fine.' Celia hesitated and furrowed her brow. She wasn't sure where Jan was going with this.

'You know she won't be staying there after Christmas?'

'Of course. The house is on the market. But what does that…?'

'I think you should talk with my brother.'

Celia's eyes widened. *What did Jan's brother have to do with her? He was to be the sperm donor for her next grandchild, if Hannah and Ingrid were to be believed. But that arrangement had nothing to do with her. What did Jan mean?*

'He's a lawyer,' Jan explained. 'He has an office in the city. He'll see you right and won't charge you and arm and a leg. He helped Anna, our sister, with her divorce when…' Her voice tailed off. Celia wondered again what that story was. As far as she knew Anna was happily married to Marcus, who was being the ultimate host here today. There was clearly a story there. But not one Jan was prepared to share.

'Thanks. If you can let me have his details. I expect Bill to make a fuss. He's not one to let go easily.'

Jan fossicked in her bag and drew out a white embossed card. 'This is him,' she said. Celia took the card tentatively. It was a big step to actually contact a lawyer. It was a decision that the marriage was ended, that she wanted a divorce. *Bob Frazer, Solicitor*, she read. It seemed innocuous, but it was something that could alter her whole life.

Celia tucked the card away in her pocket. She'd look at it later, decide if she'd contact him. But if she did want a divorce she'd need a lawyer, and she supposed Jan's brother was as good as anyone. All the others she knew were Bill's friends too, and she could guess where *their* loyalties would lie.

'Thanks,' she said, before Jan rose to leave.

Left alone, Celia gazed around the garden. It was a lovely family yard. What looked like a vegetable patch was almost hidden by grevillea bushes, and the grassy area was surrounded by beds of brightly-coloured and well-tended flowers. White gardenias and pink azaleas fought for space with orange tinted hibiscus, while a ground covering of star jasmine provided its heady perfume. She closed her eyes for a moment. The scent reminded her of Bel's courtyard. It was soothing. She felt she could sit here forever, forget everything and just float away.

Twenty-two

It was Monday morning. The rain was pelting down, sheets of water lashing the window and raindrops striking the metal roof like bullets. Bel wanted nothing more than to turn over in bed, close her eyes, and go back to sleep. But she had a shop to open and needed to check with Rod what was happening with the pest guys and, and, and… The list was never-ending.

Blinking madly in an attempt to become fully awake, Bel struggled into the shower. The stream of hot water helped revive her, and by the time she'd completed a sketchy make-up, drawn a comb thorough her hair, and dressed in a pair of blue pants with a loose-fitting blue and white striped shirt, she was ready to face the day.

'You're up with the lark,' she said, seeing Celia already enjoying coffee. Toby was munching breakfast from his special bowl.

'I didn't sleep well. I already let Toby out and I've made coffee.'

'Thanks.' Bel poured a cup, shook some muesli into a bowl and peeled and sliced a banana, before topping both with yoghurt. She joined Celia at the table.

'That was a nice barbecue. Jan has a lovely family.'

'Mmm.' Celia didn't seem to have much to say this morning.

That suited Bel who wasn't in the mood for conversation either. The weather seemed to be affecting her. She gazed out at the water pouring from the overfull gutter. One more job to do. And there would be no pest control today. She didn't imagine they could complete their treatment in the rain.

But something seemed to be worrying Celia. Bel could see how her brow wrinkled, her gaze flitting around the room without settling on anything.

'Is everything okay?' she asked, knowing perfectly well it wasn't. Although Celia was dressed and made-up as immaculately as usual, there was something about her eyes that indicated all was not well.

'Jan said something yesterday.'

'Do you want to talk about it?'

'No… yes…I don't know.' Celia wrapped both hands around her cup and gazed into the milky liquid.

'Jan gave me her brother's card.'

Bel waited for more, not sure what Celia was trying to say.

Celia picked up a business card which Bel hadn't noticed lying on the table and read, '*Bob Frazer, solicitor*. He's a solicitor. This brother of hers. She thought I might need one if I want to get a divorce.' The last few words came out in a rush, then Celia was silent.

'Oh.' Bel spooned up the last of her cereal. She met Celia's eyes across the table. 'Is that what you want?'

'I don't know. I hadn't thought… until she said it. It's a big step. It means… the end.'

'Do you intend going back to your husband?' asked Bel gently. She sometimes wanted to shake Celia and wished she could show more backbone. She seemed to flutter between being strong and behaving like an utter wimp.

Then Bel thought back to her own marriage, to that terrible time after Pete left. *Her* behaviour then had been nothing to be proud of. At one point she'd thought she was headed for a mental hospital. But she'd got through it, and Celia would too. 'Maybe you need to talk to Bill,' she suggested.

'That's what Han says. But I don't know how I can face him. What if…?'

'What is it you're afraid of? You said he's never been violent towards you.'

'Only with his words. He can be so scathing; he can make me feel so worthless. And I'm not!' She drew herself up, straightening her shoulders. 'I'm not!'

'Of course you're not. In the short time I've known you, I've been impressed by your efficiency, professionality, your resilience.'

Celia grimaced.

'Well, maybe not right now.' Bel hid a smile. 'But most of the time. It's not easy to end a marriage. And you have to be very sure that's what you want.'

'It is. I feel so much better now I've made the move. You've been wonderful, given me a home and a job. But you have your life too, and I know I'll need to move on. That's what's so difficult. I need to step out and begin again. Living here, working at Isabella. I love it. But, deep down, I know it's a crutch. It will take me a few steps, then I need to learn to walk alone, to be self-sufficient, to find out how I want to spend the rest of my life.'

Bel didn't speak, content to allow Celia to talk through her dilemma. There was silence in the room apart from the sound of the rain outside, tyres screeching on the road in the distance, the quiet snuffling of little Toby, and the hum of the refrigerator.

'Han's right,' Celia said at last. 'I *should* speak to Bill. But not at the house.' She shuddered. 'And not with a solicitor. I'm not ready for that. Not yet. Somewhere there are people. A public place. And maybe… Would you come with me?'

Bel's stomach lurched. *Come with her? Didn't she have enough to cope with; Pete coming back into her life, Matt on the other side of the world…?* 'If you think it would help,' she found herself saying.

*

Celia screwed up the courage to call Bill and arrange a meeting. At Bel's suggestion, she called on the shop phone. She'd finally taken Han and Chloe's advice and was now the proud owner of a new iPhone. She shrank from contacting Bill on it. Best he wasn't able to reach her too readily. He was aware she worked at Isabella, so calling from there presented no problem. The surprise was that he hadn't tried to confront her in the shop. Maybe the atmosphere was too feminine for him, or maybe he'd prefer to get her alone.

Well, that wasn't going to happen. She was glad Bel had agreed to accompany her. They were to meet after work on Thursday, at quarter past five in the local wine bar. Celia thought the place would be pretty quiet at that time, but not deserted. She'd debated the wisdom of meeting in a place where alcohol was served, but Bel had persuaded her that it was a good neutral venue, coincidentally, the one where she'd taken Pete for coffee.

*

Thursday rolled around almost too soon, and by four o'clock Celia was becoming nervous. There was an empty feeling in the pit of her stomach and her mouth was dry. She tried to put the meeting to the back of her mind as she helped a customer decide between a sleeveless shift and a strappy sundress. When she finally completed the transaction and farewelled the shopper, she saw Bel appear from the back of the shop carrying her bag.

'Ready?'

Was it time already? The last hour had passed in a flash. 'I'll just...' Celia put her hand to her hair.

'You look wonderful, as always. And it's Bill, remember. He's used to seeing you...'

'I know, but I'll just freshen up. I need my full warpaint on if I'm to face him. It always gives me confidence.' She disappeared to reappear wearing fresh lipstick, and with an added layer of eye shadow and mascara.

'I'm ready now,' she said, feeling as if she was about to go into battle.

'Let's go.'

The two women walked briskly along the road till they came to the wine bar, where Celia hesitated. 'What if...?'

But Bel took her by the elbow and pushed her through the door.

Celia blinked in the dim light inside the bar and glanced around warily. 'He's not here yet.' She wasn't sure whether she was pleased or disappointed to have arrived first.

Bel appeared to have no such qualms. 'Good. Let's claim a table in the far corner. I'll get the drinks. A glass of Chardonnay?'

'Do you think?'

'I do. You need some Dutch courage, and I wouldn't mind a glass of something too.'

While Bel went to the bar to order, Celia saw the door open and felt her scalp prickle as a tall figure walked in and scanned the room. He was here!

'There you are.' Bill pulled out a chair and leant heavily on the table. 'Not drinking? Too timid to order by yourself? Waiting for your husband to buy your drink? Not before we thrash things out.'

'I…'

'You must be Bill.'

Celia looked up gratefully, feeling the knot of tension in her neck begin to loosen. A smiling Bel placed the two glasses of wine on the table. 'You need to order at the bar. They serve coffee too.'

'And you are?'

Celia saw Bill's eyes rake Bel up and down. She was glad she hadn't come alone.

'Bel Davison.' Bel held out a hand which Bill studiously ignored.

'Celia's employer,' he said with a sneer. 'This is between my wife and me.'

'I think that's for her to decide, don't you?' Bel sat down and rearranged the scarf which had slipped from her shoulders. She smiled and leant back as if she had all the time in the world. 'Celia?'

'I asked Bel to be here.' Her voice faltered for a moment, then gained strength. 'She can hear anything we have to say. She knows my situation.'

'My situation,' he mimicked. 'I need a drink.'

When he went to the bar, Bel whispered, 'He's not as tough as he makes out. Take deep breaths and keep calm.'

That was easier said than done, but now they were all here, Celia just wanted to get the discussion – or whatever it was they were to have – over.

Bill returned and slammed a glass of beer down on the table. 'Right. What's this all about?' he asked belligerently. 'You say you're going to visit those two slags of yours, then disappear. And don't think I didn't notice you came back and cleaned out the cupboards. I could have you for theft. I have a lot of valuable items there. How did you get in? I suppose you helped her then too?' He turned on Bel with a leer.

Bill's vitriol enraged Celia and freed her from fear. Bill Ramsay was just a blustering idiot who didn't know squat. She opened her bag, took out her house keys and threw them down on the table. 'I used my keys. It's my house too, remember. I have just as much right to be there as you do. And I only took what was mine. I wouldn't touch any of your so-called valuable collections with a barge pole. You can have them. I never intend to set foot in that place again.'

Grasping the cold keys in her hand and the act of throwing them on the table gave Celia an inordinate sense of satisfaction.

Bill's eyes bulged. He seemed about to burst. Then he took a gulp of beer, settled his glass down gently and changed tactics. 'Come on, honey. You don't mean all this. You're my wife. We've been married a long time. Sydney's Golden Couple. That's what they used to call us. Remember? Has this woman been putting ideas into your head? What's she been saying? Is she one of those…?' His lips turned up in distaste. 'Like that daughter of yours. But *you're* not like that. I should know.' He smirked, his double chin sliding into his neck so that they were almost indistinguishable from each other. 'Come back home with me and we'll forget all about this little episode.'

'I'm sorry, Bill. It's too late for that, and I resent the implication in your remark. Bel's here as a friend – a good friend and my employer. Neither she nor I are lesbian, though it would be nothing to be ashamed of if we were. Hannah is *your* daughter too. She's in a loving relationship, a better one than I had with you for all those years. One in which she's respected, treated as an equal.

'Sydney's Golden Couple we may have been called by those who didn't see what happened at home. I knew better, and it's to my shame that I kept quiet all those years for the sake of our girls. But you managed to ruin even that relationship. I'm glad I came to my senses before I lost them for good. That place isn't my home any longer. I think we're done here.'

Bill half-rose, then slumped down in the chair. He opened his mouth as if to respond.

Celia emptied her glass and rose to her feet.

Twenty-three

The slamming of a car door wakened Matt from a nap. He'd been dreaming of Bel, her sweet face, her gentle smile and her warm body. He sat up with a start, and Hamish began to bark before running to the door. Matt rose and followed slowly, rubbing his face in an attempt to become fully awake. One of the joys of retirement was the ability to take a post-prandial nap, but it was often difficult to orient himself afterwards.

He opened the front door to find his daughter standing there, her body tense as if ready to flee. He gasped. *Was he still dreaming?* 'Elspeth?'

'Yes, it's me, Dad. Can I come in?'

Without waiting for a reply, she pushed past him. Matt followed, raking a hand through his already dishevelled hair. *What did she want? It was good she was here, wasn't it? Had Alasdair spoken to her?*

Elspeth stood awkwardly in the middle of the room, seemingly unsure of her welcome.

'Sit down. Tea?'

'Thanks.' She sat tentatively on the edge of the sofa.

Matt busied himself in the kitchen brewing tea and emptying the remainder of a packet of shortbread biscuits onto a plate.

'Here you are.' He handed her a cup and took a seat opposite. 'Well?'

Elspeth put her cup down on a low table and twisted her fingers. 'I… Alasdair says I owe you an apology. I saw the doctor.' She paused. 'I suppose you've heard all about it. Kirsty was with me. There seem to be no secrets in this family.' The words held a hint of her former bitterness.

'We care about you,' Matt said gently.

'Yes, well... Anyway, Alasdair says you've offered to take Fi and Robbie the week after next. Let us have a break. It's good of you.'

'Not at all. I'm happy to have them. So, you and Alasdair are taking a holiday?'

'He's booked us into Gleneagles.'

Matt suppressed a smile. He might have known his son-in-law would do it in style. No cosy highland cottage hideaway for him. 'Sounds nice.'

'I don't know.' Elspeth picked up her cup and put it down again. 'He says we can play golf. I ask you? Golf! I haven't played since...'

'You might enjoy it.'

'Hmm.'

There was a long pause during which Elspeth drank some tea, and Matt helped himself to a couple of biscuits, breaking off a piece from one for Hamish, who snapped it up greedily.

'Alasdair said you'd spoken. He said you'd mentioned Mum?'

'Yes. She went through what you're going through at about the age you are now. You were at uni at the time.'

Elspeth's brow furrowed, as if trying to remember. 'Didn't she...?'

'Yes, she had a hysterectomy. But that doesn't necessarily mean you will.'

'No. The doctor has put me on medication to reduce my symptoms. Maybe it'll make me easier to live with.' She grimaced. 'Have I been really bad, Dad?'

'A bit more difficult than usual.'

'Can you forgive me?' Elspeth smiled, reminding him of her mother.

'Of course, sweetheart. It was never my choice to be alienated from you and the children. I knew you'd be back. I hoped you would. And now you are.' It sounded simple when he put it like that, but inside he was a mass of contradictory emotions. *Was Elspeth only here because Alasdair had forced her to come, because he was taking Fi and Robbie for a week? What about Bel? She'd made no mention of her. Was she still so obdurate about her presence in his life?*

Matt wanted to ask her, but feared losing their new-found relationship.

'I should go now.' Elspeth rose.

'So soon?'

'I need to pick up Fi.'

At the door, Elspeth turned back and gave Matt a hug. 'Thanks, Dad. I've missed you.'

Matt stood watching the departing car with surprise. Whatever he'd said, Alasdair had done the trick. Or, he wondered, as he returned inside, had it been Kirsty who'd worked her magic?

*

'You'll be good for Grandpa, both of you?' Elspeth stood watching as her two children made their way into Matt's house, Fiona in her wheelchair and Robbie sauntering along gazing at his mobile phone. Neither replied.

'I don't know why we bought him that thing,' Alasdair complained. 'You may not hear a word out of him all week,' he said to Matt, as the three adults stood looking at the pair. But, once at the door, Matt noticed Robbie looked up from the phone to help Fiona inside.

'They'll be fine,' he said.

'But will *you* be fine? It's a long time since you had teenagers, and you're on your own now.'

'I'm not decrepit yet. Don't you worry. Away and enjoy yourselves. And I want to see some fresh colour in your face when you come back,' he said to Elspeth, giving her a warm hug. 'Now you get off. I'd better go back inside before they wreck the place.'

He saw an anxious look on his daughter's face, before she relaxed.

'Oh, Dad!'

'We'll see you next Saturday,' Alasdair called through the open window as they drove off.

'What shall we do, Grandpa?' Fiona wanted to know, once they were all inside. 'Oh, this is going to be fun! Don't you think, Robbie?'

But her brother had disappeared into his own world again, checking Snapchat or texting.

'Let's get you both settled into your rooms, then we can make some plans,' Matt suggested.

'Can we go to the old lady's house again?' Fiona wanted to know as she made her way into the room she called hers.

'In good time. Maybe next week.' It would be a good idea, thought Matt. He should check over how the work was progressing, and Fiona did have a vested interest in the place.

'Why do you want to see an old house?' Robbie asked, kicking the skirting board on the way past.

Matt bit his tongue. His grandson needed to be taken down a peg or two. He wondered what he could manage in a mere week.

The day passed uneventfully. A brief walk after lunch was followed by a quiet period. Fiona picked out a book from Matt's shelf – a Robert Louis Stevenson, he was pleased to note – and lost herself in that, while Robbie disappeared to his room as expected. Matt made use of the time to write a long email to Bel, filling her in on Elspeth's apparent change of heart, even though Bel's name hadn't been mentioned.

He remained hopeful Elspeth would gradually come around to the idea of another woman's presence in her dad's life. *Surely, once she was on an even keel again, she'd see reason? Surely she didn't want her old dad to fester away here, growing old on his own?* Matt conveniently forgot that was exactly what he'd intended to do before he met Bel. He'd eschewed the various women who tried to befriend him, refused all invitations to their social gatherings and behaved like the old curmudgeon he was fast becoming.

'What's for dinner?' a small voice at his ear asked. Matt turned around quickly to see Fiona sitting there, looking so much like Elspeth as a child he felt his eyes moisten. *What had happened to the lovely little girl his daughter had once been? When had she become the embittered woman who was suspicious and jealous of anyone who might want to share her father's affections?* Not anyone, he corrected himself, any woman, one particular woman – Bel.

Matt considered the little girl's question. His cooking skills were pretty limited. He doubted whether scrambled eggs, salad or steak would suit the more sophisticated tastes of these teenagers. They were accustomed to not only their mother's well-known skills in the kitchen, but also their frequenting of some of Glasgow's best restaurants. 'What do you fancy?' he asked, pulling on her ponytail. 'How does pizza sound?'

'Yay! Mum and Dad don't…' Fi buttoned her lip as if afraid of being too critical of her parents. 'Robbie! Gramps is getting pizza for dinner!' she yelled, steering herself toward the hallway and Robbie's room.

'Pizza? Really?' Robbie appeared, mobile in one hand, the other pulling out his earbuds. 'What sort?'

Stunned his choice was so popular, and slightly amused how easily he'd fallen into the indulgent grandparent mode, Matt pulled out a menu from the back of a kitchen drawer. 'We have to drive down to Balloch, to Cucina,' he said. 'We could eat there or…?'

'Oh, let's have a takeaway,' Fiona said. 'We never do, and can we…?' she threw a sidelong glance at her brother.

'Can we have Coca Cola with it and eat in front of the television?' finished Robbie.

'Maybe.' Matt was surprised how easy it was to please these two, though he guessed he'd have to make some effort at cooking on other nights. They couldn't survive a week eating pizza.

When they arrived back home with, not only two large pizzas, but a container of ice cream cones, Matt managed to turn a deaf ear to their pleadings to eat in front of the television. He set the table with three places and soon they were enjoying large slices of Margherita and Hawaiian pizzas.

'Better not tell Dad,' Fiona said through a mouthful of her favourite Hawaiian.

'Nor Mum,' Robbie agreed. 'They'd only make it one more thing to argue about.' He gave a world-weary sigh.

Matt remained silent. Were family secrets about to be revealed?

'Why doesn't Mum like Bel?' Fiona asked. 'I think she's nice. And she's promised to tell me more about Australia. And bring me some books at Christmas.'

'*I* think…' Robbie began in his supercilious voice, which, this time, amused Matt. The young boy took another bite and chewed reflectively before continuing. '*I* think Mum's jealous. She's jealous of everyone these days – Gramps, us, Dad.'

'She's not jealous of us,' Fiona interrupted. 'How could she be?'

'Well, maybe not us. But Dad because he stays late at work all the time and Gramps because he has Bel.'

Matt wondered if he should say something, but decided to let them continue. It was interesting to get their perspective on family matters.

'Mum loves to cook,' Robbie said. 'She likes to look after us all. I think she needs that. Maybe it makes her feel important or something. And when Dad comes home late, dinner's spoiled and she gets angry.'

'So, she brings food here instead,' Fiona said. 'But we haven't been here much recently, and Mum's been sad.'

'Maybe this week away will make her happy again? Maybe *we're* making her sad.' Robbie drained his drink with a dreadful slurping sound.

Matt decided not to comment about the slurping, but did feel it necessary to correct his grandson. 'No, son. Your mum's sadness had nothing to do with you. She hasn't been well, and she and I had a bit of a disagreement. But,' he mentally crossed his fingers, 'that's all sorted now. And she's getting better. This wee holiday will do the trick and she'll be back to ordering you about as usual before you know it.'

Matt decided this conversation had gone on long enough. 'Ice cream, anyone?'

'Yes please! I'll fetch it.' Robbie was out of his chair in a flash, all the angst about his mother quickly forgotten.

By the time Matt had managed to get the children off to bed with strict instructions not to read for too long – Fiona – and not to be on the Internet for too long – Robbie – he was ready to turn in himself. He let Hamish out for a last-minute run around the yard, then locked up the house and went to bed. As he fell into a deep slumber, his last thought was that he was going to enjoy getting to know his grandchildren better. Without their parents present, who knew what secrets they might reveal? He'd been saddened by Fiona's whispered, 'Why does Mum cry so much?' as he turned off the overhead light. He had no answer. But he hoped, with proper care, all of that, plus her antagonism to Bel, would soon become a thing of the past.

*

The happy sound of children's voices awakened Matt next morning, and he went into Fiona's room to find both children busily texting.

'It's Mum and Dad,' Fiona said excitedly. 'They've sent us photos of their hotel. It looks very grand, and Mum says she's going to the spa, they're going to play golf and...'

'Go cycling,' Robbie added with such a look of surprise, one might have imagined he'd said going to the moon.

'They used to do that together a lot,' Matt said, 'Before you two were born.' And before your dad became so engrossed in his work, he thought, delighted Elspeth and Alasdair seemed to be rediscovering their earlier loves.

'Mum sounds happy,' said Fiona wistfully. 'Do you think... now that they don't have us to bother about...?'

'No, I don't. And you don't either.' He tousled her hair which had escaped from the ponytail overnight. 'Let's get you up and out of there, and you can get dressed too, Robbie. I think a big Sunday breakfast is called for, then we can have some adventures of our own.'

The children were eager to discover what he had in mind, but Matt refused to be drawn. It was only when they'd scoffed breakfast and were in the car en route to their destination that they had an inkling of what lay ahead. He began with a game of twenty questions at which Fiona proved the more competent, infuriating her brother. But it was Robbie who finally guessed.

'I know,' he yelled, 'It's that place with all the sea creatures. Tommy Burnside had his birthday party there when I was sick, and I missed it. Dad promised to take me, but...' He pursed his lips as if to indicate his dad was not in the habit of keeping his promises.

'Well guessed,' Matt said as they found a parking spot and he helped Fiona into her wheelchair again. 'Now you're in your chariot, we can head on in.'

Three hours later, Matt thought they must have seen all the exhibits several times over, Robbie preferring the sharks, while Fiona was enraptured by the cheeky otters.

'What are we going to do now?' Robbie wanted to know, clearly eager for more excitement.

But Fiona had had enough. 'Can we go home now, Gramps? I'm hungry. And Hamish must be lonely.'

Matt thought he heard his grandson swear under his breath, but let it go for now. He didn't intend to get into a dispute on the first day of their visit. But he decided to keep his ears open for any repeat. He wasn't sure how their parents handled them, but while they were in his house, it would be his rules.

'Maybe you can take Hamish up the muir after lunch,' he suggested. He loves a run and it'll give Fi and me time for a wee rest.' His granddaughter threw him a grateful glance, but Robbie merely kicked the ground and looked mulish.

After a lunch of sausage rolls and baked beans however, Robbie seemed resigned to taking a walk with the little dog. They set off across the gorse, and the other two settled down to rest, Fiona with the copy of *The Master of Ballantrae* she'd begun the previous evening, and Matt with a well-worn-copy of Dickens' *David Copperfield*, a favourite with both him and Bel.

Reading it brought her closer. It was from that book he'd quoted *Barkis is willing* to apprise her of the depth of his love. But, much as he loved the book, he found it difficult to concentrate on Dickens' beautiful prose. Bel's gentle face kept coming between him and the words on the page, until he finally let the book drop onto his chest and fell asleep.

Twenty-four

The week passed quickly. Matt enjoyed the company of his grandchildren, and they appeared to enjoy the change of scenery and change of pace living with him provided. The weather was a mix of heavy downpours of rain interspersed with beautiful clear cool days. When the weather permitted, the three of them ventured onto the muir, Matt and Robbie taking turns at driving Fiona along in what she liked to call her chariot. The ground was a bit rough underfoot, but they managed to avoid tipping her over, and she loved the bumpy ride, yelling out her encouragement.

Fiona made inroads on the collection of books on Matt's shelves while Robbie, when he could be weaned away from his devices, helped Matt around the yard, chopping wood, fixing fences and generally tidying the place up.

Friday morning proved to be another clear day, a weak sun shining through the clouds and a sprinkling of frost on the grass.

'How about a trip into the city?' Matt asked, when they were eating their porridge and he was fortifying himself with a cup of strong coffee.

'What'll we do there?' Robbie asked. 'The city's boring.'

'I need to check on a few things and I thought you two might like to join me.'

'Can we have lunch at McDonald's?' Robbie wanted to know. 'Please, Gramps.'

From the pleading in the boy's voice, Matt deduced this was another of Elspeth and Alasdair's banned foods. He grinned. 'We'll see.'

'Why do grown-ups always say that?' Robbie complained.

'Are we going to visit that house again?' Fiona asked, her face lighting up.

'Clever girl. I had an email from the architect, and he wants to meet me there.'

'It's real neat, Robbie. This old woman died, and her house is being fixed up for people like me.'

'Smart alecks you mean?'

Fiona threw her napkin at him. 'Takes one to know one.'

Just in time, Matt foiled Robbie's attempt to return the favour with a paper which was lying on the table. 'That's enough, you two. Keep this up and there'll definitely be no McDonald's.'

'What's so special about this house?' Robbie asked.

'Fi's right. It did belong to an old lady. You met her here one day, but you may not remember. Bel was with her.'

'Bel?' Robbie seemed to be working it out. 'The lady Mum calls a bad word? Is she your girlfriend?'

'Don't be silly, Robbie. Grandpas don't have girlfriends. She's not a girl. She's his special friend. She's lovely, she lives in Australia and she'll be here at Christmas.'

'Right.' Matt was amused by Fiona's summing up of the situation. 'Well, when Isobel, the old lady, died she left it to Bel who was her niece, with the agreement that it would be modified to be a place where children with a disability could live.'

'Why can't they live with their parents?'

'Most can – like Fi. But some don't have parents, or their parents aren't able to look after them. And some parents need a holiday from time to time.'

'You mean like us staying with you now?' Fiona asked thoughtfully.

'Exactly.'

'How do you know about it?' Robbie rounded on his sister. 'Are they going to send you there?'

'No, stupid!'

'Fi visited with me and the architect one day. She was a big help in letting us know what was needed to help other children in wheelchairs.'

'Hmm.' Robbie quickly lost interest, asked to be excused and disappeared in the direction of his room and no doubt into his iPad again.

'Leaving in thirty minutes,' Matt called after him.

*

'This is it,' Matt parked the car outside the Kelvin Drive house and stared up at the façade. It didn't look any different than it had in Isobel's day, apart from the bay windows which looked naked without the thick curtains that had protected her privacy. He could almost imagine she was still there sitting in her favourite seat by the window, watching out for his arrival, ready with a caustic remark.

Then, more recently, Bel would be with her, lending her gentle presence, providing a sense of hope, of anticipation.

The door opened to reveal the tousled red head of Andrew Forrest. Matt shook his head to rid it of the images of the two women who, in his mind, still belonged here.

'It's yourself,' Andrew called. 'And who have you with you today?' He came down the stairs as Matt stepped out of the car. 'Oh, I know this young lady. Come to give us more of your valuable advice?'

'Hello,' Fiona said shyly. 'This is Robbie, my brother.'

'And have you come to check us out too, young fellow?'

Robbie hopped out, and Andrew shook his hand. 'We can always do with another opinion,' he said.

Meanwhile Matt helped Fiona into her chair, and they made their way into the house, Matt and Andrew manhandling the chair up the steps.

'Ramp!' Fiona said.

'On its way.' Andrew pushed his glasses up his nose and thrust a hand through his untidy hair. 'Matt, a word.'

'Can you two have a look around for a bit while Andrew and I discuss something?'

'Come on, Robbie. I'll show you the kitchen.' Fiona set off, Robbie following more slowly.

'You might find some biscuits and lemonade through there,' Andrew called after them.

'So,' Matt said when the youngsters had disappeared, 'what have you got me into town for? It sounded serious.'

'Upstairs.' Andrew led the way to where a ladder was leaning against the opening to the attic.

Matt raised his eyebrows. 'Damp?'

Andrew nodded. 'I don't think anyone's been up there for years. The rain's been seeping through and…'

Matt climbed up and as soon as his head entered the roof cavity the smell struck him.

When he climbed down again, he stuck his hands in his pockets and rocked on his heels. 'What's the damage?'

Andrew scratched his head. 'Could be worse, I suppose. It's fixable. We'll need to get a structural engineer up there to take a dekko. It's a miracle the ceiling hasn't fallen down.'

Matt frowned. Isobel would have been most upset if she knew her beloved old house was in danger of collapsing around her. He was glad she hadn't lived to find out. On the other hand, if she had discovered the rot earlier, it could perhaps have been caught in time. From what Bel had told him, the entire upper part of the house hadn't been lived in for years, one bedroom only having been opened up for Bel's visit.

'We'll need to have the whole roof checked,' Andrew continued. 'The water's been getting in somewhere. There may be some cracked or missing slates – I imagine, given the age of the place, it's a slate roof. Then the trusses may need replacing. It's a big job. Costly.'

'There's money. But…' Matt sighed. 'We didn't take something like this into account.' He rubbed the back of his neck. 'You'd better get it checked out. Get some quotes. Everything else going along well?' They'd reached the hallway again and could hear the two children arguing in the kitchen.

'Like a dream. Once we have this fixed, we'll be back on schedule. Should be ready for the residents in March or April. I'm sorry about this, Matt. With a house of this age, I should have foreseen… Had it checked out earlier.'

'Aye.' Matt let the word sit there for a moment. 'Well, we know now. I'll need to let Bel know.'

'She's still back in Australia?'

'Aye.'

As he spoke, Fiona came barrelling through the hallway, Robbie running behind her. 'This place is great, Gramps. Did you know there are benches and shelves and things at Fi's height and there's a big well behind the stairs. Fi says it's for a lift. I've never heard of a house with a lift in it.'

'Ah, this is a very special house, Robbie. For special people. And your sister is the one who gave us all the right measurements.'

'Thanks, Andrew.' Matt shook the architect's hand. 'Let me know the results. Let's go, kids.'

They piled into the car, waving to Andrew as they drove off.

'McDonald's?' asked Robbie.

Matt detected a note of doubt in his voice. 'Oh, I think we can manage that.' There was a murmur of satisfaction from the rear of the car.

*

The rest of the day passed quietly. By the time they reached home, the clouds were gathering and there was just time to take Hamish for a quick run before rain began to fall.

'This week's gone too fast,' Fiona said, as Matt fitted a DVD into the player.

'Sorry to go home?' Matt asked.

'Yes and no. It'll be good to see Mum and Dad again. But I'll miss all this…' She let her eyes roam around the room, cosy with the curtains drawn across the high windows, the slate floor gleaming in the firelight. 'And Hamish.'

At the sound of his name the little dog stretched and padded over to plop down at Fiona's feet.

'I'll miss you guys too. This place will seem empty without you.' *Just like it did when Bel left*, he thought. *But not for long. Only nine weeks to go and then…* He could barely wait. He only hoped Elspeth would have come around by then, and they could enjoy a family Christmas without any recriminations and backbiting. 'We might have to send your parents away again,' he said with a grin.

*

150

Next morning Fiona insisted on making a pilgrimage to all her favourite spots to say goodbye, an exercise which was loudly ridiculed by her brother.

'You're not leaving for good,' he said scoffing.

'I don't care. We may not be back for a while. It depends how Mum...'

Matt was stunned by the perceptiveness of the girl. She was right. Maybe the holiday would have put Elspeth in a better frame of mind, and their regular visits would be resumed. But maybe not. He could only hope. As agreed beforehand, he hadn't been in contact with his daughter or son-in-law all week, so he was awaiting their arrival with a modicum of anxiety.

It was almost six and beginning to get dark by the time the black car drove up to the lochside home.

'Dad.' Alasdair got out of the car first and slapped Matt on the shoulder in a friendly gesture. 'Sorry we're so late.'

'Having too good a time? We thought you'd forgotten you had children.'

Alasdair had the grace to look embarrassed. 'We had a game of golf and time got away from us. Have they behaved themselves?'

'Perfectly. The place will seem empty without them.'

'But not for long.' Elspeth had followed her husband out of the car and stood, wrapping her arms around herself. 'Are they packed and ready?'

Was Elspeth referring to Bel? Matt tried to gauge her expression, but failed. It had been a long time since he'd been able to read his daughter's mind.

'Why don't I make dinner for you here? I have steaks and can boil some spuds and carrots. I'm not completely useless, you know. I do feed myself from time to time. I've looked after these two for the past week, and they haven't starved.' Matt saw a look pass between the two, before Elspeth nodded and they all went inside.

Happy to be reunited with their parents, the children vied with each other to recount their adventures.

'So you managed to separate Robbie from his iPad,' Alasdair said.

Robbie laughed.

'And I read four books,' Fiona crowed.

'Well, maybe we need to leave you with Grandad more often.' Alasdair ruffled his son's hair as Robbie tried to move out of his reach.

'And what about you two?' asked Matt. 'Did Gleneagles live up to expectations?'

'Oh, Dad. It was wonderful. We slept, ate, cycled, swam, golfed, walked.'

'And don't forget those spa sessions you had while I was fishing,' Alasdair reminded her.

'So, a worthwhile week.'

'Absolutely!'

Matt saw Elspeth throw a secret look in her husband's direction. All was well there, then. That was good.

'Dad...' Elspeth's voice was tentative. 'Alasdair and I... we talked... about you and... Bel.'

Matt listened without speaking.

'I... it seems... maybe I was too hasty... misjudged the situation. I want to say that I'm sorry I was so hostile. Alasdair had made me see I wasn't myself. The medication is helping, I think. I should have tried to see your point of view. Can you forgive me? I'll try to...'

Matt didn't wait for her to finish. 'Of course, pumpkin.' The pet name slid naturally off his tongue. 'It's forgotten already.'

Matt couldn't wait to share Elspeth's apparent change of heart with Bel. Then he remembered about the dry rot at Kelvin Drive. It wasn't all good news.

Twenty-five

'Have you done anything about Bill yet?'

Bel and Celia were enjoying an after-dinner glass of wine in the courtyard. The cicadas were creating their usual cacophony in the surrounding gum trees, the sound of flute music drifted across from a neighbouring house, and the air was heavy with the scent of jasmine. It was a typical Sydney evening.

'No.' Celia sighed, stroking the damp glass with a finger. 'I still have that card Jan gave me. I keep taking it out of my bag, then putting it back in again. I suppose I should contact him.'

'It's your call. But if you've no intention of going back to Bill, wouldn't it make everything simpler if you got a divorce? I mean...' Bel wondered how to phrase it, then decided it was best to be blunt. 'It would sort out your finances. Not that it's any of my business,' she added quickly. *It would serve her right if Celia called her an interfering old bat.*

'No, you're right. I can't go on like this. I need to find a place of my own. I know I can't stay here forever. You won't be here. And I need to find the money for a bond before I can rent anywhere.'

'I wasn't trying to get rid of you.'

'I know that.' Celia took a gulp of wine. 'I'll call this solicitor tomorrow. I guess it doesn't do any harm to see what he has to say.'

'You haven't heard from Bill?'

'Not since that night in the wine bar. But I've heard on the grapevine he's been on a bender and badmouthing me to anyone who'll listen.'

'That figures. My guess is he's never had anyone stand up to him before. He didn't expect it from you and he didn't like it.'

'Maybe.'

'Don't forget the pest guys are coming tomorrow. They said they'd be here early – around seven-thirty. Maybe we should go out to breakfast, though I'm not sure what to do with Toby. I was planning on taking him to the shop, but…'

'Why don't I give Chloe a call? She should be home tomorrow, and I'm sure she'd love to have him for the day. Si would probably enjoy it too.'

'Would you?'

'I'll do it now.'

While Celia made the call, Bel took the empty glasses into the kitchen. Standing at the window, looking out at the elegant woman sitting by the table, she wondered what the future had in store for her. While she pretended to be strong, Bel had often been privy to the more vulnerable side of Celia Ramsay. Maybe the divorce would help her, force her into making decisions about her future. At the moment, she seemed to have settled into Bel's home and shop as into a comfortable cocoon. But that cocoon wouldn't be there forever, and, like the chrysalis, Celia would have to be strong enough to emerge and fight for her own future.

'It's done!' Celia joined Bel in the kitchen. 'She'd be delighted to have him for as long as you want. Her only proviso is that he won't disturb Bindi. How is he around cats?'

'Oh, hell. I don't know. He's never had much to do with them. Do you think…?'

'I think it'll be fine. Bindi's pretty self-reliant and she can always jump up out of harm's way. We can drop him off as soon after seven-thirty as we want.'

'Thanks.'

'Where did you have in mind for breakfast?'

'I thought maybe Avenue Road Café in Mosman. It's handy for Isabella, opens early, and they usually have a good range.'

'Sounds good. Well, I think I'll call it a night.' Celia yawned and stretched her arms over her head. 'See you in the morning.'

Before retiring herself, Bel opened her computer. It would be early morning in Scotland. Sunday morning. Maybe she'd be able to catch Matt on skype. They hadn't arranged a call today, but she'd had to laugh when she received his last email. The fates really did seem to have it in for her. Termites in Sydney and dry rot in Scotland. It seemed as if everything was threatening to collapse around her. No, that was an exaggeration. The termite problem was going to be fixed tomorrow and the dry rot could be fixed too. Matt was sure of that. But it might take longer, and there was no saying what the cost might be.

The business with Elspeth was different. Matt seemed optimistic she'd be more willing to accept Bel, but Bel wasn't so sure.

She had no luck with skype. Matt was probably out with Hamish already. She wondered what the weather was like over there and idly googled a Scottish weather site. An early ground frost, rain, strong winds, and cloud. *What had she expected?* She pictured Matt battling the winds as he strode across the heather which would probably be squelchy at this time of year, wee Hamish running in circles around him. How she wished she was there with him.

*

Everything seemed to happen in a rush next morning. The pest men arrived ready to start work, Bel bundled Toby into the car, and she and Celia set off.

By eight-thirty, they'd had breakfast and were setting the shop up for the day. Leaving Celia to handle an early customer, Bel logged onto the computer and checked the phone for messages, her standard morning routine. She wasn't anticipating any surprises so was shocked to hear Pete Sadler's voice on the answering machine.

'Bella. I need you.' There was a pause, then the message continued. 'I need... Can you call me back?' There followed a number then the message finished. Bel leant back in her chair. Pete! She'd almost forgotten about him. Almost, but not quite. She looked at the number which she'd automatically jotted down. It was a Sydney number. So, he *was* still here. And he didn't sound well. *What should she do?* She tapped on the desk with her pen. The simplest thing would be to delete the message and ignore it. Part of her wanted to do just that.

*

Celia took a deep breath and looked at the card in her shaking fingers. She was going to do this. She was! She picked up her phone and keyed in the numbers, hesitating before pressing the green button to connect the call. When she heard it ring, she almost hung up. But something made her hang on, the hand holding the phone becoming slippery with sweat.

'Good afternoon. Wilson and Frazer solicitors. How can I help you?'

Celia gripped the phone tightly. 'Hello. Can I please speak with Bob Frazer?'

'Just a moment. I'll see if Mr Frazer is available.'

The woman's voice was replaced by bland music, the sort that made Celia want to run a mile. Where did these establishments find the stuff? Maybe it was designed to soothe, but it had the opposite effect. It made her want to throw something at whoever chose it.

She didn't have long to wait.

'Bob Frazer here. How might I help you?' The voice was reassuring. Celia immediately felt more at ease. He was only a man, after all – a gay man, she reminded herself. Not a bully like her husband. Not one of Bill's friends. And he was Jan's brother.

She took another deep breath and began to speak.

By the time she'd finished the call, Celia's foremost emotion was one of relief. Bob Frazer sounded like a nice guy. He hadn't asked too many questions, had suggested an appointment to discuss her options – she liked that – and she had arranged to meet with him in two days' time.

But a few seconds later, she was beginning to have second thoughts. *Did she really want a divorce? How would Bill react if she went ahead?* She remembered how belligerent he'd become in the wine bar when, for the first time, she'd stood up to him.

The one thing she did know was that she never wanted to return to the person she'd been when she was living with Bill. Now she could see what a vapid creature she'd become over the years. She'd lost her identity, been subsumed into the role of Bill Ramsay's wife or plaything.

She was sitting looking at the phone, her thoughts in a whirl, when Bel popped her head through the door.

'Have you done it?'

Celia nodded. 'I have an appointment on Wednesday at two. If that's okay with you?' *Maybe Bel would need her here and she could postpone the appointment? Maybe even cancel it?*

'Fine by me. What did he say?'

'That we could *discuss my options*.' She looked up at Bel, still gripping her phone tightly. 'I'm not sure what that means.'

'What it says.' Bel sat down opposite Celia. 'It's hard. I know. I've been there. Though my marriage didn't last as long as yours has. But the first thing you need to do is to talk to Bob – or someone like him. Did you get the feeling he was someone you could talk to – confide in?'

'Yes.' Celia didn't hesitate. She did feel Bob Frazer was someone she could trust.

'Well, then. Now you've made the appointment you can forget about it until Wednesday.'

'Mmm.' Celia knew it wouldn't be so easy. She knew the thought of Wednesday's meeting would sit at the back of her mind like a spider waiting to pounce.

'What do your girls think? You *have* talked with them about it?'

'They have no time for their father; think I should get shot of him – the sooner the better. They never saw the good years.' Celia began to draw imaginary lines on the desk with a finger. 'There *were* some good years, Bel.'

'I know. Believe me. Pete and I had some good years, too, before…'

There was something in Bel's voice that made Celia glance up at the other woman. 'Have you heard from him again?'

Bel nodded, and Celia saw her eyes cloud. 'This morning. There was a message on the answering machine. He wants me to call him.'

'But you won't.'

Bel drew a hand through her hair. 'No. Maybe. Hell, Celia. I don't know what to do. The man's sick, very sick, dying. Despite what he did, how he treated me. He's paid his dues. He's here in Sydney. Maybe I should.'

Bel drew a piece of paper from her pocket. It was creased, looked as if it had been screwed up, then flattened out again several times. 'He left a number to call.'

Celia had no idea what to say. Bel had divorced Pete years ago. Now he was back trying to inveigle himself into her life, playing on her sympathy, just when she'd found herself a good man and was planning a fresh start. What if the same happened to her? What if she never managed to put Bill out of her life? What if she did divorce him, only to have him keep coming back to haunt her? She'd always valued her marriage vows, made in Saint Andrews Cathedral right in the heart of Sydney with all the pomp and ceremony that entailed. Was she now prepared to throw that aside? Did she really want to end her marriage?

Twenty-six

Bel knew she was being foolish, but she also knew she'd never forgive herself if Pete died alone in some dive in Sydney when she could have done something to help. She didn't know why, but her imagination was working overtime. She pictured him lying, ill, in a rundown boarding house. She knew he'd told her he was staying in a hotel in North Sydney, but that had been some weeks ago. What if he hadn't been able to stay there? What if...? She smoothed out the scrap of paper and picked up the phone.

'Good morning, Harbour View Hotel, North Sydney.'

Not some seedy dive, then. This was an upmarket hotel with – as its name suggested – views of Sydney Harbour. Bel almost put down the phone. Was this Pete's way of wheedling his way into her life again? If so, he was out of luck. She hesitated, irresolute. What should she do?

The hotel receptionist spoke again. 'Can I help you?'

'I believe you have a guest – Pete Sadler. May I speak with him?'

'I'll just ascertain if he's in the hotel, madam. I won't be a moment. Please hold.'

The sound of a morning talk show blasted Bel's eardrums. She was deciding if he was out, she'd tear up the paper and leave him to stew, when the receptionist spoke again, 'Putting you through now.'

'Hello.' It was the voice of a sick man. *He couldn't be playacting, could he? How could he know it was Bel on the phone?*

'Pete?'

'Bella! I knew you'd call.'

He knew her better than she knew herself, if that was the case.

'What do you want of me? You've made your atonement or whatever. We had our talk. I thought you planned on going back to Melbourne. Didn't you say so?'

'That fell through.' His voice was weak, much weaker than when they'd met only a few weeks ago. 'I need to see you, Bella. One more time. I'm dying.'

Bel had been standing by the kitchen window. Now she sat down with a thump. Not another death! Was she the only person Pete could turn to?

'Why me?' The words burst out without thinking.

'You're all I have left.'

Pete sounded so mournful, so sorry for himself, that she forbore to remind him he didn't have her, hadn't had her for years.

'What we had was a long time ago. Another lifetime.'

'Would you reject a dying man?'

Bel bit her lip. Pete had always been good at getting around her in the past. He'd put on that little boy lost expression, and she was gone. At least she couldn't see his face right now. But she could imagine it. She pictured Pete as she'd last seen him. – a pale shadow of his former self – and, against her better judgement, knew she'd agree to see him one more time.

'All right. I can get away for a few minutes at lunch time. Where do you want to meet?'

'Can you come here? I haven't left this room for days. I don't think I can face the dining room downstairs.'

Bel gasped. His hotel room? That was a big ask. Then she recalled the lunchtime buzz in Harbour View. She'd eaten there many times and, at lunchtime, it tended to be full of local business-men swilling beer and talking business, interspersed with bright young women in their tightly fitting suits and dresses. It certainly wasn't somewhere conducive to anyone who wasn't in the best of health. Reluctantly, she agreed.

*

Bel was already regretting her decision as she drove her little Volkswagen into the underground parking lot, grabbed her bag and locked the car. She straightened her pale blue tunic top before making her way up to the foyer where she was directed to Pete's room.

'You came!' Pete greeted her at the door, then dropped into an armchair strategically placed by the window.

'I said I would.'

'I ordered lunch to be brought up – room service. I presume you still eat pasta?'

'I didn't expect food.' Bel walked across to the window and stared out at the wide expanse of water spanned by the famous Harbour Bridge. It was one of her favourite parts of Sydney.

'Remember?' Pete asked.

Bel knew exactly to what he was referring. They'd spent one New Year's Eve in this very hotel, in a room much like this one. Young, in love, and full of the joys of life, they'd toasted in the New Year with champagne and watched the fireworks, before spending the night in each other's arms.

'Nineteen seventy-five,' he said.

Bel turned sharply. She didn't want to remember those days – days when she'd been giddy with love for him, when she'd have done anything to please him, and he her, when it had seemed the world was their oyster.

'We made a promise to each other that night,' he continued. 'We promised that, whatever happened, we'd always see each other right.'

Bel's lips tightened. *Why was he referring to that promise now? It was one he'd broken many times over.*

There was an almost inaudible knock at the door.

'That'll be lunch.'

Bel opened the door to a hotel employee who carried in two covered platters which he deposited on a small round table. They drew up a couple of chairs and removed the covers to reveal an enticing plate of gnocchi with pumpkin and ricotta under one and a boiled egg with a slice of toast under the other.

'I'm not eating much,' Pete said. 'I seem to have lost my appetite. But eat up. You used to like gnocchi. Do you still?'

'Yes.' But Bel had little appetite for what was one of her favourite dishes. She opened the bottle of water that accompanied the meal. She picked at the pasta, before laying her cutlery aside. 'I'm sorry. It was a lovely idea, but I'm not very hungry.'

She folded her arms.

'Why am I here, Pete? You didn't ask me here to eat pasta.'

'No.' Pete's eyes flitted around the room before finally settling on Bel. 'I find myself in a bit of a pickle.'

That was nothing new, Bel thought. It was the story of his life. But he'd always managed to come out unscathed – apart from the time he'd ended up in prison.

'You see, the place in Melbourne. The one in palliative care I told you about. There's been a bit of a disaster.'

'What sort of disaster?'

'A bushfire. It was on the news. They had to evacuate.'

Bel vaguely remembered seeing a news item. Below average rainfall and above average temperatures had resulted in a spate of bushfires around the southern city. It had never occurred to Bel it would have anything to do with her. Why should it?

'So?'

'I've nowhere to go.'

The room was silent while Bel digested this latest piece of information. *What did he expect her to do about it?*

'You seem pretty well set up here.' She gestured around the well-appointed room, the magnificent view. 'What's wrong with this?'

'Oh, Bella, Bella.' Pete shook his head. 'This is a hotel. They don't cater for sick people. They don't understand. They don't have room for me. They don't want their guests dying on them. I need to move out, move on... to somewhere else.' He gave her a glance from under his hooded eyebrows, his lips tilting up just a little in a pleading moue.

Bel suddenly realised the enormity of what he was suggesting. No, she was wrong. He couldn't be... But he was.

'That's why I needed to remind you of your promise,' he said. 'For better, for worse. Whatever happens, we'll see each other right. We never thought it would come to this, but it has. I'm begging you, Bella. I'm a sick man. I don't have much longer. Let me see out my days with you until a place comes up in a nursing home.'

Bel wanted nothing more than to get up, go out the door and run – as far away as possible. But she was stuck to her seat.

*

Bel arrived back at Isabella with little recollection of how she got there. The shop was busy and remained that way for the rest of the day, so it wasn't till closing time that she became conscious of Celia's eyes on her.

'Are you all right? Since you got back you seem to have been on auto-pilot.'

'Sorry. No, I don't think I am.'

'You need a drink. Wine bar.'

When the two were seated with glasses of the best Shiraz, Celia said, 'Now what's the matter? Where did you disappear to at lunchtime? You came back looking like death warmed up. Did someone die? No, sorry. That was stupid of me. I know you lost your aunt recently.'

'No one's died. Not yet.' Bel's lips took on a grim line. 'I went to see Pete.'

Celia's eyes widened. 'I thought…'

'I know. I said I never wanted to see him again. But I did. He's in North Sydney. At the Harbour View.'

'Very nice.'

'Yes. The thing is. He can't stay there. And he's lost his place in Melbourne.'

'He doesn't…' Celia looked horrified.

'He does. And I don't know what to do.'

'But aren't there places?'

'He says not right now. He's probably speaking the truth. And he mentioned something about a waiting list.'

'Hell!'

'Exactly.'

'But you?'

'We were married once.'

'Bill and I are still married, but I can't imagine giving him house room ever again.'

'Not even if he was dying?'

The two women's eyes met in recognition of Bel's dilemma.

'Well, it's not going to be decided today,' Bel said. 'But he's here in Sydney and he's not going away. I do need to make up my mind if I can bear to take him in, to look after him in his last days, weeks, however long he has left, or until he finds somewhere else.'

'What about Matt – and Scotland?'

'I don't know. Maybe it was never meant to be. Maybe I'm too old after all. Maybe…'

'Another wine?'

'No. We should get home.'

'I promised to call in on the girls tonight. Will you be okay on your own? I can cancel.'

'No. Don't change your plans for me. I have a lot of thinking to do and I'll do that best on my own. You enjoy your evening and give young Simon a hug from me. It's tomorrow you meet with your solicitor, isn't it?'

'Yes.' Celia didn't elaborate, but Bel knew she was dreading the trip into the city.

'Maybe if you do divorce Bill, you should get a clause in there to ensure that he'll never come back to you with a dying request.'

*

Celia dressed even more carefully than usual. She'd discovered long ago how her self-confidence increased in direct proportion to her satisfaction with her reflection in the mirror. Satisfied, she gave a final pat to her already immaculate hair, called out to let Bel know she was leaving and walked up to the bus stop.

She'd decided to take public transport today rather than drive, partly because of the difficulty in finding a parking spot in the city and partly due to the butterflies tumbling around in her stomach. She'd feel much safer if someone else was behind the wheel.

Once in the city, she found the solicitor's chambers without difficulty and, after a moment's hesitation at the foot of the steps, wondering if she really wanted to do this, she boldly climbed up and pushed open the door.

She was early, so was asked to take a seat. Picking up a magazine, Celia pretended to read, but merely flicked through the pages, unable to concentrate. This was worse than going to the dentist. Finally, a tall, dark-haired man appeared.

'Hello. I'm Bob Frazer. You must be Celia Ramsay. Come through.'

He wasn't what she expected, not at all like his two sisters, both of whom were blonde. They talked for an hour, or rather she talked, and Bob asked the occasional question and took notes. By the end of the hour, Celia was glad she'd come. She felt she could put her trust in this man. She left the office with a long list of questions to consider, the most pressing of which was whether she was willing for Bob to contact her husband to sound him out about the prospect of divorce.

*

'How was it?' Bel greeted Celia as soon as she walked in.

'I'm not sure. Can I tell you later?' Celia felt too strung out to talk now. She needed to digest what Bob had said. She'd thought about nothing else all the way back on the bus, his words whirling around in her head like little Si's spinning top. She could see the sense in his approaching Bill as her lawyer, to test the water. It didn't commit her to anything. It wasn't as if he was going to serve divorce papers on him – not yet.

But that was her intention. As Bob told her, it was the only sure way to have their assets fairly divided. And she wanted that, didn't she? Hell, she needed it. While she didn't want to be mercenary, she needed money to set herself up in a new apartment. She'd be homeless when Bel tootled off to Scotland. Christmas wasn't far away.

She worried about it all afternoon in between serving customers, though she was sure they must have wondered what was on her mind. Bel had to remind her several times of what she was doing. But by closing time, she'd come to a decision.

'Now sit down for a second.' Bel faced Celia in the office as she was fetching her bag. 'You've been on another planet all afternoon. What on earth happened in Bob Frazer's office to put you in such a muddle?'

'He wants to contact Bill – to sound him out about a legal separation. He said… since I have no intention of going back to him, that's the first option. I've been thinking about it ever since and I've decided. I'm going to tell him to go ahead. There are all sorts of financial ramifications, and I'm worried Bill may not agree. But I can only get a divorce without his agreement once we've been separated for twelve months. We have to start somewhere.'

Bel hugged her.

'I'm glad you've made a decision. That's often the hardest part. It won't be easy. He'll most likely fight you every step of the way. But I think you're doing the right thing.'

'And what about you? Have you decided what to do about your ex?'

Celia saw Bel hesitate before asking quietly, 'Would you help me prepare the other spare room?'

Twenty-seven

Matt stared at the blank computer screen in disbelief. Had Bel really told him she was stuck in Sydney for the foreseeable future, and he should maybe not count on her being there for Christmas? Had she cancelled her flight? He shook his head as if he could shake away her words. He was hurt, saddened, disappointed. Hell! He pushed himself away from the computer, his chair skidding on the slate floor and causing Hamish, who had been lying at his feet, to leap up with a yelp.

He was angry!

What right had this guy – this ex-husband of Bel's, to turn up and expect her to look after him in his last days? As if she hadn't suffered enough seeing Isobel die. To be faced with this. And with a man she thought she'd seen the last of. Why had she agreed?

That's what rankled. She'd agreed. He was moving into her house.

Matt brewed a cup of strong coffee and dropped into his favourite armchair. Sensing his master was out-of-sorts, Hamish settled himself on Matt's feet and gazed soulfully up at him.

Matt replayed the conversation. First, they'd talked about the engineer's report on Kelvin Drive and Bel had shared news of the successful pest control on her house in the Sydney suburb of Cremorne. Matt had never been there, but Bel's lyrical descriptions of the tree-lined suburb close to the harbour had fired his imagination. He could picture her home so clearly, the sundrenched courtyard, the light airy rooms, her study. Even the white picket fence and her little Toby. *He* hadn't been there, but now this Sadler guy would be.

Unable to sit still, Matt began to pace up and down. There was something else bothering him – something sitting on the edge of his consciousness. Then it struck him! *Surely Bel would only have agreed to give her ex house room if she still had feelings for him? Was that what all this was about? Was this the brush off? Was Bel regretting what they had found together? Was she in love with her ex-husband?*

He was striding around when he heard a car draw up. Who…? Then he remembered. Duncan had arranged to drop in to discuss a tricky problem he had with a client.

The pair went into the study and settled into the two easy chairs Matt had designed for just such a collaboration. Usually he enjoyed these meetings – evidence he still had a few gems of advice to offer the younger man. But today he had trouble keeping his mind on the issues relating to a boundary dispute between two local landowners.

Finally, Duncan laid down his documents and said, 'What's the matter, Dad? You're not with it today. Something on your mind?'

'Sorry, son.' Matt drew a hand through his hair. 'I had a disturbing call from Bel this morning. I can't seem to think straight.'

'Is she all right?'

'She is. But…' Matt proceeded to tell Duncan what Bel proposed to do.

When he finished, Duncan steepled his hands under his chin. 'And now you're doubting her good Samaritan act, wondering if she still has feelings for him?'

'Got it.'

'Well.' Duncan leant back in his chair, a smile on his face. 'Seems you only have one thing to do.'

Matt was baffled. How could Duncan see a solution when he'd been puzzling over it all morning.

'You have to go there. To Sydney. Find out for yourself what the story is.'

'But…,' Matt began, then stopped. Of course, it was so simple. That's what he must do. 'You're right, son. Remind me to come to you next time I want advice, too. Now let's have another look at those title deeds of yours.'

*

While deciding to go to Sydney was simple, it wasn't so easy to arrange.

Next day, before Matt had a chance to contact the airline, he received a call from Andrew Forrest which required him to meet at the Kelvin Drive house again. Remembering this was the main reason he hadn't gone with Bel in the first place, Matt tried to curb his impatience as he drove into the city.

It was a grey day – grey skies, grey streets, grey people. No wonder Bel was taking the opportunity to remain in her adopted country. From what he remembered of his trip down-under years ago, the sun seemed to shine every day. He could clearly recall the light glistening on the sails of the Sydney Opera House, the beaches full of tanned bodies, the tall gumtrees with their scents of lemon and eucalyptus. Who in their right mind would want to give that up for this place?

By the time he reached his destination, Matt had convinced himself that the story of Pete Sadler's illness was an excuse, a convenient justification for a decision that might have nothing to do with the man at all, but everything to do with Bel's wanting to let Matt down gently.

They didn't know much about each other, after all – had only been together for a few emotion-charged months. But, he reasoned, they had been good months, even spectacular months, despite the impending death of Bel's Aunt Isobel. No, Duncan was right. Matt needed to see Bel face-to-face – in person, not on a computer screen. He knew, deep down, he wouldn't be able to settle until he knew for sure what was in her heart.

Matt took the steps two at a time and reached the door just as Andrew opened it to greet him.

'Good to see you. Glad you managed to get here so quickly. The engineer wants a word.'

The three men climbed up into the roof, and all thoughts of Bel and Sydney were banished from Matt's conscious thought as the engineer explained what was required to make the house safe for the new residents.

After the lengthy explanation about the need to replace a number of the roof trusses, the procedure involved, and the estimated costs, they climbed down from the roof.

'So, there'll be nae problem wi' that?' Bert Walker, the engineer asked, when they reached the hallway.

'No. Go ahead, book the men and order what you need. I suppose it'll put our dates back a bit?' Matt said, turning to Andrew.

'Aye. I'll rejig the plan. It'll be closer to the end of April, I'm thinking. If the weather doesn't hold us up.'

The weather. The damned Scottish weather!

'I need a word, Andrew.'

'I was going to duck down to Byres Road for a bite to eat. Fancy joining me at the Curlers? We can talk there.'

After his confusion, a lunchtime beer in his old student haunt sounded attractive to Matt. He agreed, and soon he and his companion were enjoying thick Reuben sandwiches with chips and glasses of craft beer.

When Matt broached the subject of his taking a trip which would mean he'd no longer be on call for emergencies like the one that morning, Andrew surprised him.

'Following her to Australia, are you?' the younger man said with a grin. 'Wondered how long it'd take you.'

Matt was astounded. What made Andrew think that? Until yesterday he'd had no intention of following Bel. But now he'd made the decision, he didn't know why it had taken him so long.

'Yes. A short trip.' Matt didn't know what made him say that. He had no idea how long he'd be gone. All he knew was that he had to see Bel again, find out from her what the real story was and… But there he drew a blank.

'No need to worry about this project while you're gone. It should be smooth sailing from now on, and I can email you if we have any dramas. You'll be back for Christmas.'

It wasn't a question. And Matt realised his family would expect that. His family! How would Elspeth react to the news he was going all the way to Australia, going to see Bel? Well, he'd soon find out. Better to strike while the iron was hot. He'd drop round to Anniesland after lunch and see if he could catch her before school was out. Elspeth had mellowed since their Gleneagles trip; her medication seemed to be having the desired effect. But his heading off to the other side of the world might rekindle all of her misgivings. Hell, he wasn't looking forward to breaking the news to her.

*

'Dad! To what do I owe the pleasure? It's not like you to turn up unannounced.'

'I was in this neck of the woods. Had to meet the architect at Kelvin Drive and we had a bite to eat in the Curlers. Took me back a few years, though it's a bit more upmarket than it was in my day.'

'Yes. It's a nice spot to eat. Alasdair and I have had the occasional meal there with friends.'

Definitely upmarket if Alasdair deigns to eat there, Matt thought.

'So how have you been?' Matt had followed Elspeth into the kitchen as they were speaking, and now he drew out a chair.

'You'll have coffee?' Elspeth asked, ignoring his question.

'Thanks.' Matt gazed out the window while his daughter fussed with the coffee maker. The garden here was much more ordered than his own. Elspeth was a keen gardener like her mother had been and she'd modelled her garden on the one Ailsa had created in the old family home. It was like being back in time. Despite the wintry aspect, the yard looked tidy and cared for. The hedges had clearly been recently trimmed and the roses – a favourite of Ailsa's – carefully pruned. On the bird feeder, a couple of bright yellow-hammers were vying for space with a red breasted robin.

'Been doing some work outside?' Matt gestured to the garden.

'Yes.' Elspeth smiled as she carried two mugs of coffee to the table and joined him. 'I find it helps me. I can lose myself caring for my plants.' She looked down for a moment then raised her eyes again and pointed to three shallow bowls Matt hadn't noticed.

'Let me guess. Hyacinth bulbs and… tulips?'

Elspeth laughed. 'Almost right. Hyacinth and crocus.'

'You always did like crocus. They remind me of Easter.'

'And Easter picnics. Remember we used to go to Kelvin Park on Easter Monday to roll our eggs?'

Matt did. He remembered the years when Elspeth and Duncan were little, even younger than Fiona and Robbie were now. Every Easter Monday without fail, he and Ailsa would pack up a basket with corned beef sandwiches, apples, hard boiled eggs, lemonade and chocolate Easter eggs. The family would spend a large part of the day in the park and, after lunch, the children would find a small slope and roll the hard-boiled eggs down again and again until they cracked and were ready to be peeled and eaten.

Matt nodded. It was going to be even more difficult to bring up his proposed trip in the midst of these memories.

'I still miss Mum so much,' Elspeth's eyes moistened. 'I wish…' She dashed away the tears. 'Sorry, Dad. I get weepy rather easily these days. They tell me it's *that time of life.*' She grimaced. 'As if that makes it any better.'

'I miss her too, sweetie. Every day.' He sighed. 'But life goes on.'

Elspeth sighed too. 'And you didn't come here because you were having lunch in Byres Road, did you? What did you want to tell me?' Elspeth had regained her composure and had seen through Matt's not-so-glib explanation for his visit.

'You're right.' He put his mug down and leant on the table with his elbows. 'You know I miss your mum. I always will. But she's been gone for five years now, and I get lonely out there by the loch. It's a glorious spot and I love the peace and ambiance of the place. But, when I met Bel I knew she was the companion I wanted to spend the rest of my life with. I'm glad you seem to be warming to the idea of our friendship.'

Matt paused to take a breath. He glanced at his daughter to gauge her reaction. It was difficult to tell. Elspeth was as still as a statue, holding her coffee mug in both hands. Her eyes didn't meet his. He ploughed on.

'The thing is, Bel's having a few challenges down there in Aussie land, and I've decided to take a trip to see if…' Matt's voice died away. He wasn't exactly sure how much he wanted to share with Elspeth. Telling her about the arrival of Bel's ex-husband wouldn't endear her to his new love, while his doubts about Bel's commitment to him might reignite her earlier antagonism. '…I might help,' he finished.

'Oh!'

Matt waited, but there was silence.

'Finished?' Elspeth rose and took the mugs over to the sink. Matt watched as she carefully rinsed them and placed them in the dishwasher, before turning her eyes in his direction. 'It's your life, Dad. And if that's what you want to do, I guess you'll do it. You *will* be back for Christmas, won't you?' Her eyes clouded with worry. 'With or without her.'

Damn! Matt knew right away she'd seen through his subterfuge. But he decided to continue the ploy. 'We should both be back for a family Christmas. I remember you said it was my turn this year, but I'm counting on your help with the catering. Otherwise it'll be Marks and Spencer or Waitrose.'

'Dad!'

But Matt was glad to see his remark had raised a smile. His daughter hadn't completely lost her sense of humour.

However, as Matt drove back home, he knew Elspeth still bore a grudge that her beloved mother might be replaced. He could only hope that, once she got to know Bel, she'd understand what he saw in her and would come to regard her as a friend.

Twenty-eight

Matt was coming here! Bel wasn't sure how she felt. Everything seemed to be happening at once. Pete was moving in next day, Celia was arranging her separation, and now Matt was arriving in two days' time.

She needed time to take stock. Celia, she didn't need to worry about, although she did. The woman had had a raw deal and was trying to claim her life back from the bully she'd been married to for too long.

But Bel's own life seemed to be going into freefall. The thought of having both Pete and Matt under her roof at the same time would be laughable if it wasn't so serious. Reading between the lines of Matt's email – he'd been too cagey to tell her on skype – she received the distinct impression he was doubting her willingness to make good her promise.

'Celia!' she called, hearing the front door close.

Bel knew she had to let Celia know Matt's plans. She felt bad about it. When she'd offered the woman succour – a safe haven from her bully of a husband – it had been to share a house with another woman. Now she was going to be sharing it with not one, but two men. How would she react? Bel wouldn't blame her if she decided to leave. But where would she go? She'd already decided she couldn't stay with her daughters.

Bel exhaled loudly as Celia dropped onto a chair with a sigh.

'I'm glad today's over.' Her eyes met Bel's, her brow furrowing. 'Was there something else? What did I forget?' She began to rise again, but Bel signalled her to stay.

'It's Matt. He's coming here.' She rubbed her forehead.

'That's good. Isn't it?' Celia added, clearly noting Bel's frown.

'I'm not sure,' Bel said slowly. 'I'm pleased he's coming. Of course I am.' *So why did she feel as if she was trying to convince herself?* 'He wanted to come with me, but it made more sense for him to stay, to look after things there.'

'So now he can get away?'

'So it seems.' She shook her head. 'The thing is, Celia, he hasn't said exactly why he's coming. Why now, when Pete's moving in too? It all seems so…' Bel waved her hands in the air.

'You think he's jealous?'

'Maybe. But he's not the jealous type. At least I didn't think he was. Perhaps this just demonstrates how little we know each other.'

'Mmm. Better to find out now.'

Bel agreed with Celia but hated that she'd pointed it out.

'When does he arrive?'

'Thursday.'

'Sheesh! That's only two days away.'

'I know. It seems to have been a sudden decision. He didn't even tell me to my face. He emailed his travel plans and asked me if I could meet him at the airport. No consideration of the fact I have a shop to run.' Bel could feel her temperature rising.

'You're angry?'

'No!' But Bel's tone belied her words. 'Well, maybe – a little. I wish he'd taken time to discuss it with me – to tell me why he decided to come at this point. I'm more upset than angry.'

'I can look after the shop while you go to the airport,' Celia offered.

'Thanks. I know that. I guess I'm not thinking straight. And there's Pete to organise tomorrow, too.'

'How's he getting to the house?'

'Taxi.'

'Right. Is there anything you need me to do?'

'No, you've done enough. I don't know how I'd have managed all this without you. If I'd been on my own, it would have been more difficult, maybe too difficult. That *would* have given Matt something to be concerned about.'

'But he can't really think… Pete's a sick man. You wouldn't have offered otherwise.'

Bel thought she could hear a question in Celia's voice. 'And it's only until we can get him into a nursing home. God knows, I'm no nurse, but the poor man has nowhere else to go.' *Or so he says*. Not for the first time, Bel wondered if she was being played yet again by Pete Sadler.

*

Bel arrived early at Sydney's Kingsford Smith airport. She was a bag of nerves. It was weeks since she'd farewelled Matt in Glasgow. He should be welcoming her back there, instead of which here she was heading across the airport bridge to the arrivals lounge.

Carrying a cardboard coffee from a nearby stand, Bel took a seat within sight of the gate, watching as the various travellers struggled out, some pushing carts piled high with luggage, others wheeling one small case. On her side of the barrier, families were waiting impatiently to be reunited with loved ones, limousine drivers held up placards or iPads inscribed with the names of their passengers, and excited children rushed around, tripping over bags and getting in everyone's way.

She checked her watch and wandered over to the arrivals board. Matt's flight had landed, but so had many others. Sydney International Airport was a busy place, and she remembered only too well the large queues at customs and immigration. Bel bought another coffee and resumed her seat, prepared for a long wait.

She thought about Pete. When he'd arrived the previous evening, he seemed to have found a new lease of life. The invalid she'd met in the hotel room had morphed back into the man she'd lunched with in the Botanic Gardens.

Their conversation played out again in her head.

'So this is where you are? A nice set-up.' Pete had dropped his bag on the bed and rubbed his hands together. 'You certainly have done well for yourself, Bel. And all without a man in your life. What's this man you told me about thinking of, letting you come back here to be all alone? He can't be…'

Bel had twisted her hands together, knowing she had to tell Pete.

'His name's Matt – Matt Reid – and he is *coming here. Tomorrow, actually.' She saw Pete's face fall.*

'*He…*' *he began, then seemed to think better of it.* '*Well, we'll have to see who's the best man, then, won't we?*' *he said with a lopsided grin.*

Bel almost laughed out loud. This was like the old Pete, the one she'd lost her heart to, the one she'd seen the shadow of at Harbour View Hotel, the memory of which had led to her agreeing to offer him a room.

Her phone buzzed.

Just picked up my bag. Joining the queue now. Can't wait to see you. Mx

Bel smiled, all thought of Pete forgotten. Her heart raced. The butterflies which had been flying around in her stomach since she awoke that morning began to dance in formation. This was Matt. He was here! All of her doubts and misgivings disappeared. She stood up, unable to stay still. The sense of excitement in the air began to make sense. She was one with the crowd, waiting to see her beloved walk through the gate.

She paced up and down. Then. Suddenly. He was there. Matt's familiar figure, pushing a small wheeled case, was walking toward her beaming. Bel moved forward, her approach hindered by others greeting their own loved ones. Then he was standing in front of her. His arms were around her. She felt his lips on hers, his cheek brushing against hers; she inhaled his familiar aroma and knew with absolute certainty everything was going to be all right.

*

Pete glanced up when Bel and Matt walked in arm and arm. He half-rose, then collapsed into the chair again as if the effort had exhausted him.

'So this is him?'

Bel tightened her grip on Matt's arm. 'This is Matt. I told you he was arriving today.'

'So you did. All the way from Scotland are you, mate? A long way to come.' His eyes raked Matt up and down.

'Good to meet you.' Matt held out a hand, but Pete waved it away.

The pair gazed at each other for all the world as if they were two dogs itching for a fight. This is ridiculous, Bel thought. They're grown men, old enough to know better. She glared at Pete who only seemed faintly amused.

'You can put your things in the bedroom.' Bel decided to ignore Pete's expression and led Matt to her room where he took her in his arms.

'I've been longing for this ever since you left,' he murmured.

'Me, too,' Bel breathed, as her body moulded to Matt's, the almost forgotten aching desire reasserting itself. But for some reason she felt uncomfortable in Matt's embrace when Pete was sitting only a couple of rooms away. She extricated herself and slid open the wardrobe door. 'You can hang your clothes here. I've made room. And there are drawers…' She gestured to the tall boy on the opposite wall. 'Sorry, I'm babbling.' She sat down on the bed with a thump.

Matt joined her and grasped her hand, entwining his fingers with hers. 'I know it must be hard – having both of us here. I've been trying to understand your reasoning. I came because…'

Bel put a finger on his lips to stem anything further. 'There's no need to explain. It's enough that you're here.' She had a good idea why he was here, why he'd chosen to come now. But she didn't care. If it had taken Pete's arrival in her home to force Matt into this trip, then so be it. All she knew was that she was delighted to see him.

Bel gazed at Matt silently, her eyes feasting on his face – the eyes such a deep brown a woman could happily drown in them, the gentle expression with which she'd become so familiar, the lines around his eyes and mouth which lent the face character.

'I can see how sick he is. I hadn't realised. But what I don't understand is why he's here.'

Bel hesitated. She really didn't understand either. She just knew it was something she had to do. Despite everything, Pete had been an important part of her past and she couldn't leave him to die alone. 'It's just till a place comes available,' she murmured.

She gazed down at her fingers linked with Matt's. His hands were so strong, still tanned from being outdoors all summer. The sight of them brought back memories of days spent on the muir with Matt and Hamish, hours tramping through the heather and gorse, a time when she'd felt so removed from her life here in Australia, she'd wondered if she ever wanted to return to her adopted land.

'We can't stay in here,' she said, rising and disentangling herself. 'I should get back to work. You must be tired after that long trip.'

'A nap would be good. Will...?' he gestured to the room where Pete was.

'He's not going anywhere.' Bel wondered about the wisdom of leaving Pete and Matt together, alone, in the same house. But surely... They were grown men, after all – one sick and one exhausted. 'You're okay with that?'

'Sure.'

Bel dropped a kiss on Matt's forehead, stroked his cheek and paused for a moment to reassure herself of his presence before going out and closing the door.

'So that's your Scottish guy? What's he got that I haven't?'

Suddenly Bel felt her frustration boil over. 'He's more of man than you ever were. He'd never get himself into the mess you did. Never leave me to clear up the mess. Never...' She ran out of words.

'No. *He's* a lawyer.' Pete's voice contained a bitter note she hadn't heard in it since he came back into her life.

Was this the real Pete? Had the weakness he'd shown her been a facade designed to bend her to his will? Had he fooled her yet again?

'Well, you're both here now. And if you want to stay, you'd better play nice. I'm warning you, Pete.'

'Oh, you're warning me, are you?' He grinned. 'Don't worry, Bella. I know on what side my bread's buttered. Beggars can't be choosers. I promise to behave. Scout's honour.' He held up a hand as if to demonstrate his sincerity.

Bel decided to ignore the sarcasm. 'Matt's having a nap. I need to get back. I'll see both of you around five-thirty or six.'

*

'He arrived safely? I can tell. You're positively glowing,' Celia greeted Bel with a knowing grin.

'Yes. He's having a nap. It's a long trip. But I don't know how wise it is leaving the two of them together.' Bel frowned. 'I may have misjudged Pete. He became quite bitter.' She bit her lip. 'I was actually glad to get out of the house.'

'Are you regretting inviting him to stay?'

Bel thought for a moment. 'Not exactly. But I'm beginning to feel I may have been used – yet again. I guess a leopard doesn't change his spots. But there's no getting away from the fact he's sick, dying. And he had nowhere to go.'

'You believe that?'

'Yes. You only have to look at him. And on the plus side, Matt's only here because Pete is.'

'And you *are* pleased about that? You seemed to be in two minds.'

'Now he's here, I wonder why I even thought twice about it. Anyway, now I'm back, you can go to lunch.'

'What about you? Can I get you something?'

'Maybe a ciabatta with ham.'

'Will do.'

Left alone, Bel had time to reflect on the scene she'd left. While she couldn't wait to get back to Matt, she dreaded more signs of what now appeared to be Pete's resentment of her new relationship.

All too soon it was time to close up for the day and the prospect of her return home beckoned. Bel and Celia left the shop together but, as often happened, Celia was heading to have dinner with her daughters, so Bel drove home alone, her heart in her mouth. What would she find waiting for her?

Twenty-nine

Bel arrived home and opened the front door cautiously to be greeted as usual by a delighted Toby, the little dog's tail wagging as if it was in danger of falling off. Apart from the dog's barking the house was silent.

Walking through the hall, Bel peered into the living room where Pete had been when she left. Empty. She dropped her bag on the hallstand and continued into the kitchen. It was empty too.

She needed a drink.

She was pouring a large glass of Chardonnay when there was a sound behind her. Bel turned quickly into Matt's arms.

'Oh! You gave me a fright.'

'Steady on. You didn't used to be so jumpy. What happened to the woman I met in Scotland, the one who said she loved me?'

'I'm still here.' Bel closed the fridge door with her free hand. 'It's just that everything…' She peered around Matt. 'Pete?'

'I heard a door close. I think he's in his room. We need to talk about that.'

'Later. Would you like a glass of wine? Did you sleep? How are you feeling?'

'Which one do you want me to answer first?' Matt laughed and caressed Bel's cheek with one finger. 'It's so good to see you. You've no idea.'

'I think I have. It's been hell for me too.' She allowed herself to sink into his embrace. 'I've missed you so much. And I was worried about

Elspeth, that you might decide it was all too difficult. I don't want to be the cause of trouble with your family.'

Matt stopped her words with his lips, and Bel was once again caught up in the tumultuous emotion his kisses unleashed. It was several minutes before the pair separated.

'Now,' Matt said, when they were seated in the courtyard with large glasses of Chardonnay. 'Pete. What's it all about? Why you? Why now?'

Bel sat quite still for a moment enjoying the fact that Matt was right here with her in Sydney. A slight breeze was blowing the lilac blossoms of a neighbouring jacaranda tree over the deck to provide a carpet of purple, and the cicadas were filling the air with their noise. She loved evenings like this.

'I don't know why now – maybe because he's dying. But why me? Maybe because he did the dirty on me all those years ago and wanted to make amends. At least, that's what he told me. But, in the last little while, I've begun to wonder if he was spinning me a line; if he's still the sad bastard who's only out for himself; if yet again, he's regarded me as a soft touch.'

'How so?'

'It's a long story. Suffice to say, I fell right in. He's here, at least until a spot becomes available for him in a nursing home.'

'He's on a waiting list?'

'I…' Bel realised she'd only taken Pete's word for it, for a lot of what he'd told her. 'Shit, I don't know if anything he's been telling me is the truth. Apart from the fact he's ill. Anyone can see that.'

'True.'

'And you? Why are *you* really here? I thought we'd decided you were needed back in Glasgow?'

'When you told me about Pete, I saw red. All I could think was that you'd gone back to your ex. I had to come to see for myself.'

'And if I had?' Bel toyed with the stem of her glass, interested to hear what Matt had to say.

He exhaled. 'I don't know. I love you more than life itself, but I'd probably have gone home with my tail between my legs. I'm too old to get into a fight over a woman, no matter how much…' His voice died away.

Bel smiled inwardly at this admission of devotion, but also felt a pang of disappointment at the revelation she wasn't worth fighting over.

'Anyone home?' a voice called from the kitchen.

'Out here,' Bel replied, mouthing 'Celia' in response to Matt's raised eyebrows.

'Hello, you must be Matt. I've heard a lot about you.' Celia was a vision of elegance in a tailored white linen suit, the collar of a red shirt peeping out from the neckline, her blonde hair carefully styled, her make-up immaculate.

Bel tried to stifle the twinge of jealousy that surged up uninvited. Celia was her friend; she had her own cross to bear. But she was beautiful, sophisticated and twenty years younger. Bel forgot Matt was, like Bel, in his mid-sixties and would have nothing in common with someone like Celia. For a full ten seconds her mind was filled with *what if*.

The sound of Matt's voice brought her back to her senses.

'And you must be Celia. Bel's told me about you too.' His knee found its way to rub against Bel's under the table in a silent message that *she* was the one for him.

'I won't interrupt,' Celia said. 'I just wanted to tell you, Bel. I called the solicitor to get things moving with Bill.' She threw an apologetic look at Matt. 'Sorry. You've only just arrived. You don't want to hear my sordid story.'

Matt appeared bemused. 'I'm a lawyer, too. I've probably heard every sordid story there is in my time.'

'Are you okay?' Bel asked.

'A bit fragile. But I had a drink with Han and Chloe and they're right behind me. My daughters,' she added to Matt.

'Why don't you join us?' Matt asked. 'I'll get another glass.'

'Are you sure?' Her doubt-filled eyes met Bel's.

Bel nodded faintly.

'I can fetch a glass.' Celia disappeared again.

'Thanks,' Bel whispered, all her jealousy forgotten. 'She looks as if she could do with some company. She's having a difficult time.'

'Looks to me as if you've become a refuge for waifs and strays.'

Bel chuckled. 'You make me sound like the local dog and cat home.'

When Celia returned with a glass, she had a strained look. Bel noted the dark circles under her eyes that even her skillful make-up had failed to conceal. Feeling suddenly guilty for her earlier suspicion, she asked, 'Do you want to talk about it? Get a second opinion?'

Celia ran a jerky hand through her hair while Matt filled her glass. 'Oh, I don't know. What's the point? And I'm sure you don't want me to spoil your evening.'

'Nothing could do that.' Matt threw an adoring glance at Bel who basked in its warmth. Just having him here made such a difference. She wasn't alone any-more. Matt's presence filled a gap she hadn't been aware of, but which had been there ever since she'd returned, opening up like a festering sore. Now it was healed. It was as if she could actually feel the raw ends joining together again. She squeezed his hand under the table.

'Well...' Celia twirled the stem of her glass in her fingers, clearly oblivious of the undercurrent of desire between the other two. 'It's the old story – a marriage made in haste, two children, my loss of a career and hence identity, his unfaithfulness and bullying. Then,' she smiled across at Bel, 'Bel came to my rescue. Now I've decided to make it a complete break and my solicitor is going to see about getting a legal separation as a precursor to a divorce.' Her voice shook on the final word, and she took a gulp of wine.

'Sounds like you're doing the right thing consulting a local guy. I'm not familiar with the family law situation here. Where I practice – used to, I should say – we adhere to Scots Law. Things are probably very different in Australia.' He peered at Celia whose eyes were flitting around the yard as if unable to settle. 'How do you think your husband will react?'

Celia gripped the stem of her glass so tightly it looked as if it might snap. 'That's just it. I think he'll go ballistic.' She took a deep breath. 'He tends to lose his temper if he doesn't get his own way. I don't want either of you to be in the firing line.'

'I think we're tough enough to cope. More wine?' He held up the bottle and Celia accepted a refill, emptying it in one swallow before rising to her feet.

'I'll leave you two alone now. You must have a lot of catching up to do. Thanks for listening. You have a good man here, Bel.'

When she'd gone, Matt filled Bel's glass again too, then drew her into his arms and rested his chin on her head. 'This feels right,' he whispered. 'But it's a bit different from home.'

'Home,' Bel murmured. *Where was home?* She'd been struggling with this question ever since her plane touched down at Sydney airport. Relaxing into Matt's arms and closing her eyes to enjoy the warmth, it came to her. Home wasn't only a place. Home could be a person, too. And, here in Matt's arms, was where she wanted to be, where she felt at home. She snuggled into his embrace.

*

Next morning, Bel crept silently out of bed, taking care not to disturb Matt with whom jetlag seemed to have caught up. He'd almost fallen asleep during dinner last night and had barely managed to make it to bed before he'd fallen into a deep slumber. So much for a passionate reunion, she thought, as she dropped a kiss on his brow and brushed back a lock of hair.

But, she reminded herself, they had the rest of their lives to satisfy their hunger for each other. And she had a shop to run. She sighed, but after a quick shower, dressed in a pair of wide-legged white pants topped with a bright pink tunic, she closed the bedroom door gently and made her way to the kitchen.

Celia and Pete were sitting in silence at the kitchen table, while Toby was eating breakfast oblivious to the tension in the room.

'Good morning.'

At the sound of her voice, the little dog scampered over to greet her, and Celia looked up, her eyes full of what appeared to be relief.

'Where's lover boy this morning?' Pete's voice held a note of the same bitterness Bel had heard the day before. She winced. *Had she made a mistake inviting him to come here? Or was the mistake in allowing Matt to come too? But could she have stopped him? Would she have wanted to?*

'If you're referring to Matt, he's still asleep.' As she spoke, Bel poured herself a coffee and filled a bowl with muesli, topping it with a generous helping of yogurt. Then she joined them at the table.

'How did you sleep?' Bel asked Celia, noting that the woman's eyes appeared clearer today, a sure sign she'd been able to pass a restful night.

'So-so. I heard the clock chime every hour until three,' she said referring to Bel's grandmother clock, a gift her mother had bought her on her one trip to Australia to remind her of the house she'd grown up in. Despite the bad memories the clock occasionally provoked, Bel had never found the heart to part with it.

'Oh, dear. Would you like to stay home today? I can probably manage.'

'No, I'll be fine. It's better I keep busy. I need something to keep my mind off things.'

'It's like a circus in here,' Pete complained. 'And I have no idea what's going on. People coming and going, keeping me in the dark. You seem to be living here too,' he said to Celia. 'Is Bel turning the place into a hotel?'

'I'm right here,' Bel said. 'You can talk to me. There's no need to take your bad temper out on Celia. Just remember this is *my* house. You're a guest here.'

'Oh-oh. That puts me in my place.' Pete gave a wry grin, then a flash of pain crossed his face. 'I think I'll lie down for a bit.' He shambled off.

'Is he in much pain?' Celia asked when she and Bel were alone again.

'I really don't know.' Bel picked up her cup, then put it down again. 'He won't talk about his illness. I wish I knew more. I don't even know if he's on medication. I suppose he must be. But when I try to ask him about it, he closes up. Pete was never good at sharing things. And that hasn't changed.' She let out a sigh. 'I'm glad you're here, Celia. It's good to have another woman to talk to. Though I know this isn't what you expected when you moved in.'

'I'm grateful to be here, regardless of how many men you decide to add to the mix. Though we'll run out of rooms soon,' she chuckled.

Bel stared at her for a moment, then joined in, glad to see the funny side of it. 'I suppose it might seem as if I'm running a hotel. And one I hope to sell soon,' she added, sobering up.

'No sign of a buyer?'

'No. I must get back to Rod. He was hoping the original buyers might come back, now that we've fixed the termite problem, but they bought elsewhere. He'll probably want another open house, but how we can organise that with an invalid in the house, I'm not sure. We'll see what Rod has to say. Oh, Celia, I wish it was all done with, and Matt and I could head off back to Scotland.'

'And the shop?'

Bel leant her elbows on the table and rubbed her eyes. 'Don't mention it. I don't dare to think about what I'm going to do about it. I guess I'll have to list it with a business broker. I don't know where to start. I've been hoping the other shopkeepers would come to the party, or the developer would be willing to buy Isabella in the hope of persuading them. It's a good business. It'd be a shame to see it go.'

The two women sat in silence, each lost in her thoughts. Finally, Bel sighed and stood up. 'This won't get us anywhere. I have a few things I need to take care of.' She ran a hand over her hair again. 'I'm sorry. I'm a bit behind today. Would you mind…?'

'I can open up.' Celia rose and collected the empty dishes, carrying them to the dishwasher. 'Take as long as you need.'

*

When Bel reached the shop, she was pleased to note Celia had already begun to change the window display. She stood back to admire it. Her new assistant certainly had a flair for this business. It was such a pity… She gave herself a shake and pushed the door open.

'Rod Miller called,' Celia greeted her. 'He'd like you to call back.'

'Oh, hell. I bet he wants another open house. How am I going to manage that with Pete around? Matt would be happy to go out for the duration, but I don't know about Pete.' Bel trudged into the office feeling weighed down by the demands of everything and everyone in her life. She picked up the phone and pressed redial.

'Bel. Good news,' Rod's voice boomed in Bel's ear, his words triggering a spark of hope.

'Yes?' She fiddled with a couple of paperclips as Rod continued to talk, his voice exuding energy and optimism.

'Can we arrange a viewing? I have a couple who're very interested in buying in the area and they're looking for something just like yours. They're visiting from interstate and short of time. Can we do it today?'

Today? Bel envisaged the house as she'd left it. Both men still in bed, the kitchen a bit untidy, though the breakfast dishes had been cleared. She tried to remember what the rest of the place looked like, but the image escaped her. This was what she'd been afraid of. It was important for her to get a sale, and previously, she'd left the house spotless, even going to the trouble of having fresh flowers, a welcoming smell of baking and… She became aware Rod was waiting for her response.

'I…'

'They're serious buyers, Bel. They've sold their Adelaide house, and he's taking up a local teaching position in January. I think they're going to love your place.'

Bel made a spot decision. 'Can we make it this afternoon?' She'd go back home and do a quick run around the place. Matt could help, and Pete… Maybe Matt could help there too – get him out of the house. It would only be for a short time.

'Great.' Bel heard the relief in Rod's voice. 'I'll tell them two o'clock. Will that be all right?'

'Should be. You have the key. I'll try to make sure it'll be empty.' Bel hung up before Rod could ask any questions.

Walking back into the shop, Bel was met by Celia's raised eyebrows.

'There's a couple want to look at the house. Today.'

'Oh.'

'They're from South Australia and only here for a short time. Can I impose on you again?' Bel threw a pleading look in Celia's direction.

'On you go. I can cope. But what about Pete?'

'I'll deal with him.' Bel tightened her lips. That man had caused her enough grief. She wasn't going to let him stand in the way of a potential buyer for her house if she could help it.

On the way home, she stopped to buy a couple of bunches of fresh flowers, reckoning the tulips, freesia and chrysanthemums would both brighten up the rooms and provide a pleasant fragrance. As she put her key in the door, she crossed her fingers she could bring it off.

She was in luck. Matt was sitting at the table eating breakfast. He was dressed and ready for the day, looking refreshed and every bit as handsome as she'd remembered.

'Come back to check up on me?' he asked, with a grin.

'I need to ask you a favour.' Bel joined him at the table and laid out her plans. 'I know it's a big ask. And I guess Pete won't take kindly to the idea, but I can't have him here. I can't trust him.'

Matt held up a hand. 'It's okay. I understand. I can take him out to coffee or something. Don't worry. How can I help you right now?'

By one o'clock, the house was spotless. Matt had even helped set up and start the bread maker, and the house was beginning to fill with the delightful aroma of freshly baked bread.

Pete too was dressed, but was full of objections, pleading his invalid status as a reason to stay home.

'Don't worry. Trust me,' Matt said, ushering Bel out. 'I have something up my sleeve. We'll both be gone by two. See you later.' He pulled her into his arms, and their lips met in a long kiss. 'That should keep you going till then.'

Two o'clock came and went, and, although kept busy with customers, Bel felt she was performing automatically. All the time she was making pleasant conversation, complimenting customers, wrapping purchases and managing payments, she was wondering what was happening back home. Had the buyers arrived? Did they like the house? Had Matt managed to get Pete out? From time to time, she surreptitiously checked her watch. Would Rod call? Was it too soon for her to call him?

'You'll be a nervous wreck if you go on like this,' Celia said when there was a break in the rush, and they were taking the opportunity to drink herbal tea in the office. 'Call him, why don't you?'

'Rod or Matt?'

'I meant Rod. But maybe Matt too, if it'd set your mind at rest.'

Matt, Bel decided. No doubt Rod would be in touch if there was any news. She fingered the silver necklace she was wearing, rolling the chain round and round in her fingers as she pressed speed dial for her home number and hoping Pete wouldn't pick up the phone.

'Hello?'

Bel felt a rush of relief as she heard Matt's Scottish burr. 'It's me. Did you manage?'

'Oh, ye of little faith.' Bel heard the amusement in his voice. 'I said I would and I did. We took a cab to Balmoral Beach and had coffee overlooking the ocean in a place called The Boathouse. Pete didn't say much. He seemed to be lost in his thoughts.'

'Oh!'

Balmoral Beach had been a favourite with Bel and Pete in the early years of their marriage. Maybe it had brought back memories – pleasant ones of a time when they'd been happy together. Before he'd ruined it.

'Is everything all right?'

'Yes.' Bel shivered, memories jostling with each other for supremacy – running along the beach hand-in-hand, swimming out through the breakers, drinking champagne together on her birthday. She shook her head to dismiss them. It was all a long time ago. Another lifetime. 'What's he doing now?'

'Lying down. The trip seemed to tire him out. We didn't argue, if that's what's worrying you. The agent left a card, so your buyers obviously arrived. Any word?'

'No.' Bel chewed on the inside of her cheek. 'Not yet. Well, thank you so much, Matt. I'll see you soon.'

She pressed to end the call and sat looking at the phone. How she hoped this would prove to be the sale of her house. That would be one hurdle over. And a few more to go, she was reminded by a jolt of something akin to foreboding. What else could go wrong?

Thirty

It was a glorious Sunday morning, the sort of morning that makes you glad to be alive. Bel turned her head on the pillow to look at Matt's sleeping figure. A warm glow enveloped her. If she'd had any doubts about her love for Matt, the past few days had totally dispelled them. And last night had been even more perfect than any of those that had preceded it, better even than those early nights of passion in Scotland.

Matt had completely recovered from the jetlag that had plagued him during his first couple of days in Sydney. His passion was that of a much younger man. They'd made love well into the night, Bel trying hard to avoid the sounds that had escaped her in their earlier lovemaking, the sounds of raw passion which had shocked her. She was aware that they weren't alone in the house and had no intention of disturbing either Celia or Pete.

Pete! She was beginning to wish she hadn't given in to her knee-jerk reaction to provide him with a home – or rather a staging place until another one could be found. One which would be his last. It was a morbid thought.

Pete wasn't proving to be the passive house guest Bel had anticipated, and she was fast losing patience with his moods and bad-temper. Surprisingly, Matt seemed to be finding it easier to communicate with him. Maybe it was a male thing, Bel thought, or maybe Matt had developed skills in his legal practice.

As she studied the man beside her, she glowed with pleasure despite feeling several unaccustomed aches, unused to such energetic activity as she'd experienced the previous evening.

Now, Matt's eyes opened, and his arms wrapped around her. Bel sank into his warm embrace, tucking her face into his shoulder and inhaling his distinct aroma – a mixture of soap and the tang of the outdoors.

'Shall we do something special today?' he asked, hugging her tightly and dropping butterfly kisses on her eyelids.

'Mmm.' Bel wondered if they could leave Pete yet again. Then decided she couldn't – wouldn't – allow her life to be ruled by her ex's whims. 'It would be a beautiful day to show you more of the harbour. Headland Park isn't far away. There's a great little café there – Frenchy's – and the views are superb.'

'Tell me more.' Matt leant his chin on her head, and she snuggled closer.

'It's the site of an old army hospital and barracks and – you won't believe this – but the army built the facsimile of a ship out of rock and concrete, to practise loading and unloading.'

'What's there now – just the café?'

'No. The old buildings are used as artists' studios and galleries. Lou – a friend of mine – and I often used to go there on Sundays for lunch, then wander around the galleries afterwards. Lou's had an exhibition there.'

'And this is Sunday. And Lou? You've mentioned her a few times. Am I going to meet this wonder?'

'Maybe one day.' Bel was wary of introducing Matt to her friend, given Lou's acerbic comments about him, and her skepticism concerning their relationship. Lou wasn't known for her tact. God knows what she might say to Matt.

*

It took them no time to drive along to their destination where they parked the car and walked across to the still half-empty café, finding seats at a small round table under a shady umbrella.

Despite Matt's protests, Bel had decided they leave Toby at home. She wanted Matt all to herself today, and hadn't been sure of the cafe's policy about dogs.

After a leisurely lunch of quiche and salad, Matt and Bel wandered hand-in-hand along the pathway above the harbour. The water was a deep blue, its surface interrupted only by the multicoloured sails of weekend-sailors' yachts. After a while, they chose to sit on one of the many wooden benches along the path, enjoying the view across the bay to the eastern suburbs and South Head on one side and to the cliffs of North Head on the other.

They gazed through the spiky casuarina trees and the tall gums at the white wake of a speed-boat and the harbour ferry, the only sound the occasional hoot of that same ferry, each lost in their own thoughts.

'You're going to miss this,' Matt said after a long pause, his arm around Bel's shoulders.

Bel was silent, then said, 'Yes. I probably will. But, at my stage of life, people are more important than places, and you are the one person I want to be with. I think I can cope with Scotland and the Scottish weather to be able to do that,' she said with a teasing smile.

Matt only grinned, pulled her closer and tightened his grip. 'And when were you thinking of coming home with me?' he asked.

'Oh!' Bel pulled herself out of his arms and met his eyes, a shadow in hers. She paused for a second before replying, just long enough to see the glow in his eyes dim. 'That depends... I mean...' She wrapped her arms around her body, suddenly feeling as if a cold breeze had wafted between them. 'I can't leave just yet. There's the shop, the house, Celia.' She bit her lip. 'And...'

'Your ex,' Matt finished for her. 'How long are you going to let that leech prey on you?'

'He's sick,' Bel protested, but knew it was a weak justification. Her home was no place for someone who was as sick as Pete purported to be. And he had no right to be there.

'Hmm.' Matt stood up and walked over to the edge of the pathway, standing with his hands in his pockets to stare out to sea.

'I thought you two were getting on okay,' Bel said, following Matt and wrapping her arms around his waist.

'To some extent.' He turned and rested his chin on her head, clasping her to him. She could sense him searching for the right words. He sighed. 'Sometimes I feel as if we're two dogs fighting over a bone. Not that I'm suggesting you're...'

'I've never thought of myself as a dog's bone,' Bel laughed. 'But I know what you mean. 'When we're all in the same room I feel torn.' Bel silently chided herself. She'd known deep down that things weren't going well between the two men. How could they be? But she'd tried to pretend to herself that they were grown men, and surely they could be civil to each other. Maybe she'd been expecting too much.

'Torn?' Matt raised his head.

'No, that's the wrong word. I feel as if I'm being split in two. Even if nothing's being said. There's a tension.'

'Would you rather I wasn't here?'

'No!' Bel met Matt's eyes, seeing more anguish than she'd thought possible. 'Never that. It's just… difficult.' She turned away.

Thirty-one

'I'm afraid it's not good news.' Bob Frazer looked down at the papers on his desk as he spoke, and Celia's heart sank.

She wasn't surprised. Had she really expected Bill to let her go easily? In her heart of hearts, she'd known he'd balk at the mention of separation, never mind divorce. But she'd hoped. God, how she'd hoped. 'So, what can I do now?' she asked, steeling herself for Bob's reply.

He looked up to meet her eyes, twirling a pencil in his fingers, then tapping his teeth with it. 'It's a bit of an odd situation. He… your husband… It seems he's…' He coughed.

Get on with it, Celia thought, wondering what was the worst Bill could do. He couldn't force her to return to him, could he?

'It seems,' he repeated, 'he's in some sort of negotiation with one of the large publishers to write his memoirs, and he can't afford to have any adverse publicity while that's going on.'

Celia almost burst out laughing with relief and a sense of the ridiculous. 'Bill? Write his memoirs? He can barely put two words together on a page. He was a football player, for God's sake, not a writer.' The relief she felt was enormous. If this was the best he could do…

'I believe he has a ghost writer – someone who'll do the actual writing for him,' he added. 'A lot of celebrities do that. They provide the material and pay…'

'I know what a ghost writer is,' Celia interrupted. 'It's just that the thought of Bill…' She laughed. 'Sorry. I'm finding it difficult to imagine there being enough in his life to fill an entire book, his bloated face on the cover.' She recovered her equilibrium. 'Though I suppose he'd use an old picture, one when he was young and fit, the darling of the media. So where does that leave me?'

'With no legal recourse at present. It'll be a year before you can divorce without his agreement.'

Celia slumped in the chair, her laughter forgotten. A year! She needed things settled now. *How was she to survive for a year once Bel sold the shop and moved overseas?*

'However…'

Celia looked up, a tiny sliver of hope in her eyes. Did Bob have a solution?

'I think we may be able to do a deal. With your agreement, naturally.'

Celia straightened up, her head erect, and crossed her fingers in her lap. 'Yes?'

'It seems this publisher wants to present him as unblemished to the public, *his* public.'

Celia snorted, but kept listening.

'So, it seems to me that *he* needs your cooperation and *you* need money. Maybe we can do a deal.'

'You mean?'

'You agree to play the devoted wife for any media appearances in return for an advance on any future divorce settlement.'

Celia thought for a moment. 'It wouldn't mean going back to live with him, would it? I definitely won't do that.'

'We'd have to draw up an agreement which both of you would sign, then…'

'How much?' Celia's mind immediately went to the bottom line. How much would she need to start over, to pay a bond or put a deposit on a unit? How much would Bill be prepared to pay to get his way on this?

'Enough. Let me handle it. So, I can tell his man – Julian Clarke – that we may have a deal?'

'Julian bloody Clarke. I should have known he was involved. They've been best mates since they were new boys together at King's School. Yes, please try and make a deal – as long as you can screw enough out of him.' Celia bit her lip, wondering if she'd sounded too grasping. She didn't usually care about money. She hated being so vulnerable and needy.

'Don't worry. I can handle the pair of them.'

For some reason, Celia believed him. Bob Frazer might appear to be your friendly man-next-door, but there was a steel core to him that wouldn't suffer fools gladly. Though Bill and his mate Julian weren't fools. Far from it. They were wily manipulators. But, Celia thought, they might have met their match in the man sitting across the desk.

'So that's it?'

'I'll be in touch when I have a document that requires your signature.' Bob rose, shook Celia's hand and ushered her to the door.

*

'You look as if you've lost a penny and found a sixpence as my old granny would say,' Bel greeted Celia as she pushed through the shop door. 'Good news?'

'Yes and no.' Glad the shop was empty, Celia dropped her bag on the counter and collapsed onto the small chair strategically placed to cater for the odd husband who might accompany his wife into the shop. All the way back on the bus, Celia had been turning over the meeting in her mind wondering if she'd made the right decision.

'Want to talk about it?'

'No thanks. Not now. I need to get my own head around it first.' Celia gave an apologetic smile. She did need to discuss it with someone, but, at the moment, it was too fresh in her mind. She needed to think about the ramifications; to decide if she could really bear to play happy families with Bill, to pretend all was well in front of cameras; to consider how much money would make it worthwhile, if any amount would. 'Maybe later.'

Somehow, she got through the afternoon, planning to share her dilemma with Bel after work. But she'd forgotten that, with both Matt and Pete in the house, it was nigh impossible to find a private moment. When, after dinner, Pete retired to his room and Bel and Matt settled in front of the television, she knew she couldn't bear an evening cooped up with those two who were obviously so much in love. Not when she was so unsure about appearing in public with the man she now considered her ex-husband. Deciding she needed some fresh air, she picked up her bag and popped her head into the living room.

'I'm going over to see Chloe and Han. Be back later.'

Once outside, breathing in the scent of the jacarandas which lined the street, Celia began to feel better. An hour or so with her girls and young Si were just what she needed to take her mind off Bill and the weirdness of this proposed memoir.

To her surprise, she recognised Jan's car outside the girls' house and felt a hint of disappointment before shrugging it off and walking up the path. Jan had as much right to be there as she did. Simon was *her* grandson too. Celia usually enjoyed Jan's company, but tonight, she'd wanted to get Han and Chloe to herself. She knew Ingrid would have tactfully withdrawn at the slightest sign from Hannah. Well, she consoled herself, as she heard steps in the hallway and saw Chloe's outline through the stained glass of the door, maybe Jan wouldn't stay long.

'Celia, how lovely to see you.' Jan rose to kiss Celia on the cheek while Hannah moved to hug her mother.

'We didn't expect you tonight,' Hannah said, raising her eyebrows. 'Everything all right?'

'Yes.' Celia took a seat beside Jan on the sofa and held out her arms to her grandson who raced into them almost toppling over in the process. She picked him up and gave him a big hug.

'He's still a bit wobbly at times,' Chloe said, coming into the room. 'I put the kettle on. Tea, Mum?'

'Thanks.' Celia buried her face in young Simon's hair and inhaled the sweet smell of the little boy. If only all of her problems could be resolved as easily as picking up little Si.

'You don't look as if everything's all right,' Hannah said. 'Out with it, Mum, we're all family here.'

Jan looked awkward. She half-rose. 'I can go, I was about to leave anyway. You won't...'

'No.' Celia put a hand on her arm. 'Don't go. It's thanks to you that...' She swallowed. Despite her earlier concern at Jan's presence, it was thanks to her that she'd gone to see Bob Frazer.

Jan's eyes widened. 'What did I do?'

'You gave me your brother's number.'

'Oh, that?'

'That.'

'Let me get the tea. For you too, Jan?' Chloe asked.

'Please.'

Little was said while Chloe left only to return a few moments later with a tray containing mugs of tea and a plate of odd-shaped cookies. 'I tried my hand at baking and they taste okay, even if they don't look up to much,' she said.

'Now, Mum. You went to see Jan's brother again today?' Hannah asked.

'Yes. It was a bit of a surprise. Your dad's planning to publish a memoir.'

'What?' Chloe and Hannah spoke in unison, while Jan gently touched Celia on the shoulder.

'It came as a surprise? How does that affect *your* plans?'

Celia threw Jan a grateful glance and began to recount her meeting with Bob.

'The bastard!' Hannah spat out, when Celia paused for breath. 'And he expects you to act as if everything is fine and dandy?'

'I need to put Si to bed, Mum,' Chloe interrupted, reaching over to relieve Celia of her burden. 'My views are probably the same as Han's. I'll see you again before you go.'

'Night-night, little fellow,' Celia said, handing him over to Chloe who paused to allow Jan to kiss him goodnight too.

Once they'd left, Ingrid, who'd remained silent all this time asked, 'And are you happy to do this, Celia? How will you feel standing beside him and smiling to the camera as if you were a happy couple?'

Ingrid had got to the heart of the matter. That was exactly what had been on Celia's mind since she left Bob's office.

'You can't do it, Mum!' Han yelled. 'It's exactly what he wants – to get you back under his thumb, doing his bidding. He's sly enough to think that's what'll happen. You won't, will you? Surely you're not that hard-pressed for cash?'

How little Hannah knew. But she was right about one thing. Bill did probably see it as a way to force her back. But Bob had said he could handle him. She had to believe that.

'We'll see. I think I know your father as well as you do, maybe better. I lived with him for a long time.'

'Too long,' Hannah muttered so low Celia could barely hear her.

'I did what I thought was best at the time – and he's still your father, even if he doesn't always act as if he is. I should go.' Celia gathered her bag, fumbling a little with the long handle, and stood up, surprised when Jan joined her.

'Me too,' she said.

The two women made their goodbyes, calling out to Chloe as they left. Once outside, however, they paused together at the kerb.

'You look as if you could do with something stronger than what they were serving in there,' Jan said. 'What say we stop off at the wine bar, if you don't need to hurry back to Bel's?'

'No. I'm afraid the loved-up couple aren't exactly what I want to go home to tonight, never mind the prospect of Bel's ex appearing like the ghost at the feast.' She gave a wry chuckle. 'But don't *you* have to get back?'

'Graham and Andy are at a movie. They won't be back for ages. I think you need someone to talk to – a sounding board. Correct me if I'm wrong, or if you think I'm not the right person.'

A wave of relief flowed over Celia. Jan, with her own challenges behind her, was exactly the right person. She had no agenda, no real connection to Celia or her future. 'In that case, yes please,' she said.

*

Once they were settled in a corner table away from the hustle and bustle of the young crowd of drinkers, chilled glasses of Chardonnay on the table, Jan leaned forward.

'Ingrid was right, you know. And what she said seemed to strike a chord. Hannah and Chloe are your daughters, and I know they have your wellbeing at heart, but Bill's their dad, the dad who rejected them. It's only natural they want you to have nothing to do with him. But what do *you* want?'

'I just want to get on with my life.' Celia sighed. 'Your brother – Bob – he's a good man, a good solicitor. He thinks…' She began to draw circles in the drops of moisture on the table top. 'He thinks we can do this deal. It might give me enough to start again properly. Bel's been great, but she's not going to be here forever. I'll need to find somewhere to live, another job.' She looked up to meet Jan's eyes. 'It's not easy at my age. There's not much call for a former model.'

'I know. I remember what it was like when I left Graham that time. Bel came to *my* rescue then too. We oldies need to stick together. But you're younger than I am.'

'Bill made me feel I was useless, that I didn't exist apart from him. I was Bill Ramsay's wife. Full stop. That's part of the trouble.'

'You mean you think if you go along with this memoir stuff, you'll lose your identity again?'

'Mmm.' Celia was weighing up the alternatives and couldn't decide which was worse. 'The trouble is I don't know which way to turn.'

'Bob knows what he's about. If he says he can pull off a deal, he probably can. How much would it take to make it worthwhile for you?'

Celia blanched at the blunt question. But Jan had a point. How much would it take? How much would she sell out for? No, that was putting it a bit strong. But it came to the same thing. How much was she prepared to do in return for an unspecified amount of money. 'It makes me sound like a whore,' she said.

'Not at all. You have something he wants, and Bob is going to find out how much he's willing to pay for it. Sounds like a straightforward business transaction to me. So, how much?' she repeated.

'Oh, I don't know. Enough for a deposit or a bond, a bit more to keep me going till I find a job.'

'One hundred thou, two hundred?'

'Not that much, I don't think.' Celia was stunned by Jan's estimates. Would Bill be prepared to part with that amount of money for her silence? And her participation in promotional events, she reminded herself with a shiver. But she was good at those, and she'd kept up the pretence of being happily married for years. Surely she could do it a few more times if it gained her the freedom to start again?

By the time the two women left the wine bar, Jan had almost convinced Celia it would be in her best interests to go along with whatever Bob proposed. Almost, but not quite. However, she had given her food for thought.

Thirty-two

Matt wakened early. The sun was just beginning to peek through the slats of the blind, and he could distinguish the loud cackling laugh of Bel's resident kookaburras. Bel was still sound asleep so, after watching her for a few minutes, he decided to surprise her with an early morning cup of coffee.

Slipping out of bed, he drew on his jeans and a tee-shirt, raked a hand through his hair, and left the bedroom, closing the door silently behind him.

From the kitchen window Matt had a clear view of the eucalypts that had caused Bel such heartache. They were beautiful tall trees – lemon-scented gums, Bel had said – seeming to stand guard over the courtyard. The two birds he'd heard earlier were sitting on the fence and, as he watched, they flew up and disappeared leaving silence in their wake.

He set out two mugs, filled the reservoir in the coffee machine, and turned it on. Matt smiled to himself, remembering how Bel's body had felt against his last night – warm and inviting. For what must have been the millionth time, he gave thanks to old Isobel for bringing then together and to whatever God there was that Bel reciprocated his feelings.

He was about to fetch the milk, when he heard a movement behind him.

'No nookie this morning? Cut you off, has she?' Pete Sadler's coarse comment broke into his thoughts.

Startled, Matt turned to see Bel's ex open the fridge door and remove the milk carton.

'What's that?' *Had he heard correctly? Surely even Pete couldn't be so crass?*

'You heard me.' Pete waved the milk in the air. 'Think you've got it all sewn up, do you? Just wait. I'll see you off yet. You'll be back in Scotland, and Bella will still be here – with me.' He tottered and grabbed the still-open fridge door for support. 'She invited *me* to stay, didn't she? Did *you* get an invite?'

Pete must have seen Matt's expression change. He continued, his voice becoming louder and louder. 'You'll see, mate. When the chips are down, it'll be *me* who stays here, not you. It'll be *me* who…'

Matt forced himself to remain civil. He wasn't going to let the bastard get to him. 'Don't you think you'd better keep your voice down? You'll waken the whole house.'

'And you wouldn't like that, would you? Oh no, Mr Scottish *solicitor*, Johnny-come-lately. Think she loves you, do you?' Pete sneered, his voice rising an octave as he continued to wave the milk around. 'She loved *me*. Let me tell you about my dear Bella.'

'Stop that!' Matt was surprised to hear his own voice rising to match Pete's. He was worried the milk was going to pour all over the kitchen floor. He wanted Pete to stop talking. He wanted to close his ears to his words. He knew the other man was sick, and most probably only trying to get under Matt's skin. Well, if that was the case, he was doing a pretty good job of it.

*

Bel reached across to the other side of the bed, expecting her fingers to touch Matt's warm body. Instead, her outstretched hand found only an empty space. She opened her eyes to see the covers folded back and heard the sound of harsh voices coming from the other end of the house.

Matt and Pete!

She rose hurriedly, slipped into a towelling robe and, without taking time to put anything on her feet or to draw a comb through her tousled hair, she rushed into the kitchen.

Matt was standing by the coffee machine clearly in the process of brewing his morning caffeine hit, while Pete was by the open door of the fridge waving a half-full milk carton in the air and looking as if he was about to collapse.

'What on earth…?'

'Sorry. Did we wake you?' Matt asked. 'I was making coffee. I planned to surprise you with a cup in bed when…'

'This fellow's acting as if he belongs here,' Pete broke in. 'I… I…' He tottered across to a chair and collapsed onto it, still grasping the milk carton.

Bel suppressed a smile. They were like a couple of children fighting over who was best. She could almost hear the *I was here before you* argument culminating in some instances that defied belief.

'Well, it's not a surprise now, but a good strong coffee is what I need and…' she extricated the milk from Pete, handing it to Matt, 'I think *you* need to lie down,' she said to her former husband. 'I'll bring you in some breakfast.'

'Maybe,' he replied, getting to his feet again and lumbering toward the door. 'But…'

'I won't have any of this silly bickering. Can't you try to get along? I permitted you to come here because you said you'd nowhere else to go. I can just as easily show you the door if you can't behave. Matt has as much right to be here as you do. More,' she added throwing a smile at Matt. 'But he'll go too if he doesn't behave,' she threatened, amused to see Matt raise his hands in entreaty. 'The same rules apply. What were you arguing about anyway?'

Matt busied himself with the coffee maker to avoid replying, while Pete tried to slink off, a downcast expression on his face.

'What's going on? I heard loud voices.' A fully dressed and elegantly coiffed Celia entered the kitchen and gazed at the tableau wide-eyed.

'Nothing I can't handle,' Bel said, accepting a coffee from Matt with relief. 'Thanks.' She took a long draught, sat down on the seat Pete had vacated and glowered at Matt. 'The pair of them were behaving like stupid little boys, not grown men who should know better. You didn't tell me how you got on yesterday,' she said, turning to Celia.

'Another time. I caught up with Jan last night, and we had a long chat.'

'Right.' Bel peered at Celia who seemed less stressed this morning. Maybe the chat with Jan had done her good. She drained her coffee, flinching as the hot liquid hit the back of her throat. 'I need to get showered and dressed, then take some breakfast in to the so-called invalid.'

Matt followed Bel into the bedroom, closed the door and took her in his arms. She slithered out of the embrace and went into the ensuite discarding her robe on the way. After what she'd seen and heard in the kitchen, she was in no mood for romance.

'I'm sorry.' Matt was at her side before she stepped into the shower. 'I don't know what came over me.' He rubbed a hand over his hair. 'He hit a hot button, tried to remind me *he'd* been married to you, *he* had a right to be here, while I had none. He even suggested there were still feelings between you. Can you forgive me?'

Bel paused, one foot in the shower well, realising how ridiculous they must look – her, naked apart from a pink floral shower cap, and Matt wearing a little-boy-lost expression, his mouth turning up in the way she loved. 'Oh, get away with you. But never again. I have enough to cope with without the pair of you feuding right here in my home.'

'Well, if I'm forgiven, maybe I can show my remorse?' Matt began to divest himself of his clothes, while Bel stepped under the stream of warm water and began to laugh. By the time he joined her, all thought of Pete, the quarrel, and her annoyance had vanished, and she relaxed, allowing herself to revel in the combined sensations of his hands soaping her, his lips travelling across her face and neck and the evidence of his desire pressing against her.

When they finally emerged, Bel was glowing with pleasure. This was what she'd longed for – to begin every morning in this man's arms. What had she been thinking when she'd doubted their relationship? What was Pete, the shop, the delay in the sale of the house, when weighed against this?

'Better now?' Matt asked as he blotted the water on Bel's body before towelling himself dry.

'Yes.'

Standing there, water dripping from his hair, droplets beading on his skin, he was more like a young Adonis than a sixty-seven-year-old Scotsman. And he loved *her*! Bel caught sight of herself in the mirror, amazed yet again that he could find her aging body beautiful. She grimaced at the signs of age – the blue veins beginning to show on the insides of her legs, the creases around her belly, the slightly drooping breasts, the…

As if reading her mind, Matt appeared behind her, put his arms around her waist and met her eyes in the mirror. 'I love you exactly the way you are. These lines…' He gently stroked her face, his fingers moving down to her neck and breasts. 'This shape… It's a sign you've lived, experienced life. What would I do with a younger woman – one who didn't share the same memories, the same music?'

Bel turned, and their lips met in a long kiss, his tongue reaching into her mouth provoking a swift ache of desire.

Matt was the first to step away. 'I suppose you're going to tell me you have a shop to open. But, if you decide to stay home we could spend the day in bed. Mmm?' He moved toward her again and nuzzled her neck, cupping her face in his hands.

For a moment, Bel was tempted. Then she remembered her responsibilities. Pete was in the other room, Celia in the kitchen. She did have a shop to open and several matters to take care of. She wasn't in a position to take the day off for her own pleasure. Not yet.

*

Once Bel and Celia had left, Matt brewed another cup of coffee and took it out to the courtyard. He leant back in the cane lounge chair and gazed up at the tall gum trees that formed a border to the garden. They were close to the large jacaranda in the neighbouring yard which had showered down its purple blossoms to add to the carpet of lilac on the paving stones. It was so different from home, gentler somehow. Though the birds were anything but gentle. The raucous calls of the native parrots echoed through the air as they flew overhead and perched in the high branches.

Sensing a movement at his feet, he leant down to scratch Toby behind the ears. Bel's little dog reminded him so much of his own Hamish. How he missed his furry companion.

A light breeze unleashed another cloud of blossom which rained down on him covering the table. A few of the petals fell into what remained of his coffee. He peered into the mug with a grimace, wishing he'd drunk it more quickly.

At eight o'clock on this November morning, the heat was already beginning to build up. It was strange to think it would soon be Christmas. Matt wondered idly what it would be like to spend Christmas here, at the bottom of the world, in summer. He'd read of beach picnics, of barbecues, of eating prawns, even of those who tried to replicate a northern hemisphere Christmas complete with turkey and all the trimmings.

But he wouldn't be here for Christmas. Nor would Bel. She'd made him a promise, and he intended to see she kept it. He felt confident she would, and they could travel back together, unless… The image of Pete forced itself into his head. He picked up the mug and went back inside, blinking as his eyes adjusted from the bright sunlight to the dimness inside.

He rinsed his mug and set it on the draining board, then carefully pushed open the door to the room currently occupied by Bel's ex. Pete was lying on his back sound asleep, a low snoring sound coming from him. Matt studied the recumbent figure. Asleep, it was easy to see he was a sick man. While awake, Pete might sound belligerent, and it was easy to think he was malingering. But asleep, his face appeared more cadaverous, and Matt could detect the lines of pain around his mouth. Lying on his back as he was, he seemed to almost disappear into the bedcovers. Matt withdrew, pulling the door closed behind him.

So, Pete hadn't lied about his illness, but even after only a few days in his company Matt had the distinct impression the man was lying about something. He wandered back through the house at a loss for something to do. He wasn't accustomed to this sort of inaction. Noticing the kitchen floor bore evidence that he'd brought in many of the purple blossoms on his feet, he sought out a broom and swept the floor.

Then he went into the study and was checking his emails on Bel's computer when an idea occurred to him. Nursing homes. Hadn't Bel said something about Pete being unable to get a place in a nursing home, being on a waiting list or some such thing. He wondered if she'd checked.

Matt suspected she hadn't. Bel had so many other things to take care of right now, he'd be willing to bet she'd taken Pete at face value. Well, this was something he could help her with. He googled Nursing Homes Sydney, and was stunned by the large number of options that popped up, many of them specifically for aged care. He guessed Pete didn't exactly fit into that category, but... He leant back and decided to brew another coffee before taking any action. As Bel's machine – which was similar to his own – hissed and gurgled, he reflected that he'd drunk more coffee in his time here than he did in a couple of months back home. But Bel favoured these herbal teas which he couldn't stomach, so coffee was his best option.

Taking the mug of caffeine back to the study, Matt examined the list again. It occurred to him he should also do a search for palliative care facilities. Those would be more appropriate for the man currently asleep in the next room. He needed to devise some sort of system, contact them one by one to determine if they had vacancies, and if Pete Sadler was on their waiting list. Good. He rubbed his hands. This was more like it. He had a plan.

The morning passed in a flash as Matt set up a spreadsheet and began to call the various facilities. Deciding he needed company, Toby settled himself at Matt's feet and proceeded to fall asleep making occasional grunting noises as he no doubt dreamt of catching some small creature.

At first it appeared that Pete may have spoken the truth when he'd told Bel they were no places available. While this was the case, so far none had admitted to having a Pete Sadler on their waiting list. But, he realised, perhaps they wouldn't due to confidentiality issues. He should have thought of that. He cursed his ineptitude at the haste with which he'd set about this search. He decided to pretend he was Pete's carer. That way, he should have more chance of success.

Finally, towards lunchtime, he discovered Margaret Rose House, a hospice in a place called Fairfield which predicted they'd have a space available in a week or so. The woman Matt spoke to was very circumspect, saying she really couldn't say for sure, but if he wanted a place kept she'd be willing to take a name. Matt let out a sigh of relief. He had no compunction in giving her Pete's name.

'And what is your relationship to the gentleman?' she asked. Matt hesitated for only a moment before replying, 'I'm his solicitor.'

He did experience a pang of guilt as he finished the call, but justified the lie to himself with the thought that it was all in a good cause.

He was about to continue in his quest, when he heard a door open behind him and returned to a perusal of his emails just in time.

'You still here?' Pete muttered, bumbling through the room. 'Thought you'd have found some other woman to batten on by now.'

'I was thinking about lunch. Would you like me to make something for you?' There was no sense in antagonising the man, and it *was* lunchtime.

Pete followed Matt into the kitchen, put a hand to his head and collapsed onto a chair. 'That'd be very… kind of you,' he said as if the words stuck in his throat. 'I'm not feeling too grand. Maybe some water?'

'Surely.' Matt fetched a glass of water, then returned to fossick in the fridge and pantry, working out what he could make for lunch that would satisfy both of them. He settled on some slices of wholemeal bread spread with cottage cheese and filled with tuna, and set a few slices of tomato on the plates beside each sandwich.

'How long do you intend to stay?' Pete asked, as the two men began to eat.

Matt noticed his companion took only small bites and followed each with a long draught of water. 'I'm not sure. It depends…'

'On Bel, I suppose. She's a good woman,' he said to Matt's surprise. 'Not everyone would have taken me in like she has.'

'She is that.' Matt agreed. 'And how long do *you* intend to stay?'

'I don't have long,' was the ambiguous reply.

Thirty-three

By the time Bel returned home from work, Matt had managed to contact every nursing home and palliative care centre on his list. None of them had heard of Pete Sadler. But Pete had been right about one thing. All were full. In fact, the only one which offered any hope was the one in Fairfield which had agreed to put Pete on their waiting list. Matt rubbed his chin. He knew what that meant. For a place to become available, someone had to die. It was a sad fact of life – and death.

He heard a car draw up, followed by the sound of the gate latch, then the opening of the door. Toby began to bark and rushed to greet his mistress. Matt followed at a more sedate pace.

'How was your day?' He drew Bel into his arms and kissed her warmly on the lips.

'Glad it's over.' Bel returned Matt's kiss with fervour, then put a hand on his chest as if to push him away. 'Did you two manage to get through the day without any more wrangling?'

'I was on my best behaviour. But there's something you should know.'

'Can you tell me later? I need a shower before I can feel human again.' Bel kissed Matt again on the lips. 'Could you pour me a glass of something cold while I do that and change?' She slipped out of his embrace and into the bedroom.

Matt gazed after her with longing. For a moment he wondered if he should follow for a repeat performance of their morning in the shower.

But his good sense got the better of him and he decided instead to do as she'd asked. He found a bottle of Bel's favourite Chardonnay in the fridge and poured two glasses. Then, remembering an earlier visit to the local deli, he filled a platter with some cheeses and fig and pecan crackers, set them all out on the table in the courtyard and sat down to await Bel's return. It was pleasant out here in the early evening. The heat of the day was beginning to diminish and there was a slight breeze. He'd remembered to cover the platter to shield it from any falling blossoms, but it seemed that even they had ceased to disturb the ambiance of the evening.

As he took a sip of the chilled wine, Matt wondered how best to approach Bel with the results of his day's work.

'This looks lovely. Thanks, honey.' Bel appeared in the doorway, freshly dressed in a pair of white pants and a long loose lilac garment, matching the jacaranda blossoms and looking altogether as if she'd spent a relaxing day.

'Feeling better?' Matt handed her a glass.

'Much.' Bel dropped into the seat beside him and took a long sip of wine. 'Mmm. So what did you get up to today? You sounded mysterious earlier.'

Matt cleared his throat. He still hadn't decided how to broach the subject. 'Pete,' he began.

'I thought you said all was well between you two?' Bel's eyebrows shot up. Then a frown appeared between them. 'Don't tell me...'

'No. I told you the truth, but...'

'Not all the truth,' Bel conjectured, putting down her glass, and folding her arms on the table. 'What else do I need to know?'

Matt leant back, thinking how beautiful Bel looked when she was angry, but he could see from the way she was tapping her foot that she was in no mood for compliments.

'Did you think to check with the nursing home? The one he said had him on its wait list?'

Bel appeared confused. 'No. I guess I didn't. He...' A strange look appeared in her eyes. 'You don't think he'd lie about something like that? No. Not even Pete would...' Her voice trailed away, then she asked, 'Did he say something to you?'

'Not exactly. No. Pete didn't.'

'Then what...?' Bel's eyes widened, realisation dawning. 'You didn't...?'

'*Mea culpa.* I was at a loose end and had the distinct impression your ex was lying about something. He's definitely a sick man, so he wasn't lying about that.' Matt took a deep breath. 'So I began to wonder about his story of being on a waiting list. He's found himself a comfortable spot here, and clearly resents my arrival. Was it just possible he intended to remain here until...' Matt met Bel's astonished eyes.

'What did you do?' Bel said, her voice full of tension.

Matt quailed. He hadn't expected this response. Though he wasn't quite sure what sort of response he had expected. He remained silent.

'What did you do?' Bel repeated in a louder voice. He could see her fingers gripping the stem of the glass tightly.

'I called them.'

'What? All of them? There must be...'

'A lot. It took me all day.'

'And what did this investigation of yours discover?'

'He was right. There are no vacancies.'

Bel seemed to relax.

'But neither did any of them have his name on any sort of list.'

Matt picked up his glass and took a gulp of wine, then cut a piece of camembert and placed it on a cracker. But, before he could take a bite, Bel spoke again.

'And what was Pete doing all this time?'

'For most of it he was asleep.'

'Have you spoken to him about it?'

'No.' Matt looked down at the table, and the uneaten cracker in his hand. 'I wanted to speak with you first.'

'Shit!' Bel's hand reached up to her forehead and she propped her head on it. 'What do you expect me to do?'

'One of them, in a place called Fairfield – nice name – has a potential vacancy so I put Pete's name down.'

'You did what?' Bel glared at Matt. 'How dare you take matters into your own hands, make decisions for Pete and me, act as if...'

'As if I'm your future partner?' Matt asked in a strained voice before carefully placing his glass on the table and walking back inside the house.

*

Bel heard the front door close. Matt had gone out. She let out a long sigh, picked up her glass and drained it. How had her life got into such a mess? How had she managed to provide house room to two men as different from each other as chalk and cheese? She shook her head in disbelief. Why had she ever succumbed to Pete's entreaties, believed his lies, knowing full well how often he'd lied to her in the past?

But that was *her* problem. It didn't excuse Matt. She ignored the small voice telling her Matt was only trying to help her. What he might see as help, she viewed as interference, as a sign that he didn't respect her judgement, that she couldn't make wise decisions, that... Thoughts were whirling around in her head. She picked lethargically at the biscuits and cheese still sitting there, but they tasted like dust. Bel pushed the platter away. She didn't feel hungry. She felt sick. She wanted... She didn't know what she wanted. She wished they'd all go away and leave her alone.

If only Aunt Isobel was still alive. Bel needed some of the old woman's sage advice. It would be so good to be able to share her misgivings; to hear Isobel's reassurance that it would all work out for the best in her forthright Scottish manner. Why, oh why, did her aunt have to die just as they were becoming friends?

'Anyone home?'

Bel started to get up, then sank down again. Maybe if she didn't speak, Celia wouldn't notice her. But the steps came closer, and soon Celia was standing in the doorway.

'Oh, there you are. Where's Matt – and Pete?' Celia gazed around as if expecting to see one or both of the men suddenly appear.

'I think Pete's in his room, and Matt left.' Bel couldn't help the note of despondence in her voice.

'Left?' Celia sat down opposite Bel and cut a piece of cheese. 'This looks nice. Did you...?'

'We had an argument,' Bel said shortly. 'I don't know... Oh, Celia, what am I going to do?'

'How about another glass of wine and... have you eaten?' She looked pointedly at the still full platter of cheese and biscuits.

'I'm not hungry. Did you have early dinner with Hannah and Chloe?'

'Yes. Chloe made a pasta dish. She's turning into a good little cook. But this is about you.'

She went back into the kitchen returning a few moments later with two brimming glasses of wine.

'Do you want to talk about it?'

'You don't want to hear all my troubles.'

'Well, you've heard all of mine, so maybe it's your turn to unburden yourself.'

Bel considered Celia's words for a moment. Maybe it would help to share the gist of her argument with Matt. Maybe Celia could examine it objectively. 'It's like this,' she began.

'So you see,' Bel finished. 'He acted as if…'

'As if he was concerned about you,' Celia finished. 'He did what any concerned partner would do. And that's what he is, isn't he? Your partner?'

Bel shifted uneasily in her chair. 'Well, I suppose. It's just that…'

'You've been on your own for so long and you hate it when anyone – Matt – tries to take over, to do what you know you should have done. And maybe when he questions your judgment?'

Bel bit the inside of her cheek to prevent the caustic reply that shot up. She recalled only too well, how, back in Scotland, she'd enjoyed being taken care of, welcomed Matt's concern. *What was different now? Was Celia right? Was Matt right? Was she, Bel, the one who had everything back-to-front? And where had Matt gone to? Had she ruined everything with her pig-headedness?*

Thirty-four

Matt was lying beside Bel when she awoke early next morning. She looked fondly at the familiar figure, relieved he'd returned at some stage during the night. But where else would he have gone? She slipped out of the room, showered and dressed and made her way to the kitchen which was deserted this morning.

After eating breakfast –orange juice and toast – she checked on the computer to see the results of Matt's endeavours the day before. It wasn't difficult. He was perhaps the most organised man she knew – probably a result of his legal background.

She scrolled through the recent documents. Yes, there was the spreadsheet of nursing homes listed alphabetically. Fairfield, she remembered. There was an asterisk beside one in that suburb. Bel was just jotting it down when Celia popped her head in.

'You made me think – what you said last night. And you were right. Matt was only trying to help me. It seems I'm a difficult person to help.' She saw Celia's mouth turn up in what looked like a smile. 'Well, I'm going to leave you on your own again today. I want to check out this nursing home he thinks he's found for Pete. It's way out in the western suburbs. How on earth he thinks…' She fell silent. Of course, if she was in Scotland she wouldn't be able to visit anyway. But would Matt still want her in Scotland after the way she'd behaved last night? And would she want to visit Pete, even if she was still in Sydney? Why on earth hadn't the bastard stayed in Melbourne? Why had he decided to come and disrupt her life?

*

'You're not booked into any nursing home, are you?' Bel had pushed open Pete's bedroom door. He was sitting on the bed, a folder open on his lap. 'You lied to me. You wanted me to take pity on you, to let you stay here till…' Her voice broke. She couldn't say the word.

'Well, well. So that's what he was up to – busy on your computer yesterday. I thought there was something up the way he shut it down when I looked in. And you'd rather believe *him*, I suppose.'

'It's true, isn't it? Just how sick are you?' Bel quivered. She could feel the heat flush through her body. *Matt had been right!*

'Yes, I'd hoped…' For an instant Bel saw another glimpse of the old Pete, the one she'd fallen in love with, then it was gone, and the cunning expression was back. 'But I'm a sick man. See here if you don't believe me.' He threw a sheaf of papers at Bel, the pages scattering around her feet.

She bent to pick them up.

'I suppose you're going to turf me out now,' he said, shuffling to the door and disappearing in the direction of the kitchen.

Bel sat down and leafed through the document. It appeared to be a medical assessment from a GP in Melbourne stating that the patient, Pete Sadler should be admitted to a nursing home or palliative care facility and detailing a list of medications.

She'd known. Of course, she had. Pete had told her that very first evening. But to see it written there in black and white brought home his mortality. Whatever, Pete had done in the past however she felt about him, Bel's eyes began to fill at this confirmation of his imminent death.

*

As she manoeuvered her way through the commuter traffic along Epping Road, Bel had time to reflect on exactly what Matt had done to provoke her anger. Finally, as she was driving along the M4 behind a line of trucks, she came to the conclusion that Matt was just being Matt – the Matt she'd fallen in love with. *She* was the problem. Since she'd returned to Sydney her life had been so beset with challenges, she'd lost sight of what it was she really wanted.

She'd become so involved with Pete, Celia, the issues with the sale of the shop and her house, that she'd all but forgotten why she'd returned, forgotten her promise to Matt, forgotten how safe and secure she'd felt in his arms, in his house. Suddenly she longed for his presence, for his home on the loch – the home that was her future. If she hadn't spoiled it all with her outburst the night before.

Bel stopped the car as she entered Fairfield. She had to decide what she'd say when she reached her destination. Thoughts of Matt filled her head, so much so that she took out her phone, ready to call him, to apologise. But, before she pressed the button, she thought better of it. No. She'd get this visit over first. Find out what the place was like. He might still be asleep anyway. Worse still, Pete might answer the phone. She tucked her mobile back into her bag and restarted the car.

There were gardens on either side of the driveway which led up to a small single level building surrounded by trees. This was Margaret Rose House, named after the late Princess Margaret, if the website was to be believed – a sign of the lingering love of royalty that still existed in many corners of Australia.

Bel parked in the visitors' car park and took a deep breath before getting out of the car. She looked around. It appeared peaceful. There was a low wall with the name *Margaret Rose House* etched in black and surrounded by carvings of roses. So far, so good. But it didn't hide the fact that this was a place people came to die. The list Matt had compiled included both nursing homes and palliative care centres. This was one of the latter.

Bel walked in to a deserted entrance hall. A bowl of roses sat on a low table filling the air with a delightful scent. There was a small bookshelf alongside several easy chairs and a box of children's toys. To one side was a reception desk, almost hidden behind a large vase of blue hydrangeas.

'Can I help you?'

Bel turned quickly as a young man in jeans and tee-shirt, his black hair standing up in spikes, appeared behind her.

'Sorry. Did I startle you?'

'I didn't hear you coming,' Bel looked down at his feet to see he was wearing a pair of black sneakers. 'You're...?'

'I'm Brad.' He held out a hand. 'I'm one of the nursing staff here. We choose not to wear uniforms to put our guests more at ease,' he explained, clearly seeing her looking askance at his outfit.

'Right.' This wasn't what she'd expected. If she'd had any expectation at all, it was that she'd find a dark, depressing building smelling of urine and disinfectant. This place was a pleasant surprise.

There was the sound of a throat being cleared, and Bel realised Brad was waiting for a response.

'I'm following up on a call we made yesterday.' Bel decided the small white lie was in order. 'About my... about Pete Sadler. I understand he's now on your waiting list and I wanted to have a look around.'

'Ah, you'll be Mrs Sadler. You need to speak with Arlene. I'll see if she's free.' He disappeared through a door Bel hadn't noticed before she could correct him. *Mrs Sadler*. It sounded strange. It was a long time since she'd been that.

Before long, a cheerful woman who looked to be in her forties and was wearing a multicoloured caftan bustled in.

'Mrs Sadler! Brad said you'd come to check us out.' She grinned. 'I'm sure your husband will be happy here. As I told your solicitor yesterday, we should have a place soon.' Her face softened. 'Well, you don't want to hear about that. Can I get you some tea? We just take a few guests at a time. We're a small facility, as you see, and we try to make it as much like home as possible.'

While she was talking, she led Bel to the armchairs and gestured for her to be seated. A few minutes later, Brad appeared with two mugs of tea. Bel accepted one in a trance. She had the distinct feeling she'd been taken over.

'I'm not...' she began.

'I know it's hard to let your loved one go,' Arlene said. 'But really it's for the best. It's good you've made the decision. Do you live close by?'

'No. I'm in Cremorne.'

'That's no distance really.' Arlene chatted on, giving Bel the history of the facility and describing the care Pete would receive when a place became available, scarcely drawing breath. Bel gave up trying to explain she was no longer Pete's wife and just nodded at what she deemed to be appropriate times, while sipping the welcome tea.

'Now,' Arlene said, when their mugs were empty, 'let me show you around.'

Bel rose and allowed herself to be given the guided tour – one which her companion was clearly accustomed to undertaking. The tour took them back to the front door, but not before Bel had been impressed by the layout and the homely nature of the rooms, each of which had its own theme which was reflected in the décor and colour schemes.

Bel left her details as the contact person, choosing not to respond to the surprised look on the matron's face when she gave her name as Bel Davison.

As a result of her earlier altercation with Pete, she was able to provide Pete's medical assessment and to complete most of the application form, but floundered a little when asked questions regarding Pete's medical insurance. She promised to email the details through later in the week, which meant another discussion with Pete that she wasn't looking forward to.

As she drove back across the city, Bel was filled with guilt. She'd been too quick to dismiss Matt's attempt to find a suitable venue for Pete to end his days. Her home was definitely not it. She'd never intended that it would be. But it seemed Matt was right in believing that Pete had other ideas. She couldn't wait to see Matt, to apologise for her anger, to make things right.

*

The sunlight was streaming through the window when Matt awoke. He cursed to himself, realising Bel must already have gone to work. Was she still angry with him? It had been well after midnight and she'd been sound asleep when he crept into bed somewhat the worse for drink. It wasn't like him to drown his sorrows, but Bel's unexpected reaction to his attempt to help her had knocked him for six. Maybe they didn't know each other as well as he'd thought. How well do we ever know another person?

He desperately needed to talk with her. As soon as he was dressed, he'd go to Isabella and try to set things straight. Hopefully, now she'd had time to reflect, he'd be able to make her see his point of view. If not… But he wouldn't let himself even consider that possibility.

Matt was fixing a quick coffee and checking his phone – maybe Bel had left a message – when Pete ambled into the kitchen and dropped into a chair. He looked terrible – as if he'd aged even more overnight.

'Should you be up, mate?' he asked, amused to hear himself using the Australian term but, before he heard Pete's mumbling reply, he noticed several missed calls on his phone. They weren't from Bel. They were from another number he knew by heart. His son, Duncan.

Pete tried to say something, but Matt held up a hand to silence him. 'Got to take this,' he said, pressing *voicemail*.

Matt's face blanched as he listened to his son's message. What the hell! How had he been so stupid as to leave his phone behind when he stormed out last night – and too drunk to check it when he returned? Elspeth was in hospital. Duncan had called to tell him, to entreat him to return. It appeared she'd begun to haemorrhage and had been rushed to hospital for an emergency hysterectomy. His baby. His little girl. Undergoing major surgery. He needed to be with her.

Pete was still muttering, but whatever he was saying fell on deaf ears. Matt dashed into the study and fired up Bel's laptop. Googling flights to Scotland – or any airport in the UK, Matt's pulse raced as he tried to book a flight, only steadying slightly when he managed to find a seat on one leaving early that afternoon. It wasn't a Glasgow flight – it was to Newcastle-upon-Tyne on Malaysian Airlines, but it would have to do. He could hire a car and drive up from there. The timing would be tight, but he could just make it.

'Gotta go,' he said in Pete's direction, not caring whether or not the man heard or understood.

He called a cab, dived into the bedroom and threw his belongings into the case he'd stowed away on his arrival. Back in the kitchen, he dashed off a brief note telling Bel of Elspeth's emergency surgery, explaining why he'd left, and giving details of his flight. He stuck it to the fridge using one of Bel's collection of magnets. He didn't take time to call Bel, planning to do so on the way to the airport, sure she'd understand, and confident she'd get his message.

Matt was on tenterhooks all the way to the airport. He wanted to speak with Duncan or Alasdair, find out more about Elspeth. How had the surgery gone? Was she okay? But it was after midnight over there and, hopefully, all was well and they'd all be asleep.

But he could call Bel. He took out his phone to make the call only to discover the battery was flat. He cursed himself again for his stupidity the night before. Not only had he failed to make things right with Bel, he'd forgotten to charge his phone, he'd missed the crucial calls from Scotland and now he was on his way home with no idea what he'd find waiting for him and no way of contacting anyone.

Thirty-five

There was no word from Matt all day. Bel was worried. She knew she could call him – *should* call him. But something held her back, perhaps a misplaced sense of pride. She knew she'd been in the wrong, but she'd been stunned by the way he'd stormed out. *Was this a side of Matt she could live with? With one failed marriage behind her, dare she risk her future with another? Was love enough? Was she really willing to change her lifestyle, give up everything she had here for this man she hardly knew?*

He hasn't asked you to marry him, she reminded herself. But Bel knew marriage was on the cards. They were both pretty conventional when it came to living together and, although it hadn't been put into as many words, Matt's repeated assurance that *Barkis is willing* was tantamount to a proposal of marriage.

'Shall I close up?' Celia's voice broke through Bel's thoughts, and she looked up from her computer to see the younger woman's face peering round the office door.

'Yes please. Will you be home for dinner tonight?'

'If it's okay with you?'

'Sure.' But Bel wasn't sure at all. She suffered from guilt feelings that, since Pete and Matt had arrived on the scene, she'd abandoned Celia who had responded by spending more and more time with her daughters.

'The girls are all going out tonight. Han and Ingrid have some do on, and Chloe is off to Jan's for dinner. I feel I've been monopolising them. Probably not a good idea. I need to make a life for myself.'

'No word from your solicitor?'

'Not yet.' Celia let out a sigh. 'It's a worry, but I guess I just need to be patient. What is it they say about a watched pot? I think the same can be said for any legal action. I'll see you at home then. I'll lock the door when I leave.'

'I won't be far behind you.' Bel returned to her computer to check the emails she hadn't made time for earlier in the day.

Most were spam which could quickly be deleted. She dealt with the others, printed out a couple of invoices, then noticed one from Miller's Realty. About time, she thought. She'd been waiting to hear from Rod ever since that viewing when she'd had Matt take Pete out of the way. She opened it warily, unsure how she'd handle another request to view the house. Pete seemed to be becoming less mobile each day, and it was a lot to ask Matt to take care of him yet again.

But it wasn't another request. It was an offer.

The couple had returned to Adelaide, discussed the house, talked with their bank and solicitor and made an offer. Bel took off her glasses and leant back in the chair. She wasn't sure how she felt. Relief? She supposed so. But it was so sudden, so unexpected. Though why unexpected she wasn't sure. The house was on the market. She'd wanted to sell it. Had she changed her mind?

No, not that. But she'd be sad to leave. That house had been her refuge, her bolt hole for so many years. It would be a wrench to leave it. And the thought of packing up everything was a nightmare.

Although she'd begun to sort through her belongings, she hadn't got very far. First Pete, then Matt had got in the way, and she'd been sailing along forgetting all about it. She looked at the offer again. It was a good one, and Rod was recommending she accept it. Well of course he would. That was his job.

Bel dithered. Should she try to negotiate, see if the couple would increase their offer? No, she decided, and typed Accept, pressing *send* before she could change her mind. That was one less thing to worry about. Now she just had to sort out Pete and apologise to Matt.

As she drove home Bel rehearsed what she would say. The traffic on Military Road was particularly heavy that evening, so she had plenty of time to consider her approach. By the time she parked in the driveway she thought she'd almost got it right, but as she stepped out of the car, she had a sour taste in her mouth and felt slightly dizzy.

Walking through the hall, she saw Celia sitting in the living room, her mobile to her ear. Seeing Bel, she paused her conversation. 'Pete's in his room,' she said. 'I don't know...'

Relieved, Bel dropped her bag. 'Matt!' she called, heading to the kitchen. It was empty. She poked her head outside. No sign of Matt. Bel went next into the bedroom. But he wasn't there either. Beginning to tremble, her eyes fell on the bedside table where Matt had taken to leaving his loose change, his spare glasses, the book he was reading. It was bare.

Bel stood in the middle of the room. What had happened? Where was Matt? Surely he hadn't been so upset with her, he'd left for good? She threw open the wardrobe door, to where only this morning, his shirts had hung alongside hers, his conservative beige pants and jeans hanging side by side with her more colourful ones. Now the empty hangers swung to and fro as if to mock her. Her hands went to her cheeks.

Nooo! Had she yelled out loud?

Maybe... Rushing out into the kitchen, Bel searched high and low with a sense of *déjà vu*. This couldn't be happening to her again. There must be a note. Matt wouldn't have left without some farewell or explanation. He wasn't that sort of man. Not like Pete.

At the thought of her ex-husband Bel whirled round and pushed open the door to Pete's bedroom. 'Where's Matt?' she demanded of the man in the bed, a newspaper lying open on his stomach.

Pete gave a sly smile. 'Not such a lover boy now, is he?'

Bel swallowed and tried to regain her composure. 'When did he leave? Did he say where he was going?'

'Why would he tell *me*?' Pete asked in his usual belligerent tone, though this time with a hint of malice. 'He left in a cab in the middle of the morning. Looked like he took all his stuff with him. Managed to scare him off, did you?' Pete closed his eyes, a smirk on his face.

Bel felt herself crumple. Matt had gone. He'd really gone – and without a word.

She walked back into the kitchen, collapsed onto a chair and dropped her head into her hands. She had only herself to blame. What had possessed her to become so annoyed with him?

Bel went back over her conversation with Matt, the words she'd spoken before he turned and left. Had she been too abrupt? Too demanding?

All he did was try to help. But he acted as if I wasn't capable of making my own decisions. He went ahead and did something I should have done. And for that, I blew him up as if he had no rights at all. As if he was a stranger. I acted as if he was a stranger, not the man I hope to marry!

'Are you thinking of dinner?' Celia stopped in her tracks at the sight of Bel's forlorn figure. 'What's the matter?' She moved closer and put a tentative hand on Bel's shoulder. 'Where's Matt?'

'Gone!' Bel roused herself from her stupor. 'I chased him away with my damned independence. He's cleared out. Pete saw him get into a cab. He's probably on his way back to Scotland by now.'

'That doesn't sound like Matt.' Celia's voice was reasonable as if trying to calm Bel. 'He must have left a note. Maybe something else happened. Did he and Pete have an argument?'

'No. It's all down to me. He stormed out when I had a go at him for checking out nursing homes for Pete.' Bel rubbed her forehead. 'I knew I shouldn't have believed the bastard when he said he was on a waiting list, but I wanted to. I wanted to believe he'd turned over a new leaf, that the man who'd left me all those years ago, really wanted to make amends. Having him here was my way of... Hell, I don't know what it was. And now look where it's got me!'

'He'll call,' Celia assured her. 'Matt's a decent guy. He may have had to leave in a hurry for some other reason. He may even have left a message with Pete?' She raised her eyebrows.

'Well, if he did, Pete's not saying. He's taking great delight in my being left in the lurch a second time.'

'Have you tried calling him?'

'No, I haven't, I...'

'Then do it now,' Celia said.

Bel looked at her concerned friend. *What if he answered and told her to go to hell. What then? What if...?*

'Stalling won't make it better. Please, Bel, give him a call.'

She was right, of course. Her hand trembled as she took her phone from her bag.

'I'll be outside,' Celia said but Bel held a hand up to stop her.

She pressed speed dial, brought the phone to her ear with her heart thumping. It went straight to voicemail.

Please leave a message…

Bel hung up. 'Voicemail,' she said.

'Then you can try again later,' Celia said, 'So, dinner?'

'I'm not hungry. I don't think I could stomach food right now.'

'Well there's no sense in sitting here feeling sorry for yourself.'

Bel raised her head to meet Celia's determined gaze.

'How about I boil an egg for his lordship, and you and I head out?'

'I couldn't ask you to do that,' Bel said, already regretting she'd fallen into the habit of cooking for Pete since he'd arrived. At first it had been easier to include him in their meals. Then, as he'd become weaker, he'd been eating in his room, his meals prepared separately and delivered by Bel. He really had been using her, Bel realised. But what else could she do? Once she'd agreed to have him here, she couldn't ignore him, leave him to fend for himself.

'You didn't ask me. I offered,' Celia said. 'Not that he deserves it. I do feel you've gone beyond the sense of duty where that one's concerned. I don't know if I could do the same for Bill if I were in your position.'

'It's surprising what we find ourselves doing. I never thought I'd give the man house room. Yet here we are. And he may have cost me my future – such as it was.'

While Celia organised Pete's meal, Bel tidied herself up. It felt strange to have the bedroom to herself again. In the short time Matt had been here, she'd become accustomed to his masculine presence. His scent was still on the pillows and in the bathroom, where the tang of his shaving foam still lingered, she could imagine he was standing behind her just as he used to, his arms around her, his face in her hair, his…

Stop! she told herself. He's gone. It wasn't meant to be. If one argument can scare him off, you've had a lucky escape.

But she couldn't quite believe that of Matt. Not of the man she'd known in Scotland, the man her Aunt Isobel had put her faith in, had encouraged Bel to fall in love with.

Putting her confused thoughts aside, Bel joined Celia and the pair spent the evening at a local bistro where Bel was persuaded to nibble on an omelette and drink a glass of wine.

'Feel better now?' Celia asked, as they finished their meal with two cappuccinos.

'A bit,' Bel acknowledged. 'Though I still don't understand.' She furrowed her brow. 'Oh, let's go home. Tomorrow is another day.'

Thirty-six

Matt drove the hire car out of Newcastle airport into driving rain which turned to sleet as he headed north. The windscreen wipers were making little headway and, given the number of trucks on the road, Matt knew he should take a break. It could be a three-hour trip, but he'd decided to try to shave off some time by taking the A74. That may have been a mistake.

He'd called Duncan from London where they'd had a layover and he'd managed to charge his phone. He'd been able to discover Elspeth's surgery was over and she was back in the ward but still drowsy. He'd tried to call Bel too, but there had been no reply and he'd hung up, frustrated.

Matt hadn't taken time for anything to eat or drink before setting off, had just passed Carlisle and was beginning to feel weary when the sign to *Welcome Break Gretna* loomed up. He gratefully took the exit ramp, parked the car, leant back and closed his eyes. He was exhausted.

He hadn't got much sleep on the plane crowded with expats travelling home to the UK for Christmas – a reminder, if he needed one, that the day he'd planned to spend with Bel wasn't far away. And the layovers at KL and London had been too short to do anything but pace around, worried about what was happening in Glasgow and Sydney. He'd tried to call Bel again when they landed at Newcastle, but again there was no reply. That stunned him as it was early evening there, and she should have been having dinner around then.

Half an hour later, sustained by a strong coffee and with a ham and cheese sandwich under his belt, Matt set off again. As he sped up the motorway his thoughts returned to Bel. He was filled with regret at his hasty action. He didn't know what had got into him. He wasn't usually so quick to anger. There was a dull ache in his chest as he remembered how he'd strode out. That was Bel's last memory of him. He wouldn't blame her if she didn't want to speak with him.

But Matt knew he couldn't leave it like that. He had to contact her, talk with her, explain, and beg her forgiveness. It would be the middle of the night back in Sydney by the time he reached Glasgow, but he could call in her early morning. Surely he'd be able to reach her then?

He allowed his thoughts to wander. Hopefully, Elspeth would make a speedy recovery, Bel would see sense and follow him to Scotland and they could have the family Christmas he'd planned. He was glad he and Elspeth had settled their differences before he'd left. But it was bad it had come to this. Although her mother had experienced the same early symptoms, her surgery hadn't been classed as an emergency and had gone well. He consoled himself with the thought that it was a fairly routine procedure – he'd googled it during his four hours at KL, when he'd found it difficult to rest or concentrate on the thriller he'd bought at the airport.

He considered emailing Bel while he was logged in, then decided he'd be better calling when he was back home and had some news. At this point there was nothing to add to the message he'd left.

Finally, Matt reached the outskirts of Glasgow and, twenty minutes later, breathed a sigh of relief when he entered the multi-storey hospital car park. He texted Duncan to let him know he was on his way, wishing he could buy flowers for Elspeth, but he seemed to remember some controversy about bedside flowers. There would be time enough when she was home, and they could spoil her.

He checked his phone as he entered the main building. There was no reply from his son, but he was able to find the ward number on an earlier message and followed the signs. As he inhaled the unique smell of the hospital, he was reminded of visiting his dad here just before he died. It wasn't a pleasant memory. Bob had lingered for weeks before finally succumbing to the cancer.

Matt was out of breath by the time he reached the corridor and was carefully checking the ward numbers when he saw a huddle of people standing by a doorway. Alasdair's familiar bulk loomed over the other couple who were surely Duncan and Kirsty. But what were they doing standing out here? Why weren't they at Elspeth's bedside?

Matt quickened his pace. As he drew closer, he could see Kirsty's arms around Alasdair's shoulders which were shaking. The loud sound of men weeping met his ears.

No! It couldn't be... Elspeth couldn't be... Matt couldn't even think the word, never mind say it. But when he reached the group, their faces told the story. His beloved daughter had gone; Elspeth was dead.

A ragged wail rent the air and Matt looked around in anguish before realising it came from him.

'She's gone, Dad.' Duncan came towards Matt and enveloped him in a warm hug. 'Our Elspeth... my sister... she left us.' He sobbed, his face wet with tears just as Matt knew his own face must be. He knuckled them away and turned to face Alasdair who seemed to have aged in the time since Matt had last seen him.

'But what? How?'

'They said the surgery went fine,' Alasdair spoke through his tears. 'Then...' He seemed unable to say more.

'There were blood clots – a pulmonary embolism,' Kirsty interrupted. 'They couldn't save her.'

Matt felt his body sag. It was as if he'd suddenly taken on a heavy load and had no way of shifting it. 'The children – Robbie and Fi?' Hell, what would it do to them? To lose their mother? And Fi? She depended on Elspeth for so much.

It was Alasdair who spoke. 'They're with my parents. Hell, how do I tell them?' He looked wildly around as if the answer was hidden somewhere in the air of the sterile hospital corridor. 'I... I can't...' He broke down.

Matt put an arm round Alasdair's shoulder, Duncan joined the pair and the three men shared their grief. They'd all loved Elspeth in their different ways. For Alasdair she was a beloved wife and mother of their children, the girl he'd fallen in love with when they were both students; for Duncan the older sister he'd teased and been bossed around by, and for Matt, a treasured though sometimes infuriating daughter, an ongoing reminder of the wife who'd left them, also too soon.

When they broke apart, all three men still had tears in their eyes and could barely speak. It was left to Kirsty to say, 'We can't do any more here, and the children should be told.'

Alasdair nodded absently.

'Would you like me to come with you?' Matt asked. He didn't relish the task any more than he imagined Alasdair did, but the thought of his two grandchildren being told they'd never see their mother again was like a shard of glass in his heart. He'd have done anything to spare them the hurt.

Thirty-seven

There was a loud groan from the room Pete had made his own.

What now? Bel opened the door and peered in, but the figure in the bed had his back to her and didn't stir. She closed the door gently and left, planning to take in his breakfast when she and Celia had eaten theirs.

'Thanks for last night,' she said, when Celia appeared, immaculate as usual. 'I did need to get out of the house.'

'Did you sleep?'

'Not a lot.' Bel wouldn't admit to the number of times she'd turned over expecting to find Matt's warm body, only to have her hand touch an empty space. She'd buried her face in his pillow inhaling the remaining scent of the man she missed so much it hurt.

At that moment the phone rang, and Pete lumbered into the room, staggering from side to side in what seemed like a drunken torpor, though Bel knew he hadn't touched a drop of alcohol since he'd arrived. She tried to help him into a chair and answer the phone at the same time – not an easy feat.

'Hello? Yes, this is Bel Davison. I'm sorry. Who did you say you are?'

Bel listened intently, taking a few seconds to recognise the name of the matron at Margaret Rose House, then a few more to grasp what she was telling her.

'A place has come available. Your... Pete Sadler is top of our list. He would need to take it in two days' time. Do you wish to take it up?'

Bel shot a glance at Pete who was leaning heavily on the table and seemed to be trying to catch his breath. How was he going to take this? 'Yes, please. Can I get back to you with the arrangements?' She listened while the other explained that they'd need details of Pete's medical insurance and how he – or Bel – intended to pay, then hung up.

'Good news?' asked Celia.

'Mmm. Tell you later. Now, Pete,' she said to the man still breathing heavily, 'Don't you think you'd be better in bed? I can bring you in some breakfast. Can you help me, Celia?'

The two women manhandled Pete back to bed.

When they returned to the kitchen, Celia gave Bel a questioning look.

'It was Margaret Rose House – the place I visited in Fairfield, the one Matt found.' She grimaced at the irony of this. 'They have a place for Pete.'

'That's good, isn't it?'

'Good for me, yes. But how am I going to tell Pete? How can I convince him it's the right thing to do?'

*

Two days later, after much mumbling and grumbling on Pete's part, Bel drove him to the hospice where he'd spend his final days. It had taken a long discussion before he'd agreed to the move, and Bel was forced to entertain the thought that he'd continue to refuse. But, finally, when she reminded him the house had been sold, he'd reluctantly produced details of his private medical insurance and waved away any suggestion he might need financial assistance.

'I've a good bit put by,' he'd said, 'And, as I told you, what's left will go to you when my time's up. Though, I'd thought I'd see out my last days here with you. Still,' he added, with a touch of his old humour, 'I can see I'm not wanted here with you and Celia. I'm the thorn between two roses.' He tried to laugh but ended up almost choking.

'Is this it?' Pete shifted in his seat and peered out the window. 'Margaret Rose House. That's a pretty fancy name for a place people come to die.'

Bel forced her face into a smile. 'Ready?'

'As I'll ever be. I suppose you're glad to get rid of me – you and that woman you've got living with you?'

Bel tightened her lips and remained silent. Would Pete never give up baiting her? His initial attempt at being nice had soon deteriorated into his customary belligerence. She sighed inwardly. Despite her guilt feelings, she *would* be glad to be rid of his negative presence in her house.

They were greeted by the same Brad Bel had met on her earlier visit, and the male presence seemed to reassure Pete, as did the pleasant surrounds. The room they were shown to was decorated in a subtle mix of blues and browns and Bel noted that Pete sank gratefully into the easy chair in front of a long window.

She stood and gazed out at the lush gardens, while Brad explained to Pete how the house operated and booked him an appointment with their consulting medico the following day.

His part over, Brad left and, as Bel turned to go too, Pete stretched out a hand towards her. 'Bella. You've been good to me. I knew it couldn't last, but I'd hoped... Can I ask one more thing of you?' he pleaded, his eyes watering.

Bel stopped in her tracks. Surely she'd done enough? What more could he want?

'Will you visit me? We had some good times, didn't we? Before I ruined it all. You've always been the only one for me, Bella. Please? Can you satisfy the wish of a dying man?'

'You're asking a lot, but...' Bel hesitated. What harm would it do? She knew he hadn't long to live. 'Okay.' She took the hand that was offered, stunned at how skeletal it had become. There was barely any flesh on it. How had she not noticed?

*

Back home, Bel felt restless and decided to strip the bed Pete had been using and to remove all signs of his presence. He'd caused so much trouble, she wished she'd never let him move in, wished she'd never agreed to meet with him at all. That's when all the trouble had started, when Matt had become jealous and decided to come to Sydney.

Bel was feeling angry with herself as much as with Pete as she pulled the sheets and pillow-cases off the bed and dumped them into the washing machine. She returned with the vacuum and, as she manoeuvered it around the bed, a piece of paper fluttered to the floor. Bel stopped and picked it up. She was about to throw it into the wastepaper basket, when she caught sight of her name written on it.

Turning off the vacuum, she looked at the paper more closely. That was Matt's handwriting! Her heart in her mouth, she opened the folded scrap of paper. It was creased and torn on one end as if it had been scrunched up and thrown away. She read Matt's words quickly, then read them a second time.

Bel's hand shook. Matt hadn't abandoned her. He had left a note. And… Pete must have taken it. The bastard! He could rot in hell for all she cared.

But that was days ago. Why hadn't Matt called? He'd have reached Glasgow by now. She read it again. It was his daughter. Elspeth had been taken to hospital. He said he'd call as soon as he could. But he hadn't.

*

'So I agreed I'd visit him,' Bel said to Celia when they were settled in the courtyard. Dinner was over, and they were enjoying a chilled glass of wine, the cool evening air wafting around them and the gentle sounds of music flowing across from the neighbouring house. 'I felt sorry for him. Lou would say I'm too soft. I guess that's what got me into this mess in the first place. Now I wish I hadn't.'

'Maybe, or maybe you were just doing your civic duty. I'd like to think I'd do the same, but I don't think I have your generous spirit. I've heard from Bob Frazer again, by the way. So maybe I can have *my* mess fixed up soon too and get out of your hair.'

'You know I'm happy to have you here. Though, now the place is sold…'

'The house is sold, Pete is taken care of. Now you need to make things up with Matt – eat humble pie and admit he was right. What did his note say?'

'His daughter – Elspeth – was taken into hospital, emergency surgery. He needed to be with her. I understand all that. But I don't understand…'

Now she'd read his note, it rankled that she still hadn't heard from him. 'No, you're right. I should…' Bel knew one of them had to make the first move.

'Why don't you try ringing him again?'

'Now?'

'No time like the present.'

Bel checked her watch. It would be between twelve and one there. Matt would probably be sitting down to lunch. She pictured him, sitting in that warm room, a weak winter sun shining in through the glass, Hamish at his feet, and an ache of longing welled up in her almost forcing her to cry out in anguish.

Clearly sensing Bel's mood, Celia rose. 'I'll leave you to it.'

Left alone, Bel poured out another glass and took a sip before pressing Matt's number.

She sat patiently while the call was routed through to Scotland, then a warm glow enveloped her as the familiar voice sounded in her ear.

'Matt Reid.'

'Matt. It's me.'

There was silence, then the sound of the connection being cut.

Thirty-eight

Matt looked at the phone in his hand as if he'd never seen it before, his thumb still firmly on the off button. His hand had moved faster than his mind.

Bel!

He couldn't speak to her now. They'd just had Elspeth's funeral, and the family had come back to her house – Alasdair's house now – to do whatever one did. He knew he should have called Bel before now, told her about Elspeth's death, but there was a part of him that felt guilty he'd been with her when Elspeth was dying.

Matt should have been *here*, not on some stupid imagined jealousy trip. He should have been here to say goodbye to his darling Elspeth and, although he knew it was crazy, a part of him blamed Bel. If she hadn't invited Pete Sadler to move in with her, Matt *would* have been here, not on the other side of the world.

His gaze moved from the device in his hand to the rest of the room. It appeared alien to him, filled as it was with a host of friends and neighbours – all here to commiserate about Elspeth's death or celebrate her life as the minister had said during the service. Matt didn't find any cause for celebration in the loss of a cherished daughter, wife, sister and mother.

He'd helped Alasdair sort through photographs to select those most appropriate to be shown on a large screen during the service. But when they'd flashed up, he could barely look at them.

Goodness knows how Fi and Robbie had coped. They'd insisted

on being present to farewell their mother and, surprisingly, Fi had taken her death better than Robbie. She'd quietly said, 'She'll be with Grandma now, won't she? They'll both be looking down on us.' The tough, often arrogant, Robbie had gone quiet. It was impossible to know what he was thinking as he'd brushed away all attempts to offer sympathy or to distract him.

Matt worried about the boy, but Fi assured everyone he just needed time, and that he'd come out of it when he was ready. How had she become so mature and sensible? It was a testament to her mother's refusal to allow the young girl to dwell on her own disability. It seemed to have given her not only an inner fortitude, but an uncanny insight into the minds of others – not least her brother.

'It's a sad day.' Alasdair's father, a large white-haired man who was more at home on the golf course than in a living room, approached Matt, a glass of whisky in one hand a bottle in the other. 'A refill?'

Matt looked down and realised he was holding an empty glass. He had no recollection of having drunk its contents. 'No thanks.' He had to get out of here. The atmosphere in the room – in the house – was stifling him.

He threw on his coat and walked out into the garden. It was a cloudy day. Snow had fallen overnight and left a scattering of white patches on the grass and on the leaves of the shrubs, the shrubs Elspeth had planted with such pleasure the previous spring. There had been snow on the ground at the cemetery too, leading Matt to wonder how difficult a job the gravediggers had had, even as he'd flinched from the thought of the clods of earth that would soon cover his daughter.

The image of Elspeth's face floated into Matt's consciousness, and he felt her presence as clearly as if she was standing in front of him. He could almost hear her voice telling him that Fi would be right, and asking him to keep a close eye on Alasdair and Robbie for her.

*

It amazed Matt how quickly everyone else seemed to be ready to return to some semblance of normal. Kirsty had promised to drop in to see Alasdair most days. Fi and Robbie had returned to school despite the suggestion that it was so close to Christmas they could take an early holiday. 'Mum would want us to keep going,' Fi had insisted, and untypically Robbie had gone along with her.

Alasdair himself had been back at the office the day after the funeral, his excuse being that he needed to keep busy, to have something to fill his mind other than his loss. Seeing how lost he was without Elspeth, Matt was filled with guilt for his earlier suspicions of his son-in-law, who was now obviously wracked with grief.

Matt had offered to help with Fi and Robbie, given they'd managed so well for the week he'd had them stay. Alasdair had refused politely, but firmly. He wanted to start as he meant to go on, he said, and if he needed help he was perfectly able to pay for it. Although he knew it was partly the grief talking, Matt was hurt.

It was Sunday, and Alasdair had agreed to bring the two children over for lunch. Duncan and Kirsty were coming too with Jamie. As Matt struggled with preparing the roast he was determined to cook, he reflected how it had taken Elspeth's death to bring the family together again for Sunday lunch – the tradition which had disappeared when her mother died.

Lunch was a sombre affair, everyone conscious of the empty chair. Even though they'd spread out around the table, it was clear to Matt that Elspeth was on everyone's mind.

'Grandad.' Fi followed Matt when he went out to the courtyard after lunch, wheeling her chair through the French windows and across the pavers with her usual dexterity, and managing to avoid Hamish who scampered out of her way. The serious expression on her face told Matt she had something serious to say.

'Yes, sweetheart?' Matt took a seat, his eyes now level with the little girl's.

'Two things.' Her pretty face was solemn, the slight frown between her eyes only serving to emphasise the gravity of what she had to say.

Matt wondered what was coming, but prepared to listen intently. Fi was an intelligent child, who often took things to heart, but who sometimes could be very insightful.

'Firstly,' she said, tapping one finger. 'Dad needs help. I know Aunt Kirsty drops in, but she has her own family to take care of.' She paused. 'And Gran Pauline comes too. But…' She bit her lip. 'She isn't a big help to me. She does her best, but she doesn't do things the way Mum did.'

Matt stifled a smile. Alasdair's mother was well-meaning, but she did have her own way of doing things and could never fill Elspeth's shoes.

'So what do you suggest?' Matt knew Fi would have a solution.

'I think Dad should get someone to live in the house. One of the girls in my class told me they have a French girl who looks after them. We could have one of those, then Dad wouldn't have to worry. She could take me to school, do the cooking and cleaning. It would be just like it used to be, except...' Her bottom lip trembled.

'No one could take your mum's place.'

'I know that! So will you talk to Dad?'

Matt promised, though he doubted Alasdair would be open to bringing a stranger into the house so soon. But it did present a possible solution. Fi was right. It would have been difficult enough for Alasdair to cope with two able-bodied children, and Fi did need extra help.

'And the other thing?'

Fi threw him a sideways glance before speaking.

'What happened to that nice lady? The one from Australia? Mum didn't like her, did she?'

Out of the mouths of babes.

'Your mum was still missing *her* mum and she felt...'

'But *you* liked her, didn't you?'

Damn Fi's perceptiveness. And today of all days.

'Yes, I did. I do. But Bel's back in Australia now and...'

'Is that where you went before Mum got sick? She wouldn't tell us where you'd gone, but *I* told Robbie...'

Damn the child. Did she have second sight?

'Yes, I did. I went to visit Bel in Sydney.'

'Why didn't you bring her back with you? Was it because Mum didn't want you to? I thought she was coming for Christmas.'

How to answer that one? Fi was leaning forward, her head tilted to one side. For her it was a simple matter of liking or disliking. If only adult relationships were that straightforward.

Matt took a deep breath. 'I came back because Mum was sick. Bel... she was busy.' But Fi's question reminded him of the call he'd quickly cancelled. He should talk to Bel. She deserved an explanation. It wasn't fair to have left her without one. But now wasn't the right time. He wasn't sure when that time would be. He had to get over that niggle of blame that marred the memory of his trip to Australia, to adjust to a life without Elspeth in it, then he could consider his own future. Whether or not it could include Bel was now in the lap of the Gods.

Thirty-nine

Celia was already eating breakfast when Bel walked into the kitchen. She'd barely slept a wink. The sound of Matt ending the call reverberated in her head, making sleep impossible. How could she have so misjudged him?

'There's fresh coffee. You look as if you need it.' Celia paused, coffee cup half-way to her mouth.

'Thanks. Just what I want to hear.' Bel helped herself to a cup and slid a slice of bread into the toaster. She didn't know if she could stomach anything, but she'd try.

'Did you call?'

Bel extricated the toast, dropped it onto a plate and took a seat. 'He hung up on me.'

'What? But he said something first. Did you argue? Did you tell him…?'

'He hung up as soon as he heard my voice. I don't want to talk about it.'

Bel picked up a knife and began to spread vegemite on the toast as if her life depended on it.

'I thought you didn't like vegemite?' Celia asked.

Bel looked askance at what she was doing. She must be more distraught than she'd thought. Celia was right. Bel had never managed to develop a taste for this Australian icon. It wasn't Celia's favourite spread either. It had been Pete who'd demanded they add it to the shopping list, and Matt had tried it once before stating it wasn't a patch on Marmite.

Bel pushed the plate aside. 'I wasn't hungry anyway.' She gazed across the kitchen, out to the courtyard where she and Matt had loved to sit. She was aware of Celia speaking.

'What did you say?'

Celia fiddled with her phone. 'I've had a message from Bob Frazer. He wants to see me today if possible. He's heard back from Bill's solicitor.'

The words gradually permeated through the fog that was Bel's brain. 'Of course. You must go.'

'He wants to get everything settled by Christmas.'

Christmas! It would be Christmas in only two weeks. The Christmas she was to spend with Matt. The Christmas that was to be the beginning of their life together. Not anymore. Bel's stomach lurched. What was she to do? The house had sold. Come the New Year, she'd have to find somewhere else to live. She couldn't even think about that right now. Everyone else was getting settled. Pete was in the hospice, Celia was meeting with her solicitor. And Bel's life was descending into chaos.

'When does he want to see you?' she asked.

'He's suggested four. Would that work for you?'

'Fine.' It really didn't matter to Bel when Celia went into the city, but late afternoon would be good. It meant she'd be there for the busiest part of the day. Their regular clients tended to arrive mid-morning, before lunching with friends. These days they were keen to purchase new outfits for the festive season or suitable for beach holidays.

*

After Celia left for her appointment, Bel stood in the middle of the shop and looked around. Now she'd be staying in Sydney, there would be no need to sell. Part of her was glad about that. But another part – a small voice – whispered to her, asked her if this was really what she wanted to do for the rest of her life. She wasn't sure. Before going to Scotland, it had never occurred to her that her life could be any different from what it was. She'd become an independent business-woman, built her boutique up from scratch, developed a group of friends, a pleasant lifestyle. She'd been happy.

So why did she now feel so discontented? Why did she hanker for something more? What was it about Scotland and her meeting with Matt Reid that had unsettled her, made her dissatisfied with her life?

With a sigh, Bel opened the computer to the Qantas site and found her flight booking. There'd be no need for that now. Clenching her jaw, and stemming the tears which threatened to engulf her, she cancelled the flight, and with it her hopes for the future, for a fresh start with the man she'd thought was her soulmate.

Bel was still feeling low when Lou breezed into the shop at closing time.

'I haven't seen you in an age,' she said. 'Can you join me for dinner? I thought we might go to The Oaks again.'

Bel was about to refuse, when she considered the alternative. Celia had said she'd go straight to Hannah's from the city as the girls would want to know what Bob recommended – what Bill was offering. Returning to an empty house wasn't an attractive prospect. She didn't know why. She'd lived alone for years – enjoyed the solitude, enjoyed being in control.

But lately – since Celia had moved in, then Pete, then Matt – she'd enjoyed the company.

'Okay. I'll just finish up here. Won't be long.'

'I'll browse while I wait. Might find something I like.'

Bel grinned. Lou's taste and hers differed so much. Her friend had never purchased one garment from Isabella, always telling Bel they were too smart, too chic, or too expensive. Instead she favoured what she called the casual look which meant loose caftans, jeans and tee-shirts that hid her shape completely.

They drove along to Neutral Bay in Lou's car, finding a parking spot not far from the hotel. It was a balmy summer evening and a pleasant walk to the courtyard which was already filled with a noisy crowd.

'They must be celebrating Christmas already,' Lou said as they squeezed into one of the last empty tables between large groups enjoying bottles of champagne and exchanging gifts.

There it was again – Christmas. Bel recoiled from the word as if she'd been stung.

'What's up? Weren't you supposed to be in Scotland by now? I wondered why you hadn't been in touch. Last I heard you'd taken pity on that poor sod, Pete, and your he-man had arrived to whisk you off back to Bonnie Scotland.'

'About that... I'm not going.' Her stomach lurched. She felt slightly sick. The next day was the fifteenth of December – the day she should have been on her way to Scotland.

'What?' Lou's voice rose to a crescendo making the group at the next table turn around. 'This needs a drink. I'll be back. Don't move.'

She rose and made her way to the bar. Bel had no intention of moving but sighed at the thought of having to relay the news of Matt's defection to her friend. She could imagine her response.

Bel was right. Two glasses of Chardonnay later, she finished her sad tale.

'I told you so,' Lou said. 'Never trust a man. But you thought you knew better. Huh!'

Their meals arrived at that point, and Bel discovered she was hungry after all. She remembered throwing away her toast at breakfast and skipping lunch. As she cut into the steak Lou had ordered without asking, she hoped her friend had finished dishing out her advice.

'So,' Lou continued. 'You've sold your house, you have your baby on the market and you're not going anywhere? That's a fine howdy-do.'

Bel almost smiled. Trust Lou to find something amusing in her situation. Despite her habitual distrust of men, Lou was a good friend and could always be counted on to find humour in the most bizarre circumstances. But this circumstance was Bel's, and there was nothing funny about having her life turned upside down.

'I can take Isabella off the market,' she said, chasing a cherry tomato around the plate. 'But...' she hesitated, 'I'm not sure I want to.'

Lou stopped eating. Her eyes widened. 'You don't? What will you do?'

'I don't know.' Bel tried to make sense of her thoughts. 'Maybe this is a wake-up call or something. Oh, call me daft. You're the one who usually talks of signs and portents. But...'

'You can always stay at my place while you sort yourself out.'

'Thanks.' Bel was grateful for the offer, but the thought of camping out on Lou's sofa had little appeal. Her friend lived frugally in a one-bedroom unit in North Sydney. It wasn't designed for guests.

'Will you retire?'

Retire? It had a sort of final note to it. Bel supposed she was the age many people did retire. But, without Isabella, what would she do? How would she fill her days? After the debacle with Matt, she needed more to do, not less. 'Probably not. What would I do with myself?' she asked, unconsciously echoing Lou's sentiments. 'Anyway, it's not something I have to worry about right now.'

But Bel knew it was something she'd need to consider pretty soon.

*

Bel had just arrived home when Celia burst in. The previously distraught woman appeared to have found a new lease of life. She was glowing with a barely suppressed excitement.

'Good news?' Bel guessed. She could certainly do with some. Dinner with Lou had been completely unsatisfactory, with her friend repeating all the reasons why she'd never put her trust in a man and assuring Bel she'd been lucky.

It wasn't what Bel wanted to hear. Despite Matt's curt response to her, she still harboured feelings for him, and a tiny part of her still wondered if perhaps he had a good reason for his behaviour. But she'd never know.

'You'll never guess?' Celia trilled. 'I thank my lucky stars Jan put me onto her brother. The man's a miracle worker.'

Bel burst out laughing. This was so at odds with what she'd been listening to all evening. 'I'm glad *one* man is able to do the right thing,' she said. 'He got a result for you then?'

'And what a result. I never imagined…' Celia dropped her bag on the floor. 'You'll never guess how much he's managed to get for me? Of course, I'll have to come to the party with media appearances and such, but I think it'll be worth it. Han and Chloe think so too. I can't believe it.'

'How much?'

'Five hundred thousand. It's enough to… I don't know. Certainly enough for me to find a flat and to keep me going for a while. What do you think?'

Bel remained silent, but her mind was going round in circles. Five hundred thousand was the price the broker had put on Isabella.

Forty

It didn't seem like Christmas. The day Matt had planned to be one of celebration, when Bel would be introduced to the family as his new partner, passed like any other since his daughter's death. The only concession to the season was a Christmas tree which sat in the corner of the room as if accusing Matt of not grieving sufficiently. It was there at the urging of Fi and Robbie who'd demanded its traditional presence as being 'what Mum would have wanted.'

Matt wasn't too sure about that, but had succumbed to their pleading, and there it sat, the star on the top of the tree a reminder of other Christmases before the family had become fragmented.

How did you grieve for a daughter gone too soon? Matt was at a loss. He found himself wandering around the house, Hamish at his heels, unable to sit still, unable to do anything.

There would be no celebration here this year.

Matt had driven into Glasgow and delivered gifts to Fi and Robbie on Christmas Eve. The children had been subdued, missing Elspeth who'd always made a big thing of the celebration. He intended joining them at the Christmas Eve carol service, but couldn't face it, citing the threat of snow and the need to get home as his reason for declining.

Now it was Christmas morning and Kirsty was preparing a Christmas lunch for the family. Matt dressed slowly, knowing Elspeth would be missed even more today. It had been the same when Ailsa died. For the first few Christmases, all he'd wanted to do was lie in bed, cover up his head and wait for the day to be over. It had been Elspeth who'd brought him out of it then. He had to think of her, what she'd want. And she'd want everything to go on as usual for the sake of the children. But it wasn't usual. How could it be when there was a gaping hole at the table where she should have been?

'Dad.' Duncan hugged Matt as he shook the snow off his coat and stamped his feet before entering the house. 'Good to see you. Can I get you a drink?' He led Matt into the large living room where Alasdair was standing, his back to the fire, hands behind his back, and the three children were engaged in a board game in the far corner. The room was so quiet Matt could hear the clock ticking.

'Thanks, son,' he said, and went over to clasp Alasdair on the shoulder. 'How are you? Getting much sleep?'

'Not really,' Alasdair's red-rimmed eyes focussed on Matt. 'It doesn't seem to get any better. And at this time of year…' He shook his head. 'Why her? The surgeon said they do these ops every day. Why did Elspeth have to be the one to go?' His voice broke, and he turned away.

'Here, Alasdair. Have another.' Duncan offered his brother-in-law a glass of whisky, but he shook his head.

'I'm driving.'

'Yours, Dad.' Matt accepted the crystal glass of tawny liquid. He was driving too, but not till later and he'd need something to help him through this day. 'You can always bunk down here, Dad,' Duncan said as if reading Matt's mind.

The silence hung in the room like a living thing. Duncan cleared his throat. 'How're you coping, Al? And the kids?' He nodded to where the trio were vying with each other at the Scrabble board.

'Oh, you know,' Alasdair said, a faraway look in his eyes. 'One day at a time. Fi's been a wee trouper. She had this idea we need to get an *au pair*. Can you imagine?' He essayed a laugh, but it came out as a croak.

So Fi had taken the bit into her teeth. Matt had delayed acting on her request till at least Christmas was over.

'She mentioned it to me too – that Sunday you all came to lunch. It might not be a bad idea.'

'A stranger in our house? What would Elspeth say?' Then Alasdair's eyes hooded over in recognition that Elspeth would never say anything again. 'We're managing just fine.'

But the talk of an *au pair* and Fi, reminded Matt of the other thing

Fi had spoken about – Bel. She should have been here with them, today of all days. That had been the plan. She'd promised, had her ticket booked, and he'd let her down.

They were interrupted by Kirsty appearing to hustle them all into the dining room where the table was groaning under the load of all the usual festive fare. There was the turkey with stuffing, roast potatoes and vegetables, small chipolatas wrapped in bacon, and a platter of sliced ham. She'd refused to give in to the mood of the group, perhaps in the hope she could shake them out of their grief, even if only for one day or one meal.

Despite downing a couple of whiskies along with several glasses of good red wine with lunch, Matt decided to set off for home. A short nap and a strong mug of coffee convinced him he was safe to drive, so he left the city with lots of hugs and urgings to drive carefully.

Snow continued to fall as he sped up the A82, the white flakes flurrying across the windscreen and hindering visibility. Matt cursed as he slowed to a snail's pace and concentrated on the road ahead.

Despite the annoyance, there was something beautiful about the world encased in a white wonderland. Tree branches were patterned with a delicate tracery of white, while the road itself was a pristine carpet in the sections untouched by vehicles, compared to the brown slush from the tyre treads. But Matt couldn't wait to get home where Hamish would be waiting impatiently for his return.

It had been a difficult day. They'd all tried their best to be cheerful for the sake of the children, but even *they* had been much more subdued than usual. Matt gave a sigh of relief when he finally turned into his driveway, glad he'd had the foresight to leave a light on outside the door. He battled his way through the icy blast and closed the heavy door behind him.

As anticipated, his little dog was delighted to see him and leapt up on Matt's legs before he could remove his coat.

'I'm pleased to see you too, Hamish, but would you let a man get in before you start your mithering?'

Once he'd fed his pet and made sure he had enough water, Matt poured himself a glass of whisky, settled down in his favourite chair, and picked up the copy of Ian Rankin's latest book he'd been given for Christmas. But today, the exploits of his beloved Rebus failed to retain his interest. The book dropped to his lap as the image of Bel forced itself between him and the pages. He couldn't put her out of his mind.

He shouldn't be sitting here all alone on Christmas night. Bel should be seated opposite, a glass of wine in her hand, a loving smile on her face. They should be toasting the beginning of their new life together. They even had Elspeth's blessing.

He remembered his son-in-law's words. Just before he left the family gathering, Alasdair had taken him aside.

'A word, Dad.'

Matt had looked at him askance, before the younger man had continued. 'It may be water under the bridge but, before she went into hospital, Elspeth said something. I think you ought to know. She was sorry...'

Matt wondered what was coming. What did Elspeth have to apologise for?

'She was sorry about how she'd behaved about your...' Alasdair cleared his throat. 'Bel, isn't it?' He struggled on. 'She said when Bel had gone back to Sydney, she'd been glad. But she'd come to accept you needed someone in your life and thought you'd gone back there to fetch her. She said... she said she'd be happy to see her at Christmas. But I guess that wasn't to be either.'

Kirsty had appeared on the scene just then, fussing about coats and scarves and preventing Matt from replying. But Alasdair's words had stayed with him and now, as he enjoyed the light bite on the back of his throat from his favourite malt, he remembered how they'd gone straight to his heart.

He knew he should contact Bel – at least give her an explanation for his actions. He was the one at fault here. Matt had long since decided he'd acted rashly by walking out on her, and his departing so precipitously leaving only that brief note had compounded his culpability. He'd even dismissed his uneasiness around the fact that it might have been Bel's fault he hadn't been there when Elspeth lay dying.

No wonder she'd tried to call – and he'd hung up on her. What must she be thinking? She deserved an explanation. He wouldn't risk a phone call, and the danger of receiving the same treatment he'd meted out to her, and the time was probably wrong anyway – it would be

Boxing Day morning in Sydney. With a fleeting curiosity as to how Bel had spent Christmas Day, Matt refilled his glass, opened his laptop and began to write.

My darling Bel,
I'm writing to apologise and try to explain my actions which I know were despicable. I can only hope you'll find it in your heart to forgive me...

Forty-one

Bel slept late.

Christmas Day had been a washout. Celia had spent it with her daughters, and though Bel had been invited she'd chosen to decline, unwilling to inflict her own misery on other people on this day of celebration. It had been a typical Sydney Christmas Day with the temperature in the mid-twenties, a relief from the storms of the earlier part of the month. Bel almost wished the rains had continued – they would have been more in tune with her mood.

Lou had suggested a beach picnic, but Bel had eschewed that too. She couldn't bear to be part of cheerful family groups determined to wring the last second of enjoyment out of the day. Instead, she'd chosen to hole up by herself at home with a good book and a bottle of wine. The bottle had morphed into two as the day progressed and she tried to prevent the images of Matt and his lovely home from inserting themselves between her and the pages of her book.

She'd gone to bed early, hoping to deaden the pain, but the thought of where she should have been spending that day wouldn't disappear, no matter how hard she tried. She'd tossed and turned, hearing the clock chime every hour until at last falling into a fitful sleep just as dawn was breaking.

Something had wakened her. For a moment Bel lay still, wondering what had disturbed her. The sound came again – a dull knocking. There was someone at the door. Sighing and pulling on a towelling robe, she dragged a hand through her tousled hair and made her way to the door. She opened it a crack and peered out blearily.

'Merry Christmas!' Lou stood there, a big grin on her face, a bottle of champagne in one hand and a large package in the other.

All Bel wanted to do was say, *Go away*, but she knew Lou couldn't be dismissed so easily. 'Come in.' She led the way through to the kitchen. 'Make yourself coffee. I'll just duck into the shower. Be with you in a few minutes.'

A dowsing under a stream of cold water had the required effect of waking Bel up, but it didn't make her feel any more sociable. She would have to front up at Isabella tomorrow, having decided to start her post-Christmas sale the day after Boxing Day, thus avoiding competing with the large department stores in the city. She'd made the assumption that most of her customers would be more intent on watching the Sydney to Hobart Yacht Race than in seeking out bargains today and had planned to spend the day at home.

'That looks better,' Lou greeted her, her eyes taking in Bel's white pants and tunic, a lilac-hued scarf thrown casually around her shoulders. She'd donned the outfit to give herself a lift but failed miserably.

Bel accepted a coffee from her friend and joined her at the kitchen table.

'What did you have planned for this beautiful day?' Lou asked, straightening her own outfit – an outsized black tee-shirt teamed with baggy pants in a multicoloured fabric. 'It's too good a day to spend it inside, which is what I suspect you did yesterday. We should watch the start of the race.'

Bel did a double take. 'What? When did you develop an interest in yacht racing? And besides, every man and his dog will be on or near the harbour today.' She shuddered. 'No thanks.'

'Well, let's at least go out to lunch. We're both at a loose end.'

Bel immediately felt guilty. Of course Lou was at a loose end. In years gone by they'd always spent at least one day of the Christmas period together, bemoaning and revelling in the fact they had no families to worry about pleasing or antagonising. She let out a sigh. 'Where had you in mind?'

'I thought maybe the Northern Beaches. Far enough away from the harbour to avoid the yachties, but we might still catch a glimpse of the fleet going through the Heads.'

Lou was incorrigible. Bel managed to raise a laugh. 'Oh, get away with you. You're no more interested in the yachts than I am, but that sounds like a plan. Lunch? What's the time?' In her hurry to get ready, Bel hadn't looked at her watch or the clock since she'd awoken.

'It's gone ten. You must have had a sound sleep.'

'Not really.' But Bel didn't want to share her restless dreams with Lou. She knew what her friend would say. She'd heard it all before. And even though it had been weeks since Matt had left, even though he'd hung up on her call, there was still a part of her that wondered, that knew he *had* loved her. It hadn't *all* been a sham. It had been her last chance at a happiness she'd never imagined – and she'd thrown it all away.

*

After a pleasant lunch, Bel and Lou walked slowly to the car and made their leisurely way back to Cremorne. There was little traffic on the road, though the same couldn't be said for the harbour. They waited patiently as Spit Bridge opened to allow through a host of small yachts, their many-hued sails billowing in the breeze. Bel guessed they were returning from watching the start of the race.

The race was an Australian tradition she'd taken a while to become used to, this mad dash of maxi yachts from Sydney to Hobart in Tasmania on Boxing Day. People set up their positions hours ahead of the start time and celebrated with picnics and such like. The larger boats were accompanied through the heads by a flotilla of smaller yachts, and this was no doubt some of them. The maxis had to cross the treacherous Bass Strait and the Pacific Ocean, renowned for high winds and difficult seas, on the way to the finish line and, although no follower of the race, Bel hoped the forecast storms didn't result in any accidents.

This was another of Bel's favourite spots in Sydney. She loved the peaceful view of Middle Harbour. It occurred to her that, now the house was sold, she could make changes in her life – maybe even find an apartment with the view she'd often admired. It was certainly food for thought, though, for some unknown reason, she shied away from making future plans.

'Would you like a cold drink?' Bel asked reluctantly, when the car stopped outside her Cremorne home. All she wanted was to be alone, but she felt obligated to offer Lou some recompense as she'd insisted on paying for lunch.

'Love to.' Lou eased herself out of the car and followed Bel. Once inside the cooler house – Bel had closed up the house before leaving to protect the house and Toby from the heat of the day – Bel opened the blinds and threw open the door to the courtyard, allowing a light breeze into the kitchen.

'Iced peppermint tea?' she asked when Lou returned from freshening up. They'd enjoyed a couple of glasses of wine over lunch and Bel could feel an incipient headache. Her favourite tea should knock it on the head

'Sounds good. Celia not here?' Lou glanced around.

'She spent Christmas Day with her girls and stayed over. She should be back later tonight.' Bel spoke over her shoulder as she set the teabags to soak and prepared the honey and lemon.

'What's going to happen to Celia when the house settles?' Lou asked, when they were seated in the courtyard with long glasses of the cold tea. 'Will she go back to her daughters?'

'Interesting you should ask.' Bel remembered Celia's excited outburst. She'd put it to the back of her mind, but Lou's question prompted her. She hesitated for a moment but, since Celia hadn't sworn her to secrecy, had no qualms in repeating it. 'Her husband has made her an offer – a generous one – if she'll agree to being part of the media circus for his memoir.'

'Well done, Celia! She'll accept, of course.'

'It's more a case of well done, her lawyer. I think she will. It's a lot of money.'

'What will she do with it?'

'Find somewhere to live, start again. What else?'

'And what about you? You're in the same boat.'

'Yes,' Bel answered abruptly. She didn't want to talk about that. Not now. Not with Lou. She wanted to come to her own decision and, right now, she had no idea what that would be.

As she closed the door behind Lou. Bel let out a sigh of relief. She'd thought her friend would never leave as she chatted on about mutual friends and her own plans for the year ahead. Bel had been close to screaming. Now she was finally on her own, and the house seemed to close around her like a comforting cloak.

She was about to drop into her favourite easy chair when a sharp yap from Toby, accompanied by a pleading look, reminded her the little dog had been stuck indoors all day. 'Okay,' she said, taking his lead from its hook by the door, 'you need a walk, don't you?'

Bel let her mind wander as they walked along. She'd managed to get through the two days of holiday, and tomorrow things would be back to normal. She'd have her work to keep her occupied, to take her mind off what might have been. She needed that. It came to her in a flash that she'd be mad to go ahead with selling her boutique. Going there every day was what kept her sane. No, she'd take it off the market. It was enough she'd have to find somewhere else to live. The sale of the house would be settled late January – a fresh start to the New Year. That decided, she turned around and set off for home at a brisk pace.

Not one to let the grass grow under her feet, as soon as she arrived home, and ensured Toby was fed and watered, she opened her computer. She'd email the broker now. While it was booting up, Bel poured herself another glass of peppermint tea, took a sip and glanced at the emails which had arrived since she last checked a couple of days earlier.

There was the expected flurry of Christmas greetings – so few people sent cards these days. Then Bel's eyes fell on a familiar address and a quiver of something she couldn't identify swamped her. She knew that address so well. It was the one she'd been using daily. The email was from Matt!

Forty-two

Bel blinked twice. She couldn't believe her eyes. She hadn't heard from Matt since he walked out on her. He'd cut off her call. What on earth was he doing emailing her? Her finger hovered over *delete*, but curiosity got the better of her. What if…?

She clicked *open* and began to read, hearing his familiar voice in her ear as her eyes scanned the screen.

My darling Bel,

I'm writing to apologise and try to explain my actions which I know were despicable. I can only hope you'll find it in your heart to forgive me. I have no excuse for treating you the way I did. All I can offer is an explanation in an attempt to make you understand.

First, let me assure you of my love. That hasn't altered though, given my behaviour, you have no reason to believe me.

Yes, I was angry when I stormed out that night. I'd expected you to be grateful I'd discovered what a lying cheat Pete was. But instead, you were angry with me. Now I've had time to reflect, I understand why. I understand you felt I was interfering, suggesting you were incapable of coping with the situation. Whereas, you are the most capable and independent woman I know – have ever known – apart maybe from your Aunt Isobel.

The truth of the matter is that, instead of apologising as I should have, I left and proceeded to get abominably drunk – not something I'm proud of. I fully intended to apologise abjectly the following morning, but when I finally saw the light of day, you'd gone to work, leaving me alone with the very cause of the problem.

My next plan was to come directly to see you at the shop. That was until I discovered the missed calls on my phone. Elspeth had been taken to hospital for an emergency hysterectomy, and I knew I needed to be back here.

I left you a note. I'm sorry it had to be so brief. Why didn't I call you? I truly can't answer that. I think my brain must have fried. I fully intended to call you as soon as possible, but fate intervened in the form of a flat battery and different time zones. Then, when I did call – several times, there was no reply.

I went directly to the hospital when I arrived in Glasgow to discover I was too late. It's difficult to write this, my dear, but my darling Elspeth didn't survive. I won't go into details, suffice to say that when you called me I'd just returned from the funeral and was in no position to speak to anyone.

I realise now, how hurtful that must have been for you. It must have taken a lot of courage to make the call when I'd been such a fool. I can only beg your forgiveness yet again and hope there is a tiny part of you which still thinks of me with some kindness, even though I don't deserve it.

Christmas here was a very sombre affair, as you can imagine – far from the celebration of our love I'd planned. I thought of you on Christmas Day and wondered how you were spending it. Can I hope that you spared a thought for me too?

If you can find it in your heart to forgive this blundering idiot and are still reading this, I'd love to hear from you. The house is empty without you. I miss your ready smile, your warmth, your body next to mine.

Remember, Barkis is willing.

I remain always,

Your loving Matt

Bel's eyes blurred and began to fill with tears as she read Matt's final words. He'd called her. But there had been no missed calls. She'd have known if... Then she remembered the problems she'd had with her mobile provider. It must have been then...

She sat unmoving, wracked with sobs, scarcely hearing when the front door opened and closed.

'What's happened?' Celia's voice broke through her weeping.

Bel gestured to the computer.

'Who?' Celia's eyes widened as the realisation clearly dawned. 'You've heard from Matt? Not good news?' She moved into the room as if to offer comfort, but Bel waved her away.

Bel rubbed her eyes. 'It's not what you think. Elspeth's dead.'

'Who?' Celia's mouth dropped open. 'Oh, no! His daughter? Why? What happened?'

'She'd had a hysterectomy. A blood clot, I think, maybe. I don't know. But, Celia, the poor man! What he's been through. And her poor children, left without a mother. I met them, and...' Bel wiped her eyes. 'I can't imagine... Oh, God. That was the day I rang. It was the funeral. No wonder he hung up on me.'

'Is that why...?'

'It's part of it. Oh, Celia. He says he still loves me. What should I do? Can I believe him?'

'What do you want to do?'

'Damned if I know.' Bel grimaced. 'I'd given up hope of ever hearing from him again. Put him in the same bag as Pete. Then this.'

'Do you love him?'

Trust Celia to ask that. That was the crux of the matter. Bel *did* still love Matt, despite all he'd done or not done, despite the distance, despite everything. She nodded, not trusting herself to speak.

'And he still wants you to go to Scotland?'

Bel nodded again.

'Go for it. If you still love him, and he loves you. You always intended to go, didn't you?'

'Yes. But it's not that simple. There's...' But Bel couldn't think of the numerous impediments to Celia's suggestion. 'Do you think I could?' She sniffed.

'Why not? This house is sold. Pete's taken care of. I'll have enough money to find somewhere else to live. Not that *my* situation should enter into your plans. There's only Isabella...'

At that, Bel's memory kicked in. 'Isabella. I was about to take it off the market when I saw Matt's email. Now, I...' She looked down, supporting her head with both hands, and remembered the crazy idea that had flashed through her mind when Celia mentioned Bill's offer. Raising her head, she met Celia's eyes. 'I don't suppose? No, it's a daft idea.'

'What is?'

Bel took a deep breath. 'I don't suppose you'd like to buy Isabella?' She thought Celia was going to choke.

'Buy Isabella? Me?' Celia squeaked. 'I'd never be able to afford it. But if I could…' Her eyes gleamed in anticipation.

'Maybe we could come to some arrangement.' Bel felt a hint of excitement slither through her grief. 'I know you couldn't afford the entire asking price. We could talk to your lawyer, see what he could come up with. I'd like to see my baby going to someone I know, someone who'd care for it as much as I do.'

'Oh, Bel!' This time it was Celia's eyes that filled with tears. 'We're a right pair,' she said between sobs. 'I suppose this means you're going to Scotland?'

'I guess it does.'

*

It was too late to ring Matt that night. Bel lay awake hearing the clock chime every hour, the words in his email repeating in her head, till her resident kookaburras began their morning chorus and the first streaks of dawn peeped through the blinds.

Her heart was racing as she picked up the phone and checked facetime. She wanted to see Matt's face, needed to be sure he really meant what he'd said in his email. What if he'd had second thoughts? What if she'd taken too long to respond? The email had been sitting there while she'd been out with Lou. What if…?

She pressed his number and waited impatiently, listening to the call being rerouted, until…

'Bel?'

Matt's voice filled her ears, his Scottish burr so familiar, so welcome. She wanted to cry, to shout out, to… The tension that had been building all night began to diminish. She breathed more easily.

'Matt. I got your email.'

What a dumb thing to say, but for the life of her she couldn't find the right words to convey her relief.

'I'm sorry. Do you forgive me?'

Then, as if he'd read her mind, knew she wanted to see his face, there it was. Matt's familiar face was gazing at her from her phone. He looked older, more careworn. No wonder, after what he'd been through.

'I'm so sorry about Elspeth. I can't believe... How are you coping? How...?' Bel felt the tears begin to well up and dashed them away. She wasn't going to cry – she wasn't. But she saw an answering moisture in Matt's eyes.

'Thanks. We're managing. It's not easy, especially Christmas, but we're getting through it. I'm so sorry I hung up on you when you called, but...'

'I know. You explained. I... I love you, Matt Reid.' The tears began to flow, streaming unchecked down her cheeks. 'I want to be with you. I'm sorry I lost my temper with you. You were right, and I was wrong. Pete's in the nursing home now. It's for the best. I can't believe how gullible I was, how I believed him. How... Did you really mean...?' She held her breath. What if she'd been wrong to call? What if...?

'Yes, I did. I love you so much. I can't believe we let all this get in the way of our relationship. It took wee Fi to make me see what I wanted. I want you. I need you – here, with me, always.'

'Oh, Matt! Bless her.' Bel sniffed, smiling through her tears.

'Here, you're not still crying, are you?'

'Sorry.' Bel sniffed again. 'I'm just so happy to see you, to hear your voice, to know that...'

'I wish I could reach out and touch you.' Matt's voice broke. 'Does this mean you'll be coming back to me – to Scotland?'

'Yes, please!' Bel beamed and was rewarded by an answering grin from Matt.

'When?'

'As soon as...' Bel thought of all the things she'd need to do before she could actually step on a plane. 'As soon as I can. The house is sold. Celia is taking over the shop. There's nothing to keep me here. I just need to pack up, buy a ticket, arrange for Toby, and...' She began to make a mental list, realising it was true – there was nothing to keep her here. Her love for Matt was so all-encompassing, so complete, that everything else in her life faded into insignificance. This was the man she wanted to spend the rest of her life with. Home was where he was. Home was *what* he was.

'Organised as ever,' Matt teased. 'But don't take too long. I've been without you for too much time already. We need you here – me, Hamish, Fi and the others.' Matt paused. 'I've been so lonely without you, Bel. I want you to make my life complete again.'

Bel still had tears in her eyes when the call ended, but they were tears of happiness.

*

After that, things moved quickly.

Celia and she contacted Bob Frazer who drew up a contract which satisfied both of them. Celia would take over ownership of the boutique at much less than the original asking price while Bel would retain a percentage of the profits, leaving Celia the option to buy Bel out completely at some future date. Celia had been so overwhelmed, she'd hugged Bel and cried.

Now, Bel existed in a bubble of happiness.

Each morning she awoke to see Matt's face on her computer, to hear his voice as he constantly reassured her of his undying devotion. She began her preparations, began packing up a lifetime of goods and deciding which to sell, which to give away and which to pack in the packing cases which now filled her hallway.

She moved around in a daze, expecting to wake up and find it had all been a dream.

On the day Celia came home with the news she'd found an apartment, Bel knew it was actually going to happen. She was leaving Sydney. The pair spent hours in Isabella with Bel explaining ordering procedures and her finance software. Heather took her out for coffee to congratulate her on her decision, while Lou continued to be her skeptical self.

'Are you sure?' Bel found herself repeatedly asking Matt, as she pinched herself at her good fortune, while feeling a sense of loss as she looked around her in the house that had been her home for so long.

*

It was close to the end of January before Bel was ready to leave. Despite Matt's urging, and her own desire to make the move, there were various matters to be taken care of. She had to stay till the house settled, she had packed up, sent those belongings she couldn't live without ahead of her to Scotland, and disposed of the rest either in a garage sale or by donation to charity. She'd already bought her own ticket, but had to arrange for Toby to be transported.

When the morning arrived, she cajoled him into his special travel crate and sent him on his way, standing in the gateway as she watched the carrier drive down the road and disappear around the corner. Then she returned to the empty house. Matt would be collecting Toby at Glasgow airport and taking him home to meet Hamish.

Now her pet had gone, the packing cases were ready to be picked up and Celia had moved out, the house didn't feel like home anymore. It had become an empty shell.

Bel shivered as she locked the door and slid into the car to put in her final day at Isabella.

A couple of days later, Bel experienced another sad moment when she finally handed over the keys to Rod Miller and arranged for the house to be cleaned ready for the new owner. She took one last look at the home she'd been happy in for so many years before turning her back on it, getting into her car and driving away. She planned to spend her last few days in Sydney in Celia's new home – a spacious modern unit with the Middle Harbour views Bel had always admired.

There was one more thing to do before she left. She had to see Pete one last time. He was a part of her life she'd prefer to forget, but she felt she owed him a proper farewell.

When Bel entered the room, she was shocked at the change in Pete in such a short time. The man who'd once been her ideal had become a shrunken skeletal figure who appeared lost in the single bed.

'This will be my last visit,' she said.

'Given up on me already?'

'I'm leaving. I fly to Scotland tomorrow.' She moved closer and stroked a fold in the bedcover.

'So he's won,' Pete said in a slurred voice.

'Won? It wasn't a competition. I'm not a lucky dip prize.' But Bel knew that, to Pete, everything was a competition. He wasn't unlike Celia's Bill in that regard. Both men saw women as prizes to be won, possessions to be flaunted. The surprising part of it was that Pete saw Bel that way, even after all those years apart.

Bel left soon after. She almost wished she hadn't come, sure Pete wouldn't have bothered if the boot was on the other foot. But I'm not Pete, she reminded herself, and it was the right thing to do. Now I can leave with no regrets.

She drove back to Cremorne with a clear conscience. All was ready for her departure next day, and Celia had organised a small farewell party that evening. This time tomorrow, Bel would be on the plane, on her way to Scotland, to Matt. She could hardly believe it was actually going to happen, almost sure something would occur to prevent it.

Matt had repeatedly told Bel how he'd be waiting for her at the airport, how Fi couldn't wait to see her again, how Hamish and Toby were looking forward to her arrival.

Toby had already arrived in Scotland. Matt reported that, after a few awkward moments, he and Hamish had taken to each other and were already firm friends. But Bel was keen to see how the two dogs reacted to each other, which one would become dominant. She suspected it would be her own Toby, but no doubt Hamish would want to lord it over the newcomer to his territory.

Bel was sorry Elspeth had died. She knew how devastated the whole family must be. Their lives would never be the same again. She wondered how Matt could forgive himself for being in Sydney with her when it happened. Maybe that had been preying on his mind too.

She thought of her own recent loss. But her Aunt Isobel had been an old woman; she'd been ready to die. Elspeth was a young woman. She'd had so much to live for.

Bel would have liked the opportunity to make friends with Matt's daughter, who Matt told her had finally come around to the idea of Bel in her dad's life. But it was not to be.

The children appeared to be coping as well as could be expected, though Bel was sure Fi cried herself to sleep at night – maybe Robbie too. She imagined he wasn't as tough as he pretended to be. Matt said Alasdair was contemplating hiring an *au pair* at Fi's insistence. Bel wondered if it was too soon to introduce someone else into the family, though they would need help.

The evening went well as Celia, Jan, Heather and Lou toasted Bel's new life. The only sour note was when Lou took Bel aside to ask if she was sure about this. But Heather stepped in to reassure her that sometimes we need to take a risk on happiness and that no one knew what the next day might bring.

Bel fell asleep with a smile on her face. She would miss her good friends, but they'd keep in touch, might even visit her in Scotland. She'd enjoy showing them her new home.

Lou drove her to the airport – a remorseful Lou who apologised for her negative talk the night before. 'It was the wine talking,' she said, though Bel knew it was typical Lou, and her dear friend would never change.

As the plane lifted off, she looked down on the red roofs of Sydney, remembering her homecoming only a few months earlier. So much had happened since then. But here she was, fulfilling her promise to return, even if Christmas was over. She and Matt had the rest of their lives to spend together.

It was a long flight with only a brief stopover at Dubai, but sleep eluded Bel, allowing her to only doze fitfully. She was keyed up – filled with anticipation, yet tentative about the enormous change she was about to embark upon. Images of the harbour city, her home for the past forty-odd years vied with memories of the time she'd spent with Matt in his highland hideaway.

When she thought of Matt, a warmth that had nothing to do with the temperature in the cabin filled her with a mixture of excitement and dread. What if she'd been wrong? What if she couldn't adjust to living back in Scotland on a permanent basis? What if…?

She closed her eyes and tried to make her mind a blank, then, realising the impossibility of such a task, opened her book again. For the trip, she'd chosen the latest Caro Ramsay – an author both she and Matt enjoyed, and the book was one which Matt had recommended highly. But even that failed to engage her, so she was left with her memories and her misgivings.

It was a relief when she finally heard the captain announce they were about to land and, moving her seat to the upright position, Bel peered out the window hoping to catch a first glimpse of Scotland. But all that met her eyes were white clouds and a pattering of water drops on the glass. She closed her eyes again. It was too late for doubts.

Bel must have dozed off for a few seconds, as the next thing she knew the aircraft had touched down and come in to a halt at the terminal, and there was a buzz in the cabin as other passengers began to collect their belongings. As she stuffed her book and glasses into her bag, Bel's stomach began to churn with excitement. She felt dizzy and had to pause for a moment, her hand on the back of the seat in front, to regain her equilibrium.

By the time it was her turn to make her way along the line of passengers waiting to alight from the plane, Bel's heart was racing, and she was too excited to think straight. All the tiredness from the flight had disappeared. She felt wide awake, rejuvenated by the thought that soon she'd see Matt again. She could scarcely believe this was really happening. She was about to take a leap of faith.

The slog through customs and immigration seemed to take forever. Bel was grateful she'd brought only one suitcase filled with those of her clothes she considered would serve her in a Scottish winter. She'd sent everything else by sea and looked forward to a shopping spree in Glasgow once she'd settled in. The years of Sydney weather had made her soft and hadn't prepared her for the icy coldness she knew she was about to experience on this side of the world.

As she stepped through the barrier, Bel's eyes scanned the faces in the crowd, sure Matt's would stand out. For a moment she couldn't see him. She faltered, stopped, then her face broke into a wide grin as she saw the placard.

Barkis is willing.

Then she was in Matt's arms, feeling the roughness of his morning stubble against her cheek, his warm lips seeking hers, and all her doubts disappeared.

*

It was late, and darkness had fallen when Bel and Matt arrived at the house on the loch. There was a flurry of snowflakes on the windscreen as Matt stopped the car, leading him to remind Bel of his promise of a white Christmas – even though Christmas was over.

The light spilled from behind the tall, glass door, on the inside of which Bel could see two small white furry faces pressed against the glass.

They were all home. Together. At last.

THE END

From the Author

Dear Reader,

First, I'd like to thank you for choosing to read Isobel's Promise. I hope you enjoyed Bel's journey and, if you've already read The Good Sister, I hope you enjoyed meeting Bel and Matt again. I really enjoyed continuing their story in this book.

If you did enjoy it, I'd love it if you could write a review. It doesn't need to be long, just a few words, but it is the best way for me to help new readers discover my books.

If you'd like to stay up to date with my new releases and special offers you can sign up to my reader's group and you'll also get a FREE book.

You can sign up here
https://mailchi.mp/f5cbde96a5e6/maggiechristensensreadersgroup

I'll never share your email address, and you can unsubscribe at any time. You can also contact me via Facebook Twitter or by email. I love hearing from my readers and will always reply.

Thanks again.

Read a Preview of
The Good Sister

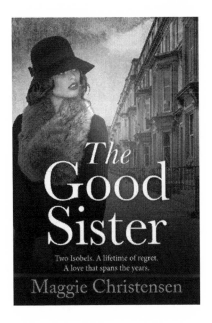

Prologue

Isobel – 2015

I was always the good sister.

I lean back in my favourite armchair and sigh looking at the words I've written. It may not matter anymore, but I want to get everything down, just as it happened. Maybe knowing what I do now, I'd have behaved differently – maybe not.

If Doctor Ramage is right, I don't have much time left, but maybe long enough to make things right. Not for me, but for my namesake

Isobel – Bel as she calls herself these days – my sister Nan's daughter; the daughter I might have had if…

My name was never shortened. Father wouldn't permit it. He regarded it as common. But this Isobel is of a different generation and she likes the shortened version.

I twist the garnet ring on my finger, the tears trickling down my cheeks. It's all I have left, all except the memories.

It began seventy-five years ago when I was only twenty. It would take another forty for me to discover the truth.

'Are you Isobel MacDonald?'

In the hours when sleep won't come, I can still hear that shrill voice echoing through my head. It was so long ago I should have forgotten it, relegated it to the past where it belongs. But now that I know my days on this earth are numbered, I need to tell someone my story. My only remaining relative is young Isobel who had the sense to leave this godforsaken land for fresher pastures. Maybe she'll understand why I behaved as I did and allow me to die in peace, to believe what I did was right – that I *was* the good sister.

One

Bel – 2015

Bel climbed out of the black taxi and stood looking up at her childhood home while the driver unloaded her case. The house hadn't changed much. It was still an imposing structure guarded by black railings, its oriel windows gazing down on the River Kelvin with what had always seemed to her a jaundiced expression. The grey stone facade she remembered had gone, replaced by a patina of soft pink sandstone. Bel supposed it had always been there, underneath, hidden by years of smoke and dirt.

She'd read about the transformation of Glasgow, but now it was right in front of her eyes and she was astounded at the metamorphosis. Bel hadn't been home since her mother's death more than thirty years earlier. She had to expect to see changes.

'Your case?'

Bel turned in surprise. She'd been so absorbed by the old house that she'd forgotten the taxi driver.

'Thanks.' She fumbled in her bag for the fare, paid the driver, then picked up the case and mounted the steps. They didn't seem nearly as steep as she remembered.

The faded lettering on the enamel centrepiece of the bellpush brought back memories, its surrounding brass plate showing signs of wear but still as bright as ever. Bel remembered polishing it till she

273

could – to use her granny's words – see her face in it. She followed the now faint instruction to *press*. A bell chimed in the distance.

A gust of wind rustled some leaves in the gutter. Bel shivered. She'd all but forgotten how cold it could be in Scotland, even in summer. From the other side of the door came the sound of footsteps and the tap-tap of a cane. The door opened to reveal the tall figure of Bel's aunt. A loud Scottish voice greeted her.

'Hello, hello. Aren't you a sight for sore eyes? Come away in. You'll be needing a cup of tea.'

Bel dropped her case and stepped into an enveloping hug. She inhaled the remembered violet fragrance of the Evening in Paris cologne that had always been her aunt's favourite. 'It's good to be here at last,' she said, returning the hug. Then she held the older woman at arm's length and studied her. 'You haven't changed a bit.'

But, as she'd expected, there was a frailty about the old woman that hadn't been there on Bel's last visit all those years ago.

'Och, away.'

The familiar Scottish expression took Bel back to her childhood. Almost as tall as Bel, Isobel still held herself erect, albeit with the aid of a walking stick. Her now completely white hair was fashioned exactly as Bel remembered, the long plait coiled into a tight bun at the back of her head. Her eyes had lost the piercing blue, which, when Bel was a child, seemed to see everything. Now they were rheumy and partially hidden behind a pair of half-moon glasses, and the skin on the cheek which had touched Bel's was papery thin.

'In here.' The older woman led the way through a door on the left of the wide hallway. As she followed her aunt, Bel glanced up at the imposing staircase she'd slid down as a young child, and descended more elegantly in her teens and early twenties, before she'd made the decision to emigrate.

'Oh, it's just as I remember it!' Bel looked around the large room. The wide oriel window was flanked by two floral-covered armchairs between which sat a low table piled with books and papers. So, her aunt was still an avid reader. Opposite the door, partially hidden by a sofa covered with a multitude of cushions, the old fireplace had been boarded up to house a gas fire with artificial coals, while on the other side of the room sat the old sideboard. The place still smelt the same too – an odd mixture of furniture polish and an elusive aroma Bel couldn't quite identify, one unique to her childhood home.

'You still have it!' Bel walked over to run her hand across the well-worn surface of the sideboard. 'I remember this so well.'

'That old chiffonier is part of the family,' Isobel said fondly. 'But I don't know what'll happen to it when I've gone. No-one wants good furniture these days. It's all that Ikea stuff. And there's no family but you, and you're on the other side of the world.' She laughed hoarsely, the laugh turning into a cough and she leant heavily on her cane as she tried to regain her breath.

'Are you all right? You'd better sit down.' Bel led her aunt to one of the armchairs and settled her into it, covering the old lady's knees with a tartan travelling rug which had been hanging over its back. 'I should've thought.'

In her excitement at seeing her aunt and the changes to the old house, Bel had almost forgotten the reason for her visit. Aunt Isobel had written detailing her illness and asking Bel to visit "before it was too late". She wanted Bel to help her "sort things out" before the inevitable.

'I'll be fine in a wee minute,' her aunt said, breathing heavily. 'It just gets me that way sometimes. I'm sorry you had to see me like that so soon after you got here. Some days are better than others, and I've been having a good day.' She wheezed a little, then raised her head. 'Maybe if you could fetch me a glass of water? Through there.' She pointed to the door leading to the hallway. 'The kitchen's where it always was. I spend all my time down here. I can't get up the stairs these days. But you'll find your room up there. I had Betty make it up.'

'Won't be a tick.'

But Bel's progress was interrupted by a wheezy instruction, 'And if you could just put the kettle on while you're there.'

Bel smiled. Aunt Isobel had always been a little formidable, even though she'd tried so hard to be friends with Bel and her mates. She hadn't changed.

Opening the door, Bel found herself in a familiar corridor leading to the old kitchen. She filled both a glass and the kettle wondering what had happened to the rest of the house and where her aunt slept. It was a big house for one person.

*

By the time Bel returned, her Aunt Isobel had regained some colour and was sitting upright in the chair clutching the rug. She allowed her niece to help her guide the glass to her lips, then pushed it away. 'It's my lungs,' she gasped. 'They're going to be the death of me,' she chortled, reminding Bel of an old friend and client back in Australia.

Heather suffered from emphysema and sounded exactly like Aunt Isobel, including the same sense of humour. 'Too many cigarettes,' the older woman continued. 'No one told us they could cause this. But I've had a good innings, not like some. They're all gone now.'

Bel followed her aunt's eyes to the sideboard, the top of which was covered with family photos: her mother, aunt and grandparents – all now dead.

'Don't know how I managed to outlive them all, especially our Nan,' she said, referring to Bel's mother. 'They say the good die young, so what does that say about me?' she chuckled and coughed violently into a handkerchief.

Bel couldn't be sure, but thought she saw a trace of blood on the white cotton. Before she could comment her aunt spoke again.

'Is that tea ready? I could fair be doing with a cup. One sugar and plenty of milk. And you'll find some ginger snaps in the tin by the stove. I remember you used to like them.' Her voice was coming clearer now, so Bel felt more confident to leave her while she made the tea.

She smiled as she poured the tea and set out the biscuits on a flower-rimmed plate. The last time she'd eaten a ginger snap had been right here in this house. As a child, she'd cracked them with her elbow to see if they'd break into three pieces so she could make a wish. Bel hadn't thought of them for years. She was touched her aunt remembered.

'Now, how are you really?' Bel asked, when their cups were empty and she'd eaten several of the biscuits to please Isobel. Her aunt had refused to have any herself saying they were too hard for her false teeth to manage.

'So-so. I've defied all the doctors and specialists so far, but I know I can't do it for much longer. I don't expect to make a hundred. The Queen can save her stamp,' she laughed, then her voice took on a more serious tone. 'I don't think I'll see the year out. That's why I wanted you to come. There are some things I want to set straight before I go, and there's someone I want you to meet. I need to make sure everything's done the way I want it. I...' She began to cough again, but waved away an offer of more water.

Bel half-rose, unsure how she could help. How on earth had her aunt been managing to live on her own – to take care of herself?

'There's a bottle of whisky over there in the sideboard,' the hoarse voice instructed. 'I'll have a wee tot and you may care for one yourself.'

Bel hurried across the room and opened the door of the sideboard to discover the bottle of a good malt whisky hidden behind some boxes. It had always been tucked away like this – kept for medicinal purposes only. Some things never changed, except she guessed the "medicinal requirements" were called on more often these days. There were some glasses there too, crystal. Most likely Edinburgh Crystal, Bel thought, recalling how, as a young woman growing up in Glasgow, she'd had it instilled in her that crystal was one of the few good things to come out of Edinburgh. As a child, she'd mentally added Edinburgh Rock to the list too, loving its soft crumbly texture and the way the pink and yellow sticks melted on her tongue.

She poured her aunt a generous measure, hesitated before pouring another smaller one for herself, then joined Isobel by the window. It was close to six o'clock and still bright outside. Bel had always loved the long light summer evenings in Scotland; something she missed in Sydney where the sun set much earlier all year round, even during daylight saving.

'There's a steak pie in the fridge. It only needs heating up. And some potatoes and peas... I'd planned...' Isobel's voice died away and she took a sip of her drink. 'Ah, that's better. Nothing like a wee dram to perk me up.'

'I can manage dinner,' Bel said.

Steak pie – always the standby for special occasions in the family. She guessed her arrival counted as that. Since her mother had died, there was only Aunt Isobel left here in Scotland and Bel herself on the other side of the world.

At one time, this house was teeming with life – her mother, two aunts, grandparents and a couple of great aunts who'd lost their fiancés in the First World War. Now it seemed like a ghost house.

'Not just yet.' Isobel's claw-like hand grasped Bel's. 'First I want you to tell me about your life down there in Australia. Letters don't say everything. I want to picture it.' She closed her eyes while Bel sipped her own drink and began to speak.

'I live in Sydney. In a place called Cremorne. My house is quite different to this one, smaller, red brick with a veranda all around and separated from the road by a white fence. It's within walking distance of Sydney Harbour. As you know, I have a dress shop just like you and Mum had – I call it a boutique.'

She saw the old woman smile and continued, 'It's in a classy suburb called Mosman not far from where I live. I've been lucky that a friend called Jan is minding it for me while I'm here. She's had a rough time, lost her elder son, but is managing to get through it.' Bel paused remembering how Jan had arrived in her shop to apply for a temporary position. Now the two were firm friends and she had no qualms in leaving Jan in charge for however long she needed to stay in Scotland.

'It's a world away from all this,' she continued. 'The weather for a start. We get a lot of sunny days and it can be very hot in summer – and humid, which can be pretty awful, so most homes have air-conditioning and sometimes fans too. I don't think I could survive the summer without them. We also have big storms, often after a really hot day. Then there are the beaches. Not like those here, or even in Europe. We have long stretches of golden sand and big waves. Lots of surfing and we have to watch out for sharks.'

'And your little dog?'

'Toby's still there, and Jan's looking after him too. Her younger son, Andy, loves him and begged to be allowed to be in charge of him. So, everything there's being taken care of and I can stay for as long as you need me.'

At those words, Bel felt her aunt's grasp loosen.

'You'll miss him and your home.'

'I guess so, but there's so much here that's different, very different from what I remember. And I'll be too busy spending time with you, so I won't miss it too much.'

'Mmm.' Isobel's voice was fainter. The older woman had dozed off. Bel gently removed the glass which was dangling from her aunt's hand, stood up and stretched. She was tired after the long flight, but was determined to stay awake until a decent hour. That way, she'd be sure of a good night's sleep and would hopefully wake up refreshed.

Now that her aunt was asleep, Bel decided to investigate her room. Climbing the stairs, she pushed open the door to what was now clearly the spare bedroom, all set up for her with a single bed, a heavy old wardrobe and chest of drawers. It smelt musty from lack of use, though intermingling was a hint of lavender. Someone, no doubt the mysterious Betty, had placed a vase holding a sprig of lavender on the bedside table. Bel smiled.

She began to unpack, hanging the few items she'd brought with her in the old mahogany wardrobe, storing the smaller items away in the tall chest of drawers and laying her Kindle and iPad on the bedside table. Closing the wardrobe door before she left the room, Bel caught sight of herself in the fly-spotted mirror. *Not too bad after such a long flight*. She examined her tall figure so like her aunt's but topped with the smooth helmet of silver hair, instead of the coiled white plait. A closer inspection showed her the havoc the trip had wrought. Her eyes, usually a clear blue like her aunt's, were red from tiredness and the skin on her cheeks appeared dehydrated. She grimaced. Nothing a good night's sleep wouldn't fix.

When she made her way back to the kitchen Bel found the steak pie on the middle shelf of the fridge. This one was shop-bought, judging by the wrapping. It was unlike those she remembered from her childhood, served in an enamel ashet provided by her grandmother and filled by the local butcher. Bel also managed to unearth potatoes and a tin of peas. She turned on the oven and peeled the potatoes, reflecting how little had really changed in all these years.

Apart from the newish refrigerator and a few appliances, it was still the kitchen she'd grown up with. The same old gas stove sat against one wall with the metal rack above where Bel remembered the dinner plates sitting to warm; the green cupboards against the other wall hadn't changed at all. The kitchen table sat in the middle of the room where it had always sat, it's smooth surface showing the result of many scrubbings over the years. The tile-patterned linoleum was now faded, wearing thin in places and curling up slightly on one corner. It all felt so familiar yet strange. It was as if she'd travelled back in time.

Bel thought the kitchen seemed to be stuck in a time warp. Given the state of her bedroom, she was guessing the rest of the house hadn't changed much either, only the curtains changing with the seasons as they had throughout her childhood – velvet for winter and floral for summer.

She set the table and returned to the living room to sit by the window, turning her chair to enjoy the view across the river to the Botanic Gardens which used to be a favourite spot where she could escape the confines of her family and this house.

Bel hadn't found it easy growing up in this house surrounded by adults, and had taken every opportunity she could to get away. Finally, in her mid-twenties she moved all the way to the other side of the world. Her childhood hadn't had been unhappy, quite the opposite, but the house full of adults was also full of rules and expectations and she'd been glad to leave those behind.

That and the broken heart she'd been at pains to keep secret. It had been a relief to find the independence she hungered for and to start afresh in a new country.

There was a movement beside her.

'I must have dozed off. Did you…?'

'Dinner's on and should be ready soon.'

'Good girl.' Isobel picked up her glass and raised it to her lips again, beamed and leant forward. 'It's so lovely to have you here. I don't get out much, but we must try to do a few things. Maybe…'

'Don't worry about me. I can see Glasgow any-time. I'm happy just to spend time with you.'

'You're a good girl,' Isobel repeated and slumped back into her chair. 'Matthew will be here tomorrow. He's the one I want you to meet. He takes care of things for me.' She nodded. 'He's a good man, clever too.'

'Matthew?' Who was Matthew? Surely Aunt Isobel wasn't going to try to introduce her to someone she deemed *eligible* for someone in her sixties? Bel had tried marriage once and wasn't about to get involved with a man again at her age.

'Matthew Reid. He's my lawyer. A lovely young man.'

Bel breathed a sigh of relief. *Her lawyer. Of course.*

Two

Bel – 2015

For a moment Bel lay still. She missed the shrill birdcalls and the early morning snuffing of Toby, her little westie, back home. All she could hear was the gush of water in the distance. She opened her eyes and blinked at the unfamiliar room, the large wardrobe looming over her like a giant ready to pounce. Of course, she was in Scotland, in the old family home, and the water she heard was rain pouring down outside. Yesterday's sunshine had disappeared. Glasgow had decided to put on its special summer weather for her.

She rose, pulled her wrap around her and, drawing back the curtains, peered out of the window. A sorry sight met her eyes. It must have been raining all night. Water was flowing in the gutters, the pavement was covered with puddles and passing cars were creating waves as they sped through the sheet of water lying on the roadway.

Bel turned back into the room, shivering. She was reminded again how cool Scotland could be, even in June. Picking up her toiletries, she went to the bathroom for a quick wash, then dressed quickly in a pair of blue tailored pants topped with a pink striped shirt.

Once she'd fixed her make-up and brushed her hair into its usual neat style, Bel felt ready to face the day. Making her way into the kitchen she was surprised to see her aunt already seated at the table with a steaming bowl of porridge and a pot of tea.

'So, you're up at last! Did you sleep well?'

'Yes thanks.' Bel crossed to give the old woman a kiss on the cheek. 'And you?'

'I don't sleep much at night. I suppose it's because I nap during the day. One of the nuisances of getting old. But I've always liked the early morning, even as a young girl.' She paused, gazing off into space, then seemed to return to the present. 'Make yourself something to eat. There's porridge, if you like it, or bacon and eggs in the fridge. And help yourself to a cup of tea. I suppose you like that fancy coffee? I've never taken to it.'

'Tea'll be fine, thanks. And maybe some toast if there's bread.'

'You won't get fat on that. You're like me. One of Pharaoh's lean cattle.'

Bel smiled at this saying which she remembered from her childhood when she had indeed been thin... tall and thin – what her grandmother had called a skinny Lizzie. Taking a seat opposite Isobel, Bel realised again how like her aunt she was. Both had the same tall build with wide shoulders and a long face with a square jaw. Bel remembered her aunt's black hair in years gone by, just like her own had been before it turned to its present silver. But Isobel had kept the long hair of her youth, whereas Bel had chosen to keep hers short and neat.

'You'll meet Matthew today,' Isobel reminded her, pushing aside her empty bowl. 'He'll be bringing over some papers.'

'Right.'

'You're looking very smart. A good advert for your shop. What do you call it again?'

'Isabella.'

Isobel smiled. 'Our name, though you've fancied it up a bit. I suppose they do that over there. Your mother, Kate, and I had no such notions.'

'I liked the name of the shop you three had. Plain and Fancy.'

'It suited the times.' Isobel's eyes closed as if remembering bygone days, then snapped open again. 'Now, we need to get breakfast cleared away. My cleaning lady comes this morning and she doesn't like to find the breakfast dishes still on the table.'

'Keeps you in order, does she?' Bel chuckled at the thought of anyone trying to keep her aunt in order. 'I can do some cleaning up while I'm here.'

'No, no. That would annoy Betty even more. She has her ways, her set times for everything and does everything I need in her two days. It doesn't do to get in her way or upset her routine. She'll be doing the living room first. We'll be talking with Matthew in there and there are some nice chocolate digestives in the pantry. He likes them with his tea.'

Obviously a much-liked and spoiled young man. Bel cleared the table without a word. She'd barely finished and was emptying the teapot when there was a loud ringing in the hallway and the sound of a door opening.

'That'll be Betty. She's been with me for years and has her own key, but she always likes to give me warning that she's arrived.'

Sure enough when the door closed there was a loud, 'Hello there. It's only me,' followed by the arrival of a short wiry woman in her fifties, dressed in a yellow raincoat and wielding a dripping umbrella. 'It's fierce out,' she said in the soft lilting accent of the Highlands. 'I'm drookit and thought I was going to be blown away coming up the road. This'll be your niece, then?'

Bel was conscious of the woman's eyes examining her. 'I'm Bel.' She held out a hand.

'I'll no shake it till I've dried off. No sense in both of us being sodden. I'll just take this off and get started, shall I?' She looked at Isobel as if for confirmation, but didn't wait for a reply and proceeded to remove her wet garments and carry them back into the hall.

'She's a canny woman,' Isobel said in her absence. 'Came to me after your mum passed away and she's been with me ever since. Every Tuesday and Friday without fail, except for when her man had his accident and was in hospital for three weeks. Even then, she popped in when she could between visiting him. I don't know what I'd do without her these days.'

'Now then.' Betty was back wearing a wrap-around overall and carrying a bucket with several cleaning implements and bottles sticking out of it. 'You're not going to sit in here, I hope. I can't get on with folks under my feet. And you said you had yon solicitor man coming today too. So, I'll need to be getting the room ready for him.'

'That's right,' Isobel answered. 'We'll get out of your road. There are some things I want to show you,' she said to Bel. 'In my room. We can go in there while Betty's doing this part of the house.'

Isobel rose and, picking up her cane, slowly led Bel into her bedroom. Bel gazed round the room which had once been the dining room. Clearly reading Bel's thoughts, Isobel answered her unasked question, 'Yes, this was the old dining room. I tend to eat in the kitchen these days and it made sense to turn this into my bedroom. It saves me the stairs. It's all shut up there now, except for your room. Maybe you'll be wanting to look around, but no one's been up there for years, other than Betty.'

Bel stifled a smile, imagining the dust and cobwebs she'd find if she ventured beyond her bedroom.

Isobel settled herself in a chair by the bed and indicated to Bel that she should pull up a small stool. Once Bel was perched awkwardly at her aunt's side, Isobel drew a well-worn photo album from a drawer in the bedside table. The cover was faded leather in a shade that had most likely been red, and was cracked from use and the passage of years. Isobel patted it like an old friend.

She opened the book at the first page and rubbed her forefinger lovingly over the photo. 'I want to show you this so you can understand what life was like back then,' she said, 'Here we are, the three of us. I was twenty in this photo, your mum was nineteen and your Aunt Kate was twenty-four. My, we thought we were the bee's knees in those outfits.' The picture showed three young women similarly dressed in spotted dresses topped by three-quarter length jackets with wide shoulders. The waists of the dresses seemed to be pulled in as they were very narrow. Their hair was coiled up behind their ears and all three were wearing hats sporting little feathers.

'You all look very elegant,' Bel said, peering at the three figures. 'That's Mum in the middle, isn't it? And you're on her right? Were you going somewhere special?'

'We were. We were all dressed up to attend the Empire Exhibition.'

'The Empire Exhibition – in Glasgow?'

'It was held in Bellahouston Park and was the most exciting thing we could imagine. I remember that summer – it rained and rained – but it didn't stop us. We travelled all the way across town to see the exhibit. There were pavilions from all over the empire and an amazingly high tower. I seem to recall it was over four hundred feet high.'

'Wow, what happened to it?'

'It was demolished the following year. Such a pity.' Isobel shook her head. 'It was 1938. What a year that was. It was a year before the war began, a year where we all thought we were invincible, that the world was our oyster. Your mum was walking out with your dad, Kate had just completed her business course and was all set to be a career woman and…' Her voice trailed off.

'And you, Aunt Isobel? What were you doing?'

'I was being good.' Isobel suddenly closed the book with a snap. 'I'm sorry, dear. I thought I could do this, but I'm not ready to… It may be best you read it. I've written it down. It's all in here.' Isobel reached back into the drawer to take out a sheaf of papers covered in spidery writing. 'Take these back to your room. Young Matthew will be here soon. I'll just see how Betty's doing and make sure she has the kettle on.' Leaning on the arm of the chair, she eased herself up, grasped her cane and slowly made her way out of the room, leaving Bel staring after her in astonishment.

By the time Bel had taken the papers to her bedroom and returned to the kitchen, the kettle was boiling away. Betty had laid a tray set with an embroidered cloth with three gold-rimmed china cups and saucers, and a matching plate containing a stack of chocolate digestive biscuits.

'We'd better be away through. Betty's done in there, and he'll be here in a minute.'

Smiling inwardly, Bel followed her aunt, curious to meet the young man who occasioned such minute preparation and appeared to be such a favourite of both her aunt and Betty.

'Here he is!' Isobel had taken her usual chair by the window and angled it so she could watch the road.

Bel glanced out to see a low-slung sports car draw up. Clearly young Matthew wasn't short of cash and was a bit of a lad. She wondered how Isobel had discovered "young Matthew" and why she'd chosen him when there must be many more conservative and experienced lawyers in Glasgow.

The sound of the bell was followed by Betty's hurried footsteps and a loud, 'I'll let him in,' before the door was flung open and Betty announced with a flourish, 'Mr Matthew.'

The man who entered the room was nothing like Bel's imaginings.

For a start, he wasn't young. He was closer to her own sixty years and towered over Bel who'd stood up to greet him. Wearing the typically Scottish tweed jacket with a checked open-necked shirt and a pair of jeans, he looked as if he'd be more at home in a paddock than in a drawing room or office. His dark thatch of grey hair was shot through with silver and glistened with raindrops, and his square-cut jaw lent him a determined appearance. She supposed he did have an office, no doubt somewhere in Glasgow, but obviously made house calls too. He immediately went over to Isobel and planted a kiss on her cheek.

'How's my best girl this morning?' he asked.

'All the better for seeing you. Are you not wearing a coat in this rain?'

'Too tough. I left my umbrella in the hall. Didn't want to leave puddles on your good carpet.'

Isobel chuckled. 'I want you to meet my niece. She's all the way from Sydney, Australia.' Her outstretched hand gestured in Bel's direction.

Matthew turned his glance towards Bel who had been listening to this exchange with amusement. 'So, this is Bel.' He held out his hand to shake hers and she felt his eyes rake her up and down. 'Another braw MacDonald lassie,' he said at last.

Bel couldn't help but feel he'd overdone the Scots accent for her benefit and reddened. 'I grew up in this house,' she said defensively, though not sure why she felt the need to explain herself.

'Of course you did. Matthew knows that. I filled him in on his last visit. So you can stop pretending to be a yokel.' Isobel directed her last remark to Matthew.

'Your aunt's told me all about you – how proud she is of you, Very successful, aren't you?.' Matthew's eyes, which Bel now saw were the hue of dark chocolate, twinkled as he spoke as if daring her to contradict. Why did she feel as if he was throwing down a challenge?

'Now sit down, both of you. Betty'll be bringing in the tea,'

'I can fetch it,' Bel offered, eager to leave the room and regain her equilibrium.

On her way to the kitchen, Bel stopped for a few seconds in the hallway, hands to her flaming cheeks. What was the matter with her? Why did she have the impression her aunt's solicitor was mocking her? Was it the way he'd spoken or some tacit message she'd seen in his eyes? She met Betty at the kitchen door, the loaded tray in her hands.

'I'll take it, Betty,' Bel said, her cheeks cooling as she relieved the woman of her burden.

Back in the front room, her aunt and Matthew were chatting about some local identity who'd been featured in that day's paper. Bel placed the tray carefully on a low table and poured the tea.

'Matthew takes his black with two sugars,' Isobel instructed, 'and I'll have mine with one and milk.'

While they were drinking tea, and Matthew was making a hole in the plate of biscuits, Isobel inquired about Robbie and Fiona, who Bel gathered were Matthew's children or grandchildren. This appeared to be a regular routine in which both engaged. So it wasn't until the cups were empty and Betty had been summoned to clear them away, that the real purpose of his visit became apparent.

Isobel straightened her back and began to speak. 'Matthew here knows my wishes. He has it all written down. I want you to know them too, so there won't be any mistakes.' She nodded. 'He's helped me write a living will. The law's a bit of an ass about this in Scotland, so I want you to make sure it'll be upheld if – when – I'm no longer able.'

'You mean you want to refuse medical treatment?'

'In a nutshell. I've had a good life. When my time comes, I don't want the doctors trying to keep me alive with all their medications and interventions. I want to go peacefully. I feel it's going to be soon and…'

Tears began to well in Bel's eyes. Why hadn't she visited before now? Why had she been so caught up in her own life that she'd kept postponing a trip to Scotland? But in her heart of hearts she knew. She'd been afraid – a sixty-year-old woman afraid of the memories this house held for her.

Matthew must have recognised Bel's anguish. He held out a large handkerchief which she clutched gratefully, throwing a teary smile in his direction. 'Thanks.' She made an attempt to return it, but he shook his head.

'Dinnae fash yourself,' Isobel said in a brisk voice. Bel smiled inwardly at the Scottish term for worry she hadn't heard for years. 'It comes to us all and I'm ready to go. And, if possible, I'd like you to be here when my time comes. Matthew here is a good man, but he's not family. You're all the family I have left. That's why I wrote to you and why you're here.'

Bel studied her aunt. She looked so well, so alive, sitting upright in her chair, the watery light from the window illuminating her hair like a halo. It was difficult to accept that she was calmly discussing her demise. She swallowed and took a deep breath. 'I'll stay as long as you need me, Aunt Isobel. You know that.'

'I know nothing of the sort,' the older woman replied. 'That's why I had Matthew come along this morning. I needed you to understand a few matters. There's this house for example.'

'The house?' Bel glanced around the room. The rain appeared to have stopped and the sun had moved and was now throwing a fine shaft of light across the faded carpet. Bel remembered it had once been bright with a floral pattern.

Matthew cleared his throat. 'What your aunt means is that she has willed it to you, along with certain responsibilities.'

'Responsibilities?' Bel repeated, thinking she sounded like a parrot. 'Maybe you could explain?'

Matthew looked at Isobel as if asking her permission to continue. She nodded.

'Over the years your aunt has donated to several charities. One of those...' he hesitated.

'Oh, for goodness sake, man! What he's trying to say, Bel, is that I'm leaving the house to you with certain conditions attached. I know you won't want to live here. Your life's in Australia now. But I would ask that you – and Matthew – set up the house as a home for disabled children and their carers. It would need some modification, but...'

'Your aunt has already had plans drawn up.'

Bel's eyes moved to Matthew at his interruption. She felt an ache in her throat. How did Isobel know about Bel's own commitment to helping disabled children back home – or did she? Was this simply a coincidence? 'I'd be happy to fulfil your wishes,' she said, 'but surely it won't be soon? I mean, you're looking so well and...'

'I do put a good face on it, don't I?' Isobel said with a smile, brandishing her cane to emphasise her words. Then her face became more serious. 'But, according to Doctor William Ramage, I don't have long. My lungs are filling up with fluid and it seems I'll drown or something equally terminal. So...' she took a long breath, 'I want you two to get to know each other.'

Bel cast a furtive glance at the man who was now regarding her with what appeared to be amusement. Just what was Isobel suggesting? Surely there was no further need for Bel and Matthew to talk until the worst happened. If her aunt was to be believed, then she – Bel – would still be here when Isobel passed away. That would be when she and Matthew needed to liaise, not before, not now. But she'd counted without the man himself.

'Sounds like a good plan,' he said, rising and planting a kiss on Isobel's cheek. 'Maybe you'd care to come for a drive tomorrow – weather permitting?'

Bel felt her mouth fall open. 'I…' she began, intending to refuse, to explain she'd come to spend time with her aunt, not to go gallivanting around the countryside with a solicitor who looked more like a farmer.

But before she could utter another word, her aunt intervened. 'Capital idea. You can show her that bothy of yours,' she said, turning to Bel and adding, 'Matthew has a place out towards Loch Lomond. That's why he looks so disreputable.' She chuckled. 'Pretends to be a man of the land, instead of a respectable lawman. Sometimes I think he's missed his calling.'

'But…'

'There's no Mrs Reid. If that's what you're thinking.' Isobel chuckled, then burst into a coughing fit.

Bel hurried to provide her aunt with a glass of water and, without quite knowing how it happened, by the time Mathew left, she'd agreed to go for a drive with him next day.

Matthew's visit appeared to have tired Isobel out so, while she was having a nap after lunch, Bel retired to her room and, picking up the sheaf of papers, began to read.

Three

Isobel – 1938

'Let's go and have our fortunes read tonight.' My sister Nan, brimming with excitement, was clearly going to brook no refusal. 'I've heard this woman is really good. She lives only five minutes away. I've already set up an appointment, but we need four girls to go. You *will* come, won't you?'

It was the last thing I wanted to do. I was on my feet all day at the hair salon and when I got home I liked to put my feet up and have a cup of tea. I didn't believe in fortune tellers anyway. I thought it was all a load of old rubbish, a way of cheating young women like my sister out of their hard-earned cash with stupid notions of meeting tall, dark and handsome heroes who'd sweep them off their feet, just like they saw in the cinema or read in *True Romances* or *True Story*.

'Say you will. It'll be fun. Jeannie's coming and you could ask Eileen, couldn't you?'

I sighed. I knew I was going to have no peace until I agreed to go along with this. My best friend, Eileen, would agree. She was always up for anything.

'Okay. I'll telephone her,' I said reluctantly. Our telephone was relatively new and we were still thrilled with the novelty of being able to contact our friends from the privacy of our own home, even though Father cautioned us from using it too frequently.

*

The four of us were giggling and pushing each other with a combination of nerves and excitement as Nan rang the bell. It was a dank November night and the rain was belting down. We were anxious to get out of the weather while being unsure what we were letting ourselves in for. Eileen was just asking, 'Do you think this is the right place?' when the door opened and we were shown into a small lounge room.

After waiting impatiently, sitting on an overstuffed sofa which had seen better days, we took turns to go into an adjoining room while those of us left behind chatted nervously and drank cups of tea.

When my turn came, I picked up my empty teacup as I'd been instructed, and entered warily. The room looked as if it had once been a bedroom. The floral curtains were drawn across the solitary window, and the woman we had come to see was sitting in front of a low table opposite an empty chair. I perched on the edge of a low chair and handed over my cup, wondering what on earth I was doing here.

The woman bent her head over my tea cup pretending to see goodness knows what in the collection of soggy tealeaves stuck to the edge of the cup.

Okay, I thought, *bring on the dark handsome stranger and let's get this over.*

'…Who's Bob Smith?'

I stared at her without speaking. I'd been letting the woman's voice flow over me, when the name grabbed my attention. Okay, it was a very common name, but I didn't expect to be given an actual name. It would be all too easy to disprove.

I shook my head. This wasn't supposed to happen. She was supposed to talk in generalities; the tall dark man from across the sea, weddings and babies. That's what I'd expected when I stood at the dark green door with my three friends just an hour earlier.

Her voice reverberated around my head as I gazed down at my hands. I tried to ignore the ringing in my ears and looked up at the face opposite me. She was a small woman whose faded blonde hair lay in wisps around a prematurely wrinkled face, the brightly coloured earrings and the red lipstick making an incongruous statement. Her eyes, behind gold-rimmed spectacles, seemed puzzled and the red mouth opened and repeated the words, 'Who's Bob Smith?'

She peered at me, clearly taking in my shocked expression. 'You haven't met him yet, then? You will, and you'll think you're set for life.' She stared into the teacup again. 'He'll leave you. It won't last.' She put the cup down. Short and sweet, I thought, shaken despite my cynicism.

I didn't wait to hear any more. 'Thanks,' I muttered and left. Back in the lounge room, I prepared to fend off questions and thought of what I'd been told. There couldn't possibly be anything in it, could there? I put it out of my mind. The woman had said it wouldn't last anyway.

'What did she tell you?' It was Eileen, always the loudest. Sometimes I wondered why she was my best friend; we had so little in common. My mother always said it was because she dared to do the things I'd like to do, but I knew that there was more to our friendship than that.

We'd met on our first day at primary school. I'd been hiding nervously among the coats in the cloakroom when she'd caught sight of me and pulled me out to join in the class line. It seemed she'd been doing that ever since – pulling me out of hiding, that is.

'Well?' Eileen's voice had become impatient. I shook myself and tried to think of what to reply. I certainly wasn't going to repeat the name I'd been given. That would just be asking for trouble. I knew I'd never hear the end of it.

'Just the usual,' I replied, shaking back my hair. I'd been trying a new style, at Eileen's urging, and it wasn't working for me. My naturally straight black hair defied every attempt to fashion it into anything stylish.

'There is no usual. Don't be so coy.' Eileen's eyes flashed, and I knew I'd have to come up with something fast or she'd never give up.

'She said I'd meet someone, a man, tall, dark hair and that it wouldn't last,' I improvised.

'Mine's going to be blonde,' Nan interjected, 'and older.' I turned around. I'd missed hearing about my sister's fortune while I was listening to my own.

'Maybe that one with the blond curls in the choir,' I joked, only to see Nan blush. It was true that there was a tall blond fellow in the church choir who'd been giving her the eye, but I hadn't thought she was interested. Well, well!

At that point Maisie, the spey-wife, emerged from the bedroom. 'Is that all of you now?' she asked. She looked different in the brightly-lit living room, surrounded by the shabby three-piece lounge and side tables filled with family photographs; less fey somehow and more ordinary. It was odd to think she'd spent the last few hours pretending to foretell our futures.

We bundled ourselves up in the hats, scarves and gloves we'd taken off only a few hours earlier and went out again into the dreary night. The rain had stopped, but the remaining clouds hid the moon and stars leaving us to find our way home by street-light.

'It's going to freeze tonight,' predicted Jeannie. She'd been quiet all evening, but chose now to become chatty. 'I think she was good, don't you?' She turned to Nan, her best friend. 'I'm glad you let me come along,' she added to me, as if I'd had anything to do with it.

*

'You were very quiet on the way home. Did she say something you didn't tell us?' Nan wanted to know. We were back in the living room drinking cocoa by the fire. Mother and Father were in bed, so we were whispering. The room was still warm, though the fire was dying down and the embers cast long shadows around the room. They flickered across the solid furniture which had been in the family for generations.

We huddled close to the fireplace, like we had as small children when we imagined shapes in the flames and the thought of being tall enough to reach the top of the mantelpiece was unimaginable. The difference was that now we huddled there so that the smoke from our cigarettes went straight up the chimney. Mother and Father would kill us if they caught us smoking.

'Just thinking,' I replied, hoping that would satisfy her. I had no intention of giving away any more details. Bob Smith! She might as well have said John Brown or some such. 'Well I'm for bed. I have an early start tomorrow.'

I lay very still in bed pretending to be asleep. I shared a room with Nan and our other sister Kate. We were all old enough to have our own rooms, and the house was certainly big enough, but we liked being together and often used the darkness to share confidences. The barnlike dimensions of the upper level of the old house echoed in the night. When we were younger, Kate had scared us with stories of ghosts, though none of us had ever seen or heard one.

Kate hadn't gone with us to the spey-wife. She had more sense, I thought. She was determined to *make something of herself* as our mother put it. What she meant was that Kate was the clever one. She was the oldest and had always been given more responsibility. Afternoons spent playing in the garden were not for her; she had work to do. She was actually only four years older than me in age, but light-years older in her attitude. She worked at the local cooperative like Nan, but had almost completed a business course. Then, as Mother said, the world would be her oyster, and she wouldn't have to put up with these stuck-up customers anymore.

I could hear the gentle snores of my two sisters, but was too excited to fall asleep immediately myself. The name Bob Smith kept going around and around in my head. It was all very well to rubbish fortune tellers and tell my sister that it was all a lot of codswallop but what if…?

I lay there imagining meeting this Bob Smith. What would he be like? Tall, dark and handsome, of course. And where would I meet him? It would have to be some romantic setting, like the couples in *True Romance* magazine. Maybe he'd save me from drowning, or from a runaway horse, or … It didn't occur to me that there was little chance of drowning or meeting a runaway horse in our part of Glasgow.

I closed my eyes tight and hugged myself.

I was twenty and had never had a real boyfriend. I'd kissed a few boys in kissing games at church socials, but had always wiped my lips afterwards and pretended it hadn't happened. They hadn't meant anything to me.

Nan was the pretty one with her blonde curls, blue eyes and pointed chin. I was… I thought about that. I suppose I wasn't exactly plain but there wasn't much you could do with a long face and straight black hair. Now that I was grown up I tended to wear my hair in a roll behind my ears, not very glamorous, but it was too long to leave down in the salon and the clients expected us to look neat, *soignée* Lillian called it, but then it *was* her salon.

It was a few months later and I'd completely forgotten about the evening and the spey-wife's prediction. I'd attended a couple of church dances and had been walked home by boys I hoped never to see again. Eileen telephoned me at the salon, her voice shrill with excitement.

'I've just met this gorgeous guy, and he's got a friend.'

'Not again.' I'd been down this route before and discovered that gorgeous guys usually had friends who were not so gorgeous. Eileen's idea of gorgeous wasn't mine anyway. 'I told you I wouldn't be in it again.'

'You've got to come. You'll like him. He's a teacher.' A teacher. Was that supposed to be an incentive? Sounded staid and boring to me.

'Well, what do you say? Saturday night? We're going to the cinema.' Eileen clearly couldn't understand my silence.

'Okay,' I replied slowly, trying to work out if this was a good idea or not, but unable to come up with any excuses. Eileen knew I had nothing else planned because we usually spent our Saturday nights together.

*

Although I wasn't expecting to like this blind date, sure he'd be like all the others Eileen had produced, I took more care than usual with my appearance. I borrowed a skirt and bolero top of Kate's and managed to coil my hair into some resemblance of the latest fashion. Father had refused to allow us girls to bob our hair, so I was stuck with these long locks. I donned my hat and gloves, checked myself in the mirror and rubbed a touch more rouge into my lips before slipping out the door.

Eileen was waiting for me at the corner and we walked quickly to catch the tram that would take us into Sauchiehall Street.

'We're meeting them outside the Odeon,' she said, beaming. 'Oh, I know you'll like him.'

'Have you met your fellow's pal?'

'No, but Alan says he's quite a catch. You're too fussy by half,' she added, referring to my rejection of the "good sorts" her own short-lived romances had produced in the past. 'And they're showing the latest Clark Gable. You said you wanted to see it.'

I sighed. It was true. Clark Gable was my pin-up, and I'd been dying to see his new film.

When we reached the cinema, there was a long queue stretching along the side of the building and no sign of the two men. 'Do you think…?' I began, wondering if we should take our place in the line, when Eileen grabbed my arm and pointed to two figures crossing the road.

'Here they are,' she said, her voice rising with excitement.

As the men came closer. I gasped. One of them could have been Clark Gable himself with his dark hair brushed back from a wide forehead and a neat dark moustache. He had to be Eileen's date. As they approached, I turned my gaze to the other. He appeared pleasant enough, a pretty ordinary sort of guy with sandy-coloured hair, freckles and a wide grin. He looked as if he might be good company for an evening at least.

But when they joined us, it was the sandy-haired fellow whose arm Eileen took. 'This is Alan,' she said with a grin, 'and this is…'

'Bob,' the Clark Gable lookalike said, taking my outstretched hand. 'Bob Smith.'

To read more you can purchase *The Good Sister* here
books2read.com/u/bpWqkX

Acknowledgements

As always, this book could not have been written without the help and advice of a number of people.

Firstly, my husband Jim for listening to my plotlines without complaint, for his patience and insights as I discuss my characters and storyline with him and for being there when I need him.

John Hudspith, editor extraordinaire for his ideas, suggestions, encouragement and attention to detail.

Jane Dixon-Smith for her patience and for working her magic on my beautiful cover and interior.

My thanks also to early readers of this book – Karen, Helen, Louise, Cynthia and Anne for their helpful comments and advice, and to Annie of *Annie's books at Peregian* for her ongoing support.

And all of my readers. Your support and comments make it all worthwhile.

About the Author

After a career in education, Maggie Christensen began writing contemporary women's fiction portraying mature women facing life-changing situations. Her travels inspire her writing, be it her frequent visits to family in Oregon, USA or her home on Queensland's beautiful Sunshine Coast. Maggie writes of mature heroines coming to terms with changes in their lives and the heroes worthy of them.

From her native Glasgow, Scotland, Maggie was lured by the call 'Come and teach in the sun' to Australia, where she worked as a primary school teacher, university lecturer and in educational management. Now living with her husband of over thirty years on Queensland's Sunshine Coast, she loves walking on the deserted beach in the early mornings and having coffee by the river on weekends. Her days are spent surrounded by books, either reading or writing them – her idea of heaven!

She continues her love of books as a volunteer with her local library where she selects and delivers books to the housebound.

A member of Queensland Writer's Centre, ALLIA, and a local writers group, Maggie enjoys meeting her readers at book signings and library talks. In 2014 she self-published *Band of Gold* and *The Sand Dollar, Book One of the Oregon Coast Series,* in 2015 *The Dreamcatcher, Book Two of the Oregon Coast Series* and *Broken Threads,* in 2016 *book Three of the Oregon Coast Series, Madeline House,* and in 2017 *Champagne or Breakfast,* set in Noosa on Australia's Sunshine Coast, in which characters from the Oregon Coast books make a reappearance. In 2018, she also published *The Good Sister* which follows the story of Bel who readers first met in *Broken Threads,* when she returns to her native Scotland to visit her terminally ill aunt.

Isobel' Promise continues Bel's story and is the sequel to *The Good Sister.*

Maggie can be found on Facebook, Twitter, Goodreads, Instagram or on her website.

www.facebook.com/maggiechristensenauthor
www.twitter.com/MaggieChriste33
www.goodreads.com/author/show/8120020.Maggie_Christensen
www.instagram.com/maggiechriste33/
www.maggiechristensenauthor.com/

Also by Maggie Christensen

A relationship after a failed marriage. Can Anna love again? Does she dare?

Anna Hollis believes she has a happy marriage. A schoolteacher in Sydney, Anna juggles her busy life with a daughter in the throes of first love and increasingly demanding aging parents.

When Anna's husband of twenty-five years leaves her, on Christmas morning, without warning or explanation, her safe and secure world collapses.

Marcus King returns to Australia from the USA, leaving behind a broken marriage and a young son.

When he takes up the position of Headmaster at Anna's school, they form a fragile friendship through their mutual hurt and loneliness.

Can Anna leave the past behind and make a new life for herself, and does Marcus have a part to play in her future?

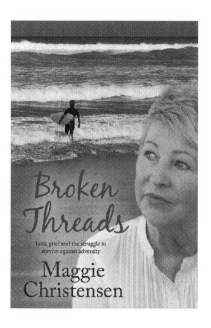

A story of loss, grief and the struggle to survive against adversity.

Jan Turnbull's life takes a sharp turn towards chaos the instant her eldest son, Simon takes a tumble in the surf and loses his life.

Blame competes with grief and Jan's husband turns against her. She finds herself ousted from the family home and separated from their remaining son, Andy.

As Jan tries to cope with her grief and prepares to build a new life, it soon becomes known that Simon has left behind a bombshell, and her younger son seeks ways of compensating for his loss, leading to further issues for her to deal with.

Can Jan hold it all together and save her marriage and her family?

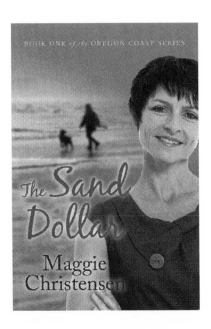

A well-kept secret and a magical sand dollar. Can Jenny unravel the puzzle of her past?

What if you discover everything you believed to be true about yourself has been a lie?

Stunned by news of an impending redundancy, and impelled by the magic of a long-forgotten sand dollar, Jenny retreats to her godmother in Oregon to consider her future.

What she doesn't bargain for is to uncover the secret of her adoption at birth and her Native American heritage. This revelation sees her embark on a journey of self-discovery such as she'd never envisaged.

Moving between Australia's Sunshine Coast and the Oregon Coast, *The Sand Dollar* is a story of new beginnings, of a woman whose life is suddenly turned upside down, and the reclusive man who helps her solve the puzzle of her past.

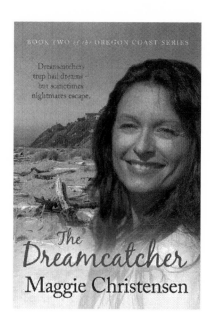

Dreamcatchers trap bad dreams – but sometimes nightmares escape.

Ellen Williams, a Native American with a gift for foretelling the future, is at a loss to explain her terrifying nightmares and the portentous feeling of dread that seems to hang over her like a shroud.

When Travis Petersen – an old friend of her brother's – appears in her bookshop *The Reading Nook*, Ellen can't shake the idea there's a strange connection between her nightmares and Travis' arrival.

Suffering from guilt of the car accident which took the lives of his wife and son, Travis is struggling to salvage his life, and believes he has nothing to offer a woman. But Ellen's nightmares come true when developers announce a fancy new build, which means pulling down *The Reading Nook* – and she needs Travis' help.

Can Ellen and Travis uncover the link between them and save her bookshop? And will it lead to happiness?

A tale of dreams, romance, and of doing the right thing, set on the beautiful Oregon coast.

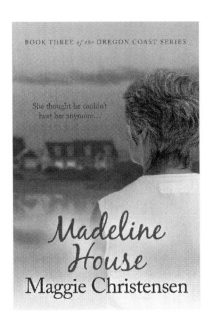

Madeline House

Maggie Christensen

She thought he couldn't hurt her anymore – she was wrong.

When Beth Carson flees her controlling husband, a Sydney surgeon, and travels to Florence, Oregon, she is unsure what her future holds. Although her only knowledge of Florence comes from a few postcards found in her late mother's effects, she immediately feels at home there and begins to put down roots.

But Beth's past returns to haunt her in ways she could never have imagined. Distraught over alarming reports from Australia and bewildered by revelations from the past, Beth turns to new friends to help her.

Tom Harrison, a local lawyer, has spent the past five years coming to terms with his wife's death, and building a solitary existence which he has come to enjoy. Adept at ignoring the overtures of local women and fending off his meddling daughter, he is intrigued by this feisty Australian and, almost against his will, finds himself drawn to her when she seeks his legal advice.

What forces are at work to bring the two together, and can Beth overcome her past and find a way forward?

Set on the beautiful Oregon Coast this is a tale of a woman who seeks to rise above the challenges life has thrown at her and establish a new life for herself.

Rosa Taylor is celebrating her fiftieth birthday with champagne. By the river. On her own.

After finishing her six-year long affair with her boss, Rosa is desperate to avoid him in the workplace and determined to forge a new life for herself.

Harry Kennedy has sailed away from a messy Sydney divorce and is resolute in kick-starting a new life on Queensland's Sunshine Coast.

Thrown together at work, Rosa and Harry discover a secret. One that their employer is desperate to keep hidden. To reveal it they must work together, but first they must learn to trust not only each other but their own rising attraction.

Are these two damaged people willing to risk their hard won independence for the promise of love again?

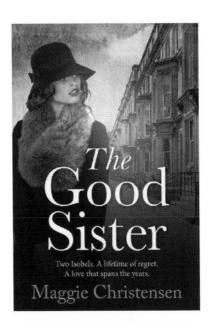

Two Isobels. A lifetime of regret. A love that spans the years

In 1938, as the world hurtled towards war, twenty-year-old Isobel MacDonald fell madly in love. But fate and her own actions conspired to deny her the happiness she yearned for. Many years later, plagued with regrets and with a shrill voice from the past ringing in her ears, she documents the events that shaped her life.

In 2015, sixty-five-year-old Bel Davison returns from Australia to her native Scotland to visit her terminally ill aunt. Reading Isobel's memoir, she is beset with memories of her own childhood and overcome with guilt. When she meets her aunt's solicitor, events seem to spiral out of control and, almost against her will, she finds herself drawn to this enigmatic Scotsman.

What is it that links these two women across the generations? Can the past influence the future?

Made in the USA
Columbia, SC
16 May 2020